SAFE IN CLUA

Elle Wylee

Cover design by Wild Star Covers

DEDICATION

This one's for anybody suffering at the hands of those supposed to love you. I see you. You are not alone. You are worth so much more and are so much stronger than you know. Don't lose hope. Reach out. Get help.

CONTENTS

A LITTLE HEADS UP

Safe in Clua deals with domestic violence and death of a spouse. It contains some scenes that may be upsetting to some readers. Though the book is about so much more than just those scenes, I thought it only fair to give you a little heads up before you start.

ONE

Laia

If something seems too good to be true, kick back and enjoy until it blows up in your face.

Words to live by, according to my dad. Probably a good thing he didn't see quite how spectacularly things did blow up in my face.

Arms wrapped around my middle, I rest my hip against the door frame and tilt my head onto the whitewashed wood. Regardless, right now, his words have never been more apt.

I have a garden. And decking. And nothing but a low wooden fence separating them from the most picture-perfect beach I've ever seen.

The warm breeze pulls a curl from its knot on top of my head and, in the confines of my sneakers, my toes wiggle, begging to be released and sunk into the pristine white sand.

Paradise. It's the only word to describe this place. Clear turquoise water rolls against the postcard-perfect shore, just yards from where I stand.

There must be some mistake, there's no way this place is meant for me.

"Peaceful, isn't it?"

"It really is." I chew the inside of my cheek as I turn to my new landlord—savior—hero-in-a-pink-mumu. "The last place Women's Aid fixed me up with was a basement Studio in Arizona with no AC and a family of cockroaches under the fridge."

Women's Aid. An organization for women with nowhere else to turn, that helps them escape a life that's become too dangerous. That sets them up with a new place, away from the danger, the violence, the *pain.*

Not an organization I ever thought I'd have on speed dial, far else have to use.

But here I am—new life number two, thanks to them.

I take in the sparkling clean kitchen we're standing in. It might be dated, but it's a massive step up.

Butcher-block worktops wrap the whole room. And the oven—I could fit at least four pie tins in that thing. That thought alone stops me up, picks at some forgotten scab I'd almost convinced myself had healed.

It's been years since I baked. Years since I even let myself think about baking.

Rubbing my thumb over the gold pendant around my neck, I meet Mrs. Devon's powder-blue stare. "I have the money for the rent."

Her thin lips lift into a smile. "Women's Aid can take care of that until you're on your feet, Laia. That's what they do." The stack of silver bangles on her wrist jingle as she lifts her hand to the pure-white braid that hangs over her shoulder.

"No. It's enough that they found me this place. I can pay my way." I'm not rich by a long shot but I have savings, and if all else fails I have the inheritance my parents left me. The one secret I had the sense to keep from Damon even before things went south between us. That's way more than a lot of women in my position.

"Okay then." Mrs. Devon nods, her gaze dropping to my twisting fingers. "You'll be safe here in Clua, I promise."

My eyes sting with exhaustion, relief, *fear,* and a whole host of other emotions I have no intention of dwelling on today. It's hard to believe that only twenty-four hours ago I walked into my tiny studio apartment back in Arcsville, Arizona, weighed down with groceries and caught the terrifyingly familiar scent of aftershave. Sweet. Musky. Unmistakable. I can still feel the bags slipping from my arms. Hear the glass jars breaking against the white tile floors as my world tilted, the fear I'd been living with for the last year shocking me numb.

I hollow my cheeks in a useless effort to stop my chin from wobbling.

He'd been there. In my house. Amongst my things. My stomach folds into itself like one of those origami swans. I blow out slowly and shake my head. Or maybe he hadn't been there at all. Maybe the smell had been nothing more than a memory triggered by a stupid prank call I'd received at work that afternoon.

The jingling sounds again, seconds before fingers cover my hand where it's gripping the neck of my travel-grubby tank top. My heart thumps. I step back, away from Mrs. Devon's touch.

She doesn't even frown. Not one crease adds to the fine lines that paint the rich dark skin of her face and not for the first time I wonder what her story is, how she got involved with Women's Aid, with helping women like me. Part of me wants to ask, but another part, a bigger part, isn't sure I have the capacity to take on her story on top of the disaster that is my own. So, I don't ask, I just force a smile. It's brittle and watery, but she returns it like she just … *understands.*

"This place is yours for as long as you need it. My son has just relocated to Hawaii with work." Her smile falters. "There's a fancy new hotel opened just outside Clua town. I've spoken to the owner and, if you want it, you have a trial for a receptionist job the day after tomorrow."

I can only imagine what my face must do in my struggle to keep from breaking into ugly gratitude sobs. "A job on top of all this?"

"This island is small." Her hand moves to touch me again, but she drops it before it makes contact. "It's not what you know around here, it's who."

The island's small all right, I hadn't even known it existed until the tinny voice on the other end of the phone told me to get myself to some back-of-beyond Mexican port and board the first ferry leaving for Clua. That a Mrs. Devon would be waiting on the other side.

I nod—I think, tiredness seeping into my bones from the top of my head down to the tips of my toes. I'd be lying if I said I'd made Arcsville my home this last year, but still, there's something to be said about the familiar. The thought of starting over again, even in paradise, feels pretty insurmountable right about now.

I'll do it, though. I don't have a choice.

Half an hour later, I've been shown around and settled in and I'm on my own again, doors and windows locked up tight.

The sun's barely set, but my eyelids droop heavily. It's been a long, long couple of days. I flop down onto the larger of two weird flesh-colored sofas in the living room, the worn cushions hugging me in, and I finally let my eyes drift closed.

A sofa that hugs.

This place might not be meant for me, but this sofa definitely is.

It's almost, *almost* enough to stop the sharp sting of disappointment of having to leave the one luxury I let myself dip into my inheritance to buy in the year I spent in Arizona. Two weeks—just two weeks of owning the comfiest, prettiest sage green sofa I'd ever seen. It wasn't much. But it was mine. A tiny step toward actually living and not just existing in flight mode, ready to run at any second.

Sighing, I wiggle my butt deeper into the cushions. *There's no point on dwelling on things you can't change, baby girl.*

This sofa will do. This house will more than do. I got away. That's the only thing that matters.

Something scratches at my lower back just as I let my eyes drift closed again.

I lift up off the sofa with a groan and reach into tket of my jean-shorts to pull out the leaflet I picked up on the ferry las Stifling a yawn with the back of my hand, I turn the creased paper to readher side.

Fern Bay Farmer's Market.

I stare at the glossy photos of fruit and veg stalls, skimiover the other advertisements. A beach-side bar, Clua's first five-star hoten back to the red letters of the market's advert and the array of fruit stacprettily on an angled table. My thumb automatically lifts to my mouth, myh finding the ragged corner of my nail as my gaze flicks in the direction of thchen.

The want, no, the *need* to roll my sleeves up and bake ething from scratch sparks for the second time tonight.

Surely Clua has some sort of public transport that would get mher.

The bubbling of excitement that takes off in my belly amost as unexpected as the need itself. I used to be good at it. *Really* good at i

Do you really believe you're good enough, Laia? Come on now, don't go mak a fool of yourself, woman.

My bubbling excitement fizzles then sinks like flat soda. Eyes squeed tight, I shake my head to rid my mind of my ex, Damon's shitty word my fist clenching tight around the glossy flyer.

He was wrong. But what if he wasn't?

I puff out my cheeks and uncurl my fingers from the flyer, tornbetween cowering in the comfort zone *he* put me in, and trying for more. Tryirg for the life I could have had if I'd never met him.

I brush my thumb over the advert and swallow down the doubt.

New life, new Laia.

I've got this.

I survived the r ust.

Nightmares are fun.

Nightmares ab)amon, even less so.

A half-drunk of coffee warming my palms, I swallow back a yawn, lean my hip against t tchen counter and gaze out the French doors when a note stuck to the out of the glass catches my attention.

I push mys rom the worktop, scanning the backyard uneasily before I unlock the do ad peel the note free, rubbing my thumb across the mark the tape left behin

My son's o ruck is in the garage. Use it. Explore. (Left for town. Right for Fern Bay. There's a var on today) Mrs. D.

She m have come while I was getting dressed. This can't be for real.

The u to bake has me glancing back into the kitchen to the oven. There's nothing pping me.

How n I not take this as a sign?

I drur my fingers against my chin and read the note again. Definitely a sign. Today is oing to be a good day—no, a great day. I'm gonna make sure of it.

The sght that awaits me in the garage is almost enough to have me doubting my great lay conviction before it's even started.

Old truck. Not an understatement. I clutch my pendant and tilt my head. It's huge. With a bulbous front and boxy back, the color of rust—at least I hope that's the paint color—it looks not unlike something from the old western movies my dad used to make me watch.

Never judge a book, baby girl.

Dad's words have me straightening, breathing in deep, and squaring my shoulders. I've got this. Vintage is never a bad thing.

After a ridiculous battle to open the driver's side door, I finally haul myself up into the seat.

Stick shift. I blow out a long breath. Okay. Still got this.

I reach beneath me to hunt for a lever to pull the bench seat forward. Mrs. Devon's son apparently has way longer legs than me. Not hard to do, I'm only five foot five on a big hair day.

With a metallic groan, I jolt forward.

Better. Now. Clutch. I press my foot onto the chunky pedal, ignoring the memories of the last time I attempted to drive stick. With Damon. My hand tightens into a fist, the badly healed fracture on the knuckle of my ring finger throbbing dully where his special brand of teaching left its mark. I shake my head, and those memories loose before they can take hold. Not today.

Fortune favors the brave. I can do this.

Holding my breath, I twist the key, close my eyes, and pray for no hill starts or stop signs.

An unhealthy whine preempts an almighty roar, the engine vibrating the whole cab as it comes to life.

My shocked woah has me laughing nervously. This thing isn't just old, it's a fricking dinosaur. I lean forward on the bench so I can see over the hood, the skin left bare by my cut-offs squeaking on the worn beige leather.

Left for town, right for the market. I flick the blinker up then bunny-hop the truck out of the drive and onto the road.

Right, it is.

I can do this. *Slowly.*

Squinting against the morning sun, I make my way around the bends and curves of the road at a snail's pace. The farther I go, the more the lightness from earlier stretches my smile.

This. Place. Is. Amazing.

Lush green forests line either side of the sandy road, their thick canopies filtering everything with a happy green light. Arcsville's dry burnt landscape has nothing on this. I fill my lungs with fresh woodsy air, and my laugh catches me off guard.

The only thing this road trip is missing is a soundtrack.

One eye on the road, I brave taking my hand off the steering wheel and push the power button on the surprisingly modern stereo. It lights up in the dashboard. *Yes.* I twist the first dial I come to as I glance up through the windshield.

Rock music blasts through the speakers at the exact same moment a flash of sun fires through a break in the forest's canopy, blinding me with its white glare.

Holy-hell.

I slam my foot down on the brake, the truck screeching to a halt on the side of the road, my heart crashing along with the music still screaming at me from the stereo.

I blink hard, my vision adjusting to the now shadowed side of the road and fixing on a pair of very wide, very blue eyes through the windshield.

No.

I blink again.

This can't be happening.

About a foot in front of the truck, mouth opening and closing like a guppy … is a man.

You've got to be kidding me.

Neither of us move.

A full minute passes before I manage to pry my fingers from the steering wheel and shut off the blaring music.

I could've killed him. I *almost* killed him.

I should get out. Make sure he's okay. Do something other than stare at him.

Eyes, bright and unblinking beneath thick black brows stare back at me, his square jaw is clenched so tightly I can see the muscles working beneath the scruff that covers it even from here.

I swallow thickly, but before I get the chance to face round two with the truck door, he moves towards the front of the truck, slamming a hand down onto the rusted metal hood. Not good. This is not good.

He's pissed. I can't really blame him. A little faster and … I should never have left the bungalow.

Sweat prickles over my top lip, the tiny hairs on my arms raising. This is not one of the many ways I imagined things could blow up in my face today.

It's worse. So much worse.

His stare doesn't leave mine as he makes his way around to my door, his thick shoulders rolling with every step. A familiar, sickly dread seeps into my bones the closer he gets.

He's not Damon. He. Is. Not. Damon.

My limbs freeze regardless when he makes it to my window, my stomach swooping. There's no glass between us. The window's down. There's nothing between us but hot, humid air.

"You hurt?"

His rough tone turns my head. He's worried *I'm* hurt?

I shake my head in a jerky answer, pinned once again by his unamused stare. This is probably about the time I'm expected to speak. Apologize. Do something. *Anything.*

I take a breath. Then another. My brain refuses to cooperate. I try again. "I … I didn't mean … I didn't see. *I'msosorry,*" I finally force out dropping my gaze to his black T-shirt.

"Who the hell taught you to drive?" he growls then glares up the road. "Ten years and not one thing has been done to make this fucking road safer." He slams his hand against the roof of the truck, and my shoulders jump up around my ears.

"I … I'm sorry." I shift along the bench, still avoiding his glare.

Just when I think he's not going to say anything else, he inhales. "And you—fucking *tourists*, driving like maniacs with no idea where you're going." Bitterness wraps words I'm not even sure are meant for me as he drags one of his hands through his thick black hair and glares down at me.

Nothing can disguise his contempt though. I clamp my mouth shut to stop my chin from trembling and move even further along the seat away from him. Crying will help absolutely nothing. I know this. It doesn't mean the tears aren't there, just beyond my eyelids. I brush at them with the butt of my hand.

He catches the movement, catches the look on my face too apparently and his anger fades, morphing into something much, much sadder. His gaze flits from my left eye to my right and a deep line forms between his eyebrows. "You've no idea."

"No, I don't," I whisper meekly, unable to look away, but shriveling more by the second under his unimpressed stare. "I'm sor…"

Pathetic. What happened to new Laia?

Fake it until you make it. Dad's voice in my head has me squaring my shoulders.

He shakes his head with a sigh.

"I wasn't going that fast." I force my brows down and fight my knee jerk reaction to keep on apologizing. "And you were standing in the middle of the road on a blind bend. Who does that?" I tack on for good measure.

It's his turn to blink. His eyes narrow, making my cheeks heat and my palms sweat. On second thoughts, maybe now isn't the time to grow balls.

"I didn't mean, I mean … I should go." I resist the urge to apologize all over again and instead reach for the keys hanging from the ignition, allowing myself one more second to—you know—check he's not damaged before I turn the ignition.

He doesn't try to stop me, he just lifts his hands from the roof of the truck and steps back without a word.

I shoot him one last wary side-eye and grip the steering wheel, my foot trembling dramatically on the pedals as I pull away with only one tiny lurch.

Hand on the back of his neck, he watches me go.

TWO

Laia

So, this is Fern Bay Farmer's Market?

Rubbing my shoulder, I glare at the truck door. Five full minutes and a whole lot of brute force it took me to get that thing to cooperate. I walk past the hood, and my almost-road-kill's furious blue stare flashes behind my eyes. That could have been so much worse. So, so much worse.

But it wasn't. He's fine. I'm fine. It's fine.

I shove down the guilt and the embarrassment over my less than stellar attempt to stick up for myself and force myself to move away from the truck.

Dust puffs up from my feet with every step I take towards the big wooden arch that covers the entrance to the market. And with every step my mood lifts a tiny bit more. It's not even ten but the place is buzzing with life, a spicy sweetness mingling with salty ocean air. Delicious and exotic and mouth-wateringly invigorating.

In a sea of people who seem to know exactly where they're going and what they're doing, I can't help but feel like I have a massive neon tourist sign above my head, but I can't even bring myself to care. There's a man carrying a basket of mangos. *Fresh mangos.* I mentally flick through a dozen different flavors that would work amazingly with fresh mango and pick up my pace.

Today may still end up being a good day after all.

Stepping under the hand-painted arch is like stepping into another world. I've been to many, many farmer's markets in my time. It was one of my mom's favorite weekend adventures. But this place is like nothing I've ever seen before.

Each stall boasts its own canopy of intricately patterned material in a rainbow of colors.

I spin slowly, mouth open, tourist sign flashing in all its glory. I'm in love.

Not far in the distance, I spot the wicker basket of mangos held high above the heads of the meandering crowd. My face breaks into a grin as I let myself be pulled along by the other shoppers.

A couple of little girls spinning atop a low wall stop me before I get far. They giggle and spin faster, their colorfully embroidered skirts flowing around them before their mom catches them, laughing as she helps them off the wall, talking to them in a language I can only assume is the local dialect. It's almost as beautiful as they are, with curling R's and a melodic sing-song rhythm.

Everything about Clua is beautiful. Even its history.

I breathe in the salt-infused, floral air and wander a little further. The island was briefly a US territory according to Mrs. Devon. That's probably the reason everyone speaks English, luckily for me. A melting pot of race and heritage she called it on the drive from the port to the house as she told me about the island's initial discovery by ships full of people fleeing some war or other many, many years ago. That the locals share a wide range of ancestors, their traditions, and histories a rich blend of many.

I smile at the girl behind a table filled with silver bracelets and cuffs. The designs are similar to the ones decorating the material that's shading her stall. All swirls and dots. They're the same as the ones Mrs. Devon was wearing last night. I pick up a slim bangle with the most delicate engraving I've ever seen. Damon hated bracelets. Said they were slutty. I glance at my bare wrist then back to the collection of bangles on the girl's wrist. "How much for two, please?"

Five minutes later, bracelets clinking on my wrist, I head in the direction of the mango man.

I spot the mango stall, shaded by a pink fabric awning with huge white hibiscus.

The sun glints off a blond head before I get there though. *A terrifyingly familiar blond head.*

My pulse picks up and I duck down, a cold sweat beading down my back. It can't be. I'm seeing things. There's no way.

Gravel digs into my knee as I struggle to get my breathing under control. It's not him. It's not him. It's not him. I'm being paranoid.

My self-chanting almost works. My breathing slows. It's not him. It can't be him.

Shade slides over me when I go to stand, and my heart attempts to climb out through my throat. I don't look up. I can't.

A pair of white low-rise Converse appear in my line of vision. My pulse stutters. Damon wore loafers.

I lift my gaze warily to a pair of calves, one has black lines and patterns tattooed around it. And just like that my fear eases. Damon would never ever get a tattoo. It's not him. He's as strait-laced as they come. On the outside at least.

I blow out a breath and tip my head back. Then instantly wish I hadn't.

I recognize those eyes. *That scowl.* Of course. Why not?

"Everything okay down there?" The man from the road cocks his head, brows knitted, hands in the pockets of his board shorts.

"Just … laces." I pull myself up to stand but can't resist glancing past him to double check it *was* just paranoia. Relief has me releasing a long breath.

He twists to look in the same direction then back to me, his frown even deeper when he drops his gaze to my feet. "Were you hiding from someone?"

"Yes." I blink up at him. "I mean no, of course not. Who would I be hiding from?"

He turns stiffly and looks out of the corner of his eye. The worst impression of sneaky I've ever seen. "Another victim of your erratic driving?"

"What? No." My cheeks blaze, the need to apologize for I don't even know what almost too strong to resist. "It was nothing … nobody."

"Right." He twists to glance behind him again then smirks, the skin around his eyes creasing. "Get your flip flops tied?"

"You stopped hanging out on blind bends?" I counter without thinking.

Something flashes behind his eyes, and he drags his hand over his jaw. "Touché."

My gaze catches and stays put on the sharp angle of his jawline and the rough stubble that covers it. I force it down to the gravel by his feet. A pretty face doesn't make him any less dangerous, probably the opposite.

Silence stretches between us like an elastic band. It's only a matter of time before it snaps back, and I start stress talking. I can feel them building, climbing up my throat. Stupid, random words that will only make this situation one hundred times more awkward.

"If you followed me here to yell at me some more, I should warn you, I'm a crier." I close my eyes and pray to anyone listening to put me out of my misery. *What the hell happened to New Laia?*

He clears his throat. "A crier?"

"Snot, tears, the whole shebang. It's not pretty." *And yet I just keep going.* "Trust me, you'll hate it."

He scratches his fingers through his mess of black curls, a bemused not-quite-scowl taking over from the glower. "I guess it's a good job I didn't follow you here to yell at you then."

"So, you're here to…"

"See someone."

"That's not me." I blink up at him.

"That's not you." His lips twitch.

"Okay." I press mine together. I'm still staring. Why am I still staring?

"Okay." He stares back, the blue of his eyes bright against his tan skin.

I nod, take a step back, attempt a smile and finally remove my stare from his. "I really am sorry, you know, for before." I glance up into his face one more cringe inducing time then about turn and walk away.

The weight of his stare on my back stays with me even after I've slipped into the crowd. That was mortifying—and distracting. I'm heading in the entirely opposite direction of my mangos.

It takes me a full ten minutes and three wrong turns to calm my cheeks down and focus on what I came here to do. To convince myself not to just give up and go home. Fruit. Pies. *New Laia.* I can do this.

I puff out a steadying breath, tug the neck of my tank from my clammy skin and head back towards the slight slope to my mangos.

And, he's there. *Still there.* Not far from where I left him, helping an old lady set up her stand just one stall away from my mangos.

He hasn't seen me and there's absolutely no reason for him to. I can be stealthy.

I watch them from the side of my eyes as I pass. He's smiling at the woman as he arranges the lemons she's selling into baskets. Waist-length, silver-streaked black hair, and wide dark eyes. She's beautiful, but old enough to be his mother. Maybe she *is* his mother. Maybe she's *not.* And the fact that I'm even wondering means I should definitely look away.

I don't. He looks up and his eyebrows raise along with the side of his mouth as he picks up a lemon and smells it.

My flip flop hanks on something, and I stumble a step because apparently life just isn't on my side today.

I'm pretty sure he laughs. Can't say for sure, I don't look back even when my newly awakened baker's brain pouts over the size of that lemon.

Half an hour later with no more sightings or trip-ups, I'm making my way through the thickening lunch-time crowd towards the hand-painted wooden arch of the exit, clutching a brown paper bag filled with mangos and spices. I'm coming back next week for those lemons. And the week after. And the week after that.

I think I've just found New Laia's happy place, despite the rough start.

I swipe my hair from my face and take the step down to the sandy parking lot, my grin widening even more at the sight of the spectacular beach peeking between the palm trees that line the opposite side of the parking lot. I can taste the salt on the breeze.

Old Laia would ignore it and scuttle back to the bungalow for the rest of the day.

New Laia is going to dump these mangos in the truck, then buy one of the handmade bikinis she spotted by the exit.

The irate scream of a horn stuns me as I turn back to the market.

But before I can even begin to register what's happening, I'm hauled backwards, my mangos flying into a cloud of dust.

I cough and splutter and bat the sand from my eyes, struggling to twist to see whoever's sprawled out behind me—and around me—and under me.

"Fucking idiot," is roared from behind me, warm breath tickling my neck, the rumble of a hard chest vibrating against my back.

I scramble to my feet, cracking my head on a chin, blinking to clear my vision as I turn, my heart thudding against my ribs.

Well, nobody can claim that the universe lacks a sense of humor.

It's him. Of course, it's him.

He rubs his chin as he stands, his gaze bouncing from my feet to my knees, to my face like he's checking for injuries before that trusty old scowl of his returns.

"I thought you weren't following me," I whisper when I'm sure my voice won't wobble.

"Not following. *Saving*." He glares up the road toward the long-gone van, dragging his hand down the back of his neck as he turns back to me.

I drop my gaze to the ground, embarrassingly close to tears. My fruit is scattered everywhere and the adrenaline holding me upright is seeping out fast. My shoulders droop. My spice jars are covered with sand, so are my mangos. So is my *everything*. I attempt to brush at my dusty shorts, the paper bag still crushed to my chest. A big fat mess, that's all this day's been.

"I am an idiot." I drop to my knees, grabbing for a jar of nutmeg. "I should have known better."

He squats down before I can tell him not to. To go. To leave me alone. "You're not the idiot, the guy driving the van is."

I concentrate on the lilting way his accent wraps around his words and not on the lump in my throat threatening to make this so, so much worse.

"Hey, are you okay?" His hand covers mine.

I flinch so hard I almost land myself back in the sand, because I obviously haven't made a big enough show of myself as it is. "It's fine. Really. I'm fine."

Something between worry and pity creases his forehead beneath the black curls that just about touch his eyebrows.

"You really don't need to be here." I sink my teeth into the inside of my cheek.

"There are worse places to be."

My hand stills on the last mango and I blink stupidly at him.

His eyes widen, his mouth opening before he snaps it closed again. "I mean…" He straightens from his crouch, raking his hair back from his face, that frown tickling the corner of his lips again.

I push to my feet, abandoning my shopping and every last drop of hope I woke up this morning with, and I walk away. I just—walk away.

And I don't look back. Not even when he calls after me. Not even when I make it to my truck.

What the hell is wrong with me? I drag the truck door open on the third attempt almost dislocating my shoulder in the process and climb in. I can't even make it to a market and back without not one, but two near-death experiences□ and a fat dollop of soul-shattering mortification to boot. I drop my head onto the steering wheel with a groan.

And I left my mangos.

There are worse places to be.

He looked about as shocked to have said it as I was to hear it. I shove the key into the ignition and peel my face from the steering wheel. He didn't mean it. I'm a mess. A paranoid, clumsy mess.

A sharp rap on the window has me jumping over to the other side of the cab, my hand flying to my chest like it can stop the sudden thrashing of my heart.

It's him. And my mangos.

By the time I've managed to creak the window open, I have no other option but to look at him.

His head tilts to the side, eyes scanning my face like he has no idea what to make of me. "You forgot these." He ducks down to pass the brown paper bag through the window, his big form filling the space. He smells like mint and fresh air and the two giant lemons nestled in there with my mangos.

"You didn't have to do that." I keep my stare on the massive lemons. "And those aren't my lemons."

"They are now." He grips the bottom edge of the window, a little line appearing between his brows. "You sure you're okay?"

"I'm great." I offer him a tremulous smile. "Just one of those days." My hand trembles as I reach for the keys dangling from the ignition, my foot shaking on the clutch. "I should go."

Concern flashes in his narrowed eyes. "You shouldn't drive if you're in shock."

"I'm not in shock." I force myself to meet his concern with a scowl. "And it's got nothing to do with you."

That muscle in his jaw ticks again. "You're in no state to drive." He blows a long stream of air through his nose, then just leans right in the window, and plucks the keys from the ignition. "So, don't."

"You can't be serious."

He turns his face before he pulls himself back out of the window. His nose is just millimeters from mine. "I'm serious."

My pulse trips over itself, my eyes widening until there's a very real danger they might just give up the ghost and fall out. "You … you can't do that."

His mouth twitches, a hint of a dimple flashing in his cheek. "I just did. Come on. I'll buy you a coffee." He stands back and tries to open my door.

It doesn't budge. *Ha.* "Look, I don't know what you're trying here, buddy, but it's not working."

He yanks at the door again, the muscles in his forearm cording with effort until it finally opens with a groan. "It's not only you that uses these roads here. Think of this as an intervention."

"You cannot be serious." I repeat, because seriously. He cannot be serious.

The hard line of his mouth tells me he is.

"There are laws against this you know?" I huff but stay put. He's got at least five inches on me. Still, a punch to the manly bits would probably drop him. The moves from the self-defense class Women's Aid had me take play out behind my eyes.

I could take him.

Maybe. Probably not. But I could try.

"Speaking as a recent victim of your driving, I'd say it would be classed more as a citizen's arrest for the safety of the Cluan public."

There's no disguising it. The universe hates me. And he's officially insane.

I curl my lip and attempt to put some menace into my glare. "Give me back my keys."

He shakes his head and leans a forearm against the roof of the truck. I shift away from his nearness. "One coffee and you'll get them back."

Felix

For ten years on this day, my mornings have followed the exact same trajectory. Visit her grave, leave her flowers, then visit her mother.

No deviations, no detours, and definitely no coffees with random women.

Until today. Until this woman apparently.

A dark blonde curl hangs over one of her eyes as she wraps her fingers around a tall glass of iced coffee. It took her ten minutes to finally appear in the shaded terrace of *Clua's Coffees,* scowling like—well, like someone just stole her car keys.

Who the fuck steals someone's car keys?

I do, apparently, and she's right, there are definitely laws against this sort of thing. I take a gulp of my own black coffee, its bitterness burning down my throat.

She hasn't looked at me since she sat down, but there's no disguising her mistrust.

Me staring at her probably isn't helping matters.

Novelty. She's just a novelty. A novelty with bad luck when it comes to driving. And walking. And an aversion to people. Or maybe it's just an aversion to me, she hasn't exactly seen my best side this morning.

"So." I place my mug onto its saucer with a clink. "What brings you to Clua?"

She looks up, and along with the wariness in the deep green of her eyes, there's a healthy dose of suspicion. Understandable. I shouted at her on a country road, man handled her in the car park, then stole her fucking keys, and now I'm actually trying to make small talk.

"Change of scenery?" Her soft voice lifts on the last word. "A … a friend … had a house sitting empty and I needed one, so, here I am." Her slim shoulder lifts in an awkward shrug, and she drops her gaze back where she's folding a paper sugar packet into a tiny triangle. "Is this what you do to get women to have coffee with you?" Her nose wrinkles and her already pink cheeks flush to red like the words just fell out of her mouth of their own accord.

I snort and tilt my head up to the tied canes that shade the terrace. I suppose that is probably what this looks like. "It's not what it looks like." I scrub my hand over my jaw. "You were shaking. I couldn't let you drive."

"Why do you care?" Her brows pinch up, almost meeting in the middle, and her head tips to the side. "You don't even know me."

I click my tongue off the roof of my mouth. I could tell her that I know firsthand what can happen when someone loses control behind the wheel, the devastation it can cause, the loss of everything that matters. The hole it leaves behind that can't ever be filled.

I could, but I won't.

I don't know her. She doesn't know me. And there's no reason for that to change.

"I mean, you seem to be pretty safety conscious for a man that hangs out on blind bends." She continues when I don't reply, tucking her hair behind her ears as she glances around the busy little coffee shop from one wooden table to the next for the fifth time since she sat down.

"I was visiting someone."

"On the side of a country road?" She pushes then freezes, eyes wide at whatever she reads on my face. "Sorry, I shouldn't have…" She glances down at the sugar packet triangle, her cheeks flushing. "Sorry."

"You apologize a lot."

"I say stupid things a lot." She gnaws her lip but doesn't look up. "My ex didn't—" Her gaze jumps up to mine and the color drains from her face. "I mean, it's a long story." She sighs and twists the silver bracelets on her wrist, the weight of that long story right there in her eyes.

Seconds pass but I don't look away, hell I'm not sure I even blink. I'm not usually a curious man. Haven't been for a long time. Simplicity. I like it. And I've no interest in that changing, especially not today. "We've all got one," I finally say, dipping my head to scratch the back of my neck. "I'll make you a deal. I won't tell you mine if you don't tell me yours."

The puff of laughter that pushes out her lips catches me off guard. "Deal."

The smile it leaves in its wake is small but it's there. My chest pulls at the sight of it, a tiny barely there thing, but it's enough to have my answering smile die before it even makes itself known.

Hers fades just as quickly as it appears, like she's about as used to doing it as I am. "Thank you … for, you know … saving me from the van back there."

"You're welcome." My lips twitch when hers do. I expect her to look away, but she doesn't.

There are gold flecks in the green of her eyes, a tiny freckle to the left of her slightly fuller top lip, another just below the arch of her right eyebrow. The details pulse in, unexpected, unwanted, but vividly undeniable. I stopped paying attention to the details of women's faces a decade ago.

Something smashes a table over and she flinches so hard she almost knocks her glass over, shattering the moment or whatever the fuck that was.

"Shit—sorry." Her voice breaks, her throat contracting with her swallow before she gets to her feet, the iron legs of her chair scraping loudly across the stone paving slabs. "I need my keys back now. Please."

Zi, my weekend bartender, glances up from counting coins into the register as I pull out one of the tall stools by the bar. It's not even seven, but the beach terrace is already half full. A mixture of tourists and locals enjoying the last of the day's sun. It's busy for a Sunday. Even that isn't enough to ease the low-grade headache that has me pressing my fingers into my temples.

"Rough day, Fee." The register drawer clicks closed, and her blue eyes meet mine. She's not asking. She knows what today is. It's written in the slight downward pull to her lips. I wasn't the only person to have their worlds shook up that morning ten years ago.

She bends to open one of the fridges that run beneath the bar, grabs a bottle of Corona, then opens it with the opener attached to her wrist. "Looks like you could use one of these."

The side of my mouth lifts when she slides it across the gleaming mahogany bar to me.

I spin the cold glass bottle in my hands, and the memory of the woman from this morning doing the same thing with her glass beats me around the head. I shake my head and take a long pull of beer. Today of all days is not the day to be thinking about random women.

"What's this?"

"What's what?" I look up and barely suppress my groan.

Arms folded over her chest, Zi tilts her head like she's reading my thoughts straight from my face. It wouldn't surprise me if she could. "That look? You look…" she tilts her head to the other side and taps her fingers against her lips. "Like there's something you're not telling me."

"It's nothing." Elbow on the bar, I rub my hand over my face. "I went to see Rosemary today."

"I know, she told me." She tilts her head to the other side. "But there's something else." She narrows her eyes and leans closer, her long blond braid hanging over one shoulder. "A little birdy told me that a certain Felix Ashur was spotted in Fern Bay's Clua Coffees with an unknown woman this morning." Her brows lift. "Spill."

"There's nothing to spill," I answer honestly. "A van nearly knocked her over, so I took her for coffee to make sure she was okay. I didn't even get her name."

Something that feels a lot like regret niggles in the back of my mind followed by a sharp sting of what-the-fuck?

THREE

Laia

My fingers tap over the keyboard, and the reservation details appear on the monitor. I double check them against the pink Post-it stuck to the side of the screen, hit enter then lean back into my chair. Done. And on my first day too. Not such an idiot after all.

"See? Told you you'd get the hang of it." Kenzi, the other receptionist, pats my shoulder.

I only just manage not to shrink away from the contact. Probably best that I don't let my crazy out of the bag on my first day. That doesn't mean I don't let out a little breath of relief the second she removes it and goes to sit in her own chair.

"I'm so glad they finally brought in another receptionist." She shoots me a wide, straight-toothed smile. "It's just been me since the grand re-opening last month." The same sing-song lilt all the locals speak with colors her words, making it easy to smile back. It's a very cool accent.

The guy from the market spoke with the same curled R's and elongated vowels too. Though in his rough voice it had more of a … I blink away the memory. Not helpful. I clear my throat. "Re-opening?" Shifting to adjust the high waistband of the gray pencil skirt of my uniform, I spin my chair to face her.

Her large, blue eyes sparkle, perfectly arched brows lifting. "Believe it or not this place used to be a crappy old family-run hotel."

I smooth my hand along the polished driftwood of the reception desk. It contrasts perfectly with the gray-veined marble of the floor. And probably costs more than I'll make in a year.

There's nothing crappy about this place anymore—A normal person would have said something like that.

"Oh." Is the genius reply I come up with. Friendly. I know.

Seemingly undeterred by my epic awkwardness, Kenzi turns her chair to face mine. "They say they had the marble flown in from Italy." She clicks the low heel of her black pump against the shimmering floor. "Freaking Italy. I mean, who even has that kind of money?" She folds her arms over her white blouse identical to the one I'm wearing. "And the best of it is, nobody has a clue who it is."

She's waiting for me to talk. You know—like people do when spoken to.

Seconds pass. I swallow. Take a breath. Then say the first thing that comes to my mind. "Don't look at me. This outfit is officially the most expensive item in my life right now." I hold my hands out and drop my gaze to the uniform I changed into after my meeting with the boss, or just Pete as he insisted on me calling him. I'm not even making sense. "I mean—" I shrug lopsidedly. I should probably just shut up now. "You sure it's not Pete? He looks pretty expensive."

Kenzi eyes me seriously but shakes her head. "That's what everybody thought at first too. But it's not. And he's not talking. Not to me anyway." Her lips press together then she sighs. "It'll come out eventually. Everything always does in this place. But enough about that mystery. I wanna know about you.

How is it living in Mrs. D's son's house?"

"How do you know I'm living there?" I don't even try to control my face. My pulse roars unevenly in my ears. My address isn't even to be stored here in the hotel files. Pete assured me my details would be kept off everything. If Kenzi can get them then what's to stop anybody else from getting them?

"This is Clua, Laia. Everybody knows everything." Kenzi rolls her eyes, oblivious to the panic attack currently trying to pull me under. "Mrs. D's great, isn't she? She's like Clua's favorite aunt. I think she's taken in half the island at one point or another."

"What do you mean?" I clench my hands into a fist to stop my fingers from twisting together. By taking me in Mrs. Devon has me labeled as a charity case? So much for keeping to myself.

Kenzi's face sobers at whatever she finally reads on my face. "Mrs. D is a good woman. The best. She even took in one of my friends back when we were kids."

"Oh. Well. I'm just renting the bungalow. Nothing else to tell. No taking in of anyone. Just your everyday rental." My smile feels fake even to me. I rub my thumb over the pendant around my neck as if somehow, it'll offer me the gift of normal small talk. "What about you? Are you from here?"

Her lips pinch. "You suck at deflecting."

I hold my breath and wait for more questions I can't answer. More reasons for her to decide I'm not worth the energy it would take to be my friend. It's what usually happens. The reason I made the whole of zero friends back in Arizona.

The questions don't come though. Instead, she just blasts me with another of her megawatt smiles and shrugs. "Born and raised here. My parents live on the other side of the island. I'll take you over one day. That side's got the best beaches."

A mini tingle of hope lifts my lips into a smile—a real life, God's honest smile. Maybe I've not scared her off just yet. "I've only made it as far as the market in Fern Bay yesterday. But I'd love to explore more of the island."

"You were at the market yesterday?"

"Yeah, it was lovely. Until some jerk in a van nearly painted the parking lot with me."

Her mouth drops open then closes again in an even wider grin, and she claps her hands together and swings her chair back to her desk. "This weekend you're coming out with me. You're off on Saturday, right?"

"I am, but—" I shake my head. "I'm not really into going out."

"No buts. You're coming for a drink."

Saturday arrives way before I'm ready. I bailed on Kenzi and her night out. I'm not ready. Not yet.

Sun streams through the kitchen window, bathing the yet untouched mangos in a warm afternoon glow. They're goading me from their bowl.

It's been almost a week and I've still not done anything with them. Every time I start to, I just … don't. And it's driving me crazy.

Make the pie, Laia, just make the fricking pie.

I narrow my eyes and stalk up to the counter, grabbing a knife from the drying rack on the way by the basin. Okay. This pie is getting made. Today. I puff out a few short breaths like a boxer gearing up for a fight and reach for the fruit.

"When will you get it through that thick skull that your parents lied, Laia. They lied. You're about as good at baking as you are at everything else…"

The air leaves my lungs, and I slam the knife down on the countertop beside the hand-painted fruit bowl.

Eyes squeezed closed, I try to evict his poisonous voice from my mind. Why is it always the bad memories that linger, while the good ones, the happy ones just seem to drift further and further out of reach? Blowing out a long sigh, I stare at the intricate patterns on the ceramic bowl and the fruit it holds. One more day and they'll be too bitter to use.

Frustration burns up my throat. With myself for bailing on my first maybe friend on the island, with Damon for existing, with my parents for dying on me when I needed them the most, but most of all with these damn mangos.

I throw the knife into the basin, the steel blade clattering against the metal. I grab the bowl and stomp to the garbage bin, step on the pedal and tip it until the mangos thud out.

"Laia?"

Bowl held up in front of me, I spin around, ready to launch it towards... "Kenzi?" My head jerks back in surprise at the sight of her, one foot already inside the open French doors. "What are you doing here?"

"What am I doing? What are you doing?" she asks, staring horrified at the garbage bin and the mangos peeking above the rim. "Has nobody ever told you that it's bad luck to throw out mangos like that?" She sweeps into the kitchen and grabs the bowl from my hands. "You better hope I don't catch it through association." She tips her head back. "This had nothing to do with me."

I watch, dumbfounded, as she picks the dark red-and-green fruits from the bin and throws them back into the bowl. She's lost the plot. "Erm, Kenzi, that's kind of gross."

One brow arched, she fixes me with an exasperated frown. "No—what's gross is what happened to my aunt's boyfriend's dentist's sister." She hollows her cheeks.

"What happened?" I ask, against my better judgement.

"She died." Her lips purse, her eyes widening.

"She died," I deadpan back. "For tipping out some over-ripe mangos?"

"Yes. She died. Now come on. We'd better wash these bad boys and undo whatever awfulness you just summoned up."

"I think somebody is having you on, Kenzi," I say to the back of her head as she carefully washes each mango then places them onto a plate from the drying board.

She glances over her shoulder. "Are you willing to risk it?"

I chew on my lip and hand her a dish towel to dry her hands. Insane or not, I'm definitely not willing to risk it. "Didn't you get the night off to go out?"

"I did." She finally seems to take in my black yoga pants and scruffy tank top. "We are."

"Kenzi, I already told you. I'm not really in the mood." I glance over to the unopened bag of flour on top of the microwave and lift my thumb to chew on the corner of my thumbnail.

She follows my line of vision. "You're trying to blow me off for a bag of flour?"

"No. Yes. I don't know." I twist my hair up onto the top of my head then secure it using the hair tie from my wrist. "I thought I'd make—something." I wave my hand around the kitchen and wait for her to tell me I'm stupid. Or weird. Or weird and stupid for preferring to bake on a Saturday night off than party.

"Fine." Lifting the plate of mangos from the draining board, Kenzi carries them over to the worktop. "What are we making?"

My mouth opens. Then closes. "Pie?" I wait for Damon's voice to sound again in my mind. It doesn't come so I move to stand beside Kenzi at the work top and reach to the cupboard above our heads for a mixing bowl.

I open the drawer by my hip and pull out a sieve and a rolling pin.

Still no Damon.

"I love pie." Kenzi nudges my shoulder with hers and slices one of the mangos in half. "Pie will totally reverse your bad-mango-luck. I'll chop, you mix."

It's not long before the sweet and tangy scent of boiled fruit and cinnamon fills the small kitchen.

Cheeks flushed pink, Kenzi grins while stirring the filling. "You know what you're doing, huh?" She brushes back a strand of hair that's come loose from her ponytail then returns her attention back to the stove. "Who taught you?"

"My mom." I pause, my fingers lifting from where I've been pressing the soft pastry into the waved edges of the pie tin I found in the back of the cupboard, to touch the gold pendant hanging around my neck. "She worked in a bakery." The image of her tucking her hair into her white baker's cap pops into my mind then fades like it was never there in the first place. "She died of a heart attack a few years ago."

Kenzi stops her stirring, and for an awful minute I think she might try to hug me. I'm not good at hugs. But she doesn't. I try to arrange my face into something I hope looks relatively smile-like then get back to preparing the pastry for the oven.

"I'm sorry." Her perpetually smiling mouth turns down at the corners.

I nod and keep my stinging eyes on my hands. "It's fine." It's not.

There are some people in this world who have the power to smooth over conversation bumps, or awkward babbling, or even silences with ease.

My mom was one. Kenzi, it seems, is another.

We talk about everything and nothing until the oven pings that the pie is ready.

My first pie in years.

Kenzi gets the plates out as I cut into the crisp, golden pastry.

"Careful, it's still hot." I pull out one of the mismatched wooden chairs from the kitchen table, the legs scraping across the terracotta-tiled floor.

The sun's near setting, its pink light filling the kitchen as I place a glass of white wine on the chunky wooden tabletop for Kenzi.

Rocking back on her chair, she wafts her hand in front of her mouth still chewing. "Amazing." She squeezes her eyes shut and swallows. "Ahh, but yeah, I burned my tongue." She grabs her glass and takes a massive swig. "Seriously, Laia. Who would have guessed that adding nutmeg and vanilla to the pastry would make this amazing-ness?" She cuts another chunk of pie from her plate. "You're wasted as a receptionist, woman."

Elbows on the table, I cover my mouth with my clasped hands and grin against them. I did it—with a little help—but I did it, and it tastes good.

I won't ever be able to explain to Kenzi what her showing up here has done for me. I wouldn't even know where to start. So, I settle with giving back a little instead. "Let's go for that drink."

She stops mid-chew, then jabs her fork into another piece of pie. "I thought you weren't in the mood." She wiggles on her chair and stuffs another forkful into her mouth as soon as she's swallowed.

"Maybe I am." I shrug and drain the rest of my glass. I just made pie. I can do anything. "I should probably change first, though." I lean back and brush at my flour-speckled yoga pants.

Scraping her fork along her plate to get the last of the crumbs, Kenzi examines her own outfit. Her off-the-shoulder khaki T-shirt dress is as clean as when she walked in, if you don't count the crumbs that just escaped her fork on its journey to her mouth. "Let's do this."

FOUR

Laia

The second I close the taxi door, my pie high plummets down to the toes of my brown leather sandals.

Figures.

Nerves twist into knots in my belly as I watch the taxi pull out of the parking area and take off down the road.

The Beach Hut sign in big wooden letters tops the doorway of the low building we've pulled up in front of. The sky blazes red and orange behind it. I've seen this place before. The flyer from the ferry.

Bouncing on the balls of her feet, Kenzi holds her hand out for me. "I'm so glad you came. You'll love it here, I promise."

Suddenly leaving dinosaur-jeep at home seems a bit drastic. Back at the house, it had made perfect sense. I'd already had one glass of wine. Any more would probably take me over the limit and let's face it, even sober I have trouble keeping myself alive.

Taking a bolstering breath, I force myself to take Kenzi's hand and let her pull me forward and up the three wooden steps. I can do this. New Laia has totally got this.

"Welcome to The Beach Hut." Pushing one of the swinging saloon-style doors open with her bum, she drags me into the bar.

A-mazing. My mouth falls open. And I thought the view from the bungalow was special. One side of the bar is completely open to the beach, and from here the sun looks like it's floating on the sea, its oranges and pinks reflected across the sand, casting everything in a cozy, shimmering light.

I could stand here all night. It's just—perfect.

"Oh look, there's Fee." Still holding my hand in hers, Kenzi leads us between the comfy-looking wicker sofas that fill the inside area until we reach the bar. "Laia, I want you to meet Felix." She pulls me to stand beside her. "He's the owner of The Beach Hut."

I drag my gaze from the spectacular sunset. And freeze. Completely.

Seriously? *Seriously???*

It's him.

He hasn't looked up yet. Too busy listening to the tiny brunette who's practically sitting on top of the gleaming mahogany bar. All white teeth, flappy eyes and silky, dark hair down to her bum. If I run now, I could probably make it out before he looks up. I glance down to where Kenzi has my fingers in a death lock, then up to her beaming face and the other shoe finally drops.

This was a set up. I don't know how, but this was a goddamn set up.

My face warms. I don't have to look to know he's spotted me. But I do. Obviously. Because I'm me and I have no idea what's good for me.

His dark brows raise in recognition, and he straightens, his gaze sliding down to my short red sundress. I fight the urge to tug at the hem. It's too short. Too low-cut. I should never have let Kenzi talk me into wearing it. His full lips curve into a bemused smile.

I definitely should have run.

"You?" He scratches the corner of his mouth with his thumb, then folds his arms over his wide chest, the Beach Hut logo printed across the middle of his black T-shirt.

He seems lighter than the other day somehow, that glower of his nowhere to be seen. It looks good on him—I shut that thought down before it can take root.

"Hi." I do a semi half jazz-hand wave. It's exactly as lame as it sounds, trust me.

Moments like this I wish it were possible to make myself disappear. "I mean, hey." I snatch my fingers into a fist.

"You two already know each other?" Kenzi presses her lips together like she's trying to stop herself from grinning and if there was ever any doubt that this was a set up it's gone now.

"We do." Felix smirks and shakes his head, his attention never leaving my face.

"You do?" Flappy Eyes glares down her wrinkled nose.

"We do." I twist my lips to the side and side-eye Kenzi. "Sort of."

"Small island, right?"

All three of us turn to Kenzi and an awkward silence falls over our little foursome, her expectant eyes swiveling between us.

"Apparently so." Felix shakes his head indulgently at her but steps away from Flappy Eyes, his gaze flicking to me like I might vanish the second he takes his eyes off me. "Drinks?"

"We'll both have a Pink Monstrosity." Kenzi slaps her hand down on the bar decisively.

"We will?" I jerk around to face her. "Should I know what that is?"

"Only the Beach Hut's inhouse cocktail, created by yours truly. Trust me. You'll love it." She grins wide.

And I can't help but return it. Even if she did set me up.

"These are on me." Felix grabs a couple of oversized fishbowl glasses from the rail above the bar. "It's the least I can do after last week."

A slither of abs appears with the lift of his arms. And just like that, my cheeks blaze and I can't, for the life of me, remember what he's talking about. "Last week?"

"The key thing." His lips twitch again, like he's barely restraining his smirk, when I finally return my gaze to his.

"Oh. Yeah. Right." I shake my head. "Don't worry about it."

"Is one of those for me?" Flappy Eyes fixes Felix with an unimpressed pout.

His jaw ticks when he glances her way, but he grabs another glass.

She's the girlfriend. Of course, there's a girlfriend. It's probably a good thing. A tug of something that feels scarily like disappointment has me pressing my lips together and looking away. Most definitely a good thing.

"Let's go sit over there." Kenzi pulls me away from the bar.

"I'll bring these over." Felix lifts his chin and picks up a bottle of pink liquor.

"I knew it was you," Kenzi singsongs as she lowers herself down into the cream cushions of the wicker sofa she marched me to.

"It was just coffee … and a couple of near-death experiences." I sit beside her, twisting my body to face her. "How did you even…?" I glance over my shoulder just in time to see Flappy Eyes reaching over the bar to run her fingers up his forearm.

"I told you, this island is small. So, spill. You like him? I think I saw sparks."

I force a smile, focusing on Kenzi's excited face and not the unease her assurance has set off in the back of my head. "I don't like him … I don't even know him … and there was definitely no spark."

"*Okay*." Her lips purse, her eyes narrowing on my apparently lame excuse for an easy breezy, everything's-fine smile.

I sink back into the soft cushions, my back to the man in question. "I'm not interested in sparks."

"Shame." She shrugs, staring over my shoulder to the bar. "I think you'd be good for him."

"You seem awfully interested in his love life."

Resting an arm along the back of the sofa, she tucks one of her long, tanned legs under her bum. "Me and Fee go way back." There's no disguising the warmth in her eyes. "He's more than just my boss."

"Oh." I'm helpless to keep the confused frown from my face, or the weirdness climbing up my throat. "You guys?"

"What? Ewww. No." She pretends to gag. "We lived next door to each other growing up. He's my brother from next door's mother. Seriously. No."

"It doesn't matter anyway, it looks like his sparks are directed elsewhere to me."

"Two Pink Monstrosities."

I squeeze my eyes shut and pray to anybody listening that he didn't hear any of that.

Felix

Laia's eyes widen, tracking her cocktail's journey from the tray balanced on my fingertips to the low table in front of her.

I should have known Zi was up to something when she texted me four times today to make sure I'd be in tonight. I just can't decide if I'm mad at her thinly veiled match making or not. I don't date. She knows this. And there's a particular type of woman I *don't date* with, she also knows that, even if she has made her disapproval more than known.

Regardless, finding myself face to face with this *Laia* again after convincing myself I wouldn't, and, more importantly, that it wouldn't bother me if I didn't has picked at something I don't want picked at.

She pushes her hair behind her ears and looks my way when I straighten, those big green eyes flashing the same wariness as the other day. "Thanks."

"You're welcome." Pulled by something bigger than common sense and the unfamiliar need to get rid of that wariness, I tuck the tray under my arm and drop to a squat beside her chair. "So, you're staying around here then?" I ask, ignoring Zi and the smug grin on her face.

The pink that's been staining her cheeks since she walked in deepens, her eyelashes fluttering nervously. "I … no … yes. I started in the hotel this week. That's how I met Kenzi." She nods slowly. Awkwardly as she presses her lips together and glances over to the woman by the bar. "I think your date wants you."

She's not wrong. Janice-Jane-*Jocelyne?* is glaring. She's not even my fucking date. She just showed up and parked herself at the bar. But. I scratch my jaw as I stand and look over there, she's Rosa's double. She's *exactly* my type.

Clearing my throat, I stand and spin the tray on the palm of my hand like it's a basketball as I step back from the table, refusing to meet Zi's dumbfounded stare. I should stop fucking about and stick to what I know, and this—Laia—is about as far from what I know as I could possibly get. "Enjoy your drinks, ladies."

I don't look back as I walk away. Not my type. She's not. My. Type.

"Baby. You abandoned me." Rosa-look-alike places her hand on my shoulder as soon as I'm within reach. My skin bristles under her touch. Her perfume's too sweet. Her voice, too high. But fuck. I could look at her all night.

I wave to catch the bartender's attention. "Water, Dale." I nod my thanks when he gives me the thumbs up. "And take a couple over to Zi's table when you get a minute, those cocktails are lethal."

"You seem distracted, babe."

I start at the feel of *Jill's?* hand on my inner thigh. She's forward, I'll give her that. I raise my brows at the faux innocence in her dark eyes as she runs her fingers up until they almost graze my cock through the denim of my board shorts.

"Want me to take your mind off it?"

Any other day, I probably would have taken her up on her offer. It's not healthy. Hell, it's the equivalent of chasing a ghost. But it is what it is.

Laia's laugh pulls my attention back over to their table. Her head is tilted back, her fingers wrapped around the gold necklace that hangs around her neck, and for the first time in a long time chasing ghosts doesn't hold much appeal.

"Listen. Joyce…" I grab her hand and place it back into her own lap.

"It's Jayne." Her pretty features twist into a deep scowl.

"Jayne. Right. Listen, I've got stuff to do after we close tonight."

I don't have to look to know where her glare is aimed before she hits me with a very wide, very fake smile and leans forward to plant a kiss on my cheek. "Rain check it is then." She stands and smooths her hands down her tight little body and the even tighter white dress covering it, then turns and struts away.

I drag my hand over my mouth and watch her go.

"Hey, boss." Dale grabs two of the big cocktail glasses from the shelf above the bar. "Zi just ordered two more cocktails. She said they're on you."

"Take more water over with them." I fold my arms and lean on the bar, shaking my head when Zi holds her empty bottle of water in the air above her head. Laia just looks right through me.

FIVE

Laia

Lifting the fishbowl glass of pinkie-goodness to my lips, I attempt to catch the end of the black straw in my teeth between giggles, my gaze flicking over to the bar and the man behind it before I drag it back to Kenzi for the millionth time tonight.

"You're drooling." Kenzi's glazed blue eyes hold my stare over the top of her glass with a smirk. She stopped messing about with straws two Monstrosities ago. "On a score of one to ten, how bad have you got it?" She takes an unladylike gulp of her drink then places it down between her two unopened bottles of water.

A snort escapes me before I finally catch the straw and take a long pull of the sweet frozen drink.

I've felt the weight of his stare on me most of the night too. It's been kind of … nice. I think. Not that I would ever admit that to anyone, especially not to lil ol' matchmaker over here. If my brain wasn't so warm and fuzzy, I probably wouldn't even admit it to myself. Placing my drink down beside my empty water bottles, I fix her with a serious-ish stare and lean forward. "He's perfection in surf shorts." Wha?? I slap my hand over my mouth. "I mean. Zero … minus ten."

Kenzi cackles loudly. "Perfection in surf shorts? Really?" Rocking back against the cushion, she lets out another cackle. "Oh, Laia. I like you. I think I might keep you."

I want to cry. I want to laugh. I want to climb into my glass and never come out. "Joking. I was totally joking." I chew on the corner of my thumbnail and wait for her to stop laughing. At least I *think* I was joking.

Whatever she reads on my face when she finally wipes the tears from her eyes and sits up kills her buzz. "Laia, there's nothing wrong with having the hots for Fee." She only sways slightly as she covers my hand with hers. "They say he's quite hot."

"There is if you're me." I pull my fingers from beneath hers and wrap them around the stem of my glass, my own Monstrosity-buzz dissipating rapidly.

Concern scrunches her forehead. I've said too much. *Shown too much.* Damn you, lovely Monstrosities.

"I know we don't know each other very well yet, but…" Her mouth drops open, her attention caught by something behind me before she drags it back to me. "You can talk to me, Laia, you know, if you want to, eventually."

To my complete and utter mortification, my eyes start to sting, my nose tickling with emotion. We're nowhere near me telling her about my crappy past, but the thought that maybe, someday, we could be warms something in me. "Got it." My chin wobbles. I hide it behind my fishbowl.

"Okay. Now, I really need you to turn around and tell me I'm not seeing things."

Mid-drink, I swivel on the cushion until I'm facing into the bar—and the monster of a man that just pushed through the door. Think Thor—but bigger. In board shorts and a gray T-shirt. "What? I mean, who's that?" I shift closer to her on the sofa.

"That." She leans into my side and rests her head on my shoulder with a long sigh. "Is my idea of perfection in surf shorts. I think I've just fallen in-fucking-love."

I don't know whether to blame it on the cocktails, or blame it on the pies, but an uncontrollable burst of laughter bubbles up my throat and explodes from my mouth.

I can't help it. And I can't seem to stop. My tummy aches and tears roll down my cheeks. Thank God the bar's nearing empty because I'm full-on snorting, and my hysterics, apparently, are catching. A second later, grabbing onto my hand for support, Kenzi leans forward until her head's almost on the table, her shoulders shaking with the most unladylike laugh I've ever heard.

"I. can't. Breeeeeeeeeathe." Clutching my sides, I rock into her shoulder.

"And this pair of hyenas are Kenzi and Laia."

Kenzi's laughter withers right along with my own, her fingers clamping around my wrist.

Staring down at us, matching smirks on their faces, are Felix and Thor, the man-mountain that started us off in the first place.

My cheeks are numb, my eyes, wet. I force myself not to stare at Felix and instead concentrate on the tattoos that cover his friend's ginormous left arm. Intimidating—definitely. Stunning—absolutely. I nervously glance up into his face. But his eyes are gray and … sort of kind. Startlingly so.

Books and covers. That old chestnut again.

"Ladies, this is Mylo." Felix jabs the mountain in the bicep. "We served together in the Marines." Dimples appear in his cheeks. Two of them. "Fucking surprised the shit outta me tonight."

My lips twitch, but I manage to keep my smile at bay. The man's hot when he's serious but when he smiles like that … I grab my pendant … there's nothing more dangerous.

He's with Flappy Eyes and I'm a million miles away from being ready. I need to stop.

"Ladies." Mylo lifts his chin in greeting, one side of his mouth turning up into a half smile, his gaze lingering on Kenzi.

Her lashes bat rapidly, and she squeezes my wrist. "Hi."

Felix clears his throat, and I can't help it. I look again. Bad, bad mistake. He really shouldn't look at me like that. I lick my lips, and his attention drops to them. I can't help that either. He's just—heat rushes my cheeks. I'm drunk, that's the only reason I'm noticing.

"Nice to meet you, Mylo." I cough to clear the breathiness from my voice and return to gawping up at his friend.

This is fun.

I lift my shot glass to my lips and methodically meet the stares of Mylo, then Kenzi, then Felix before slamming it back.

When my eyes release from their alcohol-induced scrunch, I'm instantly handed a bottle of water. Felix's thigh is pressed tightly against mine. Has been since Kenzi abandoned my sofa for Mylo's. I only flinched for the first ten minutes after he sat down next to me.

Now it's … I've no idea what it is—comfortable? Distracting? Dangerous? For once I don't feel like dissecting the feeling though. And I don't feel like moving away either.

"Tell me again what's with the eye contact thing?" Kenzi lounges against Mylo's massive shoulder.

"It's an old military thing." Felix leans back into the cushion behind us, his arm stretched along the back of the sofa behind me, his legs crossed at the ankle. "Supposed to be lucky."

I sway as I drink my water and my arm brushes his pec. It's—firm. Everything about him is firm. *Hard.* Thankfully, I manage to swallow my water before my snort escapes.

"What's funny?" He takes the half-drunk bottle from me and places it on the glass-strewn table then sits back, his body so close his smell wraps around me. It's a good smell. A safe smell. I like his smell.

I twist around to face him. "Just wondering what you do to get so … hard … I mean … firm … I mean…" I cover my mouth and sink further into the cushions. "Fit … I've no idea what I mean."

His laugh is a rumble of deliciousness. It slides down the back of my neck and straight to my tummy. I haven't felt this relaxed around anyone in years. I also haven't had a drink in years. Something tells me it's not a coincidence.

The flutters in my tummy multiply when he carefully tucks one of my untamable curls behind my ear. "Where did you come from, Laia?"

I still, but I don't flinch. "Arizona." Wait. What? I don't tell people that.

The first rule of living on the run—don't tell people where you're running from.

His eyes narrow at whatever my face does. Kenzi and Mylo's easy banter fades along with the crashing waves from the beach and the low background music of the bar. The voice that's become a constant in my mind for the last year niggles; *Be careful. A pretty face does not make him good.*

But tonight, there's a new voice in there too, a slightly tipsy but way more persistent … *it doesn't have to make him bad either.*

My neck heats like my cheeks and the rest of my body.

His smile is disarmingly handsome, his teeth straight and white against his deeply tanned skin. "I like your pink cheeks, Laia." He stills as soon as he says it and drags his hand over his mouth, something closing behind his eyes like my pink cheeks are the last thing he should like.

He's not wrong.

Flappy Eyes. He's thinking about Flappy Eyes. The thought is like a bucket of ice water over my head. "You're thinking about your girlfriend? The woman at the bar earlier." I suck both lips into my mouth.

His brows raise. Then fall. And just when I think I've offended him, just when the familiar prickle of fear seeps down the back of my neck, and I start to shift away from him, he chuckles roughly and drops his head onto the back of the sofa to stare up at the ceiling. "She's not my girlfriend."

I watch the rise and fall of his chest and the slow bob of his Adam's apple as he swallows. Take in the black mop of hair that curls around his ears and his thick dark lashes and for the first time in a long time, my fingers itch to touch. To press against his lips. To run over the stubble of his jaw. To trace the straight line of his nose.

As if he can hear my thoughts, he rolls his head to look at me, a sadness etched over his face I have no idea how to read. My heart trips over itself but I don't shy away from it.

I just fold my arm on the back of the sofa, rest my cheek against it and offer him the only thing I can. The only thing I need when people catch a glimpse of the secrets in my own stare.

Understanding without questions.

SIX

Laia

I peel one eye open. Then the other. This isn't the bungalow. Kenzi's. I stayed at Kenzi's. I unstick my tongue from the roof of my mouth and gingerly pull myself up until my back rests against the iron headboard, unease tightening the back of my neck. I let my guard down last night. My pulse thumps uneasily in my throat as my fuzzy brain attempts to sift through the night. The bar. Kenzi and Mylo flirting like there was no tomorrow. *Felix*. Nothing happened. Anxiety blooms in my stomach and twists around my insides regardless. I let my guard down. I should know better.

My gaze meets my own in the mirrored wardrobe on the other side of the room. Gauzy curtains the color of sunshine hang from a wooden rod, ruffling in the warm breeze.

My hair, half-in half-out of its bun, sticks clammily to the side of my face.

One strap of a pink tank that's definitely not mine hangs off my shoulder. And my eyes. God. I look like a hungover panda. My attention is caught by the massive canvas on the wall above the bed's headboard. I twist to look at it. A sunset of pinks and reds and oranges, the rippling of the water so vivid I can almost hear the waves. The muscles in the back of my neck loosen slightly. I let my guard down last night, but nothing bad happened. I blow out a slow breath. Nothing bad happened. I had fun. I'm allowed to have fun.

My tongue re-sticks itself to the roof of my mouth. Water. I need water.

I spy the white-washed wooden bedside table and the tall glass of water sitting on it. I barely remember getting home, let alone coming to bed with the foresight to bring water.

My face screws up with the effort it takes to lift the glass and down the whole thing in one go.

Okay. Better. Still blurry but better. Nothing bad happened.

I should feel worse. Probably something to do with the bottles of water that kept on appearing with every cocktail or the fact that Felix cut us off after Kenzi challenged Mylo to an arm wrestle.

It *was* fun.

"I'm rough." Kenzi's voice sounds a second before the bedroom door opens, and she weaves in, already dressed for her shift in the hotel, hair wrapped in a cerise-pink towel.

"I'm not too bad actually." I take stock of my brain now that I've managed to reel in the morning after anxiety. It's a bit fluffy around the edges, but it doesn't ache. I can handle this.

Throwing the crisp white sheets from my legs, I wiggle my toes until they appear out of the bottom of Kenzi's pink-checked pajama pants. "Maybe if you'd drank the water that came with every cocktail…"

She rolls her eyes and pulls the towel from her hair, then sets about combing it into the tight bun she wears for work. "Yeah, *perfection in surf shorts* isn't usually so attentive." Her lips quirk to the side as she winds her hair onto her head.

"I was drunk. I didn't mean it." I glance back at the painting above the headboard again in search of something to change the subject before the nerves set in again. I *was* drunk and I *didn't* mean it. "Was this painted from The Beach Hut?" Swinging my legs off the side of the single bed, I lean over to search the floor for my purse underneath my discarded dress. No purse. It's not there. I jack-knife up and look around the room. Not on the rocking chair by the window. Not the dresser Kenzi's sitting at. "Kenzi?"

"Your purse is at the bar," she mumbles, opening a drawer and pulling out a makeup bag. "Fee texted earlier. And yeah." She glances up at the painting, her brows tipping up in the middle, a not-quite-happy smile lifting her lips. "My friend painted it right from where The Beach Hut is now."

"She's really talented." Wincing at the ball of red material that used to be my dress, I fight to keep my dread in check. The Beach Hut is literally the last place I want to go this morning. Especially not in last night's clothes.

"She was." Rummaging in the dresser drawer by her knee, Kenzi tosses me a pair of gray jersey drawstring shorts and a white tank. "Here, throw these on."

"Thank you." I grab the clothes, eyeing the shorts dubiously. "I can't believe I left my purse."

Twenty minutes later, we're pushing through The Beach Hut's swinging doors. And just like last night, I freeze, mouth open at the sight that awaits me. This time it's not the view though. Well, not just the view.

Felix—fresh from the ocean, walking up the beach towards the terrace like some sort of Surf God from the deep.

"Tongue in." Kenzi nudges me in the ribs when she walks past me to the bar.

I press my fingers against my lips. How can she not be affected?

Or more importantly, how can *I* not be affected?

Drunk Laia gets on great with Drunk Felix. But in the sober light of day—

I'm not Drunk Laia.

Walk forward. Walk. Forward. I force my feet to move.

By the time I make it to where Kenzi's already skipped behind the bar, Felix is stepping in from the terrace, beads of water glistening as they weave their way over his pecs.

I try to look away. I do. Okay, I don't. At all. It's risky, and dangerous, and probably not good for my health, but the man is … I didn't think those V muscles actually existed.

He grabs a towel from the bar and wipes himself down, and I finally manage to blink my eyes up to his face. What's wrong with me? I don't check out half-naked men. I have *never* checked out half-naked men, not even pre-Damon.

"How's the head today?" His eyes do that happy, smiley, crinkly thing when he comes to a stop before me.

Semi-frozen between wanting to recapture the easy banter of last night and knowing that I can't, I just stare at him dumbly. Last night was a fluke, a fake comfort brought on by whatever was in those cocktails.

"Fine. Good. Thanks." I swallow down any of the random words forming before they make themselves known.

His gaze slides down—then stops long enough to raise goose pimples over my skin before he jerks it back up to my face.

I glance down and only just manage to stop myself from about turning and leaving. Kenzi could maybe have mentioned that this tank leaves absolutely nothing to the imagination. Heat licks up my cheeks. I might as well be standing here in my bra. I cross my arms to hide the unmistakable reaction my body's had to wet him.

The muscles in his throat contract, his jaw tight as he dips his head to run the towel over his hair. "You okay?"

"Yep." I clear my throat. "Yes."

"Good." His gruff chuckle releases some of the tension in my shoulders.

I tuck my hair behind my ears but can't quite make myself look away first despite the fact that the niggly *be-careful* voice is back and louder than ever.

His clear blue gaze scans my face, eyes to lips and back again, his brows pinched up in the middle like he's as wary of whatever happened last night as I am.

"What do you take in your coffee, Laia?" Kenzi calls over from the coffee machine.

I shake my head, trying to the disperse the—whatever that was—and force myself to move, to pull out one of the high stools by the bar and get my head out of the wet-man-shaped clouds. "Milk and one sugar, please." I lean my elbows on the bar and press my hands to my hot cheeks.

"Warm, Laia?" Kenzi frowns as she slides a mug of coffee across the bar to me. "Want some ice for your coffee?"

Felix's bare arm brushes my own as he climbs onto the stool beside me.

I flinch.

He notices, his forehead creasing. "She does look warm."

I like your pink cheeks.

My face blazes even more.

Kenzi smirks as she places a mug of black coffee in front of where he's leaning on the bar. "Is Jo in this morning?"

Who's Jo? Another Flappy Eyes?

My stomach drops before I remind myself that I shouldn't care. It doesn't matter how many Flappy Eyes he has flirting around him. The more the merrier. All the better to keep me out of his way.

"Like she is every other morning, Zi." Felix shrugs and takes a sip of his coffee. "Why?"

If there's something I've learned from a week of working with Kenzi, it's that her face tells no lies. And when she does that shoulders-up, girly grin, she's up to something.

"Laia isn't in the hotel until this afternoon, why don't you show her around the island?"

No. She did not just—I'm seriously reconsidering this friendship.

Felix's warmth shifts against my arm.

I stare resolutely ahead. "You really don't have to do that."

"As much as I'd love to"—he gulps down the rest of his coffee and stands— "I'm meeting Mylo in a bit."

I suck my bottom lip into my mouth and try to keep the sting of unreasonable disappointment from my face. I didn't want him to say yes.

I did *not* want him to say yes.

The moment Felix steps through the door behind the bar, Kenzi hops up onto the top-loader refrigerator that runs beneath the bar top and leans over. "Don't think I missed that little stare-off. I saw sparks."

I wince, checking that he's not there. Why she bothers leaning in when she's not even whispering is beyond me.

"It was ... this tank." I pluck at the stretchy material. "Thanks, by the way."

"I'm not blind," she sing-songs. "There's definitly something there."

There's no point in arguing with her. "You may not be blind, but you're about to be late?" I smile sweetly and lift my chin to the big clock hanging on the back wall.

"Shit. How is it ten to already?" She hops off the bar, the mug by her knee clattering to the ground.

"Steady on there, Zi." Felix appears through the door while dragging his T-shirt over his head and my heartbeat does a distracting little tap number. "I'll give you a ride."

The soft white material hugs his perfectly rounded biceps, making it absolutely impossible to look away when he reaches above the bar. I'm officially my own worst enemy. "I think I'll just walk." I barely manage to catch my stool before it falls when I push it back with my bum.

The questions that appear in his eyes are impossible to miss. I don't have to look to know they're there in Kenzi's too.

Questions I have zero intention of answering.

"I can give you a ride home too, no worries." He slides his sunglasses onto the top of his head then reaches back up to the shelf above the bar. "But you won't get very far without this." He hands my purse over the bar to me, the tips of his fingers brushing my wrist.

It may be my imagination, but I don't think I'm the only one that flinched this time.

He clears his throat and jerks his head in the direction of the exit. "Let's go."

The moment Felix opens the back door to his pickup, Kenzi jumps in and hauls it shut behind her. Her subtleness is outstanding.

I glare at her over-the-top grin through the darkened window when she points with both fingers to the passenger seat.

"Jump in." Felix's fingers brush the curve of my shoulder before he opens the pickup's passenger door for me.

My whole body jerks back from the unexpected touch. I suck. And going by the frown that creases his forehead before he pulls his Ray-Bans on, he thinks so too.

"Come on, Fee." Kenzi's head pokes out from between the seats. "Drop me first. Pete will have a cow if I'm late again."

I climb in the passenger seat, and Kenzi pins me with a wide-eyed stare, swiveling her eyes between me and where Felix is already climbing into the driver's seat.

I shake my head my eyes widening right back. She really needs to get off this match-making trip.

"Seatbelts," he orders while clicking his closed.

"Okay, okay." Kenzi's head disappears back between the seats again like a sulky child.

"You really do have a thing about road safety." I swipe my hair from my face and tug the seat belt across to click it into place.

"Doesn't everyone?" His jaw clenches as he turns the ignition. "Any idea how many preventable deaths there are every year on Cluan roads alone?"

I blink back my surprise at the seriousness of his tone. "Too many?" I venture quietly.

The tension radiating from him seeps into my skin, making my spine straighten and my fingers twist over each other.

"Too many." He nods but keeps his attention firmly on the road, and not for the first time I wonder what his story is.

"Laia's staying in Mrs. D's son's place up the road," Kenzi announces when we pull out onto Clua's main road in silence, the fun comfortableness from last night well and truly gone.

"How do you know Mrs. Devon?" he asks, concentrating on taking a tight bend.

"I didn't … don't, she … em … a friend put me in touch with her."

His eyes flick to mine then back to the road. "You said last night you're from Arizona?"

"I did?" I pinch the bridge of my nose between my forefinger and thumb and shake my head. I must have been drunker than I thought.

Kenzi groans from behind us.

I glance over my shoulder and force a wide grin at the hungover lump of woman that was once Kenzi, hoping like hell we're done with this particular line of questioning. "Told you, you should have drunk the water."

"You don't sound like you're from Arizona," Felix presses when I sink back into the black leather and suede of my seat. "I served with a guy from there."

My grin falls. "You must have been young when you served? You must have lived through some crazy things." I roll my eyes. Subtle. Jeez. Kenzi's right, I suck at deflecting.

"Crazy things. Cool things. Terrible things." He flicks his gaze my way with a little half-smile that barely reaches his dimples.

"I can only imagine." I keep watching the side of his face even after he returns his attention to the road. "Must be nice to see Mylo again."

His lips twitch into a smirk. He knows exactly what I'm up to. It doesn't take a genius.

"Erm, Fee." Kenzi's face appears between the seats again, a yawn splitting her face like she's just woken up from a power nap. "You just drove by my turn off."

I'm jerked forward, then back by my seat belt with our sudden stop, my purse sliding from my knees, my keys and wallet and God knows what else spilling out by my feet.

"Shit, sorry—"

"—I'm so sorry, I'm so clumsy."

Our words fall over each other, our gazes colliding.

"Why are you apologizing?" There's a hard edge to his voice like he … like *he knows.*

Impossible.

"I'm not. I didn't. Sorry." I swallow down my useless babbling, heat seeping up my cheeks.

Hand on the back of my seat, he shifts the pickup into reverse and twists to look where he's going.

I scoot closer to my door, and that crease between his brows returns when he glances at me, possibly even deeper than before.

He sees far too much. The black leather squeaks as I bend forward to pick up the contents of my purse. Wallet, lip gloss, loose change. Emergency Tampon. Seriously? Why?

Kenzi has her door open before we even pull up to the entrance of the hotel. I glance at the time flashing from the console. We made it with two minutes to spare.

"Behave, you two," she crows as she jumps out of the back seat onto the sidewalk and slams the door shut behind her.

"I can just get out here if you want." I glance at him from the side of my eyes. "I don't want to … you don't need to put yourself out for me." I chew on the inside of my cheek, far too aware of how he's looking at me—of whatever conclusions he's coming to about me. Last night was a bad idea. Getting comfortable around him was a *really* bad idea.

"No worries, I don't mind taking you." The tendons in his forearms tense and release as he drives around the fountain in the middle of the hotel's cobbled drive until we're headed back up to the main road. Tension, so thick it's overwhelming fills what little distance there is between us even if he hasn't looked my way again.

His hands flex on the steering wheel, his long fingers curling around the leather. "Why?"

My mouth goes dry at the roughness of his voice. "Why what?" I blink hard and swallow harder.

"Why do you wince every time anyone goes near you?" His fingers flex again, the muscle in his jaw ticking.

"I … its …" I wet my lips and turn to the window. "I don't wince."

It's hot in here. Too hot. I'm not ready for this, for any of it. I should have known better.

With embarrassingly trembling fingers, I attempt to press the window down button on the center console. I need air. It doesn't budge. Cars hate me. I jab my finger a little harder onto the button. Still nothing.

His hand covers my fingers, guiding them to slide the button, not jab.

I fight back the urge to shy away from the contact in an attempt to prove whatever he thinks he's figured out about me is wrong. I just about manage to still my hand beneath his. My skin tingles. My throat contracts. I can't. I pull away and clasp my hands in my lap.

The humid air now flowing in the window only adds to my discomfort, but I stare resolutely out the windshield. Mrs. Devon's house is just around this bend. I can survive this. Then never leave the house again.

"You do."

I'm already shaking my head when I turn to him. I can't—I *won't* explain myself to him or anyone. My past's my past and *I* decide who gets to know that part of me.

He holds my stare. It's only for a second, but it's enough. Something's there. He really is figuring me out. Figuring it all out.

I swallow down the urge to blurt out whatever mortifying things my stress-talking brain can come up with to deflect, but he sighs and shakes his head, eyes back on the road. "I met Mylo and Tom, the guy from Arizona, in boot camp." He side-eyes me in a way that says, *you win … for now.* "Probably wouldn't have survived my first week without them."

"Friendships forged in fire and all that?" I nod like I've any idea what I'm talking about, the relief at the change of subject so acute it almost makes my head spin. "Where's Tom now? Still serving? Or back home?" I relax back into the seat. "Maybe he'll show up out of the blue too."

"I doubt that. He didn't make it home from his last tour."

My chest aches at the tightness that pinches his face. "I'm such an idiot. I'm so sorry." I lift my hand to—I don't even know what. It drops back into my lap. "Losing people you love leaves its mark."

We slow to a stop outside the bungalow. He cuts the engine and then shifts in his seat to face me, pulling his glasses off and tucking them into the neck of his T-shirt. "You're not an idiot." He narrows his eyes at me, his lips parting before he blinks away like he's decided against whatever he was about to say. "Losing people you love doesn't just leave its mark, it changes everything about you."

The ache his words set off in my heart is almost suffocating; it blasts past the unease and the awkwardness and settles right in there. "You're right. It does change you."

Something strange, but not uncomfortable passes between us. I couldn't put it into words if I tried. He doesn't blink. Or look away. Or even twitch.

Neither do I.

Neither of us talk. I'm not sure we even breathe. The air is still thick with unasked questions, but also with a weird sort of understanding I don't think I've ever had with anyone.

We've both suffered. We've both survived. We both have scars.

Every muscle in his body has stilled, besides the drop of his eyes to my lips.

I don't move. Don't shy away. I'm pretty sure I sway towards him, pulled by something way bigger than common sense.

A car speeds by, its engine a loud rumble in the silence and the spell breaks.

I jerk back and shake my head, heat exploding across my face. I must be still drunk. "I'm sorry … I didn't … I … sorry. Thanks for the ride … I mean lift … run home." I can't even look. What the hell was that? With a little prayer that his door isn't as stubborn as mine, I lift the lever. It clicks open without a single groan, and I jump out and run-walk down the drive without looking back.

SEVEN

Laia

I woke up thinking about him, and not the *him* I usually wake up thinking about.

Felix. I woke up thinking about Felix and it's almost more terrifying than the thoughts and memories and paranoias that usually drag me from slumber.

Smiling at the woman over the fresh produce counter when she hands me my paper wrapped goat cheese, I attempt to keep my cheeks from overheating. Sex dream. I had one. About a man I barely know, and now it keeps flashing in my mind like some sort of strobe light porno—in the middle of the grocery store—all lips and hands and naked, naked skin—at nine in the morning.

What if he had actually kissed me yesterday? Right there in the car? Was that where it was going? Would I have let him? *That moment?* Did he feel it too? Was it even a moment? Maybe I made the whole thing up. I'm not sure if that's better or worse. Better, definitely better. I don't want moments, or sex dreams, or even tummy flutters. I had them. They didn't end well, and I have no interest in experiencing them again.

Dropping the cheese on top of the chocolate ice cream in the basket hooked in the crook of my arm, I head back down the dairy aisle and try to focus on the happy little jingle playing over the speakers, the cool air blowing from the AC, anything but—

I turn at the end of the aisle and my face crushes against a warm, hard, T-shirt-covered chest.

I spring back, nose filled with fresh air and peppermint and clean man, the basket falling from my arm, crashing against the tiled floor. My eyes meet the owner of the chest, and a flash of my dream, his hands on me, his lips on mine, assaults me. *Seriously?*

"Felix." My voice is a squeak, my battle with my heating cheeks lost entirely. "Sorry. I didn't … sorry."

"Laia." He drops to a squat at the same time I do, those blue, blue eyes scanning my face, his ever-present glower lowering his brows like he wanted to see me about as much as I wanted to see him. "You okay?" He reaches for my ice cream, and I flinch back like his fingers are on fire.

"Yes. Fine. Sorry." I shake my head. "I didn't see you I was…" *Trying not to think about you naked.* My face actually pulses it's so hot.

"Stocking up on ice cream and"—he lifts the paper wrapped package and frowns at it— "cheese?"

"Goat cheese," I blurt out. "It's nice in salads…" I trail off, because really, who needs to know that?

"Right." He drops it into my basket then pulls himself to standing, my groceries in one hand, his other held out to help me from my crouch.

My gaze flips from his getting lower by the second, eyebrows to his hand.

I scramble to my feet without taking it, brushing my hands down my sleeveless T-shirt dress, sure of only one thing, well, two actually. The universe hates me, and whatever moment I thought I felt definitely lands on the made-it-up side of the scale. "Why are you everywhere?" The words fall out of my mouth, making me sure about another thing too, my words are about as controllable as my cheeks.

His lips twitch into something that's not even a smile, more a bemused what-the-hell-is-wrong-with-this-woman? "I could ask you the same thing." He lifts his hand to the back of his neck, flashing the slightly paler skin of the underside of his bicep where his T-shirt sleeve stops as he scans the, thankfully, almost empty store. "I was actually hoping I'd run into you."

"You were?" My chest does a weird sort of flip and dive at the same time. "Why?" I'm frowning. I can feel it. I bet Flappy Eyes would take this moment and run with it. Flirt, or flap, or something equally pretty. I just frown even harder, the thought alone catching me up. Why am I comparing myself to her now? I don't flirt, I don't flap, and I most definitely don't do anything with moments and this man other than make them excruciatingly awkward.

The creases lining his forehead tell me he agrees completely. "You ran away."

"I did?" I don't know why I'm posing it as a question, I totally did. I ran from a moment that may or may not have been in my head, because I don't want moments. I don't want anything other than to fade into the background and not be noticed by anyone.

I drop my gaze to where he's still holding my basket, his big hand wrapped around the red plastic handle, and the spattering of dark hair that covers the tanned skin of his forearm. "I mean I did, I had to ... I'd forgotten I had something to—"

"I made you uncomfortable." He scans my face, and for the first time I wonder if the glower he always wears is because of me or it's just the way he looks at everyone. Brows down, the blue of his eyes intense with a sort of—I've no idea what—if I had to guess I'd go with loneliness? Maybe? Sadness?

Seconds pass.

I'm staring. But not talking. And he's waiting.

"What? No. Uncomfortable? Pfshhh." I wince as soon as the *pfshhh* leaves my lips. "I just. I don't do well with…" I press my lips together, staring helplessly into his face. "People."

"People?" The glower is gone, dimples tickling the stubble-covered skin of his cheeks as he tries and fails not to smile. "Not just me then?"

"No." I shake my head too fast. I almost prefer the glowering, it's much easier to look away from. "Just people." I clamp my bottom teeth over my top lip to stop this torrent of randomness. "In general." *I fail.*

His chuckle is rough and rich and filled with enough gravel to make even my cheeks halt in their heating.

My mouth plops open before I clamp it shut to stop my lips from tipping up into what I've no doubt would be a stupefied grin.

Don't smile like that. You look like something escaped from a psychiatric ward.

Damon's words come out of nowhere, stealing my fledgling grin. I lift my hand up to cover my mouth.

It doesn't go unnoticed. Felix's face sobers, his dimples disappearing, brows lowering all over again. "So, we're good?"

I nod, the unexpected brightness from a millisecond ago dimmed right back down to bad lighting and awkward shadows. "Of course."

His gaze flicks over my face like he can figure out what's going on in my head if he just glares hard enough. "Good."

"Okay." I nod again. "I should probably…" I glance over my shoulder up the aisle, already turning to walk away.

"Laia."

Shit. My groceries. I turn back to him.

He's holding out the basket.

"Thanks." I take it awkwardly in my attempt to keep my fingers from making contact with any part of him.

"See you around, Laia."

"Yep." I lift my hand in, I swear, the weirdest little wave I have ever been a part of, then turn and walk back up the aisle I've just come down.

The next week flies by, my new life in Clua taking on a realness I never in a million years expected when I stepped off the ferry that first night.

My days are filled with shifts at the hotel, making pies, hanging out on the tiny beach behind the bungalow, and coffee dates with Kenzi or visits from Mrs. Devon. In a couple of weeks Clua has started to do something Arizona never managed to do in the whole year I was there—feel a little bit like home.

And Felix was right. I do see him around. Constantly. And each time is more awkward than the last. I spilled coffee on him when I walked into Clua's Coffees as he was walking out. Dropped my ice cream when I collided with him in the ice cream shop Kenzi introduced me to in town. Almost backed my truck into his reversing out of a parking space at the grocery store. The list goes on. And on. And did I mention I'm still having those sex dreams? And I never know when they're gonna come. Like my brain will just sneak one in between the nightly Damon nightmares. One second, I'm being found by Damon, the next I'm being fondled by Felix. Both steal my sleep, though for very different reasons.

At first, I thought he was, in fact, following me, my paranoia spiking every time I found myself pinned by that growly, kind of bemused stare. But I came to realize pretty quickly that it's just a part of living in a tiny island town. You run into everyone, *everywhere*. Mrs. Devon in the pharmacy. Mylo on the beach. Kenzi on Main Street. And even Pete shopping for cushions.

Small town life—it takes a lot of getting used to, but I think I am, slowly. More than that, I think I'm actually beginning to like it.

So, when Kenzi invites me to check out *the best ribs on the island* I don't think twice.

EIGHT

Felix

"These ribs better be worth it." Mylo scratches his jaw as he checks out the restaurant over the heads of the other people waiting for a table in Mama Den's. "I'm about to hulk out if I don't get some food in me soon."

"Definitely worth it." I snort a laugh; I still can't believe the fucker showed up outta the blue. It's been good having him around. Like old times. A distraction from thoughts that are not from the old times at all. Thoughts of big green eyes and pink cheeks and, seriously, the worst habit of literally walking into me wherever I go. If it wasn't for the fact that she jumps back like I'm contagious every single time, I'd think she was running into me on purpose—I mean, I'm not exactly a small man, not exactly easy to miss in broad day light. And it just makes stopping thinking about her and her reasons for looking at me like I'm the most lethal thing she's come across even harder.

"What's with the photo wall?" Mylo's rumbling voice forces my mind back to the now.

He's turned completely in the queue now, craning his neck to get a better look at the back wall and the thousands of polaroid pictures that cover it.

I try really hard not to, the memories that wall brings with it too big to let loose. Too painful to keep close. My picture was on that wall once. *Our* picture was on that wall. I clear my throat and instead focus on the ceiling and the hundreds of blown glass light shades twinkling every color of the rainbow. If it wasn't for the ribs being *that good*, I'd have stopped coming here years ago. "Mama Den has a thing about photos. Trust me. You see her point that camera at you, you walk the other fucking way."

Mylo's staring at me when I finally look at him, eyebrows lifted in question.

"You don't wanna know." I force a smirk.

Before he can push for an explanation, I'm whacked in the elbow from behind. I scowl, turn, look down. Mama Den in the flesh.

"You two, with me." She cranes her neck back to look at us, her slashing black eyebrows in their usual unamused grimace making the deep lines that cover her face even more prominent. The tight knot of gray hair on the top of her head wobbles when she jerks her chin for us to follow her, completely ignoring the two couples waiting in front of us.

That's the thing with Mama Den's, you never know where you'll end up. With the people you come with or the people she decides to put you with. The cranky old woman just does whatever the hell she wants, and everybody lets her because, seriously, the ribs are *that* good.

We follow her tiny self through the restaurant, past the massive circular bar in the middle of the enormous space and through the tables that surround it until we come to one in the back corner that's, by the looks of things, already occupied on one side.

By Zi.

I didn't tell her we were coming here tonight. Hell, we decided on a whim and a craving for barbeque.

Awareness tickles down the back of my neck as we near, I can only see the back of the head of the woman sitting across from her, but it doesn't take a genius to figure out who it is.

I slow my steps, Mylo almost walking into my back when Laia turns at Mama Den's arrival. Her smile falters when her wide eyes lift to me, her cheeks flushing pink even in the moody lighting of the restaurant.

"Busy night. You four share table." Mama Den orders, the Japanese in her accent still unmistakable even after way more than my lifetime here. "Ladies on wall side, these brutes no fit." She scowls up at Mylo, her small stature almost comical next to him.

It takes Laia a second to react, to stop staring. Her mouth goes slack before she turns, eyes narrowed at Zi.

"Woah." Zi lifts her hands up. "This has got nothing to do with me."

Laia's less than happy reaction to the thought of sharing a table with me stings more than it should. It's been a long time since a woman's reaction to me has even registered, far else stung. She doesn't look at me again, but there's no disguising the straightening of her spine.

I open my mouth to tell them we'll go—

"I'm not complaining," Mylo cuts in before I can.

Zi presses her lips together, barely managing to hide her smile. "I bet you're not. Come on, Laia, the quicker we let these *brutes* sit, the quicker we get fed."

Laia just nods without looking at either of us and stands, brushing her hands down the back of her pale gray pants. My gaze drops, unbidden, to her ass. She may be a tiny little thing, but the woman has curves for days. I jerk my gaze away. Inappropriate. She can barely even look at me. Checking out her ass does nothing but make me look like one.

I barely register Zi and Mylo's easy banter as I pull out the chair she was just sitting in, watching her slide into the one across from me. Awkwardly, carefully, looking anywhere but at me.

"You sure this is okay?" I scan her face, waiting for her to slowly blink those big green eyes at me from beneath her eyelashes.

"Yes. Fine." She forces a smile, and I'm smacked about the head with an acute need to make her smile at me for real.

I drag my hand over my mouth and shut that need down. "So. Ribs?"

The corners of her lips quirk up.

Her eyes spark with curiosity even though they're still narrowed, still filled with mistrust. She tucks her hair behind her ears and glances over to where Kenzi is laughing at whatever story Mylo is regaling her with, that quirk growing into a real smile.

Until she returns her attention back to me.

My jaw ticks, a gnawing uncomfortableness I can't remember ever feeling over being blanked by a woman opening in some part of me I haven't paid attention to since—

I cut that thought off as soon as it catches, but it does nothing to stop the ache of loss that's never far away from expanding, spreading, reminding me that there's a reason I don't do this. That I have a type, and skittish, worried-eyed women aren't it.

"Ribs?" Her soft voice drags me back, zoning my attention her way again.

Loose curls the color of sand, the front lighter than the last time I sat across from her. The details of her face pulse at me exactly like they did that first morning in Clua Coffees, like I'm seeing in focus for the first time in fuck knows how long. There are freckles across the bridge of her nose that weren't there before too, her skin's sun kissed, healthy, like island life agrees with her.

"Best on the island." I lean back in my chair and rub my hand up the back of my neck.

"So they tell me." Elbows on the table, she clasps her hands in front of her mouth, her gaze dropping to the rough wood of the tabletop.

I reach around for something to say, something to get rid of the tightness to her shoulders. I'm rusty. It's been a while since I tried to actively engage a woman in conversation. It's been a while since I've been curious enough to. They come to me when they come. I don't chase. I don't put at ease, and I don't strike up conversations in the hope that they'll be more comfortable around me.

Mylo and Zi are already laughing over something that happened in the spa in the Castle. I click my tongue off my teeth. No help from them.

"You go to the market this week?" It takes a whole lot of effort not to roll my eyes. Smooth.

Her gaze flicks up and she lowers her clasped hands onto the table. "I did." She presses her lips together like there are words there, she just doesn't want to let them out.

"More mangos?" I raise my brows, this pull inside me to get her talking growing when her pressed lips start to curve up and she unclasps her hands.

"Mangos, berries, artisan chocolate." Her teeth flash when she bites her bottom lip, but there's no disguising the light in her eyes. "I got chilies too. I've been working on a recipe for chocolate and chili pie. Sounds weird I know, but spicy chocolate! I think I can make it work."

"You bake?" I don't know why that little fact makes me grin, but it does.

"I mean…" The light in her face dims and she blinks back down to her fingers. "*I try*. I know it's—"

"Does she bake?" Zi butts in, knocking Laia's shoulder with her own. "Only the kind of pies dreams are made of. You should totally start selling them in The Beach Hut."

I start at the sharp reminder that we're not sitting at this table alone, the chatter and clatter of the restaurant around us swirling back to the forefront of my mind. The sweet scent of Mama Den's barbeque sauce tainting the air.

"I'm always down for pies," Mylo rumbles from beside me.

Leaning back in my seat, I clear my throat, trying and failing to not look at Zi. She may not have set us up this time, but there's no disguising the smugness written in the twinkle of her eyes.

"Kenzi," Laia warns, shaking her head. "Don't listen to her, it's just … a thing I do."

I'm struck again over how little this woman likes attention. I've known women who pretend not to like being the center of attention, but when it's praise, they still preen. Not Laia. She seems to wilt under it. Visibly shy away from it.

I watch her shift in her chair, fiddle with the pendant glinting against her black top. "I wouldn't say no to trying one."

I'm pinned by her beneath-the-lashes stare as she puffs out a tiny breath of a laugh. "You don't have to."

"I'd like to."

"You'll probably be disappointed."

"By the kind of pie dreams are made of?" I shake my head but can't seem to bring myself to look away. "I don't think so."

"Mylo, let's go order drinks at the bar."

It's not Zi's words that catch me up, it's the panic that flits across Laia's face when she jerks her head around to where Mylo and Zi are already getting to their feet. And there it is again, that sting that she'd rather be anywhere else but alone with me.

"I can come," she goes to stand too.

"Nope. You two hang out, talk pie, we'll get the beer." Mylo claps me on the shoulder.

"I'm driving," she calls after them, her eyes wide as she watches them go. "Just water." She sinks back into her seat, gnawing on her bottom lip, when she looks my way again. "Sorry."

"Sorry for what?" My brows lower at the uneasy way she's watching me. It's like one step forward, two steps back trying to get her to relax around me. I'm not even sure why the fuck it even matters. Why I want her to relax around me.

"About Kenzi's outstanding subtlety." She tucks her hair behind her ears again and glances around the busy restaurant. "Does she always try to set you up?" Her cheeks flush, her gaze flashing back to me, like she did *not* mean to say that. "I mean … not that … I know this isn't … we're not."

"Never." My sigh is long. "She knows I don't date."

She presses her hands over the handles of her cutlery and blinks up at me. "You don't date?"

"I don't." My jaw ticks at the questions so clear in her eyes. "Do you?" I ask before she can ask any of them.

"Me? Date?" Her laugh is a ripple of nervousness. Her fingers curling around her pendant again. "No … I definitely don't date."

"Not even back in Arizona?"

Her face sobers, that startled, worried look freezing her features again. "No. Not there either. It's—"

"A long story?" I finish for her. "You don't have to explain yourself to me, Laia."

"You won't ask about my long story, if I don't ask about yours, right?"

"Right." I rest my elbows on the table. "So maybe now you can stop looking at me like I bite."

"I don't look at you like you—do I?" Her eyes widen almost comically.

"You do."

"I do?" She grimaces. It's cute. It's easy. It's finally unguarded.

I nod.

"I … sorry. I—"

"You don't have to apologize to me either."

"Okay." She puffs out her cheeks. "Sorr—I mean, okay." She sits back in her chair and nods. "No more apologizing." She narrows her eyes and scrunches her nose. "Do you always glower at people like that?" Right on queue her cheeks flush, like she has no control of the words that fall out of her mouth. "I … I mean—"

"I'm not glowering." I take stock of my face. My eyebrows *are* low, and my forehead *is* tensed. She's right, I'm glowering. I force the muscles in my face to relax, force my eyebrows up and my jaw to unclench. Do I always glower?

"You're not anymore." She smirks, nods, glances to the empty chair beside her like she too is completely out of practice at making small talk. "So … ribs?"

My laugh rips out of me. It's a shock to the system. To hers too, going by the hesitant grin that lifts her face from pretty to disarming.

Laia

I shift on my chair, chewing on my lip to halt my grin. His laugh is like melted chocolate on ripe strawberries. Rich, but filled with gravel. It's captivating. It's all kinds of terrifying. And don't even get me started on the eye-crinkles and dimples that come with it.

It stops as quickly as it starts, but the glower doesn't sink back into place over his features. His forehead stays smooth even when he drags his hand over his mouth, finishing with a little tug of his bottom lip.

This time his gaze on mine eases something in me I'm not sure is safe to have eased. Even the noisy restaurant around us seems to blur out.

No part of me wants to shy away from it. If I'm being really honest with myself, I kinda want to sink into it and cling to the tiny slice of normality radiating from its easiness like a normal woman, on a normal non-date. "What's so special about them?"

"Looks like you're about to find out." He takes his elbows off the table as the waiter appears with the biggest platter of barbeque ribs I have ever seen.

I blink from him to the ribs then to where Kenzi and Mylo have appeared again, Mylo with a pitcher of beer and Kenzi with a glass bottle of mineral water and a bottle of wine. They look good together. Like a matching set. Kenzi's hair is loose and perfectly tousled around her shoulders. Mylo's is up in a top-knot of a standard mine can never dream of reaching. Both tall and tanned and blond, and both grinning down at us like *they're* waiting for *us* to announce the engagement.

"We come bearing beer." Mylo's the first to move, to drop the pitcher onto the table beside the giant-sized platter of sticky, sweet-smelling goodness, froth spilling over the side and onto his massive hand.

"And I come bearing water." Kenzi cocks her head at me. "And wine. You could always scrap the good girl vibe, leave the truck and sleep over at mine tonight."

"Thanks, but sorr—"

Felix cocks his head. *No apologies.*

"Just water for me."

Now, I might be imagining things, but I'm pretty sure I see a tiny blip of pride in the tilt to Felix's lips before he scratches his jaw and turns to whatever Mylo is saying to him.

Best. Ribs. Ever.

My fingers are sticky and I'm pretty sure I have barbeque sauce on my chin, but my belly's full and I swear there's a full-blown party going down on my tongue. Damon would hate this, the mess, the stickiness, the blatant disregard for cutlery.

It was his voice in my head that had me picking up my knife and fork.

It was Felix looking at me like I was insane, holding my stare as he picked up a rib with his fingers and tore off the meat with his teeth, that had me putting them back down again.

I'm not gonna lie, my mouth had dropped open, and the heat that had rushed up my neck had nothing to do with embarrassment and everything to do with the way he watched me when his tongue slipped over his bottom lip to catch some stray sauce.

I've laughed more than I have in years—more than even Drunk Laia did last week in The Beach Hut. Stone cold sober, I've relaxed into the conversation, joined in, made jokes, asked questions, *lived* in the moment without a flinch or a paranoia in sight.

That's probably why, when, elbows on the table, Felix leans forward towards me, I find myself leaning in too.

"You've got sauce." His eyes lower, gaze fixed on my mouth as he reaches over and brushes my chin with his thumb.

If I thought the restaurant around us blurred out before I was hugely mistaken. This time it does. It really does. It's like everything stops, pauses. Kenzi's cackle at whatever Mylo is telling her. The kids fighting at the table beside us. Everything but his touch on my face, the dilation of his pupils, the slight parting of his lips, and the thumping of my heart. And this time I can't even blame it on the Monstrosities.

Then in a flash—a literal flash—it all spins back to real time.

I jerk back, my head snapping around to Mama Den. And a camera. My mouth dries, whatever easy breezy I thought I was feeling evaporating completely under a wave of what-do-I-think-I'm-doing.

"Wait. No." My head's shaking, my hand coming up to, I've no idea what? Snatch the camera the little old lady is already snapping a photo of Kenzi and Mylo with? To plead with her not to put my photo online or anywhere near social media without sounding like a loon?

The shell-shocked look on, not only Felix's, but Kenzi's face too, momentarily pauses my panic. But only for a second. *A millisecond.*

My cheeks are clammy, my palms sweaty and that party on my tongue? It's evaporated to ash. "That … she won't put that online?" I go to stand. To follow Mama Den. To get that photo deleted regardless of how insane it'll look to them.

Kenzi's fingers circle my wrist. I snatch it back without thinking. "You don't understand. I can't…"

"Laia, it's just a polaroid for the wall. I don't think Mama Den's even *has* a website."

Oh. I open my mouth. Close it again. Sit back down, embarrassment almost swallowing me whole.

Kenzi's watching me like I've just grown another head. Mylo's ever present smile has even straightened. And Felix? He isn't even looking at me. His eyes are fixed on his empty plate, brows lower than I've ever seen them, which is really saying something.

"The photo wall?" I manage to drag my attention from Felix back to Kenzi, the need for confirmation that my face isn't going to end up on the internet where *anyone* can find it too big to let go. *Anyone* meaning Damon. Where *Damon* can find it—*find me.*

Kenzi glances at Felix, her lips making an O, like what she's about to tell me is not something he's gonna like. "The wall is." She presses her lips together. "It's an island superstition." Her wince does nothing to ease the shriveling of whatever sense of freedom from my past I *thought* this night had given me. "If your photo goes on the wall" —her big blue eyes flick to Mylo, before she closes them and shakes her head— "you've found your one. It's probably nothing, I mean who even believes in silly superstitions anyway?"

Her. *She does.* She rescued my mangos from the garbage the other day because of a superstition.

Felix still hasn't looked at me. Like, at all. Like he believes, or *believed* it too.

My cheeks warm. It's not like I want him to be my *one* either.

NINE

Laia

I blow out a long breath and shove my key into the truck's ignition but flop back into the seat and press my palms against my closed eyes before I turn it.

The dinner … it didn't improve after the photo implosion. Felix barely looked at me again, and when he did that glower wasn't just back in place, it was deeper and frownier than ever before. Even Kenzi kept on glancing his way, a worried pinch to her face that only intensified when she was looking at me.

I don't care. I *shouldn't* care. We weren't even supposed to be having dinner together.

Shaking my head, I turn the key, the engine roaring to life in the darkness of the truck's cab. Maybe I should've taken her and Mylo up on their offer of going for a drink. Mylo's been staying at the hotel since he got here, and their flirty banter is the stuff rom-coms are made of. Easy, fun, not *awkward* at all—even after the photo wall revelation. All the more reason for me not to go. To leave when I did with barely a *bye* from Felix.

Pulling out of the carpark, I turn down the road towards the bungalow, my eyes constantly flicking to the rearview, to the back seat, my neck stretching to see further into the trunk. I forgot to check it. I always check the trunk.

Releasing another breath, I fix my eyes on the dark road again, cursing out the one downside to this island. As soon as you leave the town behind, you leave the streetlights behind too. And in the dark, even the lushest, greenest forests can look ominous.

Breathe. It's paranoia. Just your garden variety paranoia. Dropping my hand onto the gear stick, I keep my gaze fixed straight ahead. Keep it on the truck's double cones of yellow light. There's nobody back there. Ten minutes and I'm home. There's nobody there. Fifteen and I'm in my bath, with bubbles, and the glass of wine I didn't have earlier, forgetting all about photo walls, and island superstitions, and glowering men.

I almost manage it too. Manage to relax, to stop checking the rearview.

And then the engine splutters. My shoulders and my heart rate ratchet up. Then up again when it just … dies.

No. No no no no no. I pump my foot on the slack gas pedal and twist the key even as the truck slows then creeps to a stop. In the dark. In the middle of nowhere. Alone.

I hate the dark.

Fingers still wrapped uselessly around the steering wheel, I wet my lips, fear stretching like a rubber band across my chest. Tight. Too tight. I can't … this can't be happening. Not now. My chin trembles and I blow out a shaky breath just as the truck lights flicker then fail.

Pitch black. It's pitch black and I don't have a flashlight. I don't even have a cell phone to call anyone for help.

The panic's almost suffocating. I don't know what to do. I blow out, one two, three breaths. Back in. It's no good. I'm still panicking. And it's still dark.

It's still really fricken dark.

I press my shaking hands against my mouth. Think. Okay. My eyes start to adjust. There's a moon. It's not full. It's barely even a crescent, but I can see. Just. Flashlight. There must be one somewhere, it's a truck—a man's truck.

I reach beneath the bench, blindly rooting around. Nothing. Another deep breath. It's okay. It's just the dark. I can walk. I'll just walk home. It'll take me half an hour, tops.

Head lights flash in my rearview mirror before I've even straightened enough in my seat to take my seatbelt off. My pulse thumps up into my ears. Another car. And it's pulling up. Behind me. My brain flashes through a dozen scenarios, but they all end with one thing, regardless of how unlikely it is to be true. *Damon.* He's found me.

Move. I need to move. Locking the door, I try the key again, and again, and again, pumping the pedal like a crazy person. The hysteria climbing up my throat is making it hard to swallow, never mind breathe.

Screaming. Not something I do. Not something I've ever done, no matter how bad things have gotten. Somebody should probably have told my mouth that, because when the window is rapped on, I let loose a shriek so impressive I'm almost surprised the windows don't just give in and smash. Eyes squeezed shut, lungs open and fully functional, hoping like hell someone will hear me.

"Laia?"

I slam my mouth shut, slam my eyes shut too.

"Laia! It's me."

I turn my head, panic gone, mortification back—so back it's not even funny. It's not Damon.

It's Felix, hands pressed against the glass, the head lights from his pickup cutting across the angles of his face in yellow. Because he needed another reason to glower at me.

I wet my lips and stare stupidly at him through the window.

"Roll down the window, Laia." He taps his finger on the glass between us.

I close my eyes and release the air from my lungs in a miserable sigh. How many times do I need to run into this man on the side of roads? And why is every time worse than the last?

The window creaks its way down and he leans in, looking at me in a way I'm becoming resignedly used to. *Like I'm a liability to myself and everybody around me.* Because, let's face it, he's not wrong.

His gaze moves over my face, and I brace myself for it, the sneer, the wise crack, the insinuation that I can't do anything right. Can't even get home without help.

It doesn't come. None of it comes because he's not Damon. He's Felix. Nothing but concern flashes across his face. "Need a hand?"

"No." I glance around the darkened cab embarrassingly close to tears. "Yes. I don't know. It just died." I sniff and twist the key again, pushing my foot down on the gas pedal. "The lights won't even work."

Gaze still on my face, he leans back and grips the edge of the window. "Probably just your battery."

"Great." I drop my hands into my lap. "I don't even know if I have jump thingies in this thing."

"Jump thingies?"

"Yeah, the…" I lift my hands and do a ridiculous job trying to act out the pincer whats-its. "Thingies." I blow out my cheeks. "Or maybe you could just call someone for me, and I'll just wait here. You don't have to wait or anything."

"You don't have a cell?" There's no disguising the surprise in his voice, because seriously? Who doesn't have a cell these days? People worried their crazy ass ex can track them by it, that's who.

"I don't have a cell. It broke. I lost it. I just…"

"—don't have a cell," he finishes for me the corner of his mouth ticking up even though his forehead is creased with whatever it is that's going through his head.

"Yup." I moosh my lips together in an attempt to stop any more words from falling out. "I mean no. I don't."

"Come on. My jump *thingies* are at the bar. I'll give you a ride home then come back in the morning for the truck."

"Really?" My eyelashes flutter in the darkness as I turn to him. His up tipped brows. His ticking jaw visible even in the dim moonlight. His clean man scent tainted ever so slightly with the scent of barbecue reminding me that tonight didn't end well. Tonight ended weird and uncomfortable with him barely even looking at me while I fidgeted like a chipmunk on crack. "You don't have to do that. I can just call a tow truck, or you could call the tow truck. Or … or…"

"Laia."

"What?"

"Stop."

"Okay, sor—" My gaze jumps to his.

There's no smile there. No malice either. What is there is something I have no idea how to put a name to, something that makes my insides flip and my fear twist and morph and slip into something different. Something that tempts me to be braver, something that warms me even more than the humidity of the night, something that wants me to stop with the damn apologies.

"I mean, thanks." I glance up through a break in the forest's canopy to the twinkly stars and take a deep breath of the woodsy air coming through the window. It's fine. This is fine. He can take me home. He's done it before, and we got there in one piece. But this time it's dark. This time nobody knows I'm with him. This time I've sex dream kissed him. Seen his sex dream penis. Felt his sex dream lips on my sex dream—

"You gonna open the door?"

God only knows what my face must be doing, because the frown on his is part amused, part what-the-hell-am-I-getting-myself-into. "Okay. I should probably…" I reach for the window handle, glancing at where he's still gripping the door.

Hands clasped in my lap, cool air blowing in my face, I stare straight ahead. Awkward. *I'm* awkward. *He's* awkward. And he doesn't even know what images I have on repeat in my head.

"So—"

"—music?"

Both our heads jerk around at the overlap of words.

"Yes. Please." I try for a smile. It's just as uncomfortable as my not-smile.

His jaw ticks, but he reaches for the console.

Meatloaf blasts from the speakers. *Meatloaf?* My laugh ripples from me, unexpected but not unwelcome. It's the first non-nervous reaction I've had around him since I got into this pickup.

His chuckle is verging on embarrassed as he reaches for the stereo again.

"No, don't. Leave it." I reach for his hand without thinking, the tips of my fingers brushing his knuckles before he can turn it off. "I was practically brought up on eighties rock." I'm grinning, I can't help it. Memories of sitting behind the living room door, reading the lyrics from my dad's Meatloaf record cover and committing them to memory so that I could sing them with him wrap me in comfort.

"Okay." Amusement flashes in his eyes when he puts his hand back onto the steering wheel.

It takes a minute for me to stop grinning. A couple more for my foot to start tapping. And when *Like a Bat out of Hell* starts up—I'm singing. I can't help it. Quietly. To myself. To the window. In no way loud enough to be heard by the man tapping his thumb against the steering wheel.

By the time the song gets to the part about tearing down the road faster than any other boy has ever gone, he's singing too. Surreal. He's singing, I'm singing. Two almost strangers belting out the words to eighties rock together in the dark when, normally, we're the epitome of uncomfortable around each other.

It's over too soon. The next song on his play list fills the cab of the pickup and self-consciousness engulfs me tenfold. I lift my hand to my mouth and side-eye my unexpected partner in rock. I just sang. *We* just sang.

"Meatloaf." He rubs the back of his neck and clicks his tongue off his teeth before another of those rough, melted chocolate laughs replaces the silence. And just like back in the restaurant, it disarms me, it momentarily blurs the lines between my past and my present, my fear of well ... *everything,* and this shiny, new, kind of fledgling desire to actually move forward—no, not just to move forward—to stop looking back while I do it.

"You gotta love him." My own laugh is goofy, more like a noisy exhale of air, but it's there, and judging by the deepening of his dimples when he glances my way, it doesn't bother him. If anything, it makes his smile even wider.

I sink back into the seat, a smile that matches his still hovering on my lips. "Next you'll be telling me you're a Queen fan too."

His only answer is a smirk without looking my way as, eyes on the road, he taps the screen in the middle of the console a few times.

The first words of Bohemian Rhapsody sound from the speakers and my head snaps around to gawp at him. "Are you serious?"

"I never joke about Queen." He's still smirking, still watching the road too.

The rest of the ten-minute drive home is ... well it's completely not how I pictured it going at all. My jaw aches from laughing, my cheeks hurt from smiling and I've discovered that, if nothing else, we're more than compatible road trip buddies. Who knew?

But the music dies along with the growl of the engine when he pulls up outside the bungalow. The silence is sobering, like the come down after a hysterical laughing fit. The usual, acute self-awareness I wear around, not just him, but everybody, slides right back over my shoulders like an itchy jersey that doesn't quite fit right. I don't have to look to know his face has slid into its usual glower too. So, I don't. I press my lips together and reach for the door lever. "Thanks. *Again.*"

"You're welcome." He clears his throat, one hand resting on the steering wheel, his gaze meeting mine when I turn to close the door.

Gripping the top of the car door, my lips part … to say what, I've no idea. Seconds pass before I finally blink my stare away from his and close the door with nothing more than a weak *goodbye* before I make my way up the drive.

I spin at the sound of footsteps behind me just as I make it to the door.

"I'll need the truck keys if you want me to bring it over tomorrow." Felix is stalking up the narrow path towards me.

Back against the door, my heart thumps. In the pickup we were eye level, and, I don't know, kinda safe. Upright he's … well, he's much bigger than me.

"Oh. Yeah. Of course. Sorry." I unclip the truck's key from the house key with embarrassingly shaky fingers, then hold them out to him, blinking up at him.

"No worries." His gaze drops to my mouth. "Laia, I don't know what your story is, but…" He trails off releasing his breath. "I…" He wets his bottom lip, and his gaze flicks up to find mine.

I should look away. Flinch back. Turn around and walk away. I don't. I can't.

It's like everything slows.

I'm not imagining it, there's something there. Something that resonates somewhere. Something that I think might be making me—him—*both of us*—slightly insane.

"You?" I finally manage to make my mouth work.

He puffs out something between a laugh and a sigh, lifting his hand to the back of his neck and his gaze to the star strewn sky above us. "Nothing. I should probably go."

"Yeah." I nod, still staring even when he lowers his gaze back to me.

The moment stretches, unfurls, lays itself out between us, silent but not uncomfortable, neither of us making any attempt to end it.

And then he lifts his hand slowly—so slowly I've time to look from it to his face and back again before he brushes my hair from my face. "I had fun tonight." His stare is probing, *questioning*—looking just as stupefied by this as I am. "With you."

"Me too." Drawn by the warmth of his nearness and something way, way bigger than common sense, I lift my chin as his head dips. It's just a fraction of a millimeter but it's enough to have my heart beating wildly in my chest.

He's going to kiss me.

And I'm going to let him.

I wait for the fear to kick in, for the panic to pull me back and send me running. It doesn't come. His hand moves to my jaw, his thumb stroking my cheek, those questions, *that confusion,* still bright in his eyes, even as he leans in.

And then he brushes his lips over mine. His lips are smooth, soft, barely touching me. My eyelids flutter closed and my breath hitches.

And when the fear still doesn't kick in, I do the unthinkable. *I kiss him back.* Cautious at first, my insides flipping and swishing in the best sort of way, overriding the part of me still waiting for the other shoe to drop. For him, or me, or both of us to pull back.

We don't.

He groans, and it vibrates in every single nerve ending below my belly button—nerve endings I had almost convinced myself were no longer a part of me.

I part my lips and lean closer, tilting my head when he slides his tongue over mine in teasing strokes that steal every messed-up thought from my mind, except one—the man can kiss.

His teeth graze over my bottom lip, and my back hits the door. I pull him with me by fingers I hadn't even realized I'd threaded into his thick black hair. I arch my body into his chest, boldened by the intense sort of numbness that's blanked out my mind. His mouth seems to have had an erasing effect on all of the memories that play on constant repeat in my head. The fear. The paranoia. The *everything.*

I pant against his lips, and his kiss turns harder—surer. I feel drunk on him. I feel good. *I feel brave.*

His hand slides down my side to my hip, his big body pinning me into the door. I forget to breathe. Forget everything except the feel of his tongue against mine, the rough catch of his stubble on my chin, and the solid weight of him against me.

It takes me over. And I let it. He tilts my head back and pushes closer until there's not even a millimeter of space between us, lips to knees, heavy breaths and so much pressure. I lift higher onto my toes, suck his bottom lip and open to him again, falling into the feeling. The escape. *The freedom.*

But, way, *way* before I'm ready, he pulls back, and the delicious mind melt his mouth brought with it recedes almost as quick as it came around.

I unwind my fingers from his hair—open my mouth and try to get my brain to come up with something, *anything* to explain it.

He shakes his head, a black curl falling forward onto his forehead. "Laia—"

"That was a mistake," I finish for him and tug his hand from where it's still curled around my jaw, every reason, every iota of self-preservation ramming back into place with a thud that almost winds me. That most definitely should not have happened. "I don't … can't … that wasn't supposed to happen."

His brows do that quirk up in the middle thing, and he presses his lips together. I can't tell if he agrees or disagrees. It doesn't matter. What was I thinking?

"You … I…" I blow out my cheeks and lower my eyes to his heaving chest. "I'm sorry."

"No apologies." A ringing from his pants halts whatever else he's about to say. Probably for the best. He steps back, scanning my face like he's searching for some sort of sane reason for what just happened too.

He won't find it there.

I clear my throat and jerk my gaze from his. "You should probably get that."

He nods and pulls his cell from his back pocket, dragging his hand over his mouth as he glances at the screen. "It's the bar."

"Take it." I pull my, still tingling, bottom lip through my teeth and curl my fingers against the sudden desire to brush the hair from his face. *To kiss him again.*

His eyes narrow. "We should talk about this."

"Take the call."

"Laia." His jaw ticks, his eyebrows lowering.

"I'm fine, honestly. Please, just take the call and forget about" —I flap my hand in the space between us— "that."

With a frustrated sigh, he swipes his finger across the screen and lifts his cell to his ear.

He watches me as he listens to whoever it is calling him. I should go. *Now.* Just turn around and go inside. I don't. I stay. And stare. I watch his lips move, watch his eyes as they flick over my face. It was a mistake. It has to have been a mistake.

I'm still staring when he cuts the call and shoves the phone back into his back pocket. "I have to get to the bar to lock up. I'll be around tomorrow with the truck. We can talk about this then."

"Okay … I mean, no, we don't have to talk about … that, this. There's nothing to say."

"But we probably should." His low-browed stare scans my face once more before he nods almost to himself then turns and stalks back down the path.

TEN

Laia

I sit up in the bed, dazed and—*well rested?* With no idea what time it is. I was really out. No nightmares, just solid, black, beautiful sleep. It took none of the willpower or meditation techniques it usually does to fall asleep last night. My lids had become a delicious kind of heavy the second I'd flopped into bed and I'd just—drifted off. That never happens.

I feel good. Calm. *Revitalized.*

Until reality kicks in.

Felix kissed me. *And I kissed him back.*

That was … I sit up in bed and kick off my sheets, bringing my fingers to my lips … insane. Stupid. Reckless. *Really fricking good.*

My body tingles. All of it. Every single inch of it. The man can kiss, but that means nothing. Damon could kiss too. that hadn't stopped him from turning into a maniac the second he had me hooked. In fact, that's exactly how he got me hooked.

But this was different. Disorienting sure, but … I don't know … just … *different.* Even if it was a mistake.

Pressing the pads of my fingers against my closed eyes I shake my head then check the old digital alarm clock on the bedside table. What the? I lean closer. How can it be midday already? I'm working in an hour, and I have no truck and—I pat my head and wince—bedhead that won't go down without a fight and a shower.

By the time I've showered and made it to the front door to leg it up to Mrs. Devon's house to call a taxi, I've already half-blinded myself with shampoo and stubbed my big toe twice.

A man in a rush will always arrive late. I roll my eyes. One of my dad's more obscure sayings. I never quite managed to understand this one, but regardless, it never fails to pop into my head when I'm panic rushing to get ready.

An apple clutched between my teeth, I pull my pumps on with one hand and grab my purse from the console by the door with the other. I'm gonna be late. Whatever calm revitalization my epic sleep brought with it has well and truly evaporated. I don't even know if Mrs. Devon's in. Why haven't I bought a cell yet?

It's not until I reach for my keys, I notice my truck keys on the floor in front of the door. There's a note too.

I pick them both up, wiggling my foot the rest of its way into my shoe as I flip the small, folded paper open. A chasm of fluttering takes off in my chest when I scan the neat print. *Felix's* neat print.

I knocked but no answer. The battery's charged. I'll swing by later to talk.

Felix.

I read it again. And again. He kissed me. I kissed him back. He brought me my truck. *He wants to talk.*

I do not have time to freak out. This is a problem for New Laia. Later.

I make it to the hotel five minutes early, still far too wrapped in my post-kiss sleep daze, with the slice of pie I promised Kenzi for bailing on drinks after dinner last night.

It can't happen again—the kissing I mean. It was a one off. A lovely, crazy, but dangerous one off. I don't—can't—*won't* get swept up in a man again.

Kenzi glances up when I clunk the cellophane-wrapped plate onto her desk. Her normally sparkling eyes pink rimmed, and dull, and *hungover?*

"Man, are you a sight for sore eyes." She leans forward and takes a peek under the plastic wrap. "And you brought the pie. You're an angel." Leaning back in her chair, she stretches her arms up above her head and yawns. "So, spill, lady. Anything exciting to tell me about last night?"

I wrinkle my nose. I kissed your boss, and it numbed my brain. I shake my head. Our friendship probably isn't ready for that particular brand of crazy yet. "Nothing to spill." I shuck the strap of my purse from my shoulder and step around the back of the reception desk so she won't be able to read the whopping lie on my face.

My chair creaks stiffly as I plonk down onto it and spin to face my computer with the morning's check-ins. "Have fun with Mylo last night?"

Pressing both of her hands against her cheeks, Kenzi nods her head. "Yes, too much fun. It's such a waste." She pouts and pulls the bottom drawer of her desk open to get her purse out.

"A waste? Why? He seems nice." I lean forward, frowning. She was very *vocally* flirting with him over the ribs last night. And as far as I could tell, the flirting was mutual.

"He's so hot he almost made me forget about my man ban." She rests her elbows on her desk and massages her temples. "But I will not be fooled by biceps and lured by man-buns again. The last guy I was interested in was also hotness personified and he ended up being a douche, same with the one before that, and the one before that. So, I've decided to settle for admiring Mylo the man-mountain from afar. Besides he was the perfect gentleman-mountain—not one move did he make on me." Throwing her cell into her purse, she gets to her feet and grabs the plate. "Anyway, back to you. Don't think you're off the hook. Felix looked pretty starry-eyed when he appeared at The Beach Hut after rescuing a certain little Laia from the side of the road last night."

"He told you about that?" My cheeks do their usual blaze of admission before I can even think of a way to talk myself out of whatever it is she thinks she knows. Surely he wouldn't have. "What else did he tell you?" My thumb automatically lifts to my teeth.

"Nada. He didn't have to." She narrows her eyes at me as she steps around in front of the desk. "His starry eyes are as easily read as those cheeks of yours."

I press my hands against my still warm cheeks. "Kenzi, nothing happened."

"Don't." She lifts her hand to quiet me, a cheeky sparkle returning to her tired eyes. "You lie about as well as I say no to tequila shots, that's to say … not very well. Just know that I approve of whatever *nothing* that did or did not happen last night." She winks then wiggles her fingers. "I'm out, you little minx. I'll catch you tomorrow."

Hands still on my cheeks, I watch her go.

ELEVEN

Laia

That shift was possibly the longest shift ever known to man. I spent most of it fantasizing about what my life could be like if I were different. Normal. If my life wasn't messed up beyond all recognition. If I could kiss him all the time.

I'm *not* normal. My life *is* messed up. And I'm pretty sure I can't kiss him all the time. I yawn wide and pull the blinker down to turn into my drive before I notice the pickup. *His* pickup.

Felix.

I don't know why I'm surprised. He said he'd be here. He glances up from where he's leaning on the hood, looking at his cell, his gaze meeting mine through the truck's windshield as I pull up to the bungalow.

I need to tell him that I'm only interested in being friends. Even if he does look like he just stepped out of an ad for Rough and Rugged Weekly. Even if the way he kisses did act like a temporary off switch for my crazy.

The truck crawls to a stop, backfiring spectacularly before the engine sputters and dies.

I wince. The battery isn't the only thing I need fixed.

The difference between our two vehicles is laughable. His sleek black Ford Ranger gleams, even in the dim moonlight. My not-quite-new truck looks like a patchwork quilt, each panel more faded and rusted than the next. Not *even* the moonlight can disguise it.

I should get out. Get this over with. I put my hand on the door handle ready to shove it open but nearly topple out when Felix yanks it open from the other side.

With all the grace of a baby elephant, I practically fall from the truck.

His hands come out to stop me from smashing into him. I dodge them *and him* with a muttered, *hey*. I'm not stupid, one look into his face and my already crumbling conviction will disintegrate.

Head down, I fumble with my keys, my skin tingling with the warmth radiating from him and his uniquely-him ocean air and peppermint scent as I turn to lock the truck.

Why does he have to smell so damn good?

Taking a deep breath, I turn back to face him and lean back against the door. "Thanks for bringing the truck back this morning."

He folds his arms and leans against the pickup across from me, his gaze moving over my face. "You're welcome."

I should invite him in. A normal person would invite him in. I don't think I can. I absentmindedly rub my hands up my arms and look anywhere but into his face. Neither New Laia or Old Laia are ready for that. "You wanted to talk?"

Ridiculous. I'm being ridiculous. It's not like he's gonna fly into a rage when I tell him I'm not interested. I shiver despite the balmy night air. I can't help it.

My fears are deep rooted. And they're back in full force.

His hand lifts to the back of his neck and he looks almost nervous, watching me like that from beneath those thick, black eyelashes. It's disarming.

It's dangerous.

"I wish you wouldn't look at me like that." His voice is soft like if he were talking to a scared animal.

That's probably how I seem to him—skittish, nervous. If only I could control it, or at least hide it better. Be the girl from last night.

I sigh heavily and force myself to look at him. Really look at him. I need this done. "I've been thinking about what happened last night." I twist my fingers in front of me, the low buzz of crickets and the distant crash of waves against the shore still foreign enough to my ears that they never fail to catch my attention even after a couple of weeks here.

He rubs a finger over his lips as he waits for me to finish, and flashes of how good those lips felt on mine—how amazing they made me feel, don't make what I'm about to say any easier. All they do is steal the words I've been so carefully practicing in my head all day.

"I don't think—"

"—we're a good idea," he finishes for me, watching me carefully.

I lift my chin and attempt to put more confidence into my words than I feel. "I've just moved here and it's … it's not you—"

"—It's not me, it's you." His laugh is low and rough, his eyes sparkling in the dim light above the garage door.

The sound of it slides over my skin like a sinful breeze. I stare at my tangled fingers so he can't see the question I'm pretty positive is written all over my face. How can a simple laugh give me goosebumps all over?

"I agree."

"You do?" I look up. I can't help it. But the second I do, I wish I hadn't. His stare has clouded like he can sense the shift in my mood. Like he can see the effect he has on me. And it makes me squirm.

One of his dark brows raises. "I came here to tell you the same thing. I mean, you're Zi's friend, and I don't want this to get weird. I should never have, *we* should never have—"

"—It's fine. Not weird. Not at all," I rush out, my cheeks far too hot to be healthy.

My heart rate speeds when he pushes from his pickup, his hands dropping to his sides. If he can read minds, I'm screwed.

In two strides, he's standing before me.

I stop breathing.

He stares down, the muscle in his jaw flickering. My flight mode must be seriously out of whack with the rest of me. I'm pretty sure it should be screaming at me to get out of there—to get my ass into the house and away from him. It doesn't. So, I just stare, hot cheeked and wide-eyed.

"So, we're good." His tone is light. Easy.

"We are." I suck my bottom lip into my mouth to stop my lips from tugging down with unreasonable disappointment.

"Just friends." His attention flicks down to my mouth.

"Just friends." I nod. I should be thankful. This was my best-case scenario. "It's for the best." My words barely make it past a whisper.

"Definitely." He holds his hand out, his face void of any trace of humor.

He wants to shake my hand?

I stare dumbly. He seriously wants to shake my hand?

A nervous giggle bubbles in my chest at the absurdity of it all.

Holding my breath, I take his hand awkwardly, but the instant his fingers wrap around mine I flashback to how it felt against my cheek, on my hip, against my lips. My body reacts. Man, does it react. My nipples pebble against the flimsy silk of my white blouse, my skin flushing from the roots of my hair down to the tips of my toes.

I swear his eyes flash and his fingers tighten around mine before he clears his throat and releases my hand.

I snatch it to my chest, blinking my shell-shocked gaze from his face. "I … sorry. I should go. You should—I'm sorry."

"Hey." He nudges my chin up with his knuckle like it's the most natural thing in the world.

I don't flinch. Not even a little. I just stare up at him.

"Don't worry about it, Laia. We're good."

I nod. Shake my head, unable, no, unwilling, to force my stare from his. "Good." My scalp prickles with awareness.

"Good." He doesn't pull away. Doesn't move to leave. He doesn't even blink.

I'm kissing him again before my mind has a chance to tell me not to, and I swear it's even more mind-numbingly intense than the last time.

Felix

That was … I've no idea what the fuck that was.

I push my head back into the headrest, dumbstruck, staring at her front door, half convinced I just made the whole crazy encounter up.

She kissed me. Hard. *Again.* Her body bowing up and in until every curve of her was crushed against me. Soft, pliable, but completely in control. Her tongue.

Her lips. That fucking sighing moan. She just kissed the living shit out of me, and I did nothing to stop her. Didn't even call after her when she left me standing there like a kid with his first boner, mouth open, eyes closed, wondering what the hell just happened.

I blow out a long breath and scrape my fingers through my hair. It doesn't change anything. I'm not interested. *She isn't interested.* I'm good with that. *Great with that.*

But that kiss? I lean forward, turn the ignition, and shift the pickup into reverse.

I think I might be good with that kiss too.

TWELVE

Laia

Still in my green pajama shorts and my favorite washed-out gray tank, I poke my head into the cleaning cupboard under the sink. There must be a dustpan in here somewhere. Stress cleaning only works if you have things to stress clean with. Pressing the palms of my hands to my eyes, I suppress a yawn. Sleep came far too easily last night. So did the sex dreams. Wet Felix and that V of muscle that dips into his shorts.

Too much sleep and too many sex dreams. I feel *over-rested*, but jittery at the same time, but like I kinda want to go back to bed and make the most of my reprieve from the usual Damon nightmares.

I pull out a cardboard box and open the top flap. No dustpan, just an old house phone.

A cell. I still need to get one. My old one is hidden in the back seat of a bus, heading to God knows where, taking its traceable GPS, and hopefully Damon, with it.

I scrub my hands over my face and sigh, long and hard. The Felix effect officially fading, letting Damon's presence snake its way right back in. It takes up root in the base of my skull, radiating a hum of paranoia and anxiety down every muscle, vein, and bone in my body. My lungs even shrink in on themselves almost as if they're scared to expand fully—just in case.

Rubbing my hands down my thighs, I push to my feet and turn to take in the view from the kitchen doors. *Focus on the good.* I breathe in through my nose and out through my mouth. Take in the swaying palm trees and the deserted beach beyond them. *Focus on the good.*

The rumble of something that sounds an awful lot like a vehicle pulling up in my drive breaks through the quietness of the morning.

I squint like it'll let me hear better. The engine cuts out. A door slams closed. Mrs. Devon? Maybe? I scrape my hair back and retie it into its knot as I walk through the hall to the front door, the unease I haven't felt for two whole days prickling over my skin and drying out my mouth.

I turn the key in the front door, its *I love Clua* keyring jingling against the truck key as I open it just enough to see…

An ass hanging out of the hood of the Truck. Green board shorts, Converse, and a calf tattoo.

Tingles take the place of the unease. My fingers automatically lift to stroke across my lips—to reminisce over the feel of his mouth against them or for drool-prevention purposes, I'm not entirely sure. I lean my shoulder on the door jam. We didn't discuss this, I don't think. I was pretty hazy and kissed out by the time I floated into the house last night.

I purse my lips to the side and tilt my head until it, too, rests on the door jam, still very much staring at his ass.

Before I've quite figured out what to say, or how to feel about his unexpected presence here once again, he straightens—all chiseled, six-foot-whatever of him.

A sharp jolt of air releases from me when he turns and his stare meets mine, scratching his forehead, his bicep all kinds of bunched with the action. I swallow and avert my gaze, another little pant of air escaping.

"Hey." He grins, blasting me with his dimples when I look up again. "I was passing and"—he clicks his tongue against his teeth and twists back to look at the truck's open hood— "I figure this truck of yours could do with a proper once over."

I step out of the door, grabbing my keys as I go, carefully tiptoeing, barefoot, down the short path of flat stones to the driveway. It's still early. The air is still a little damp, the ground still cool with condensation, the fresh scent of morning still lingering. I hug my arms around myself. "You really don't have to do this."

He rocks back on his heels when I stop in front of him, gaze dropping to my lips.

I press them together.

"I'm pretty sure it's just a burnt-out spark plug. Easy fix." He absentmindedly scratches his chest.

I clear my throat and look anywhere but his hard, sleeveless-tee-covered torso, my fingers wrapping around my pendant. "Felix, last night—yesterday—I didn't mean to—"

"Kiss me again?" His smirk is amused, but not mocking, his head cocked to the side at whatever he reads from my blazing cheeks. "Don't worry about it."

I force a smile and nod. "You really don't have to fix the truck, though, I can take it somewhere."

"No need. I'm here now. Keys." He holds his hand out. "I'll have it done within the hour."

I chew on the inside of my cheek and shoot a glance to the truck and the toolbox balanced on the side of its open hood. It would be nice not to sound like a kamikaze bomber every time I pull up somewhere. My lips purse with indecision. He *is* already here.

I thrust the keys out to him before I can change my mind. "Okay. Yes. Sorry. Thank you." My eyelids flutter at the sudden heat in his stare. He's not looking at my face. I'm not even sure he heard my torrent of randomness. Good. No. Baaaaaad.

Pajamas. No bra. That's me.

The look on his face paralyzes me. It's—well, it's intense. Serious. Really fricking *hot.*

I practically throw the keys at his chest and back up. Fold my arms across my stretched out-with-age tank and turn for the house.

I suppose it's too much to ask for him not to notice how short my shorts are?

Felix

Fuck, those shorts.

I swallow hard as soon as she's in the door. The air is filled with her vanilla scent. The same vanilla scent that lingered on me all the way home last night. It's not helping. Neither is her ass in those shorts—or the thinness of that tank.

Maybe it wasn't such a bright idea to show up unannounced.

I just. I wanted to prove to myself that last night, yesterday, the way it felt to kiss her, the attraction I can't seem to shake are all just a one-off—or *twice* off. A random occurrence. Something I *don't* want to happen again. Prove to myself that it's only friendly concern that had me waking up this morning uneasy, thinking about her driving that death trap of a truck.

The curtain that covers her living room window twitches. Staring at her fucking window like a pervert probably isn't going to make her more comfortable around me. I turn stiffly and grab the socket wrench from my toolbox.

It's still there. The attraction. The interest. Just as strong. Maybe stronger. I need to focus. Get this done then put some distance between us.

Forty-five minutes later, I think I've fixed the problem. Sweat rolls down my back, sticking my shirt to my skin. I drag it off, wipe my forehead, then throw it through the back window of my pickup. With any luck, the old banger won't sound like it's about to explode when she turns the ignition now.

"I brought you some water."

Her voice trails off when I turn, her tongue peeking from between her lips, gaze slipping down my body.

The air thickens, the humidity multiplying, losing all oxygen, and I can't even blame it on the shorts. She's changed into denim cutoffs and a loose gray shirt, but still, I can't seem to look away.

Even with Rosa, it wasn't this intense.

With Rosa, it was love at first sight. She was my fucking world for the short time I had her, but this *thing* with Laia is different. Completely different. Guilt creeps into my consciousness and I wipe my hands off with a rag from my toolbox. What the fuck am I doing comparing this—this *infatuation* with what I had with Rosa?

"Thanks." I take the bottle from her and turn back to the engine. "Start her up."

Without a word, she climbs into the open driver's side door. The engine rumbles but starts the first time without a single splutter or whine, revving loudly until she cuts it.

A grin lights her face through the windshield. Unguarded, lacking the wariness she usually watches me with.

She hops out of the driver's seat as I slam the hood down and step around to meet her.

She almost crashes right into my chest.

My hands automatically drop to her hips to steady her before she topples backwards.

She jerks back, her face flushed from her hairline all the way down to where her sun kissed skin disappears beneath the V-neck of her shirt. "I … I'm sorry. It's just that's the first time I've started her up and not feared for my life."

"No worries." I tip my head back and stare at the cloudless blue sky, willing the tension from my body. I need to stay away. "Listen. I gotta go."

"Wait. Can I pay you?"

"I don't want your money, Laia." I drag my fingers through my hair. "We're friends. Right? Friends help friends around here."

She swallows, blinks, presses her pouty lips together. "I feel bad. At least take some pie."

I'm unable to keep the smirk from my face. Unexpected. Really fucking unexpected. Maybe that's the attraction. "Pie?"

"I'll pay you in pie." The second the words are out of her mouth she rolls her eyes and scrunches her nose.

I know that look, she does it whenever something random escapes her. She did it after she kissed me too. *After every time she's kissed me.* I grind my teeth and curl my fingers against their sudden urge to tug her bottom lip from between her teeth.

"Forget it. Stupid idea." She shakes her head, and her hair falls over her face. "You said the other day you'd like to … I thought…"

I go to brush it back behind her ear without thinking but drop my hand.

She flinches regardless and backs up. "I'm sorry, I just…"

Something tugs hard in my chest at her sudden uncomfortableness. "Any other day I'd love some pie. I just really gotta get going."

"Of course. You have to go." Wide green eyes peek through long dark lashes, pulling at something I'd forgotten existed—something I'm not sure I want pulled at.

"Come with me?" The words are out before I can stop them. Before I've even decided if I want her to. She's rubbing off on me. "If you're not doing anything."

"I'm not," she blurts out then holds her breath, her face scrunching. "I mean, I don't have plans."

I rub my fingers over my mouth to stop my laugh. We're like a pair of fucking teenagers.

That in itself should tell me everything I need to know. I don't do this. I do sex with no strings. I fuck, then leave before morning. This won't end well. "I need to pick some stuff up half an hour up the coast." Someone should probably tell my mouth that.

"I'll need to be back by one."

Reaching through the back window of the pickup, I grab the clean shirt folded on the back seat and pull it over my head. "It's only nine, we've got time."

She glances over her shoulder to the house. "I guess I better lock up then."

I watch her jog up the path and disappear into the house. What the fuck am I doing? I don't do this. I don't fucking do this.

"We good to go?" Her soft voice pulls me from my jumbled thoughts when she returns a minute later, a shy smile lifting the corner of her lips.

And suddenly I know exactly what it is about her I'm finding impossible to keep away from. It's the lack of pity when she looks at me. The absence of sadness in her tone when she speaks to me. It's that she doesn't know my past—can't see that I'm broken.

And as selfish as it is, I don't think I want that to change.

THIRTEEN

Laia

I try not to stare when Felix pops a hidden sunglasses shelf down from above the rearview mirror and slides his Ray-Bans on. I could pretend that it's the fanciness of the black leather interior I'm admiring, but Kenzi was right the other day, I've never been very good at lying. Not even to myself. "So, where are we going?"

"Tenting." The corner of his mouth quirks up at whatever he reads on my face. "I thought we could stop off at Tenting Falls on the way."

"Okay." I rummage in my purse for my own sunglasses. I've never had anyone look at me like that … like they can read my mind. Like they like what they read there.

This is maybe not one of my finest ideas.

Or is it?

Damon broke something in me—that's on him.

But fixing that thing? Not letting him take any more from me? That's on me.

I won't let him win. Not anymore. And if that means going on impulsive road trips with a man I really like kissing, then who am I to argue?

Sliding my glasses on, I lean back into my seat. "What kind of trees are those?" I tap my finger on the window at the thick forest that skirts the side of the road as it whizzes by.

"Bigleaf Magnolias." A small smile is still playing on his lips, but he doesn't look my way again. "They grow all over the island. Them and palm trees."

My tummy flutters. Everything said in that curling lilt sounds good. Even tree talk. I force myself to turn to the forest outside my window. "And those little pink flowers growing around them?"

"Those are Mexican Coral Vines, they weren't introduced here until a few years ago, now they're taking over."

"You know your plants."

He nods and I let my gaze linger on his profile, his lips…

"Everything okay?"

I blink my brain back into action. "I…" Is that a smirk on his face? It is. It's a smirk. "I was just … I like your sunglasses." Lame, lame, lame.

"My glasses?" The lips that got me into this mortifying mess in the first place press together. "You like my glasses."

I release a breath as subtly as I can.

A few minutes of awkward silence tick by before he talks again. "So. Pies, huh?"

I nod and twist my fingers. "My mom was a baker. It was our thing, now it's my thing. I guess … it's stupid." I hold my breath, waiting for him to agree—to laugh.

"Not stupid. It's your thing. It's good to have a thing."

"What's yours?" I turn a little in my seat to face him.

He snorts, but a dimple appears in his cheek when he shakes his head, his forehead creasing. "I don't know. Fishing maybe? Work?"

A smile tugs at my lips. "How are you still single?" The question's out before I can stop it.

His dimple vanishes before my cheeks even have a chance to flame. "I'm sorry. Too personal, I shouldn't have asked."

His fingers flex on the steering wheel. "It's fine." His Adam's apple bobs and the muscles in his throat contract.

"Felix, you don't have to answer, it's nothing to do with me."

"I'm single because" —his smile is forced when he finally looks at me— "Because I want to be."

We pull off the main road down a tight dirt road before the awkward silence that follows really gets … awkward.

Until I forget it's awkward because… "My God. This place…" My mouth falls open as we pull into a small opening surrounded by lush greenness. "Felix, this place is unbelievable." Without waiting for him, I open the door and jump out the second he stops.

A heady, unfamiliar scent envelops me along with the sticky, humid air as I close the door behind me. Vivid greens, breath-taking pinks, and stunningly bright oranges. Flowers every color of the rainbow and more drip from every one of the huge trees that surround us. Vines adorned with tiny white buds wrap around trunks as thick as two of me and as tall as a building. I sink down into a squat and inhale, stroking my fingers over the white petals of a plant. A wild orchid. This place is like stepping into another world. A different time. It's like a fairy-tale. "Is that smell those Big Leaf Gorgolias?" I stand at the sound of the driver's side door closing.

"Magnolias."

"Magnolias, right." My fairy-tale high plummets to the soles of my flip flops. *Stupid woman. You never listen.* "I'm an idiot, I never listen. Sorry."

Felix moves to the front of the pickup a couple of feet from me. He pushes his glasses onto the top of his head then folds his arms over his chest, the blue of his eyes unreadable. "You're not an idiot, Laia."

The humid heat sticks to my skin along with the millions of questions written over his face. I fan my hand in an attempt to cool my cheeks. "I mean … I didn't mean … I'm sorry."

"Don't apologize." His jaw sets, hardening.

I clamp my bottom lip between my teeth but can't seem to make myself look away from his face. He knows.

There's no way … I suck in a breath. Shake my head. "Felix, I don't … I…" *Can't explain.*

Straightening, he takes a step towards me.

I step back.

There's no smile in his eyes anymore. Just curiosity. Protectiveness. And it's gone before I'm sure it was even there in the first place. The tension in his shoulders eases, his mouth curving into an almost smile before he reaches me. "The waterfall is this way."

"How far?"

"Not far. Five minutes or so." He takes my hand before I can move from his path.

I stare at his long fingers linked through mine then up into his face. I didn't flinch. Not even nearly. I may feel sparks. Or I may be about to faint. But either way, I didn't flinch. I'm taking it as a win.

His thumb smooths across the pulse in my wrist. "You're not an idiot, Laia." He takes a step closer, dipping his head to keep my stare held in his gaze. "Stop putting yourself down."

My head tilts back. Damon's voice in my mind threatening to take all the good away, threatening to ruin everything like it always does.

I want it gone. I want him out of my head again, and I know exactly how to make that happen.

Before I can talk myself out of it, I lift onto my toes, everything inside me telling me that this'll make it better—that this man can make it better. That just once more won't hurt.

His gaze moves over my face, questions still flitting through his stare, until it fixes on my mouth, like he knows what I'm doing. But he doesn't stop me, not even when I close the distance and brush my lips over his. I breathe in his scent and suck lightly on his bottom lip. The effect is instant. No more Damon. Just Felix and his smell, his lips, and the calming effect they seem to have on me.

He dips his head, and his hands slide around my waist. I tickle my tongue over the seam of his mouth, and he angles his head to kiss me deeper, slower, better.

A low moan vibrates from his chest when I flick my tongue against his top lip.

He clears his throat and steps back without warning, his hand lifting to the back of his neck as he turns to the forest. "We should probably get going."

"Yeah." I barely resist touching my fingers to my lips. "Sorry. Yes. Let's go." I shouldn't have done that.

I pick my way over the partially overgrown walkway, the weight of his presence behind me accelerating my heart rate way more than the pace we're walking at. I should say something. Apologize for using his lips as an anesthetic to my fucked-up past. I lift my gaze to the sun-stippled canopy of palms and Big Leaf Magnolias and try to pick out one of the birds singing above us instead. How would I even put that into words?

"It's just up here."

I squint through the trees and sure enough, there's an opening a few meters ahead. A giddy excitement rises to the surface when I hear the bubbling of flowing water. I pick up my pace.

"Watch out for the..."

Before I can turn to see what I'm supposed to be watching out for, my foot catches on a rock, propelling me forward.

I'm dragged back from the steep drop down to possibly the clearest water I've ever seen before I even get a squeal out.

"I've got you." His breath tickles across the back of my neck, the soft cotton of his T-shirt brushing against the backs of my arms when he straightens behind me and pulls me into his chest.

My hands drop to cover his; adrenaline, fear and a whole lot of heat pumping through my veins. Breathe. I need to breathe. Get things clear in my head again. Clear in his too. "I'm sorry for the kissing," I whisper without looking back. "I think … I know you don't want anything … and I don't, but I can't … I just … you just…" *Make me forget.* There's no way to add that last bit without coming across as seriously unstable.

"No worries." His hands flex on my waist, and his chest stays pressed up against my back.

I swallow hard, my gaze fixed on where my hands cover his. "I don't know why I keep…" The lie falls dead on my lips. I know exactly why I keep kissing him. "I'm sor—"

"I'm good with the kissing, Laia." His long sigh brushes the side of my cheek and his hands slide to my hips turning me a little. "So, what do you think?"

It takes me a second to figure out what he's talking about—to unwrap myself from him enough to take in my surroundings.

My breath leaves me.

The sun, no longer shaded by the forest, sparkles over the bubbling water. Black, moss-covered stone glistens beneath the cascade of water, spraying a cool mist into the air around us. I tilt my head back following the waterfall to the top of the story high rock face and the back of my head touches his shoulder.

Neither of us move.

My eyes drift closed as I breathe in the sweet, fresh, floral air. "It's beautiful." I finally turn to him. "Thank you for bringing me here. I'd never have found this place by myself."

A smile tugs at the corner of his mouth. "My pleasure. I haven't been here for years. We can get down this way."

I follow him around the edge of the water. He doesn't mind the kissing. That's good. I think. Unless that means he wants to do more than the kissing. That's bad. My pulse starts whooshing in my ears. Definitely bad. I'm nowhere near ready for more. I'm not even sure I'm ready for the kissing.

"The thought of coming back to this place got me through some tough times when I was on tour." Felix hops down a drop onto the rock below, then holds his hand up for me to take. "Watch your step."

I grab his hand and jump down, thankful for the change in conversation. "How long were you in for?"

He kicks at a stone when we come to the edge of the massive flat rock, watching it as it rolls off the side and splashes into the water below. "Five years, give or take." Toeing off his Converse, he lowers himself down and hangs his legs over the side, his feet plunging into the water. "I busted my knee on a training mission and that was the end of that."

"Were you sad to come home?" Slipping off my flip flops, I sit down by his side. "Stupid question. I can't imagine ever wanting to leave somewhere as beautiful as Clua in the first place, let alone being sad to come home." I dip my toes into the water, then instantly jerk them back out. Jeez, that's cold. I try again, slower this time. "It's paradise."

"I was twenty-four and thought" —he picks up another flat stone and skims it across the water— "I thought that running away from my problems would make them go away."

I look up from the path of circular ripples his stone left in its wake, kicking my feet beneath the surface. "Sometimes there's no other option but to run."

"Is that what you're doing here?" That deep line appears between his eyebrows again. "Running from something?"

I shrug, but don't trust myself to hold his stare. I'll probably blurt out my whole sorry story if I do. "What does your tattoo mean?" I ask in a lame attempt to change the subject back onto safer ground.

After a beat, he lifts his leg from the water, turning it to either side, his calf muscles bunching and tightening under his skin, making the black swirls and patterns that wrap it shift and move like they've come to life. "It's traditional Cluan. In the fifties, they dug up some old tiles with script and images engraved on them. This is one of them."

I lean forward. Only just stopping myself from tracing my fingers along the details. "It looks almost Maori. Do you know what it means?" I glance back into his face.

He holds my stare, his lips parting like he wants to say something, but the words just won't cooperate. I know that feeling well.

I slide my hand across the rough rock until my pinkie is flush against his. "You don't have to tell me."

He clears his throat, his troubled stare flicking from our hands to my face.

Before I can overthink it or talk myself out of it, I lean across and kiss him. *Again.* Just a tentative press of my lips to his in the hope that it has the same effect on whatever's got that haunted look on his face as it does on my past.

His whole body stills and I'm pretty sure my heart stops completely. I've read this wrong, read *him* wrong. But, before I can pull back, he slides his hand around the back of my neck and kisses me back until I don't think I could even tell you my name if you asked.

I guess it works both ways then.

FOURTEEN

Laia

"I'll have an iced latte, please," I smile up at the waitress as I pull my new cell from its packaging and lay it onto the small wooden table of Clua's Coffees. Turns out there's one in every town on the island, including Clua Town. And I love them.

Huge-leafed cheese plants border the terrace giving a sense of privacy even though we're right in the middle of the town's busy main street.

"Make that two." Kenzi hands her back the menu then leans back in her chair. "And a chocolate muffin, please."

"Thanks for coming with me to pick this out." I lift my new smartphone and swipe my finger across the screen.

"I still don't understand why you didn't go on the same call plan as me."

Contracts. Names on contracts. Paranoia about having names on contracts. The list of reasons I picked a pay-as-you-talk cell goes on. I open my mouth hoping that a plausible excuse will come to me. "I don't like to have things in my name."

My eyes widen as hers narrow. What the hell kind of excuse is the truth?

"You don't like to have things in your name?" she repeats slowly.

I shake my head. "I mean, I just like to pay things as I go."

"Right."

I can tell by the way her lips have pursed that she's not buying it. The truth tickles the tip of my tongue. I could just tell her. I trace the grain of the polished wood then meet her curious stare. "It's just…" A simpering giggle draws my attention to the entrance of the coffee shop's terrace.

Flappy Eyes.

And Felix.

Mylo's there too, but the only thing I'm seeing is Felix's forearm and the hand that's rubbing it.

Kenzi's head turns to them then back to me. "Man, that woman is clingier than a fungus. You know he's not interested in her, right?"

I force a smile and tear my gaze from the faraway look on Felix's face as he listens to whatever Flappy Eyes is laughing about. "It's got nothing to do with me." I lean back and stare at the woven canes that shade the tables from the heat of the sun. "It's not like we're … anything … not really."

"Hold the bus." Kenzi covers my hand with hers. "Not really? What *not really?* The not really *thing* that happened the other night? The thing that neither of you will tell me about?"

My shoulders drop and I just about resist the urge to bang my head on the table.

"Start at the beginning." She presses her lips together like she's barely containing her excitement. "Did he ask you out? Invite you for dinner? Breakfast? A quick boink behind the bike shed?"

"Shh." I sink lower into my seat, my gaze flicking over to where Felix and Mylo now thankfully have their backs to the terrace and Flappy Eyes is still flapping at Felix. "We kissed. That's it." I gnaw at the inside of my cheek. "Nothing serious." She doesn't need to know about the other kisses. "It won't be happening again." I avoid her curious stare, feeling like an addict who won't admit there's a problem. And after twenty-four hours without his lips, I'm pretty sure that's exactly what I am.

"There's more." Kenzi leans across the table until there's a real threat that she might end up in my lap. "Tell me."

"Okay, fine. He took me to Tenting Falls yesterday, and we may have kissed some more." I sag back in my chair and press my hands to my hot cheeks. "That's it, though. Nothing else is going to happen."

Kenzi's mouth forms an exaggerated O and she flops back into her seat too. "We seriously need to work on your storytelling, lady, but wow. He took you to Tenting Falls? How did that even come about? Because I know he didn't call you." She stares pointedly at my shiny new cell.

Elbows on the table, I cover my face and peek through my fingers to check that the man in question is still safely on the other side of the terrace. "What's his deal, Kenzi? What's wrong with him? Why is he still single?"

"His deal?" She glances over her shoulder then back to me, all traces of the humor that usually sparkles in her eyes gone. "Felix is a good guy. The best…"

"But?" My stomach knots. I knew it. Nobody is all good.

Kenzi opens her mouth. Then closes it again. Then opens it again. "With Fee, it's complicated…"

I drop my hands from my face and lean in closer. "Don't you dare tell me he's married." Or maybe do. Then I might stop fantasizing about kissing him all the time. Cut it out cold turkey.

"No—no, not anymore." For the first time since we've met, Kenzi's lips turn down, a crease forming across her forehead.

Not anymore? He's divorced? There's an ex-wife? I puff air into my cheeks and rake my fingers through my hair, attempting to arrange my features into something less shocked. "What happened?"

The line across her forehead deepens and she leans in even closer. "Rosa and Felix … they were … she…"

"It's been ten years, Zi … She's not coming back."

We jump apart at the roughness to Felix's interruption. His jaw is clenched. Heck, his whole face is clenched.

Kenzi's eyebrows do some sort of lopsided arch when she looks at him.

His face settles to carefully neutral, his head shaking so slightly I'd have missed it if I weren't looking for it.

I look between them and my stomach sinks. Whatever happened ten years ago wasn't good. Whatever happened ten years ago, Felix doesn't want me to know about it.

A second later, Kenzi slouches back into her seat, shoots him another side-eye then shakes her head. "He's right. Rosa's not coming back."

"Nice cell?" Mylo tilts his chin in the direction of my phone still sliding his wallet into his back pocket as he comes to stop beside Felix. "What did I miss?" He takes in our little group. Our epic awkwardness is obviously pretty hard to miss.

"Nothing." Felix slides his hand over the back of his neck and turns to Mylo. "You wanna tell them, or should I?" He smirks at his friend, but his eyes stay curiously crinkle-free.

No more Rosa talk then. I force myself to pay attention to Mylo and whatever it is he's saying.

"…And so, it looks like I'll be needing a Clua number too."

"What? You're staying?" Kenzi's jaw goes slack. "In Clua?"

"Yup. We're heading to check out an apartment this morning." A look I can't quite place flips between Mylo and Felix before Mylo's mouth stretches into a wide grin.

"That's really great." I spin my glass between my hands and smile up at him trying in vain not to let my gaze shift to Felix. He has an ex-wife. He didn't tell me. Why would he? Why do I care? It's no good, I look. I can't help it.

"We should get going." His gaze drops from my eyes to my lips before he blinks it away. "I'll see you around?"

I nod, unable to drag my stare from him until he spins his keys on his fingers, lifts his chin towards Kenzi and turns to go.

"Laia." Mylo winks at me then pins Kenzi with a blinding, white-toothed grin. "Kenzi."

Eye's wide, Kenzi turns back to me. "He's *staying?*"

"Looks like it." I snort out a weird, breathy laugh. "Is that a bad thing?"

"How am I supposed to keep my man ban with something like *that* sauntering about town, all muscles and man buns." She drops her face into her hands.

"So…" I venture when she lifts her head again. "Felix … married?"

Kenzi pauses for a second, then lets out a long sigh. "Laia. I heart you. You know I do, but this is Felix's story to tell."

I nod. Too fast. I get it. They're friends. More than friends. Practically family. I twist my lips to the side in an attempt to hide the little stab of hurt. Or sadness. Or whatever it is that's stinging my tear ducts. Whatever happened, it was big, and bad enough that it clearly still holds weight, even all these years later. I, of all people, get not wanting to stir up a shitty past.

"Do you know what we need, Laia?" Kenzi grabs my hand, her grip only tightening when I do my usual, knee-jerk flinch back.

I puff my cheeks out. "A bullet to the head?"

She chuckles, and her grin lifts her shoulders as well.

I hold my breath and wait for whatever crazy is about to leave her mouth next.

"No bullets. Or men. We need a girl's night." The twinkle's back in her eye. "Wine. Chat. Dancing."

"We do?" My thumb sneaks to my lips, my teeth picking at a little tag of skin at the corner of my nail. The last proper girl's night I went to ended in a black eye and bruised ribs. My gut twists at the memory but I push it back into the box hidden in the back of my mind, force my hand into my lap and nod resolutely. "We do."

"That's more like it. Just us and a couple of my closest. Oh, and one more thing." She grins even wider. "We're meeting Simon, the head chef in the Castle tonight to talk about your pies."

"Wait, what? Kenzi, what did you do?" Panic snakes up the back of my neck and I pull my hands from hers. "Why does he want to talk about my pies?"

Her grin falters when she takes in what I'm pretty sure is horror creasing my face. "I let Simon taste the pie when he came around to my place the other night. He loved it. Like *really* loved it. He wants to talk to you about putting it on the menu." She leans toward me, a confused frown creasing her forehead. "I thought you'd be happy."

"I don't…" It's hard to swallow, it's hard to even breathe past the insecurity and doubt engrained right to the very core of me. I can't. I'm not good enough. It won't work. "Wait, he said he loved it?"

"Yes." She watches me warily. "But I can tell him you're not interested if you want."

"No!" I press both my hands to my mouth and try to get my stupid nerves under control. "No, don't do that."

I've got this.

FIFTEEN

Felix

Why the fuck is nothing simple anymore? I circle the cloth back over the already clean bar with more vigor than necessary.

I made Zi lie for me. About Rosa. *About fucking Rosa*!

Life was fine before. Good. Things were what they were. Me. Alone. Me *fine* with being alone.

I should just tell Laia what happened and get it over with. I shake my head. I don't need her looking at me like I'm the one that needs to be fixed. Made better. *Saved*. I should just stay the fuck away. It doesn't take a genius to figure out she's got her own past to deal with. I won't put mine on her too.

My fingers clench around the cloth and I rub a harder circle across the mahogany leaving a trail of moisture in its path. There's something there though. Something daring me to push further. Pleading with me to solve the fucking puzzle of her.

Maybe *that's* the novelty of her. She's a puzzle I want to solve. Something broken I want to fix. Something broken I *can* fix. I suck in a breath of warm salty air as I look up and my hand stills. Past the beach terrace, past the customers chatting lazily, past the pink lit sand to the setting sun as it slashes through the darkening sky with splices of reds and oranges.

Rosa. I see her in every fucking sunset. Sometimes it's comforting and sometimes—sometimes it's just damn miserable. I had the world and I lost it. I'm not stupid enough to think I get a second chance at it.

"Felix, man, you wanna wipe that scowl off your face? You're scaring the customers."

The tension releases in my forehead and I turn to Mylo. "Fuck you, man." I throw the cloth at his face. He's been helping out here for the last few nights to pass the time while he works out the logistics of setting up a surf school on the island.

He dodges it easily. "You're not my type, bro." A low rumble of a laugh shakes his shoulders, his mop of blond hair pulled back into a knot.

"The woman at the end of the bar has been wailing your name for the last ten minutes." He glances past me to the opposite end of the bar then pins me with something that looks a lot like distaste.

My chest tightens, mangling itself into useless knots of familiar starry-eyed make-believe the second I look her way.

Mylo knows about Rosa, but he never met her. If he did, he'd get it.

She looks just like her. Even the way she sits is the same. Hair pulled over one shoulder, elbow on the bar, hand tucked under her chin. It's like stepping back in fucking time—to before I knew just how much one moment can fuck up every single aspect of someone's life.

My greedy gaze drops to her petite frame and my chest loosens, the stupid fog receding. I can safely say I never saw Rosa in a dress as tight or as short as that one.

"Fuck, man, that voice." Mylo grimaces and scratches his chest through his brand-new Beach Hut tee frowning down the bar at her. "Tell me you haven't."

"I'll deal with it." I reach up to massage the twitching muscle in the back of my neck and head down the bar to where she's sitting.

"So, I've been thinking, babe." She stares up at me through her long black eyelashes. "I think we should give us another chance."

"There is no us." I press my hands flat against the bar unable to stop the scowl from lowering my brow. Her looks are where the similarities end. Mylo's right, her voice is all whine.

"But there could be." Her fingers tickle over the back of my knuckles.

I pull both hands off the bar and step back. "Listen— "

"*Jayne.*" Her glossy red lips push out into a pout.

Rosa never pouted. Unless she was kissing me. I rub my fist across the middle of my chest at the sharp pain my careless thoughts bring with them every damn time. "Jayne, I'm flattered, but I'm not interested in dating."

"Who said anything about *dating?*" A small crease appears on her pretty face and I hesitate. So like Rosa. So what I'm used to. I could just pretend. Just for one night. No complications, no expectations. She *really* fucking looks like her.

"Here." As if sensing my hesitation, *Jayne* pulls a pen from her purse and scribbles onto a napkin then slides it across the bar to me. "Take my number. Just in case you change your mind. I'm not looking for love, Felix." She runs her tongue over her red lips and lets her gaze slide down my body. "Maybe we can come to an arrangement that works for both of us."

I smile. I think I might even nod. It'd be so easy. Like escaping my head for a few hours. No risk. No stress. My fingers wrap around the napkin, and I shove it into my pocket.

"Hey, Fee. Three Pink Monstrosities and a vodka soda."

Kenzi? I glance over Rosa-look-alike's head, and my gaze instantly collides with wide green eyes brimming with hurt.

"Laia." I force my lips into the easy smile I greet all of my *friends* with. Except there's nothing easy or friendly about the sudden pinch to her face or the weight in my gut knowing I put it there.

"Felix." She lifts her chin, her gaze flicking to Rosa-look-a-like before she blinks and turns her head.

"I didn't expect to see you in here on a weeknight." Fuck, that sounded stiff. Guilty even.

Her cheeks stay resolutely sun-kissed. Not a blush in sight.

It bothers me. Way more than it should.

"Work stuff," Kenzi answers for her, curling her lip at the back of *Jayne's* head in the process. "Simon wanted to check out our cocktails." Grabbing Laia's hand, she tugs her back towards where Pete and Simon are already sitting at one of the tall tables that circle the edge of the bar.

"A double date?" Mylo grumbles as he hands a customer his change over the bar.

"Does it bother you?" I ask, still staring over to where Laia is sitting with her back to me. Her cream dress clings to the curve of her ass, the back low enough to have me wondering what she *doesn't* have on under it.

"Why should it bother me?" Mylo's big face cuts off my view when he leans his ass against the fridge in front of me, the black and gray ink on his biceps stretching when he folds his arms over his chest. "But really? Out with her boss?"

He's clearly bothered.

"Work stuff apparently." I can't help my long fucking sigh.

"A work thing? So, I know the manager but who's the other guy?"

I cough to hide my laugh at Mylo's thinly veiled jealousy.

"Pete's *husband*, Simon. He's the head chef in the hotel restaurant," I say dryly and clap a hand on Mylo's back. "Green doesn't suit you, bud. If you're interested in Zi, you should ask her out. She won't wait around forever."

"I think that advice works both ways." He looks over his shoulder, his body shifting to give me a glimpse of Laia.

She glances my way but doesn't smile. She doesn't even blink. Just returns her attention to her friends.

It stings. A lot. I drag my hand over my mouth and keep watching her, the soft curve of her spine, the curl escaping its knot and tickling down the back of her neck. There's nothing easy or simple about her.

I'm heading for risky fucking waters, but I can't seem to make myself paddle the other way.

Laia

Even with my back to the bar, I fail miserably at following the conversations around our little table. Too busy fighting the urge not to flinch under the weight of Felix's stare. I don't have to look to know he's watching me. But then he's probably watching Flappy Eyes too.

How could I *not* have seen this coming? He literally told me that he's single because he wants to be. He doesn't do serious, and I don't even *want* serious. So, what's my problem?

"Three Pink Monstrosities and one vodka soda."

His voice trails down my spine, the roughness lighting a fire under my skin. I clamp my teeth together and stare resolutely at the wooden tabletop. It shouldn't matter. It doesn't. I don't want anything from him, and he clearly doesn't want anything from me.

His hand invades my line of vision when he places the cocktails onto the table.

"Laia." Tray tucked under his arm, he leans in closer, so close his lips brush the shell of my ear. "That wasn't what it looked like."

I pull back, plastering my widest, brightest smile on and force myself to look at him. "It doesn't matter." My jaw aches and I'm pretty sure I look insane, but I keep on grinning. "Why would it matter?"

His eyebrows twitch down in the middle, black, black eyelashes fluttering as his gaze moves over my face. "Right." He rocks back onto his heels, the tick in his jaw working overtime. "Enjoy your drinks, guys." He shoots me one last unreadable look then saunters back to the bar.

I fiddle with the stem of my glass. I don't need to look up to know they're staring.

"So, *that* happened." Kenzi leans over the table and pulls my hand from my glass. "I thought you two were better than this."

I meet her unimpressed stare and raise my brows to where Pete and Simon are watching us like we're the latest instalment of Hot and Hasty Housewives: Trapped Edition.

"I get the feeling she doesn't want to talk about it." Pete leans back in his seat, resting his arm along the back of Simon's stool.

I still can't believe this is Pete. Buttoned up boss, Pete. I smile in thanks, my gaze dropping to the sleeve of tattoos visible where he's rolled up his black shirt sleeves.

Suit Pete is handsome, tattoo Pete is sexy as sin.

"There's nothing to talk about." My lips twist awkwardly around the simple words.

Kenzi's whole face puckers like she's sucked a lemon.

"Whatever you say, darling." Simon fans his hand in front of his face, in a move only slightly camper than the pink floral button-down he's wearing. "That man's got it *bad*."

"Looks like Laia's not the only one with an admirer around here." Pete winks when the others turn to the bar. "They sure do grow them big around here."

It's Kenzi's turn to scowl like a sullen teenager. Folding her arms over her chest, she shakes her head and lifts her drink. "I think that's about enough boy talk for this evening."

I couldn't agree more. I take a drink of my Monstrosity, only wincing slightly at the sweet burn of alcohol.

"You're right, let's talk about Laia's pie." Simon clasps his hands together. "When can I get my hands on it?"

Kenzi cackles. My cheeks flame. Pete just shakes his head. "Simon, have you any idea how nasty that sounds?"

Simon leans back and brushes some invisible fluff from his white-jean-covered knee. "You dirty-minded heathens. Laia, honey, talk to me. How soon can I have some samples?"

I reach for my pendant and spin it between my fingers. "After the weekend? Maybe?" The panic sliding down the back of my neck right now isn't normal. Why can't I just be normal? "I'm not sure if…" I press my lips together, doubt and fear mingling with Damon's constant assurance that I'm not good enough making it hard to breathe.

Simon's eyes narrow like he's about to ask me something I'm pretty sure I won't want to answer.

Pete cocks his head, the questions quickly replaced by concern. He picks up his husband's fishbowl glass. "Let me taste your Monstrosity, baby."

I watch them for a second, taking another long pull from my straw. If someone could guarantee that I could have that, what they seem to have together, I'd maybe—I glance back over to Felix—maybe want more than just a pair of lips to forget my past.

Felix lifts his chin but doesn't smile, and my tummy sinks as I turn back to the table. I'm not ready. Not even with guarantees.

"Just going to the ladies'." I climb from my high stool, trying to keep my hands steady as I offer what I hope is an unruffled smile to Kenzi. "Be right back."

"You okay?" She scans my face while stirring the ice in her glass. "Want me to come with?"

"No. I'm good." My smile turns genuine. Regardless of what is or isn't happening with Felix, this thing with Kenzi feels like it could be real.

I push through the door to the ladies' room and let it swing closed behind me before I lean my hands on the rustic wooden vanity. My reflection stares back at me from the wall-to-wall mirror. I look … I tilt my head … kind of like my mom, if I squint and pretend that the low bun of dark blonde hair behind my left ear is black and about a thousand times curlier. I have her eyes. And her nose. But my dad's mouth and hair.

The flat surface of my pendant catches the over-head light and I square my shoulders. I *am* good enough. Maybe I'm not ready for the man thing—but the *pie* thing, I've got. I'm good enough. I've always been good enough.

I puff out a sharp breath then nod and turn to the cubicle just as the middle of three doors opens.

My shoulders drop along with my I've-got-this smile. Flappy Eyes. *Why not?*

She straightens when she sees me, her chin lifting, thin shoulders pushing back as she struts in her five-inch wedge heels to the sink beside me. "Laia, is it?"

Even in her heels, she's not much bigger than me. The word petite was invented for this woman.

I nod and follow her gaze to the mirror as she smooths her super tight mini-dress until it sits wrinkle-free over her thighs. "He loves me in red." The tip of her tongue slides over her top teeth before she fixes me with an amused stare in the mirror.

My cheeks warm. Even my ears warm. I can feel the hurt tilt to my eyebrows, but I'm powerless to stop it. I take a breath to … I don't know, tell her I'm not interested?

Her big dark eyes don't stray from my face as she washes her hands then flicks the excess water from them, the stack of gold bracelets on her wrist jingling.

I should walk away. Look away. Do something. I don't. I can't. She means Felix. *Felix* loves her in red.

"Aw, sweetie…" She finally turns to look at me straight on and rests her ass on the edge of the vanity. "You didn't know about us?" Her slightly upturned nose wrinkles daintily. "I thought everybody knew."

I shake my head, the heat in my cheeks cooling until I'm pretty sure there's no blood left in them. I should walk away. I don't want to know. *Except I do.*

"Did you know he has a type, Laia?" She folds her arms, and her stare drops to my not-so-tiny body then snakes back up to my hair.

I was going for artfully tousled, but compared to her sleek, black, poker-straight hair, and the subtle sneer on her painted-red lips, I might as well have a bird's nest stuck to the side of my head. I curl my fingers against the need to fiddle with it. "A type?"

She snorts out a dismissive chuckle and bites her lip like she's considering her next words carefully. "Felix is *only* interested in women that look like *her.*" She shrugs and clasps her boney fingers over my shoulder. "And you don't."

I jerk my shoulder from her touch, trying to get her nasty words to make some sort of sense. They don't, or worse, they do. They're just … messed up.

"You're wasting your time, honey." She shoots me another once-over then walks out of the bathroom.

I meet my own shell-shocked stare in the mirror. What the hell just happened?

I've barely made it out of the toilets when an arm wraps around my waist.

"Felix," I squeak, half relief, half I'm-not-your-type-leave-me-alone, half why-the-hell-do-you-sleep-with-women-that-look-like-your-ex? That's too many halves. I don't care. "Don't." I push him away and try to continue down the short hallway back to the bar.

"Laia."

The hairs on my arms lift when his finger brushes up my forearm to my elbow, tugging me around to face him until my back's to the wall and he's far too close for comfort.

"What?" I'm pissed but pissed is good. Pissed I can work with. It's better than confused. And way better than hurt.

His forehead furrows. "Laia. I can explain that woman."

"No need. I get it. You have a type. I'm not it. Don't worry, I won't kiss you again." I try really hard to keep the pissed from bubbling over in the face of the emotions flashing behind his eyes. He looks like I've just kicked him in the balls. "I don't need an explanation. Or an excuse or … anything." Even my voice sounds tired. Done. Miserable. I try to walk away again. "It doesn't matter."

"Laia, wait." He plants his hands on either side of my head before I get far.

The panic comes out of nowhere, swift and paralyzing and completely unreasonable.

He's not Damon. He. Is. Not. Damon.

I run my tongue along my dry lips, heartbeat roaring in my ears, eyes widening with every pulse. It's fine. I'm fine. I know this, but my throat contracts and I press myself into the wall regardless.

"Fuck, Laia." The frustration tightening his features morphs into something else entirely and his hands drop to his sides, a horrified tug to his lips when he steps back. "I'm not gonna hurt you."

"Then back off." I let loose the breath that had lodged itself in my throat and drop my gaze to his white Converse. "Please. I can't do this." My words are barely a whisper, but I've no doubt he heard them, because when I look up, he's already gone.

I somehow manage to make my legs carry me back to the table. All eyes are on me as I sit.

"Everything okay?" Kenzi reaches for my hand.

I jerk away from her touch dramatically, even for me. "Fine." My gaze moves unbidden to the bar just in time to see Flappy Eyes launch herself at Felix before he makes it behind the bar.

Her skinny arms wrap around his neck and everything else fades to white noise. I clamp my lip between my teeth, some masochistic part of me I never knew existed until now eager to see his reaction. And maybe hoping for him to prove me wrong. Show me that he's exactly the man I thought he was. Nice. Cool. Not interested in women like Flappy Eyes.

His hands drop to her waist, and the stupid hope falls flat in my chest.

SIXTEEN

Laia

I lift the teaspoon of filling to my lips and close my eyes. Too sweet. Needs more balsamic vinegar. I stir the bubbling strawberry mixture, turn the heat down a notch then grab a different wooden spoon for the simmering pot of mango and cinnamon.

Both pie tins are primed with pastry crust. I swipe my hair from my forehead with the back of my hand and fight back my yawn.

I've been up since six. On my day off. I didn't fall asleep until four. My brain has come up with a new and improved way to torment me. Felix and Flappy Eyes.

I just don't get it. If *that's* his type then what the hell is he doing letting me kiss him so much? Pity. That's the only reason I can think of. And the thought is more than mortifying. It's pathetic.

My teeth gnaw at the rough skin on the inside of my cheek. His hurt blue eyes when I told him to back off taint me with doubt. Maybe I should have let him talk, though. Maybe I should have asked him outright.

Maybe I should just stop goddamn obsessing over a man.

I twist both rings to turn off the stove. He certainly hadn't been complaining when she practically climbed him.

I don't even want to know what happened after I left.

Okay. I do. I've almost phoned Kenzi about ten times this morning to see if they left together.

But no. Nope. No way.

I should be glad for my lucky escape. I *am* glad for my lucky escape. I grab the ladle from my new utensil rack and set about filling the tins.

Pies. I should just focus on the pies.

What if I'm wrong about them too? I mean, Kenzi liked them. She liked them enough to tell Simon about them, and he *seems* to like them, but…

People lie all the time, Laia.

I shake my head, but Damon's voice lingers along with a million reasons to believe him.

My fingers clutch the pendant around my neck, the coin-like disk cool against my clammy palm.

"She thought she could, and so she did."

My eyes well as I look from the black velvet box and the engraved pendant nestled in it to my mom's smiling face. "I love it."

"It seemed apt." She brushes her black bangs from eyes the exact same color as mine then pulls me in for one of those hugs only a mom can give. "That school is lucky to have you, Lai. I've never met anyone with your natural instinct for flavors. Not even your gran."

I smile into her shoulder and squeeze tighter. "You have to say that. You're my mom."

The ladle slips from my grasp, clattering against the worktop, spraying the counter with sticky puréed fruit and knocking the pan over. I stare at the mess, torn between memories and fears and hope and dread. Mom hadn't lived to see me turn down my place in culinary school. Even so, the ghost of her disappointment has weighed on me every day since. The woman had more faith in me than anything else in life. It's about time I started living up to it again.

I am good enough. Being wrong about Felix doesn't have to mean I'm wrong about this. I stare at the red, watching it spread in a sticky puddle over the wood.

I will do this. Make at least this part of my life work. I'll make her proud of me again.

But first I need to clean up this mess.

I grab a cloth from the sink.

Footsteps behind me have every hair on my body lifting. I know Mrs. Devon's steps. These are bigger. Heavier. My heart takes off in a gallop. I glance over to the knife stand. It's too far away, so I wrap my fingers around the rolling pin in the sink instead then spin.

"Felix?"

He holds his hands up but stays where he is under the arch that leads through to the front door. "The door was open. I heard a clatter."

"The front door was open?" My world spins slightly off its axle for a second. I haven't been out front this morning. I lower my rolling pin, eyes still fixed on Felix, and try to come up with reasons other than the one that would mean … but that would be impossible.

Felix's forehead creases, but he stays where he is. "Everything okay?"

I shake my head. "Yep. Fine … but kinda busy, what's up?"

Ugh. My easy breezy voice sucks.

He looks past me to the red goo now dripping from the work top then back to the door. "Need a hand?"

"Are you sure the door was open?" My thumb lifts to my teeth before I can stop it. I locked it last night. Just like I lock it every night. I think.

"Definitely open." His brow lowers and a tightness appears there I haven't seen before. "What's going on, Laia?"

I glance again at the mess on my worktop then through the French doors to the perfectly serene and completely empty beach beyond my little garden.

He's not here. I'm letting him make me paranoid again. Letting him win again.

I shake my head and force my face out of whatever grimace has Felix so ruffled. "I'm making pies." I glance over to the mess. "A pie."

His rough laugh shoots a jolt up my spine, as he rubs his hands down the front of his denim board-shorts then steps from beneath the arch towards me. I glance down. Black yoga pants and a black tank today … and a bra too.

A big step up from the shorty pajamas I was wearing the last time he showed up unannounced.

I step aside, an apology teetering on the tip of my tongue over the mess. I click it off the roof of my mouth instead. It's my mess.

As if it's the most normal thing in the world, he steps past me, grabs a paper towel from the dispenser and starts to wipe down the counter.

"You don't have to do that."

He smirks over his shoulder. "I know I don't." The muscles in his back shift beneath his white T-shirt when he goes back to cleaning.

He's got a type. I'm not it. "Felix, stop. What are you doing here?"

He pauses mid-wipe but doesn't turn to me. "I came to apologize. I made you uncomfortable last night."

I wrap the drawstring of my pants around my finger, but I can't seem to force myself to speak. Don't trust myself not to fall back into my perpetual need to placate. Make things easier for him.

He turns from the counter and leans back against it. "You told me to back off. I'm backing off."

I laugh. I can't help it. "This is you backing off?"

His face sobers as he watches me.

I stop laughing immediately. "I'm sorry, I didn't mean—" I square my shoulders. "Wait, no. I'm not sorry. At all." Well, that sounded way better in my head. I bring up the memory of Flappy Eyes and her tight, tight dress and bitchy, bitchy face and grab hold of the hurt that comes with it with both hands.

A dimple flashes in his cheek. "Good. Don't be."

"And while we're at it, *Jayne* told me everything. Why do you keep on showing up here if she's your type? I mean, I get it … she's…" I roll my eyes. "Tight. I mean, petite … I mean. I don't know what I mean." I press my fingers against my lips. "I just don't get what you want from me. Why you let me … why we keep…" My cheeks blaze and I shake my head. "I just don't get it."

He rocks back on his heels, and the way his T-shirt stretches over his big chest when he shoves his hands in his pockets almost pulls an apology for my apology-take-back from my lips. What is wrong with me?

He watches me like he's trying to work something out. Like he'll somehow find the answer in my sweaty face. He won't. I'm all out. "She *was* my type." His stare meets mine and there's a sureness about him I haven't seen before. "But last night I realized something."

I fold my arms and clamp my teeth to stop the words I know are about to fall out. It's no good. They fall out anyway. "Was that before or after you let her climb you?" I wince. "Not that it's got anything to do with me."

"I guess I deserve that." He clicks his tongue against his front teeth and rubs his hand up the back of his neck. "Nothing happened."

I arch my brow but refuse to give up my indignation. "Felix, I'm kind of busy, so…" I glance over his shoulder to the mess behind him.

"Types change, Laia." His jaw ticks, his face serious and one hundred percent trained on me.

Types change? Just like that, my elastic band of verbal weirdness stretches so far it snaps and leaves me completely speechless. I'm not sure what's worse. I look anywhere but into his face. It would be weird to ask for clarification, right?

"Felix, I'm not … I don't think I'm—" When I look up, he's staring at me, looking only slightly less mystified than I am.

"Where do you want me?" He turns back to the sink to wash his hands. "These pies won't bake themselves." He quirks a brow over his shoulder then grabs a towel to dry his hands.

Where do I want him? I swallow. *Where do I want him?*

His lips twitch. He can read my mind. I'm sure of it.

I press my hands to my hot cheeks but drop them when that damn dimple appears again and move to stand beside him, fighting my own smile. "I need more strawberries cut."

"I can do that." He leans around me and picks up a knife and the tub of strawberries left over from the first batch I made.

It takes me a couple of minutes to get used to his presence beside me. A couple more to calm my cheeks down. And about ten more to get everything into the pot and bubbling. The sweet, fruity smell calms me. And I can almost, *almost* forget who's standing next to me. Who's arm brushes mine every time he reaches for something. Who's listened to every one of my directions without so much as a grumble.

I grab a teaspoon and fill it with balsamic vinegar. "Did you know that balsamic vinegar was originally used as a healing elixir?" My lips move with my silent measuring as I pour, *one, two, three.* "It's so hard to find the real stuff that's not just cheap wine vinegar with corn syrup and flavorings." I pick up a different spoon and dip into the mixture, closing my eyes as I taste it. "Not sweet enough."

My nose itches. I rub it with the back of my forearm. "Pass me the honey." I hold my hand out. Then wince. "Please. Sorry."

His brow lowers as he scans the basket of bottles and jars on the worktop. "Sorry for what?" He leans forward to take a closer look at a jar then picks it up and twists the top off before he hands it to me. "I like watching you bake." The tips of his fingers brush my thumb when I take the jar. "It looks good on you."

I almost lose my breath. Almost fall back into hide-away mode.

Maybe it's the genuine tone to his words, or the slight upward tilt to his lips. Or maybe it's the effects of my pie high. But, for the first time in a long time, I *want* to talk about this. "I hadn't baked in a long time before I came here." I spoon honey into the mix then go back to stirring the pot. "My ex…" I clear my throat, my wooden spoon pausing in the bubbling red mixture. "My ex wasn't really a fan of me baking."

I glance over at him, and something softens in his expression before he returns to clearing away the cut-offs from the strawberries and the gooey mess my spoons have left on the chopping board. "Well, I'm a fan." The words are gruff, with way more weight to them than they should really hold.

"I…" I can barely speak from the size of my grin. "But you haven't even tried them yet."

The muscles in his forearms cord and flex as he wipes down the work top then throws the cloth in the sink. "Anything that makes your cheeks this pink and your eyes this bright, I'm a fan of."

I think I just melted. I blink dumbly at him.

"Who taught you?"

I twist the knobs on the cooker until the flames extinguish. "My mom was a baker. So was my gran."

He stops wiping to look at me. "Where are your parents now?"

"Em." I glance down at my fingers when they wrap around my pendant, then meet his stare. "Dead." I swallow carefully and press my lips together until I'm sure they won't tremble. "Mom died of a heart attack, then my dad of a stroke six months later."

Felix turns and leans a hip to the worktop, folding his arms over his chest, his gaze flicking over my face with something an awful lot like understanding.

I wait. Hold his stare. Forget to breathe. Somehow completely comfortable *way* outside my comfort zone.

"I'm sorry." He scratches his forehead and releases a long breath. "I know how it feels to lose someone close to you."

I swallow back the tightness in my throat at the sudden hollowness to his face and the tension that's stolen away his dimples. I shouldn't have said anything. "Felix. You … we don't have to talk about this. I was stupid to bring it up. I didn't think. I never think."

"Not stupid, Laia. It's just not something I talk about. Not with anyone."

I blow out a breath. "I can't imagine what it's like to lose people you've served with … and so young…" I crush my lips together to stop anything else from falling from them when his chest expands, and he lifts his gaze to the ceiling. Why am I still talking? It's not something he talks about.

I blink away the burn of tears behind my eyes at the visible pain etched in every hard line of his face. There's so much more he's not telling me—just like there's so much more I'm not telling him. "You can tell me anything. But you don't have to."

His smile is sad—almost bitter, that hollowness taking over all of his features when he looks at me again. "I'll keep that in mind."

SEVENTEEN

Laia

"What about this?"

"Hmm?" I nod absentmindedly at the gold sequin mini Kenzi's got held up over my plain black tank and cut-offs.

"Laia, jeez. What's up with you today? I know it's Monday and all, but we're *shopping*, for crying out loud!"

I jerk my head back and swat at the hand waving in front of my face. "Sorry." I try to reel my brain back from yesterday's visit from Felix and the fact that I really can't afford to be shopping a week before pay day. "I had a weird day yesterday."

Kenzi offers me a pity-filled smile and cocks her head to the side. "Don't tell me you're pissed over Jayne? I've no idea what Felix was thinking. Well, I do, but come on." Her lips twist like she's just got a nose full of rotten eggs. "Weirdo woman."

My tummy flattens against my lungs at the memory. "He came around yesterday morning to apologize."

"He did? And you wait until now to tell me?" Kenzi hangs the dress back onto its rail then narrows her eyes on my face. "What did he say? How did he say it? Details. *Details!*"

I shake my head. "Jayne told me that he's only interested in women that look like his ex." I sink my teeth into my bottom lip.

Her face sobers and she puffs out her cheeks. "Fucking Jayne. He didn't leave with her, you know that, right?" She sighs again and scratches her forehead. "Laia, there's something you need to know about Fee. For whatever reason, he's not talking, but I'd rather you hear this from me than any of the gossips around here."

A knot ties itself around my windpipe and my heart literally aches at the fight she's clearly having with herself over telling me Felix's story.

I pull a pink, faux leather mini dress out and hold it up against her before she takes her next breath. "Don't you dare say you don't love this."

She purses her lips. "Laia…"

I know this face. "Don't *Laia* me, I'm fine. It's fine. I shouldn't have brought it up. It's got nothing to do with me."

"If you two would just—"

"How's your new neighbor?" I cut her off. I refuse to spend the day obsessing. I won't be that girl again.

"That man…" Her eyes glaze and she stares into space, fanning her face with a coat hanger. "This morning I ran into him on my way to work. He'd been jogging. *Shirtless.* I could've come on the spot." Her nose wrinkles but her eyes are clear again by the time they meet mine. "I still can't believe that he, of all people, has moved in next door to me. *Fucking Mylo.* It's like the universe hates me."

I can't help but snicker. "Or maybe it loves you."

"Nope, it definitely hates me." She shakes her head. "Right. Anyway. Head out of the gutter, woman. I've organized the girls' night this Friday. You're coming. And make more pie. Simon's coming. Perfect time to dazzle him with more flavors."

"Kenzi, I'm not much of a partier—"

"You're coming." She pins me with her best menacing scowl.

I roll my eyes. If I say no now, she's only gonna harp on about it for the rest of the week. And now that I have a cell phone, her harping can follow me home. I know how she works. "Maybe." I concede grudgingly, not even bothering to hide my mutinous jaw-jut.

"No maybes. My friends are dying to meet you. I'm thinking drinks and nibbles at my house. Si always brings the best snacks." She grins wide. "And we'll finish the night with some dancing at The Beach Hut. There's a DJ playing. He's amazing. He mixes traditional Cluan with house music. A total local celeb. I can't believe Felix actually agreed to give me the night off." She claps her hands like an excited seal and bounces on the balls of her feet.

I'm still stuck on The Beach Hut part of her plans. Yesterday—baking with Felix—was good. It was fun. But maybe too much fun? Distance—I'm in dire need of some distance from him to keep my head straight.

"What's that look?"

I screw up my face. "Do we really have to go to The Beach Hut? I … I mean it's your night off, don't you want to go somewhere else?"

"Sure." Her eyes crease at the corners with the force of her put on grin. "If toothless pensioners are your thing, we can go to the Clua Local." She picks up a green jersey maxi dress and holds it over her sun dress. "Or there's always the Fisherman's Arms. That place is rocking if you're partial to the smell of fish and men in yellow overalls. Or there's a dive bar over in Tenting if you're into hairy bikers. Or there's the new night club by the Castle hotel … Oh yeah, it's not been built yet."

"Okay, Okay. Point made." I pull a black, wide-legged jumpsuit from the rack and check the price tag. I really shouldn't be spending this for a night out. My escape Arizona funds are almost at zero after all the pies I've been making.

"You should definitely try that on." Kenzi nods resolutely when I hold it up against me.

EIGHTEEN

Laia

I step back to check my reflection in the glass of the security door to Kenzi's apartment block and tug at the high neckline of the black, full-length jumpsuit I let Kenzi talk me into buying. It's almost completely backless. I twist to check for the millionth time that my butt crack isn't showing and the scar on the back of my hip is hidden. It's low, but I guess it is kind of flattering thanks to the built-in support system up front. The wonders of modern dressmaking didn't come cheap though. I dipped into my inheritance account to buy it. The money I promised myself I'd use to set up a business on my own one day. It feels wrong using that, even if I am nowhere as near to fulfilling that dream as I'd hoped to be when I made that promise after my parents died. In Arizona, it was a sofa. Here, it's clothes. I chew on the inside of my cheek.

You can't take it with you when you're gone, Lai.

I straighten my shoulders, the memory of my dad's indulgent eyebrow wiggle whenever he treated me or my mom to something we couldn't quite afford soothing a little of the buyer's guilt.

The door buzzes for me to open it, and, for a second, I consider running. No. I meet my stare in my reflection. I need this. New Laia needs this. My dad's right, I can't take it with me when I'm gone, and, let's face it, I wasn't a woman on the run trying to build a new life for the second time in two years when I made that promise to myself. I yank the door open, careful not to drop the pie I made this morning. *I've* got this. I'm *allowed* to have this. Tonight's gonna be worth the splurge. I hope.

Kenzi's already waiting by her open front door when I step from the elevator. "You're here." She holds out a glass of wine. "And you look fabulous, my friend. *And* you brought the pie! Come, meet the others."

I take a sip of the cool white wine and step over the threshold.

"Ladies, Laia's here." She wraps her arm around my shoulders and pulls me down the small entrance hall to the living room, taking the pie from me as she goes.

"Laia, at last we meet. I'm Rae."

I smile and hold up my hand in a mini wave at the teeny woman curled onto the corner of Kenzi's huge cream sectional because I'm cool like that, and meeting new people doesn't revert me back to my dorky fifteen-year-old self. Her accent is amazing. Half Cluan lilt, half something else. Scottish, maybe? Irish?

Wide, hazel eyes crinkle and she tilts a can of soda to me while dragging thick, auburn hair over her shoulder, revealing an intricate tattoo that swirls from the ball of her shoulder down to the middle of her forearm. Butterflies and flowers. Badass, but girly, just like the pretty floral sundress and clunky, black biker boots she's wearing.

"This is Rylie." Kenzi turns me to the raven-haired woman sitting beside Rae.

Rylie smiles wide and raises her glass to me. "Hey, girl." Her feline blue eyes twinkle as she takes a sip of her wine.

Are any of Kenzi's friends not drop-dead-gorgeous?

"And this little pixie here is Jo. She works days in The Beach Hut." Kenzi spins me around to where a petite woman is in the process of tying a red paisley bandana around her super short dark hair in the mirror hanging on the wall.

"Hey, Laia." She meets my stare in her reflection. "Great to finally meet you."

"And of course, you already know Si."

I'm spun again to where Simon's peeking his head out from the kitchen door.

"Hey, baby girl." He eyes the pie in Kenzi's hand, his white-blond hair slicked back.

I wave. "Hey, Simon."

"Call me Si, darling." His tawny eyebrows do a little quirk. "Only my mother calls me Simon. Now bring me that pie."

I glance at Kenzi for support, but she just hands me the pie back and nudges me towards the kitchen door with a wiggle of her eyebrows. "You heard the man, go show him your pie."

Clutching the plate in both hands, I step into the kitchen. "I made mixed-berry this time."

I've barely placed it onto the sleek black worktop when Simon—*Si*, comes at me, knife and fork in hand. "My Yaya made the best berry pie in Miami, God rest her soul. You've got big clogs to fill, Laia."

My stomach twists regardless of the humor tipping up the corners of his mouth as he cuts into the crust. I should have brought the mango one. That's the one he liked best. Or the chocolate one. I should have brought both. Or all. Or neither. God, I should have stayed home.

I worry my lip between my teeth.

He chews slowly, his eyelids fluttering closed.

I hold my breath, the giggles and cackles from the living room only adding to the tension headache that's beginning to twinge in my temples.

She thought she could and so she did.

I grip my pendant, my throat dry despite the giant gulp of wine I just swallowed.

Simon's eyes finally pop open as he licks a crumb from his bottom lip.

His head tilts to the side and he clicks his tongue against his teeth. "Laia." He glances at the pie then back to me. "Yaya lives on in you, girl. How the hell did you get that tangy balance to the sweetness?"

Air releases from my cheeks. "You like?"

"*I love.* You, young lady, are truly wasted as a receptionist. I need this one on my menu, too."

My mouth drops open. "Really?"

"Really. I'll need to talk to Pete. And try more variations but consider all your pies mine."

Three glasses of white wine later, my cheeks ache from laughing and my face feels pleasantly fuzzy. Kenzi's friends are hilarious, and they've welcomed me into the fold like I'm one of their own. I didn't realize how much I've missed having girlfriends. Doesn't hurt that they all loved my pie too. Tonight is shaping up to be the best night I've had in—maybe ever.

"And he dragged me out by the scruff of my neck like a wet cat." Rae's nose wrinkles, and she takes a pull from her soda. "But I could have saved myself. Obviously."

"Obviously," the other girls deadpan then break into another fit of giggles. They've been regaling me with tales of their past and the weird and wonderful ways they amused themselves while growing up in Clua.

"What?" Rae holds her hands out. "I don't need a knight in white armor. I save my own self, thank you very much."

"Someone should maybe let Jackson in on that little fact," Rylie nudges her playfully with her shoulder. "He's practically made a career out of saving your skinny ass since you rocked up fresh from Scotland."

Rae sticks her tongue out and her gaze drops to the pink straw jutting from her soda. When she lifts her head again, she's grinning big. "Let's tell Laia about the time Rylie decided to parade past the guys at Fee's place."

"Sounds interesting." I lean forward, more to get the heat off of Rae than anything. Her big grin doesn't fool me. There's more to that story. I should know, I'm a master of grinning through things.

"No, let's definitely not." Rylie lifts a cushion from the couch and covers her face.

"She stuffed Kenzi's mom's bra and stole her heels then tottered right past the boys mid basketball game. Man, Seb's eyes almost fell out," Kenzi cackles from where she's sitting on a big pink Aztec floor cushion. "Didn't Fee get a ball in the face because Jackson was so distracted by bazookas over here?"

"Stop, Kenzi." Rylie peeks out from behind her pillow. "They were the hottest guys in school, and they practically lived at Fee's house next door to Kenzi. It took me years to live that down."

"Who's Seb?" I ask, glancing between their flushed faces.

"Seb," Kenzi, Rae, and Rylie sigh in unison.

"Only the hottest guy ever made in Clua." Rylie crosses one long, jean clad leg over the other.

How she can wear jeans in heat like this, I have no idea.

"He was the first guy I ever kissed." Kenzi grins.

"And me." Rylie holds a hand up and takes a drink of her wine.

"Me too." Rae's face screws up and she scrunches her nose.

I turn, eyebrows raised, to Jo.

"Don't look at me. I didn't move here until after he left for college." Jo shakes her head dramatically. "Although, I did know a Sebastian once…" Her head tips back and she laughs at the other women's amazed stares. "No way it was the same guy. There was nothing small-island about this guy." She bites her painted red lip and grins, suddenly lost in whatever memories are running through her tipsy mind.

"I'd like to meet this Seb," Simon offers, holding his fork up from where he's digging into yet another slice of pie from the plate on the coffee table. "Cluans seem to have some sort of mystical hot man gene. If Pete wasn't so damn fine, I'd almost be jealous."

"Sooo, you all had your first kiss with the same boy?" I fail to contain my giggle-snort.

"In our defense, it was during a game of spin the bottle." Rae holds up her hands. "And Seb was the only boy."

"What about Felix?" I ask. Instant cringe. Stupid wine.

They all stop like someone's pressed pause on the party, heads swiveling my way.

"Don't tell me you've got a thing for our Fee?" Rae leans across Rylie and shoots me a toothy smile.

My face flames. Why did I have to mention his name?

"A *thing* is far too tame a word for what's going on there." Kenzi fans her face with her hand a little overzealously, nearly falling off her cushion.

"Kenzi," I warn, shaking my head, attempting to shoot some shut-the-fuck-ups from my eyes.

"You know all of our darkest secrets now, Laia. It's only fair they know your big juicy one." She waves me off. "Felix drools every time he lays eyes on Laia. And though she doth protest, our little Laia isn't much better."

I drop my head back onto the sofa and cover my face with my hands. *Why oh why did I mention his name?*

"Felix? Our Felix?"

I peek through my fingers at the shock in Rae's strangely accented voice. Surprise apparently ups the Scottish.

They're all looking at me like I've grown another head.

"Ahh, I did hear that someone had finally caught his eye. I didn't realize it was you though! Spill, Laia." Rylie leans towards me, a bottle of wine in one hand, a glass in the other.

I throw the pillow on my lap at Kenzi's head. "It's complicated."

"But you like him?" Rae opens her mouth and covers it with her hand. "And he likes you?"

"I…" I shake my head. "It's complicated."

"Then uncomplicate it, woman. Felix is *fine*—and good—*and fine.*" Rae's grin is so wide it almost doesn't fit on her face. "Do it. Uncomplicate it tonight. For real!"

"Agreed." Zi reaches over to fist bump Rae then turns to me. "Talk to him, woman."

"Talking was *not* where I was going with that," Rae screws up her face.

I take a gulp of my wine and lock eyes with Simon.

He smiles sympathetically and reaches for the radio. "Leave the poor girl alone and let's dance, biatches."

Interrogation over. The others squawk along to Rihanna's latest, but I'm still stuck on Felix.

Maybe it *is* time I stopped making things so complicated.

It's not long before everyone is prancing around the room, trying unsuccessfully not to spill their drinks on themselves as they wiggle and giggle and sing at the top of their lungs.

"Laia, get your ass up here." Kenzi holds her hand out for me.

I let her pull me to my feet, unable to stop myself from laughing.

Rylie stops mid-twerk and holds her glass above her head. "It's nearly ten, people. Let's take this party on the road!"

NINETEEN

Felix

I slide a beer across the bar to the man I'm serving and take his money.

"Felix, dude. It's packed in here," Mylo yells from where he's counting change into the register. He offered to cover when Zi asked for the night off. The only reason I gave it to her.

He's right, though. The bar is packed. The DJ's playing his own blend of Cluan folk songs and soulful house music, the locals in the crowd stamping their feet and clapping their hands to the tunes we've grown up hearing. The tourists attempting to follow the fast rhythms but failing spectacularly.

We've moved the sofas from the main bar out onto the terrace leaving the inside for dancing.

"I've never heard anything like this." Mylo dips his head so I can hear him over the music, his head bobbing to the thick beat as he scans the bar. I know who he's looking for. The girls are out tonight. *Out* out according to Zi.

"It's traditional Cluan," I mutter. I've spent the last hour watching the door too. I thought they'd be here by now.

"You expecting someone? The little receptionist from the Castle maybe?"

"No. Yeah." I rake my hair back from my face and shake my head. "Fucked if I know." I haven't seen Laia since the other day at her place. Figured space would give me some sort of clarity. That with some distance I'd be able to figure out what the hell's going on in my head. It hasn't.

"She seems like a good girl."

I scan the bar again. "It's complicated."

He glances down to where Jayne is calling out for another round of drinks. "I'd take *complicated* with Laia over listening to that voice any day of the week."

I blow air into my cheeks then take a swig of beer. "She's got a past." I shake my head.

"Haven't we all." He rolls his shoulders before pinning me with the same take-no-shit brow quirk he's used on me since the day I met him. "In my book, complicated is always better than easy."

Before I can agree—or *disagree,* the unmistakable sound of drunk women drifts over the loud music.

It's impossible to miss the way Mylo straightens the second Kenzi struts through the crowd and sidles up to him at the bar, the others tottering in behind her.

Laia's at the back of the gaggle in a black-trouser all-in-one outfit thing. Whatever it is, it looks sexy as hell on her. The high neck and bare arms leave just enough to the imagination. Until she turns to the terrace, bouncing on her toes to the music as she yells something into Rae's ear. Her hair is twisted up off her neck, leaving the curve of her spine completely bare from her hairline to her…

Holy shit that's low. I lift my chin in a vague greeting to the others, but my gaze refuses to remove itself from Laia. I shove my hands in my pockets and rock back on my heels.

"Hey, lover-boy, how about some drinks over here?" Rylie leans over the bar, her knowing gaze shifting between my face and Laia's back.

The other girls grin, nudging each other like schoolgirls until Laia turns.

Her smile is like a sucker punch to the gut. Complicated definitely wins out over easy.

Letting Mylo take care of the others, I lean against the bar and wait for her to come closer.

Slightly glazed, but startlingly green even in the dim light, her gaze flits over my face.

"Laia." I plant both hands on the bar in front of me.

She blinks, a smile tugging at her lips. "Hey."

I can barely hear her over the thumping music, but I try anyway. "You look good." I take in her outfit again.

She bites her lip, her nose scrunching, but she doesn't look away even when her cheeks flush. "So do you … I mean, you look good too." She rolls her eyes and shakes her head, but her smile doesn't shift.

My chest knots, a bemused grin stretching across my face. She doesn't look away until she's dragged backwards onto the dance floor.

I think Laia just flirted with me.

Laia

So, somewhere between wine number three and the fresh air of the short walk to The Beach Hut, I came to a vague sort of agreement with myself—tonight I stop being complicated.

Tonight is the night I get *uncomplicated*—with Felix. Uncomplicated with

Felix.

It's just a shame I forgot that I suck at flirting—like, really bad.

Despite it all though, a care-free drunken daze envelops me as I dance around to the music—hands in the air, wiggling, giggling, girls-night-out dancing. I'm having a ball.

And then when I don't think it can get any better, the backbeat to the last song fades and a dramatic acoustic guitar solo takes over.

Kenzi and Rylie jump up and down, squealing like a pair of teenagers, and Rae pulls me back a few steps until we're leaning against the bar. "Best give them room," she laughs into my ear.

"What? What do you mean?" My head swings from her to them and back again.

"Just watch." She tips her bottle of water in their direction. "Trust me."

Kenzi and Rylie get into position, still squawking and giggling like little girls. Arms held in an arc above their heads, one foot tipped, heel to the ground, the other planted flat.

The guitar stops for a beat then the thump of stamped feet on wood starts up. Slow at first—a rhythm completely foreign to me. Then, as it speeds up, the complicated clapping starts, and my mouth falls open.

A quick glance behind me tells me that I'm not the only one who doesn't know what's going on. Huge arms folded over his chest, Mylo's eyes are glued on Kenzi.

Even Felix has picked up the clapping. And seriously. *Seee-reee-ouus-ly*. I've never seen anything sexier. It's just clapping, but … his stare meets mine for a second, and something intense, smoldering, and hot-as hell wraps around me.

The guitar starts up again along with the haunting voice of a woman singing in Cluan. I shake myself from my Felix-haze just in time to see Kenzi and Rylie snap their arms down. Their feet do a little stamp hop thing, and then they're off.

Kenzi hitches up one side of her dress and swoops low, then follows the arch of her arms up and around into a spin and some sort of finger dance, all the time her feet stamping the same hypnotic rhythm as the music, Rylie moving in complete symmetry. And in those heels.

My face breaks into the biggest grin I think I've ever had as they move in time, swooping and arcing and stamping their feet. I clap along best I can, but these guys are good. These guys are master clappers. The speed of their fingers slapping against their palms is mind-boggling. My hands sting a couple of minutes in, but Kenzi and Rylie just keep on going, swooping and kicking and heel-toe tapping and twirling in perfect time with the beat. The clapping and the stamping get louder, building and building until finally the house beat kicks back in and the whole bar goes nuts. The dance floor heaves in a swoop of movement and music and dancing bodies. Rae pulls me back into the thick of it by the hand.

I don't get far before an arm wraps my middle, something cold pressing against my back. Surprise spikes my pulse from one to a million. I jerk around.

It's Felix. Just Felix.

My heart does a double backflip regardless, adrenaline firing through my veins at the curve of his far too kissable lips as he pushes a bottle of water into my hand. Every nerve ending in my body pings to attention beneath the thin material of my jumpsuit at his nearness—at the *feel* of him beside me.

He dips his head, his cheek brushing mine, his breath tickling the shell of my ear. "Drink." His hand drops to my hip and stays there even after he's pulled back.

I like that it's there, like the way his scent wraps around me, so, before I can think myself out of it, I lean into him, lift onto my toes, and press a kiss to his cheek, my throat throbbing with my pulse, my cheeks blazing with my public boldness. "Thank you."

Fortune favors the bold—it's quickly becoming my favorite of my dad's sayings.

When I drop back down, Felix's mouth is quirked, brows raised. "Laia I—"

"Felix, babe."

A familiar, whiney voice from behind me stops him from finishing. You've *got* to be shitting me.

Flappy Eyes nudges me to the side and flattens her hands on Felix's chest. "There you are, baby."

Jealousy flares white hot and blistering inside me. I grind my teeth. *Baby? Really?*

"Jayne." Felix covers her hands with his and pulls them from his chest, but she wraps both of her skinny arms around one of his and leans towards me while trying to pull him away. Her bold puts my bold to shame. "You don't mind if I steal him from you, Laia, do you?"

"Types change, huh?" Shaking my bottle, I force a smile. "Thanks for the water."

"Wait." Felix shrugs Flappy Eyes off his arm, turns his back on her and links his fingers through mine.

"Felix, don't." I try to pull my hand from his grip, horrifyingly close to bursting into drunk-girl tears. "It's cool. Really. It is."

"It's not." This time he tugs me to him, slides his free arm around my back and curves his big body over mine.

My head tips back and I blink stupidly, my heart speeding up in my chest. "Felix—"

His lips cover mine, cutting off whatever I was about to say. Quick. Hard. Soft. Slow. All of the above. My eyelids flutter closed, the scruff of his jaw prickling the palm of the hand I hadn't even realized I'd lifted to his face.

I inhale his breath and push into his hold. The fact that we're in a bar, *in his bar*, in front of everyone I know on the island niggles in some far away part of my brain, but I can't quite bring myself to care. Not yet.

"*She's* not my type." He nips my bottom lip then pulls back slowly, his forehead pressing against mine. "*You are.*"

And then he's gone. Sauntering back to the bar, leaving me standing there gawping like a guppy, wondering if that actually just happened.

I press my lips together and glance to the left.

The girls are staring, eyes wide, mouths hanging open with varying measures of shock. It happened.

I glance to the right. Flappy Eyes is glaring, lips pursed like she just sucked a giant lemon. It *totally* happened.

And finally, I glance over to the bar. Felix is already grabbing a glass from the overhead shelf. He looks over as he pulls a bottle from the rack and winks. And fight it as I try, I swear my grin almost splits my face clean in half.

"So, *that* just happened," Kenzi squeals in my ear as she man-handles me around to face them again.

I open my mouth. Then snap it shut again, pressing my lips together, but I'm completely unable to stop them from stretching back into a grin. "It did."

"Complicated, my ass." Rae grabs my hand and lifts it, prancing around in a wiggly little circle. "Now, less mooning, more dancing."

And so, we dance. And dance. And hug and sing and woop and laugh. And pass around shots and dance some more until my feet throb, my hair is plastered to the back of my neck and my cheeks ache from the kind of massive smile I never thought I'd ever wear again. Girls' nights rock. Even if I have had to dodge my way out of a few of Rylie's group selfies along the way.

The first bump to my back comes as Jo hands me another Monstrosity, sloshing the pink liquid over my hand. "Oops," I laugh, and hold it out in front of me, glancing over my shoulder to watch out for the wayward dancer.

My laugh fizzles out. Flappy Eyes and her friends are strut-dancing beside us. None of them look at me.

Kenzi links her fingers with mine and tugs me back into our little circle, shooting drunk eye-daggers into their backs.

A laugh bubbles up, but I shake off the weirdness and get back to my dancing, trying unsuccessfully to catch the end of my straw between my teeth as I go.

The second bump knocks me into Rae, propelling her backwards into where Rylie's showing Simon and Jo a complicated dance move. This time we all glare at their boney little backs but break into song when the beat kicks back in, promptly forgetting what we were glaring at.

The third bump is more of an elbow, and it catches me right in the ribs, nudging me sideways into a high table, knocking me and my glass into the wooden edge of it. The glass smashes, then falls from my grip. I hop back, frozen alcohol splashing up my legs as it crashes onto the wooden floor. Whoever's behind me gets the brunt of my hop back. I twist, an apology teetering on the tip of my tongue, just in time to see her go down, like a tree chopped from its roots, she wobbles then topples.

Somebody shouts, "Timber."

Still standing on one foot, I lift my hand to cover my mouth. Flappy Eyes. On her ass. Heels akimbo. Face contorted in a scream.

I can't decide whether to laugh or apologize, or, I don't know, help her up?

Common decency has me leaning forward to hold out my hand. She slaps it away, clawing at her friends' arms to help her onto her feet, just as Felix appears.

My eyes widen, my pulse picking up at the scowl on his face as he gets between us. "It wasn't my … I didn't mean to…"

"She pushed me, Fee," Flappy Eyes whines, her pretty eyes wide, but not quite innocent as she makes a grab for his arm again.

"Go home, Jayne. Now." His voice carries over the thump, thump thumping of the music. "Or you won't be allowed back."

Her mouth flaps, her face pinching until all the pretty just gets up and leaves it. "You and me are over, Fee. You hear?"

I watch her go, her girls on her heels, the music suddenly too loud, the crowd too bouncy, my head too woozy. Felix turns, big hands on my shoulders, face all kinds of worried. "You okay?"

Kenzi catches my arm and lifts it before I can get a word out.

"Blood." She joogles my hand above my head. "Bitch drew blood."

"I…" I look up at my hand, then back to Felix, trying to tug it back down without drawing even more attention to myself. "I'm fine."

"Zi? Tidy the glass," he shouts without looking away from me. "*You* come with me."

And then it's him who's holding my hand up. And it's him who's behind me, marching me past the flip-down hatch of the bar and through the door on the back wall.

Fear sparks, then stutters, then sparks again. It's Felix. This is Felix. I repeat it in my head as I take the concrete stair into a narrow hallway lit only by the open door at the end of it. Felix steps down behind me, still holding my hand out to the side like it might fall off if he lets go.

"Where are we going?" I turn my head but keep walking forward, the hand on my hip distractingly warm, and big, and *warm.* My tummy flits and bobs and weaves at his fresh air scent and the heat of him at my back.

"My office," he rumbles into my ear, his breath whispering over my cheek.

His office is … way bigger than I expected. And way more well equipped. A huge desk in one corner and a sofa, coffee table, TV and even a fridge in the other, but that's not what stops me in my tracks when I step through the door. It's the massive canvas painting of a sunset on the back wall. Pinks and reds and oranges and golds and so real if I were any drunker, I'd possibly be tempted to dip a toe into the rippling water lapping the shore. "Now that's a painting." A big paint-spattered jar of brushes sits on his desk beside his laptop.

Felix walks into my back, almost knocking me off my feet when I stop to stare at it.

I twist to look at him, my hand still clutched in his. "Did you paint that? Do you paint? Please tell me you paint," I blabber as he guides me into the room towards the desk. "Did you paint the one at Kenzi's house too?"

"Less talking, more moving. You're bleeding."

His hard chest presses against my back, my very *bare* back. From pecs to belt buckle, his T-shirt is soft and warm, and honestly? I don't think I'd notice if my fingers had fallen off and were rolling around the floor.

Finally, he releases my hand and spins me around to lift me onto the desk like I weigh exactly nothing. He doesn't even grunt.

"You know…" I peer at my closed fist and the trickle of blood that's escaping when he moves behind the desk and starts to pull open drawers. "This probably isn't necessary." I uncurl my fingers one by one, wrinkling my nose at my blood-smeared palm. My pointer finger and my middle finger have matching slices and—I lift my hand closer to my face—there's a cut in the middle of my pinkie too. "I think they're fine," I drunk-yell over to him, still examining them intently. He tugs my hand from my face and my head jerks up. I thought he was over there. "I think I'll live," I whisper.

"I didn't have you down as a bar-brawler." He scans my face, a smile kicking the corner of his lips up as he nudges my legs apart so he can get closer. "Let me see."

"I brawled with no one." I watch him as he examines each finger. "I don't think she meant it … meant *this* to happen."

"We'll agree to disagree there," he mutters, dark head tipped forward, gaze intent, jaw clenched tight as he gently wipes away the blood with antiseptic pads from the big green first aid case now sitting beside me. "Does that hurt?" He asks without looking up from where he's pressed the pad to the cut on my pinkie.

"Nope." I shake my head, the foreignness of his gentleness, of his *concern* almost enough to bring on the waterworks. Did I mention I may be a teeny bit drunk? "So." I lick my lips. "You kissed me."

"I did." His gaze flicks up to mine then drops back to where he's now cleaning up the palm of my hand with slow, careful wipes. "But technically you kissed me first."

"Is that … should we…? People know now." My cheeks heat, my pulse puttering in the dip of my throat as I watch him peel the back off a Band-Aid and wrap it around my pointer finger.

He bandages up my middle finger next and then my pinkie, before finally looking up at me. "Does it bother you if people know?"

"No. I mean yes. I mean … I'm not sure I'm…" I try desperately to hang on to carefree, non-complicated new Laia and her sureness that we're ready for this—for *him*. But my breathing speeds up anyway, my teeth sinking into my bottom lip, my Monstrosity buzz depleting by the second. "Just … can you do it again?" I hold his stare. "The kiss, I mean. Please."

His blue, blue gaze, fringed with lashes so thick I could get lost in them bounces from my left eye to my right, reading the shift in me loud and clear. His face sobers and his brows lower, but he shifts his body closer, lifts a hand to cup my jaw and tilts my head back. "Why?"

"It makes me forget." It's out before I can stop it. I forgot how much Drunk Laia likes to blab my secrets.

Time seems to halt, the muffled bass from back in the bar fading beneath the whooshing in my ears.

His gaze travels my face, the one question I pray to anyone out there he won't put into words written in every concerned line of his handsome face. *Forget what?*

Our silence stretches out, more loaded with secrets than anything either of us could ever put into words.

His eyes stay open even as his lips press against mine. Soft and smooth and … it's not enough, my mind stays depressingly clear and full of all the shitty reasons I should not let this happen.

I lean my body into his, my fingers gripping the sides of his T-shirt, the injured ones pulsing beneath their Band-Aids. I stretch up and press my mouth harder to his, suck his bottom lip, daring him—no, *pleading* with him not to overthink this.

A second ticks by and then he moves. His other hand comes up to the nape of my neck, his gaze flicks back down, before he angles his head and kisses me harder, his tongue pushing into my mouth, his teeth grazing my bottom lip, body dwarfing mine, wrapping my senses and doing exactly what I hoped it would do.

His hands drop to my bum. Mine lift to his neck. I hike my legs up around his waist, swallowing his rough growl when the thick length of him nudges between my thighs, pressing through our clothes, harder with every rock of his hips and every tilt of mine.

It all goes away, every memory, every fear, every reason morphed into nothing but a need to get closer to this man. To never let this stop. It's dizzying. It's spellbinding. *It's everything.* I grab at his T-shirt, dragging it up his hard body.

He breaks the kiss, breathing hard, his hands covering mine, pushing his shirt back down. "You've been drinking."

I wrap my legs tight around his waist and blink up at him. "Drinking but not drunk." I slide my hands beneath the hem and press them flat against the hard ridges of his abs, trailing them down until my fingers hook into the waistband of his shorts. Drunk Laia is also forward. She can stay.

He steps back, out of my reach, dragging his hair from his face and shaking his head. "Not like this."

Lips pressed together, I nod, powerless to stop myself from ogling him, from his disheveled black curls down to what's going on beneath his boardshorts.

My teeth sink into the inside of my cheek. An idea so completely un-me it almost makes me laugh out loud forming in my not quite sober brain. "Not like this?" My tummy knots itself with nerves I really hope are the good kind as I reach up and slip the strap of my jumpsuit over my shoulder.

"Laia," He warns, his hands lifting to his hair again as he watches me. It does delicious things to the muscles of his … everything.

"Or not like this?" I slip the other shoulder strap over the curve of my other shoulder and just … let it fall. And with no back to hold it up, it does. Completely. Cool air lifts goose pimples over my bare breasts. My eyes go wide, a laugh catches in my throat at my newly discovered boldness and the sheer shock on Felix's face.

His gaze drops, then lifts, then drops again, his tongue touching his top lip, before something way too carnal to be called a smile curves his mouth. "I won't fuck you in my office, Laia."

"No fucking then," I practically pant, my tummy unraveling its knots, then twisting up all over again when he moves back between my legs and seals his mouth over mine in a kiss so hard and so fevered, for a moment I forget everything. His name, my name, *everybody's* name. Big hands smooth up my sides, thumbs brushing the swell of my breasts before sliding around to my bare back, crushing me to his body as he rocks between my thighs with the confidence of a man who knows exactly what he's doing.

This time, he doesn't stop me when I grab greedily at his T-shirt. He curves back and lets me drag it over his head then goes right back to the kissing—the bodies-smooshed-together, mind-bogglingly-hot kissing, all skin on skin on skin on skin.

A hum of approval vibrates from my lips when his hot, smooth chest drags over mine and his hand moves to the back of my head. He kisses me deeper, better, harder, guiding me back, back, and back until my shoulder blades touch the cool wood of the desktop. His lips move to my jaw, below my ear, my neck, my collarbone. I arch and rub and wrap myself around him, still half waiting on the fear to kick in—to do something, but it doesn't come. Not even when he cups my breast and his lips close around my nipple, the hot, wet heat of his mouth sucking, licking, dragging a moan from my lips, but no fear.

"So fucking perfect." He growls the words, drawn out and rough against my skin.

I sink my fingers into his thick hair, and he pushes me further along the desk, his body blanketing mine. I bow into his hold, trying to get closer, to touch more of him, to let him touch more of me. It's drugging and heady.

And then my elbow knocks something.

The sound of glass shattering against wood implodes the moment faster than a bucket of iced water in our faces.

He freezes above me. Lifts his head, his hair a mess, his lips shining, but his eyes—his eyes are horrified.

One second, he's holding me, the next he's gone, hands on the back of his neck, staring down at the mess on the floor. "Fuck." He steps back from the desk and turns away like he can't bear to look at it, or me. "The fuck am I doing?"

My missing flight mode kicks in, swift and sobering. I scramble to get my top back in place and my ass off his desk. "I'm sorry, I didn't see, I…" I drop down to pick up the pieces of broken jar amongst the paintbrushes scattered over the floor, my brain struggling to catch up with the sudden jackknife of such an impossibly great moment. It's just a jar, a big old mason jar. I pick up the biggest piece of glass then start piling the smaller pieces on top, careful not to cut myself all over again.

"Laia, leave it."

I glance up to where Felix is already pulling on his T-shirt. "It's fine. I've got it." I grab a couple of the old brushes.

"I said *leave it!*"

I drop the brushes.

Every muscle in my body, every tendon and bone and cell curls into itself at the sudden sharpness of his roar. I'm not exaggerating. It's a roar. It cuts through the relative quiet of his office like a punch to the gut, shocking and sobering and catching me completely off guard.

I stand slowly and turn, the heat seeping from my face, leaving me clammy and cold, and barely able to force myself to look at him.

He's staring at the floor. Eyebrows tipped, jaw tight. "I'm sorry. I shouldn't have—"

"I—I should go." Tears sting the back of my eyes, confusion and alcohol making my head spin and my stomach roll. I run out the door and I don't stop until I'm in the back of a taxi.

Felix

I stare at the mess of broken glass and old paintbrushes on the floor. Rosa's. Her brushes—her lucky jar. It was stupidly big and ugly, but she wouldn't let me replace it.

I rub the middle of my chest with my fist and blow out a long breath, an ache as fresh as the day I lost her taking up root in there.

"Fee? What did you do?" Zi appears in the doorway, a look on her face that could shrivel the balls off a donkey. "Laia has left the building. And she didn't even say bye." She stops short when she notices the mess. The paint brushes. "Oh…" Her big blue eyes swivel up to meet mine. "Oh, shit."

Scrubbing my hand over my mouth, I force myself to focus, force myself not to roar at her to leave me the fuck alone too. "I didn't—fuck." I shake my head and glare at the ceiling, everything I thought I'd figured out turned upside down. "She left?"

Zi's bottom lip pops out and she nods. "I really wish you two would sort your shit out already."

"Give me her number."

"Do you think she'll want you to call?" Her nose wrinkles with a grimace and she sways back a step. "I think there were tears, Fee. Please tell me you didn't shout. Laia's like—like a little baby flower petal, dude. She's delicate. You don't shout at little baby flower petals, or they cry little baby flower petal tears."

"Kenzi, her number." I step towards her, pulling my cell from my back pocket. "And no more Monstrosities. You're wasted."

"Oh, shut up." She rolls her eyes but pulls her cell from where it was tucked into her bra, rocking back on her heels as she swipes the screen to life. "Rosa would be so pissed if she knew you were still playing the widower card. You know that, right?" Her lip pouts back out again.

No words form. She's right. I know she is. But it does nothing to shift the ache in my chest or the tension in the back of my throat.

"We all miss her, Fee." She taps her cell a few times and swipes a few more. "Okay, contact sent." She scowls again but leans in to kiss my cheek before weaving back out the door. "Be nice, or I'll punch you."

I wait for the door to close behind her before I hit call. It rings off. I close my eyes and listen to the automated voicemail until it beeps. "Laia it's me. I'm—fuck, I hate voicemails. Call me when you get this—please."

I puff my cheeks out and stare at the bits of jar Laia stacked up on the floor for a full minute before squatting to pick up each well-used paint brush until all that's left is paint-spattered slithers of glass too small to pick up by hand. It's just glass. It shouldn't still matter this much.

Dale's head pops around the door as I put the last of it on my desk. "Calling last orders now, boss."

"Yeah." I wave him off.

By the time I step back out into the bar the lights are on, and most of the customers have left or are leaving. Zi and Jo are helping the guys collect glasses while Rylie, Rae and Simon do some sort of weird moonwalk by the DJ box, cackling like witches.

"Any luck?" Zi asks as she unloads a tray full of empty glasses onto the bar top looking marginally less buzzed than she was in my office.

I shake my head. "Voicemail. I'm gonna head over now." I lift my hand to massage the knotted muscle in the back of my neck.

"Call me crazy, Fee, but if she won't answer the phone to you, I doubt she'll answer the door. Leave it to me. I'll get the girls to drop me round hers on their way home." She leans over the bar to grab her purse from the fridge beneath but stops before she drops back down. "Maybe you should make sure you're—you know—*ready* before you talk to her."

I click my tongue off my teeth, but nod. She's right. Fuck. I hate that she's right. Laia does not deserve to be messed around. She didn't deserve to be shouted at either. I scrub my hand over my face. "Fine, but go now." I glance up when she turns to leave. "And Zi? I want to be the one to tell her about Rosa."

"It's about time. I'll text you when I get there."

TWENTY

Laia

I curl my feet under me and hug one of my new throw cushions to my chest, staring at absolutely nothing, trying to think of absolutely nothing. Definitely not about me stripping my clothes off even after he told me *no*. And a hundred percent not of how it ended.

He shouted. At me. Logic. I close my eyes and blow out a slow breath, trying to dislodge the unease—the little voice in my head telling me that deep down, they're all the same—that all men have got it in them. Logic, Laia. One roar does not equal psycho. I broke something of his—something that obviously meant a lot to him. If that had been Damon…

Air leaves my lungs in a rush. If it had been Damon, he'd have broken something of mine. My teeth sink into the almost healed skin at the side of my thumbnail. Don't think. Don't remember. It does absolutely no good to remember.

Something bangs on the front door. My heart stutters, my back straightening, tummy clutching.

Fingers pressed against my lips, I glance at the door. Maybe it was just the wind. Seconds tick by. My breath gets stuck in my lungs.

The banging resumes.

I shake out the fear skirting down the back of my neck. Felix. God, it must be Felix.

My cheeks flame just thinking about opening the door to him. I flashed him my boobs. He stopped it. *He shouted.* I don't know. I don't think I can—

"Laia," a muffled voice shouts through the letterbox. "Let me in. The girls have just left in the taxi, and it's flipping dark out here."

Kenzi. I snort despite myself and drag myself to my feet.

The deadbolt thuds open as I turn the key, and the door flies open, Kenzi barreling past me into the house.

"Fucking Jesus in hell, Laia. How can you live all the way out here? I had about fifty heart attacks just waiting for you to answer the fucking door."

I shake my head, but a laugh escapes as I push the door shut and relock it. "What are you doing here?"

"I came to make sure you're okay, like any good friend would do." Kicking off her leather sandals, she weaves her way through to the living room, then plonks herself down onto the sofa. "Fee was going to come round."

I glance toward the door. "Is he?"

"I suspected that would be your reaction, so I told him I'd check in on you."

"Thank you."

"Don't mention it." She pats the sofa beside her. "Now sit."

I don't even try to stop my thumb from lifting to my lips, or my teeth from finding the little tag of skin by my nail again as I fold myself back down onto the sofa. "I don't know what happened."

"You're both as bad as each other. That's what happened. Felix is—he's like my brother, and I love you, girl. But you guys need to figure this shit out." She offers me a small smile, one of her shoulders lifting then dropping. "It's been a long time since I've seen him this wound up over anyone, and I adore you guys together, but not if you're gonna keep hurting each other."

I puff out my cheeks and cuddle the cushion to my chest again, blinking back the tears hovering on my eyelashes. She's right. It's not fair. None of this is fair. Something an awful lot like shame clunks down in my stomach. I've been using him with zero thought for his feelings. Just my own blind need to feel—or *not* feel—when I'm with him. "I should keep away from him."

"What. Ever." Her eyes roll but she squeezes my knee. "You're not fooling anyone. You like him. That's great. He likes you. Talk it the fuck out, people."

I rub my forehead. "If only it were that simple."

"Why can't it be? I wish you'd tell me what's going on with you, Laia. And I'm not just talking about the Fee thing. I'm talking about all of it. The no names on contracts, the jumping at your own shadow, this whole aversion to affection you've got going on?" She tries to take my hand, but I pull it away. Her bottom lip pouts out. "See? I'm your friend and you won't even hold my hand. Let me help you, Laia, please."

I swipe at a hair that's fallen over my forehead and take a deep breath, as tired of the lies and the half-truths and secrecy as she is of hearing them. Things I've never openly admitted to anyone are there, just waiting for me to be brave enough, to *trust* enough to let them out.

Kenzi just watches me, eyes wide, mascara slightly smudged, hair nowhere near as neatly tousled as it was when we left hers. She watches and waits. Just waits for me to burden her with the very worst parts of me.

My breath shudders its way into my lungs, the temptation to shut this down, to hide it all away again so overwhelming it makes my hands tremble. I shake my head.

"My ex…" I start before I can talk myself out of it. "He wasn't good. But in the beginning, he was. He was funny and kind and just—perfect. I was completely dazzled by him."

"Just like with Fee?" Kenzi's fingers link through mine, pulling my hand from its death grip on the pillow and into her lap, refusing to let go even when I try to pull back.

"No. I mean yeah. I guess." I shift uncomfortably, the memories I'm usually so careful to keep locked away fighting for space in my already jumbled mind.

"So, what happened? Did he cheat on you with your best friend? Because I can assure you that will not happen with Fee."

"I wish." I let out a miserable chuckle. "It started after my mom and dad passed. Just little things at first. Telling me who I could talk to, how to dress. Then gradually they got bigger, more controlling—he even called the culinary school I'd been accepted into behind my back and told them I'd be deferring so I could *grieve*." I attempt a smile, but my chin's already trembling. "*Looking out for me,* that's what he called it in the beginning."

"He hurt you." It's not a question, her eyes are already so full of sympathy, of *pity*, I can barely look at her.

"Yeah." I scratch my forehead with trembling fingers and nod. "It was bad." I release a shaky breath, unshed tears blurring my vision. "It was really bad."

Mouth opening and closing, brows tilted up in the middle, she shakes her head, her fingers tightening around my hand when I try to pull it from her grip again. "Why didn't you leave? Call the cops?"

"I don't know." I stare at my knees. "My parents were gone. I had no other family. He'd alienated all my friends. I didn't have anyone."

"God, I can't even imagine." She leans forward still clutching my hand in hers.

I nod, try to smile, but my blood has slowed in my veins, and my mind is caught somewhere between trying to keep the memories out and telling my story. "It gradually got worse. I'd never know what would set him off until one night I came home, and he'd decided that I'd been away too long."

I close my eyes, helpless to stop my mind from going too far into the memories of that night. "He was drunk." The remembered stench of alcohol on his breath is enough to make my stomach recoil. "He didn't normally drink."

My teeth sink into the inside of my cheek until I taste the metallic tang of blood, my nose buzzing. I pull my hand from Kenzi's and wrap my arms around myself. The phantom pain in my ribs where his fist connected is so real, I can practically hear the crunch ringing in my ears, *feel* the inability to catch my breath ramming panic up my throat until I'm there again, curled on the stone floor while he dragged my head up by my hair and tried to shake me into breathing right.

I blink myself back and clear my throat, meeting Kenzi's worried stare. "He beat me so badly, he left himself with no choice but to call an ambulance."

"Laia, I'm so sorry, I had no idea." She presses her fingers to her mouth, like she's trying not to cry. "How did you get away from him?"

"A nurse recognized my injuries. Noticed some other badly healed fractures on my x-rays. Told me she could get me to a Women's Aid shelter." My lips curve up. "She saved my life."

"Fuck." Kenzi holds my stare as she opens her arms to pull me to her. "I'm going to hug you now."

I flinch violently. She either doesn't notice or doesn't care. She just holds me tighter. And to my complete amazement, I let her.

TWENTY-ONE

Felix

"Is there a reason we're heading into the woods today?" Mylo side-eyes me as he throws his rucksack into the back of my pickup. "Isn't it forecast to rain?"

"It never rains when it says it will around here." I grunt and dump a box of groceries on the back seat. "We're going because I need fishing and beer. And space. Lots of fucking space. And no women."

His face sobers. "You fucked up last night." He drops his shoulders, scratching the tawny stubble on his jaw as he watches me lug my own rucksack over into the bed of the pickup.

"I fucked up." I nod, still feeling like a complete dick. I almost fucked her on a desk with a bar full of people just meters away then blew up at her for something that had fuck all to do with her. It wasn't her fault. The look on her face before she walked—no, *ran* out—flashes in my mind.

Dick move, but fuck. Rosa.

The jar breaking was like a fucking sign from above. I drag my hand over my mouth and stare at the wheel rim of my truck. Kenzi was right, I need to figure it out before I see her again. "I don't know if I'm ready for someone like her." A long sigh releases from my chest. "She's—complicated, and I'm—fuck knows what I am. I thought I could."

Mylo shakes his head. "Figure it out before it bites you in the ass, man. Or worse. Bites her in the ass."

"I think she's running from something." I rub the back of my neck and turn to face Mylo. "I don't know what, or who, but it's something she wants to forget."

"Pasts, man. Sometimes that shit is easier to hide from."

Something in the sobering of his face makes me wonder if we're still talking about Laia. He never talks about what happened pre Clua. Or the tour that finished his military career, but it must have left its mark. I jab him in the shoulder as I pass him. "We can talk about your shit too if you need to."

"Nah, man." His laugh is rough, but he shakes his head. "Your shit's more interesting."

I roll my eyes. "Beer is needed."

Laia

My nose twitches. I peel my eyes open a crack. Coffee. Someone's making coffee. I lift my head and unstick my tongue from the roof of my mouth. Pain explodes behind my eyeballs. Hangover. I'm definitely hungover.

Shoving my hands under my pillow, I wrap it around my head and roll onto my front, memories of last night needling their way into my fluffy head. His lips on mine. His hands roaming my back, *my front*. That rocking thing he did with his hips. A groan—think injured cow—escapes me and I press my face into the sheets. I had to flash him my boobs to get him to kiss me. Maybe the jar angst was just his way of getting out of it without hurting my feelings. But then the kiss. That kiss. That *hardness*—you can't fake that kind of hard. I groan again. I hate Drunk Laia. Drunk Laia is never allowed back.

"You awake?"

Kenzi's voice drifts through from the kitchen, along with the unmistakable aroma of bacon. My tummy rumbles but I pull the pillow tighter over my head.

"I hear groaning."

My tummy doubles its efforts to get me to take notice. I flip over and kick my covers off. "Coming."

Kenzi's already got the table set by the time I shuffle through to the kitchen in my old green pajamas.

She hands me a glass of orange juice and pushes me down into a chair. "Drink this, take those, and eat that."

I grab a couple of pills from the table and swallow them down with the whole glass of juice. "Thank you," I mumble, my mouth already watering at the greasy goodness on my plate.

"Don't mention it." Kenzi sits and stabs her fork into the sad-looking slice of pie on her own plate.

"Pie? For breakfast? Really?" I wrinkle my nose and pick up my knife and fork.

"Really." She nods and stuffs a forkful into her mouth, closing her eyes as she chews.

"You realize that pie is like a week old? I gave the fresh ones to Simon."

Her eyelids crack open a peep, but she just shrugs and keeps chewing. "Still tastes good."

I shake my head and slice off a corner of my crispy bacon then dip it into the soft yolk of my egg.

"Seriously, Laia, Simon is right, you're wasted as a receptionist. You need to be selling these bad boys. I can see it now. *Laia's Palace of Pies.*" She waves her fork in an arc over her head between mouthfuls. "Once you sort it out with Fee, you should totally talk to him about selling them in the Beach Hut too."

I drop my gaze to my plate.

"Lai, this is so good." My dad's face lights up and he shovels another forkful into his mouth. "Seren, have you tasted this? Our daughter's a pro."

My mom wraps her arms around my shoulders from behind and gives me a squeeze.

Pride swells my ten-year-old chest. "I made another to sell in the bakery. Do you think they'll let me?"

"So … you wanna talk about last night?"

Kenzi's gentle voice pulls me from my happy memories. It's not often the good ones are the ones my messed-up brain decides to treat me to.

I shake my head. I don't even want to think about what happened last night. "No?" So, why did that come out as a question? I really don't. Like *really* don't.

"Come on, Laia, Fee was a mess. You were a mess."

I push my plate into the middle of the table and drop my aching head into its place. "We…" My cheeks heat against the cool wood. "I may have tried to climb him after he fixed my fingers." A fresh wave of mortification rushes my fragile brain, and I hold my hand up to show her my still Band-Aided up fingers. "I think I forced him into it." I don't look up, just groan against the table. "He tried to stop me and so…" I snort out something that might be a mini cry. "I flashed boob to get him to keep going. No means no, but I didn't take no, and then I accidentally smashed the jar and I think he used it as an excuse to get me to stop. And he shouted. And I just ran away. I'm so embarrassed."

She laughs—actually *laughs* at my mortification. "You're an idiot, Laia."

I peek out from behind my arms. "You're supposed to be making me feel better."

"Laia, Fee is into you. He kissed you in the middle of his bar in front of everyone. He's *into* you." She sighs and places her fork onto her empty plate. "You left and he was worried. He would've been banging on your door last night if I'd let him."

I lift my head but squeeze my eyes shut against the incessant pounding in my brain. "It doesn't matter, I don't know if I can face him again." I stick my bottom lip out in full-on self-pity mode.

Kenzi cocks her head to the side then sighs. "You have to face him again."

"No."

"Yes."

"I can't."

"You can and you will. You're better than that." She sneaks her hand across the table until her fingers cover mine.

"I should call him, shouldn't I? Just rip off the Band-Aid." I drop my head onto the table again. "Apologize for running."

"Too late." Kenzi sweeps her finger over her now empty plate to catch some rogue filling. "He's gone."

"He's what?" I sit up straight. Gone? "Where did he go?"

"They've gone to Jackson's fishing hut for the rest of the weekend. I woke up to a message from him this morning. They won't be back until Sunday night and there's no reception."

I slump back into my chair. How am I supposed to fix things when my *fixee* has gone fishing?

"Hey, come on." Kenzi reaches over and squeezes my hand on the table again. "I've got a great idea. I'm not in the hotel this morning. Why don't we go chill out on the beach and just forget about men?"

"Isn't it meant to rain today?" I turn to look out of the French doors. Not even the palm trees are swaying. Maybe the weather app on my phone has it wrong.

"It never rains when they say it will in this place." Kenzi grins and gets to her feet, pulling me with her. "Come on. Let's get our tan on."

Half an hour later, we've set up camp on the stretch of postcard-perfect beach in front of the bungalow.

"About what you told me last night." Kenzi glances at me from beneath the huge straw hat she found in the back of my wardrobe. Mrs. Devon's by the looks of it. It certainly isn't mine.

I lift my eyebrows and pass her the sunscreen. I'd kind of hoped she'd forgotten about that.

"You know I'm here if you ever need to talk about it some more."

"I know you are." I offer her a grateful smile then stare up into the clear blue sky. Not a cloud in sight. Sitting on my towel, my knees bent, feet in the sand, I take a long breath of warm, tangy ocean air then blow it out.

"Maybe you could tell Felix." Kenzi sits up and sprays the factor thirty over her arms, it's sweet, coconut scent drifting to me on the slight breeze. "Then, at least he would know there's a reason behind your crazy."

A puff of unexpected laughter escapes me, and I dig my fingers into the cozy sand at the edge of my towel, flicking it at her feet, relieved she's not going all heavy on me.

"I don't know." I shake my head. It's not like I haven't thought about it, but it's one thing opening up to Kenzi, to see that pity on Felix's face though? I chew the inside of my cheek. I don't even know for sure what it is that I want from the guy. Or if I even have it *in me* to open up to him.

The silence of my non-answer stretches between us, the faint cries of seagulls and quiet rustle of the palm trees surrounding us. I sink my toes deeper into the soft white sand and turn to Kenzi. "I don't like talking about it. Feels like I'm giving him power over me again, you know?"

Kenzi nudges the brim of her hat up with the back of her hand again and pins me with a serious stare. "In that case, your secret is safe with me. If you decide to tell him, then great. Either way, my lips are sealed."

I swallow against the tightening in my throat. It's hard to believe I've only known this woman for a matter of weeks. "I don't know what I'd do without you."

"I know, I know. You love me." She winks, then lets her hat flop back down over her face. "It was only a matter of time."

TWENTY-TWO

Felix

The tension in my neck eases the moment I tug the blinker down to pull off the main road. I lean forward and glance through the windshield up to the sky.

A single wisp of white cloud. Good. The pickup bounces over the rough track, the bright sunlight dimming the further into the thick forest we go.

Mylo leans forward and stares out the window. "I hope you know where you're going, man."

"I know this track like the back of my hand." I lean back in my seat, my elbow resting through my open window and breathe deep. My lungs expand and my nostrils flare. Big Leaf Magnolias. Laia loved the smell. I blink away the image of her eyes. Brighter than any of the greens that surround me.

The pickup lurches down a dip in the road bouncing me and Mylo about in our seats.

"The back of your hand, eh?" Mylo grabs the handle above his window and raises his brows when we bound down another pothole in the dirt track.

"This place was our hide-away when we were kids." I turn the wheel to follow the sharp bend of the track. "Me, Jackson and Seb used to bike out here every Saturday morning."

"Have I met Seb?" Mylo frowns as if he's trying to remember for himself.

"Nah, man. Seb left as soon as he was old enough. Hasn't been back since. Last I heard he was in Miami."

"I can think of worse places to grow up." Still staring out of the window, Mylo's mouth falls open when the forest clears, and the sun once again floods the cab of the pickup as the road curves around the side of the lagoon.

The perfectly still water bounces its reflection of the surrounding forest back up into the sky.

"The first time we got drunk was out here." One side of my mouth lifts with the memory. "We were thirteen. Seb stole a crate of beer from his dad's garage. Jackson got so wasted he passed out." I shake my head. "We panicked and called my dad, convinced he was dead."

Whatever Mylo is about to say is cut off when we take the final tight turn. "Some fishing hut." Sticking his head out of the window, he lets out a long whistle as Jackson's hut comes into view. "Where I come from a fishing hut is a one room shack with an outdoor toilet."

I press down on the brakes and pull up beside Jackson's patrol car in front of the two-story log cabin. "I guess we do sell the place kinda short."

"Perfect timing." Jackson steps through the double doors and onto the covered wrap-around porch as we climb from the pickup. He's still dressed in his police uniform. "Just got here myself."

I grin and clap him on the shoulder. The man's solid. I've always had a couple of inches on him, but he was the one nobody messed with when we were young. Even before he had that gun strapped to his waist.

"Jackson. Mylo." I lift my chin to where Mylo's already got his rucksack on his shoulder and the box of groceries in his arms.

"Insane place you've got here." Mylo shifts to hold the weight of the box in one hand so he can offer the other to Jackson.

"There's definitely worse places to spend the weekend." Jackson shakes his hand. "Come in. Let's dump your stuff and get out on the water."

"Too early for beer?" I ask as I grab my rucksack and throw it over my shoulder.

"Never too early," they grunt at the same time.

Not even half an hour later we're on the water in the same old wooden rowboat we've used since we were kids.

Just what I needed.

"I could get used to this." Mylo leans back against the side of the boat and takes a swig of his beer.

He hadn't even bothered pretending to be interested in catching anything. Just dropped onto the bench that runs along the side of the boat and kicked his feet up on the opposite bench.

Sitting, legs spread wide by his feet, I flick my rod back and forth above my head until the line flies out across the water then sinks with a plop.

"So. What's up? You only ever come here when something's up." Jackson doesn't look at me as he reels his line in, but the smirk on his face can't be missed. "The little blonde receptionist from the Castle wouldn't be the reason for this unscheduled get away, would she?"

I grunt and scrape my hand over my mouth. Fucking Clua and its ears. "When did I miss us turning into a bunch of fifteen-year-old girls?" I mutter, refusing to look at either of them.

Mylo chuckles under his breath. "Women troubles make you an ass, man."

Still staring resolutely out over the water, I jab Mylo in the ribs.

He jerks back, rubbing his side, making the boat lurch, almost dumping all of us into the water.

"Hey now, calm down, people." Jackson drops his fishing rod and grabs the sides of the boat, his brows menacingly low.

Doesn't hold nearly as much weight now he's changed into black jersey shorts and a Clua Force tee, his pistol locked in a drawer back in the cabin.

"Better out than in." Mylo leans forward and rests his elbows on his knees. "We're all friends here."

"Seriously, man?" I massage the insistent tick in the back of my neck. "I should have left you at home."

"Spill," Jackson whips his line back out across the water, watching it until it breaks the surface far from the boat.

I sigh hard and shake my head. "I … fuck. Shouldn't this shit get easier the older we get?" I sigh again. "I'm not looking for anything. I *wasn't* looking for anything."

"Rosa's not coming back, man." Jackson glances up from his fishing rod, shrugging when I glare at him.

"I know that." I take a long swig of my beer.

"She'd never have wanted you to stay alone." His mouth ticks up in a sad smile.

Mylo nods. "If you were the one gone, would you want her to be alone?"

Definitely should have left him at fucking home. I should have left them both at fucking home.

"I think she'd be more upset by you chasing her look-a-likes as a form of stress release." Jackson, my oldest and soon to be ex-friend, snorts and runs his hand over his short hair, his stare fixed on my face.

Mylo straightens and pushes the peak of his cap up with his bottle to stare at me. "Ah, fuck, the woman with the voice? Dude. I never met Rosa, but I'm pretty sure she'd take offense at that."

"Fuck off." My scowl deepens at Mylo's raised eyebrows. "I have a type." I lift my gaze to the sky and shake my head. I *used* to have a type. "Everybody has a type." I glance over to Jackson for support. "*Everyone* has a fucking type."

Jackson's lips turn down to hide his smile and he shakes his head like he has no idea what I'm talking about.

"The way you kissed Laia in the middle of the bar last night makes me think your type has changed, brother." Mylo presses on.

Jackson doesn't even have to look up from his line for me to know exactly what his face is doing. And how smug his fucking grin is.

They're not wrong. I don't care. "You guys heard about Rae's new man? Word on the street is he's done some time." I lean back on the side of the boat. Low blow. Jackson and Rae have a history nobody quite gets, but his protectiveness over her is common knowledge.

Jackson instantly loses his smirk and clicks his tongue against his teeth, glaring at me from the side of his eyes. "Point made."

"Mylo, you see Zi dancing with the DJ last night? Wanna talk it out?"

Mylo glances between us and leans back against the side of the boat, pulling his cap back over his face. "Anybody watch the game last week?"

I chuckle roughly and polish off my beer. "That's more like it."

An hour later, we've settled into a comfortable silence and I'm pretty sure Mylo's fallen asleep.

But just because they've stopped talking about Laia, doesn't mean I've managed to stop thinking about her. I tug on my line and kick my feet up onto the opposite bench, raking my teeth over my bottom lip, the phantom press of her mouth still enough to send a shock of need down my spine. The memory of her shrugging her top down to get me to cooperate almost enough to drag a laugh from my throat. She's unexpected—she's everything I had no idea I'd been missing. But far too good to deal with my shit.

The longing fizzles into flat-out concern. For her *and* for me. What if I gain her trust just to realize I can't do it?

What if I let her in for her to realize *she* can't do it?

Either way, it would suck.

I miss the easy life. Just sex was easy. Just sex with Laia would be … I tilt my head back and close my eyes.

Not just sex.

Am I ready for that? Is she? Will she stop running long enough to try? *Do I want her to?*

A clap of thunder roars in the distance, dragging me back from the edge of stir-fucking-crazy.

We all look up into the sky. Angry black clouds hover in the distance. So much for the weatherman being wrong. The joys of island living. Storms can roll in out of nowhere.

"We getting back before that breaks?" Mylo finishes his beer then throws it in the plastic bag reserved for recycling.

"Yeah," Jackson scowls at the sky and starts to reel in his line. "No point in getting soaked when no fucker is even biting."

The skies open just as we make it back to the old jetty by the house.

"So, what is there to do in this place when its torrential rain out?" Standing by the window, Mylo lifts the curtain and glowers outside.

It hasn't let up all afternoon.

"Not a lot." Jackson shrugs where he's stretched out across one of the ancient brown corduroy sofas. "If it keeps up, we'll have to head back before the road floods."

Mylo turns from the window, his forehead creased. It's the closest I've seen the guy to worried since he arrived on the island. "Flooding? Dude, I've got a meeting with the council on Monday I can't miss."

I lean past him and look out into the gray miserableness. "Maybe we should head back now. We're not getting any fishing done in this. And I'd rather not be away from the Beach Hut if it gets any worse." I place my untouched beer on the coffee table. I only had a couple on the boat. I'm still good to drive. I look over to Jackson. "What do you think?"

"The roads won't be too bad yet. If we head out now, we should be fine." Jackson gets to his feet and stretches his arms out. "Better safe than sorry, right?"

It's already past eight by the time we've packed up the cars and are heading slowly down the road, Jackson following behind in his patrol car.

Visibility is zero, the rain a sheet of gray around us. The sun hasn't even set but the sky's already as murky as charcoal. "I can't see a fucking thing," I mutter, my face practically pressed up against the windshield, the wipers on full speed. We should have stayed put. I blow out a long breath and squint into the darkness. "This is unreal. I can't remember the last time we got hit by a storm this bad."

As if to prove my point, a clap of thunder roars above us, vibrating the dash, the cab of the pickup lighting with a bolt of lightning a second later. Too close for comfort.

"Fuck, man, that was close." One hand on the roof, the other white knuckling the side of his seat, Mylo glares through the windshield. "Maybe we should go back. My meeting ain't worth getting struck by lightning."

I chuckle but press on the brakes. He's right. No meeting's worth driving in this.

A deafening crash sounds above us before I can get the pick-up turned around, then everything goes black.

TWENTY-THREE

Laia

Feet tucked up beneath me, I blow on the frothy top of my hot chocolate and lift the steamy romance book Kenzi lent me closer to my face, snuggling down in the old woolly cardi I pulled on over my pajama shorts and tank. The thunderstorm is raging out there. It hasn't let up all day. Kenzi assured me that it's normal for this time of year, but that's not stopped me jumping at every deafening roar. The book is helping to keep the fear at bay. It isn't, however, helping with the low buzz of arousal that's been pulsing since my run-in with Felix last night.

That kiss. I blow out a long breath and try to focus on the pages of the book again. *I'm messing with his head.* I gnaw on my bottom lip and try to imagine letting him in. Telling him the truth. *Trusting him.*

I roll my eyes and groan. I don't even know if he *wants* to be let in. Telling Kenzi was kind of liberating, I guess. But that's different, it doesn't change anything, won't affect things between us. With Felix it would—with Felix it affects everything.

My cell rings, pulling me from the crazy hot sex scene on the page. A sex scene my brain may or may not have started super imposing Felix into. I glance at the phone, balanced on the arm of the sofa. I could just let it ring off. It can only be Kenzi or Felix. They're the only people who have my number.

Felix's cell is out of service. I had a moment of braveness before, but the snotty, automated message informed me that he was either switched off or has no network. That leaves Kenzi. And really. How much trouble could she have gotten herself into since this morning?

On second thought, I reach for the phone and swipe the screen. "Kenzi, this better be important, you're disturbing some pretty riveting reading."

"Laia. There's been an accident." Her voice cracks on the last word and I'm already on my feet. "I need to get to the hospital. Can you take me?"

"Are you okay?" I pull on my fluffy slipper boots, my cell tucked between my shoulder and my chin. "Hold tight, I'm coming."

"It's not me. There was an accident. Jackson called. Mylo's okay, but Felix" —she sniffs down the line— "he was unconscious when they loaded him into the ambulance."

My heart stops cold in my chest. "I'm on my way."

It takes me ten minutes and about seven panic attacks until I'm pulling up next to Kenzi's apartment block. She's already on the side of the road.

"Get in." I stretch over to the passenger side door and shove it open. "Where's the hospital?" I ask before her ass even hits the seat.

"Straight along Main Street until the church. It's sign-posted from there."

The rain has lessened to a fine mist, but the sky's still eerily dark. A shiver rips down my spine. "He'll be okay, Kenzi." I glance over to where she's staring straight ahead, biting her nails, her hair soaked and plastered to her head.

Her eyes dart from the road to me, and she nods mutely, face pale, as if she's in another time.

"It's just" —she takes a shaky breath— "the last time I got a call like this..."

She breaks off and shakes her head, her bottom lip trembling.

"Felix will be okay," I repeat. He has to be.

We run through the stark white corridors of the hospital, dodging people and stretchers as we go. *He's going to be okay.* I repeat my mantra over and over as we follow the directions the nurse gave us at reception.

Mylo, leaning against a wall, lifts his head as we round the corner. I slow to a walk, my tummy doing that origami trick it always does when things have gone to shit. Kenzi just keeps on running straight into Mylo's arms.

"He's awake." He cups her face with bandaged hands. "In a shitter of a mood, but he's awake."

I peek through the glass panel of the door behind them. My face goes hot, and my eyes burn, but I make myself push the door open.

"Just get me whatever papers I need to sign to get out of here." Felix drags both hands down his face then glares at the male nurse still standing with a clipboard by his bed. "Now! Please."

His big body fills the tiny bed right to the edges, his head snapping up when the door shuts behind me. The scowl on his face smooths. Okay, not all the way smooth, but close enough. He's in gray athletic shorts and a black T-shirt—not a hospital gown. That's a good sign—I think.

I hold his stare, barely managing to swallow down the nerves, or relief, or whatever it is I'm feeling before it leaks out of my eyes. "Hi." I lift a hand from where I'm clutching my cardi around myself, suddenly unsure of whether I should be here, whether he wants me here after last night. "I can … I should probably…" I turn back to the door. "I'll get Kenzi."

"Laia." His voice is hoarse. He coughs to clear it. "Don't."

"Are you okay? They said you were—I was so worried, I thought—"

"I'm fine." His brows are low, face serious.

"Good." My hand shakes as I scratch my forehead. There's a new wariness hanging between us—a wariness I put there.

I glance once more at the door then turn back to him and everything just falls out in a rush. "Felix, I'm so sorry about last night. Jayne, the kissing, the" —I flap my hand in front of my top half, my cheeks flaming miserably— "I shouldn't have pushed, and then the jar and you, and me. And I know no means no, but I just ran away." I press my lips together fully aware of how little any of that made sense. "I shouldn't have just run out on you like that."

"And I shouldn't have spoken to you like that." He reaches up and massages the back of his neck but doesn't look away from where I'm loitering between the door and the foot of his bed. "Come here."

I twist the front of my cardi, the residual, if ridiculous, wariness of him after last night refusing to budge. Logic, Laia. Logic. He's nothing like Damon. "Felix, I … I'm not good at this. I don't know what I'm doing. I don't even know if I can—"

"That makes two of us," he interrupts me before I can veer off on another elastic band stress ramble. "Can you please come and sit down?"

I shuffle over to the green pleather recliner by his bed, far too aware that I'm still wearing my short pajamas, a stretched out old cardi and ugly, fluffy slipper-boots and don't even get me started on my hair. "I should get someone else. I'm probably the last person who should be here." I lower myself down onto the edge of the seat, the padding flat from the thousands of other shell-shocked visitors who have sat here before me, and glance over to the door.

"The last thing I remember thinking about before the tree fell was you." He blurts it out like he's as shocked to be admitting it as I am to hear it.

My hands fall from fidgeting with my cardi to my lap and I just stare. No elastic snap back or random outburst, just semi-shocked, but fully confused silence. I should say something. Tell him how scared I was, how many deals I made with the universe that if they just let him be okay, I'd never push anyone away ever again. I'd stop being scared and grab onto this thing with two hands and make it work. "I…" I lick my lips. In the sterile light of the hospital with him alive and watching me, I think I may have just lied to the universe.

"Fee, don't ever do that to us again." Kenzi bursts through the door, her cheeks flushed, her hair still soaked and stuck to her head but with a hooded jumper that can only be Mylo's hanging off her.

We both snap around to face her, Mylo behind her, filling the doorway completely.

With one last glance my way, Felix lies back into his pillows and offers a tired smile to Kenzi. "Takes more than a tree to keep me down, Zi."

Kenzi shakes her head, and for a second, I think she's going to burst into tears until Mylo's hands clamp over her shoulders, pulling her back into his massive chest.

"Just ... stay away from trees from now on. And cars." She wipes her eyes roughly with the back of her hand. "And roads too."

"If you insist on signing yourself out, Mr. Ashur" —a white-coated doctor pushes the door open with his back, already scribbling something on the clipboard of papers clutched in his hand. He glances up when the door swings closed behind him, taking us all in before settling his unamused gaze on Felix—"I have to insist that someone accompanies you home." His tired, dark eyes slide to me. "Ah good, a girlfriend. Any dizziness, nausea, blurred vision and you bring him right back."

My mouth flops open. "Oh, no, I'm not—I mean we're not..."

"Well, I'm afraid someone needs to take him home, or I can't sign off on him leaving."

Felix glares at the ceiling, then back over to the doctor.

"I'll do it." I clamp my lips together when everybody turns to look at me including Felix. I meet his serious face and shrug. "I mean, I'll do it if you want me to..." I turn back to the doctor. "If he wants me to?"

He stills for a second, jaw ticking as he scans my face for long enough to have me doubting myself.

"Or not. I mean if you don't want me—"

"I want you." He cuts in, his forehead creasing even more.

He wants me. "Okay." My lips pressed together, I nod, completely incapable of dragging my stare from his.

"Okay." Still scowling, his gaze flicks down to my lips.

"That's settled then. Laia, you take him in your truck. Me and Mylo can catch a cab home." Kenzi claps her hands, snapping both our heads around. "Perfect."

TWENTY-FOUR

Felix

"Careful," Laia squeaks from where she's slid her arm around my waist, her cool fingers skimming under the hem of my T-shirt as I stand from the wheelchair they made me ride in to the hospital exit.

As if she could hold my weight.

"I'm fine. Nothing's broken," I laugh. Then wince. Pain shooting up the back of my neck to my rattled skull.

She flaps around me, her hands lifting to press against my forehead, my cheeks.

"Stop." I cover her hands with mine and pull them down between us.

"Sorry." She slips her fingers from my grip as she turns and yanks hard on the passenger side door handle of her truck until it creaks open. "Jump in."

The storm might have passed, but the air is still crisp, its usual humidity replaced by a biting freshness. The tarmac glitters wetly under the streetlights. It's cold. And Laia's in nothing but those damn pajama shorts, a knitted jacket, and a thin, *thin* tank. "You need bigger clothes."

"I know, I—" She tugs the sides of her jacket closed and steps back to let me pass her, lips turned down, gaze lowered. "I should have changed. I'm a mess, I didn't think."

"Laia, no. I mean you look cold. I didn't mean I don't like your … what you're wearing…" I trail off and drag my sorry ass into her truck before I can make her any more uncomfortable.

Seat belt on, she leans forward on the leather bench seat and turns the ignition. The engine roars to life, vibrating the cab as she shifts into gear. Forehead creased, delicate fingers curled around the big, old fashioned steering wheel, she pulls out of the parking space.

For a second, I just—look.

Laia in motion is pure nervous energy, startled glances and so many fucking apologies. But Laia focused is different. A quiet, careful confidence wraps her movements. It's in every gear change, every check of the mirrors as she drives us towards the exit of the car park. It was the same when she was baking the other morning. Gone was the skittishness that seems to plague her and in its place something else. Something special.

Tongue peeking between her lips, she glances over, the truck idling at the exit.

I scan her face—the last face that flashed in my mind before that fucking tree knocked me unconscious. My skull throbs with what that could mean. That my thoughts hadn't gone to Rosa's face, her smile, her laugh, like they always have when things get fucked up. They'd gone to Laia.

"Which way?" Her quiet question has me blinking to focus on her darkening cheeks and her wide green eyes.

"Left." I clear my throat and face forward. "Follow the road straight out of town."

We travel in silence. The roar of the engine and the patter of yet more rain against the windshield our only soundtrack.

I glance at the side of her face as we leave town and head down the winding, tree-lined road. Her slim forearms peek out of the loose sleeves of her jacket, two silver bangles on her right wrist. And her hands. No Band-Aids. "How are your fingers?"

She flexes her fingers, straightening them then curling them back around the steering wheel. "Good. Great." She glances my way. "Thank you … for last night." Her full bottom lip disappears into her mouth, a move I know means she's thinking, or worrying, or just trying not to come out with something random.

I shift on the bench to face her, my arm stretched along the back, my fingers almost close enough to catch one of the curls that have fallen from the more disheveled than usual knot on the top of her head. "Laia, last night—"

"—I was drunk." She chews on that lip, her gaze still resolutely on the road. "If I was sober, I never would have…" Even in the darkness of the cab I can see that her cheeks have flushed even darker. "Tried to make you do something you didn't want to do."

My house appears to the left of the road, slightly back into the forest before I can reassure her that my reasons for stopping last night had nothing to do with her and everything to do with me.

"This is it." I point in the direction of my driveway, not that there are any others she could mistake it for. There are no other houses for miles.

"It's beautiful." She leans forward to look out of the windshield as she pulls into the driveway, her lips parting, slightly curved up, exactly like they did when she slid her top down last night.

My dick throbs with the memory. I almost reach for her—almost forget how last night ended, how royally I fucked up.

The smile fades from her face before I get the chance. She cuts the engine, her cheeks puffing out like she's having to psych herself up to come inside.

She's nervous. My jaw clenches tight, the knowledge that it's me making her nervous winding itself around the tendons in the back of my neck making my head throb ten-fold.

"You don't have to stay." I sit back in the worn leather bench seat and rub my forehead.

"But the doctor said you shouldn't be alone." She twists the corner of her jacket around her finger.

It's impossible to miss the hurt in her voice.

I drag my hands down my face. "I don't mean I don't want you here, Laia. I just don't—I don't want you to feel obligated to."

"I don't feel obligated." She finally meets my stare. "I want to."

Nerves. Good or bad nerves, who the fuck knows, but they make themselves known, buzzing in the base of my skull. I don't bring women here. "Let's go in then."

"Okay." She throws her whole body against the rusted door of her truck to open it, then jumps out.

I watch her jog around the front but shove my door open before she tries to get it for me.

She holds her hands out like she's gonna help me down, bracelets jingling, knitted jacket falling open, her thin tank clinging to her braless chest. It's almost enough to make me forget about the pain.

"Laia, seriously, I'm fine." I climb down without taking her hand.

"Right. Sorry." She clasps them behind her back and steps out of the way to let me pass, eyes flicking awkwardly towards the front door with every step we take towards it. "This place is amazing."

Shoulder leaning against the door frame, hand massaging the ever-present twitch in the back of my neck, I watch her walk into my home and down the step into the open living area.

Her face breaks into a huge, unguarded grin and she spins in a tight circle in the middle of the hardwood floors, her boots squeaking as she moves. "It's not like anything I've seen here. It's so modern." She stops, facing me, her jacket hanging off her shoulders.

I swallow thickly and hold her stare. If it was surreal having her in the hospital, it's even more surreal having her here.

Her lips part again. I shove my hands in my pockets, unable to look away.

"Even the door is amazing." She closes the distance between us, walking back up the step to where I'm still standing.

She doesn't touch me, but she does slide her hand down the waxed barn door. "You built this place yourself." It's not a question. She sees so much more than she possibly can.

"I did." It was the only thing that kept me sane after Rosa—building somewhere that didn't have memories of her—of us connected to it.

"I knew it." Her hand pauses on the door. "It's beautiful." Her tongue sweeps across her bottom lip before she pulls it between her teeth. "It's so you."

I need to lie down. There's too much blood running in too many directions. I slip past her toward one of the big gray sofas in the living area.

"Are you okay?" She hurries behind me. "Ice. We were supposed to ice your head as soon as we got home."

I sit down, leaning back into the sofa, my eyelids heavier than they were a minute ago.

I don't have to look to know that she's standing by my knee, watching me with big, worried eyes. I do anyway, just lifting my head taking more effort than it should.

"I've taken the painkillers they gave you before. They make you drowsy." She offers me a little smile. "I'll get something to ice your head."

"The freezer's under the island," I call after her.

A couple of minutes later she's back, lowering herself onto the sofa beside me, one knee tucked under herself so she can face me.

"Where does it hurt?" A towel-wrapped ice pack in her hand, she peers down at me, her elbow resting on the back of the sofa by my head, so close the smell of vanilla and clothes softener fills my nostrils.

"Everywhere," I groan, letting my lids slide shut again.

I'm not lying. Every fucking part of me hurts, but despite the ache, her soft puff of laughter curves my lips up.

"You'll have to be more specific."

The barely-there touch of her cold fingers to my hairline shocks me still. My eyes stay closed, but the rest of my exhausted body slides into a strange sort of hyper-awareness as her gentle exploration travels over my skull, carefully probing, parting my hair, skimming for injury.

I hiss when she reaches a spot just above my left ear, a sharp pain rushing over my skull.

"Sorry." Her fingers disappear, replaced with the frigidness of the ice pack. It molds to the shape of my head better that any bag of ice cubes could. Frozen veg if I had to guess. I don't have the energy to ask. I barely have the energy to think.

Comfortable silence settles in, her slight body pressing a little more into my side with every second that passes.

"Frozen peas are better for bumps." Her soft musing breaks through my semi-sleep. "Ice cubes have too many hard edges."

My mind drags itself back from its painkiller-induced haze, my consciousness grabbing hold of her words to pull me from slumber. "Sounds like you're talking from experience."

She shifts beside me, the warm puff of her sigh tickling my jaw. "Maybe," she whispers quietly.

I feel her head rest on her elbow by the side of my face, her breath over my temple, her body pressing even closer to mine with the movement.

Keeping my eyes closed would probably be the right thing to do, but I can't make myself do it. I roll my head on the back cushion of the sofa to look at her, her hand, the one holding the ice pack, follows the lazy movement, keeping it pressed to the side of my head. "That's what you want to forget."

She watches me carefully, her face just centimeters from mine, close enough to pick out the darker ring that circles her irises and the single gold fleck just above her left pupil.

More seconds pass, each one melting away any hope I have of her answering. My eyes start to drift again, too heavy to keep open and I finally quit fighting the oblivion.

TWENTY-FIVE

Laia

I'm warm and comfy. I sigh sleepily and snuggle deeper, my eyelids fluttering open enough to see that it's still dark then closing again, completely content.

Until, one by one, thoughts sneak into my happy, snuggly, cozy brain. Memories of last night.

This isn't my house. I swallow thickly.

Or my bed.

And this definitely isn't my pillow.

Felix's house.

Felix's bed.

Which would mean. I crack my eyes open a slither and instantly wince.

When I finally got him up here last night only to realize there was just one room with a bed in it, the decision to sleep here with him was an easy one. He was pretty out of it from the pain meds. What if he took a bad turn in the night? The doctor said I was to keep an eye on him all night.

In hindsight, maybe I should have slept on the sofa.

I'm wrapped in him—I'm really, *really* wrapped in him. Seriously. I take a deep breath and try to untangle at least part of myself from his big body. My arm from beneath his neck seems like as good a place to start as any.

His sleep-heavy breathing stays even so I close my eyes and slide the other arm from where it's draped across his chest.

I've got this. I puff out my cheeks in preparation for my next move. He's still out cold, eyelashes fanned out, lips tipped ever so slightly up at the corners. Peaceful. *Oblivious.*

And that's exactly the way he's going to stay if I have anything to do with it.

Boldened by the success of removing the top half of my body from him, I shift to untangle my leg from around his hip. I should have known it wouldn't be that easy, the universe just doesn't like me that much.

With a deep rumble of a moan, his hand slips around my ass and he pulls me right back into place, fingers sinking into my butt cheek, his body wedged tightly between my legs.

I freeze.

The hand in question smooths down my thigh then hooks in behind my knee and drags me even tighter into him. *All* of him. Okay. I try to control the urge to roll my hips against the growing hardness nudging against the seam of my pajama shorts.

Nope, nope, nope.

I force myself to ignore the effects of this new position. It's hopeless. A pant escapes. It feels too good. Too tempting. It's been over a year. *Over a year.* I shake my head and go back to lifting the hand from behind my knee, watching his slumberous—and really quite content—face for signs of consciousness.

His sudden frown paralyzes me. His grip tightens and—holy shit—he settles himself even deeper between my legs with a slow but determined thrust. I stop breathing. His now fully erect cock is officially and entirely wedged between my legs. *Thank God he's wearing shorts because mine are putting up zero fight.*

My lips part and my belly clenches. This was *not* the way I imagined this morning going.

Holding my breath, I try once again to sneak my leg free.

This can't happen. Not like this. Not after what happened in his office. Who molests a sleeping man? If he wakes up now, he'll think it's another boob-flash moment.

I don't get far in my leg retraction before he shifts again, and this time it's worse. So much worse.

The grip on my knee tightens, his other hand slips under my waist, and before I have a chance to do anything other than let out a muffled squeak, his whole body rearranges itself, his face nuzzling—yes *nuzzling*—right. Between. *My boobs.*

Must not molest the sleeping man. Must. Not. Molest. The sleeping man.

For better or worse my body is humming like that's exactly what it wants to do.

From this new position, his sigh heats the already hot skin of my left breast even through my tank.

I look down at his unruly black hair. It's sticking up adorably. I curl my fingers against the urge to run them through the thick strands and I just … lie there, my whole body pulsing traitorously, my mind whirring from one outcome to the next. All of them X-rated. All of them surely illegal with a sleeping man.

Waking him would probably be the wise choice here.

He rocks into me, deliciously slowly. The friction—oh god the pressure. I bite back my moan.

Waking him is the *only* choice here.

"Felix," I whisper, my voice strained as his hips just keep on moving in those really nice little circles. "Felix, you need to wake up," I whisper again, a little louder, shaking his shoulder.

"Mmmmmcomfy." His mumble vibrates against my skin, flushing me crimson from the ends of my hair to the tips of my toes.

I curse into the semi-darkness. "Felix." My voice comes louder now.

He stirs but pulls me closer with another of those slow, perfectly angled thrusts.

"Felix," I squeak. If he keeps this up, I cannot be held responsible for my actions. I shake his shoulder harder.

With a grunt, he finally lifts his head and opens his bleary eyes. His pupils expand then focus, sleep visibly clearing as consciousness returns.

His fingers flex on my leg and confusion settles over his sleep-ruffled face. "Laia?"

"Morning." Head tipped forwards, I peer down into his face.

Eyes bluer than any summer sky blink up at me, his whole body stilling, locked in confusion. If I listened hard enough, I'd probably hear the cogs turning, his brain struggling to rearrange the happenings of last night that led him here, to this moment. Waking up in his own bed wrapped around a pulsing, trembling, barely breathing me.

His eyelids lower, his thick black lashes long enough they cast shadows over his cheeks as he turns his attention to the boob said cheek was just mooshed against.

I wait for him to move, to jerk back and roll away. Seconds pass. He doesn't move, he just watches me, his forehead furrowed like he's still trying to piece together the steps that could have led him here but coming up blank.

And I just hold still, petrified to break the loaded tension, the thick spell of whatever it is that's happening. One thought beating out the rest. I want this. I want him.

Slowly—so slowly that at first, I don't register what he's doing, the hand still holding my leg hitched up around his side starts to move. Starts to smooth its way up my thigh. He scans my face, his throat contracting when his slightly calloused palm meets the scrunched-up material of my shorts. When I don't flinch away or make him stop, he keeps going, keeps sliding his hand up until it comes to the skin of my waist.

Goosebumps flair, but I don't look away or pull back. My thighs contract where they're still wrapped around him. He's hard—so, *so* hard—and still pressed against me. It's dragging up feelings and wants and needs so intense, everything in me is softening, swelling, begging for this to happen, for me to get out of my own head for once and just let it happen.

His fingers skim the bottom curve of my breast through my tank, his eyes still pinning mine, probably still waiting for me to stop him. I don't. Not even when his thumb finds my nipple and brushes over it then back, teasing it to an even tighter peak. Or when his stare finally releases mine and drops to watch as he slowly tugs the neck of my tank down, his knuckles brushing my skin until the thin cotton is stretched beneath my breast, the hard thudding of my heart pulsing in my throat.

His lips part. Mine press together, torn between just letting go—and the sudden, but acute awareness that I haven't brushed my teeth. It's stupid. But the thought stays put no matter how hard I try to convince myself to relax into this—to just let go.

Lips brush, his tongue swirls, and the wet, warm suck of his mouth on my nipple shoots a jolt of tingling, perfect, eye-rolling energy from my breast to my core. A direct line that jerks my body into his, forcing the rigid thickness of him to rub with more pressure against my sadly neglected sex. Even through our clothes, the sensation is enough to drag an embarrassingly needy moan from me.

And then his lips are at my neck, my jaw, my chin. But when his heavy-lidded stare finds mine the heat there cools instantly, his brows lifting in question. "Too much?"

Slipping my hand up the barely-there space between us, I cover my mouth, feeling like the biggest idiot that ever walked the planet to be stopping this over something so basic.

"I thought … shit, I'm—" His hands fall from me, his big body tensing to move.

"—No." I shake my head and grab his shoulder before he can unwrap himself from me. "No. It's not. I just—" I cover my eyes, then my mouth again before I speak, my cheeks far too hot to be attractive. "I just need a moment—

and maybe a toothbrush?"

The tension releases the muscles of his face, his expression softening, mouth curling into a ridiculously amused smirk, before he sucks his bottom lip between his teeth and nods, laughter written in every crinkle around those eyes. "Top drawer, under the sink." He rolls off of me and throws his arm over his face with a rough laugh, kicking the sheets from where they're tangled around his legs.

I pause for a moment and just *admire* the hard lines of his body, the defined V of muscle that disappears into his athletic shorts. And the unmistakable hardness straining against the thick cotton.

"Laia?"

"Hmm?" I glance up to where he's watching me from beneath his arm.

"Quit staring and brush."

The good-humored tone to his voice pulls a grin to my lips and my butt off the bed.

His bathroom is the stuff dreams are made of. The dirty kind. The shower sex kind. Polished concrete floors. Oversized, deep gray wall tiles and a shower so big I'm pretty sure I could move my bed in there and still have room for a TV. I run my hand along the double sink with charcoal stone surrounds. Even the faucets are sexy—those modern, flat silver things. And the bath. Oh, my days, the bath. It's huge. Massive. And made of black granite by the looks of it.

Catching a glimpse of my pink cheeks in the sink-to-ceiling mirror stops me short. Teeth. Toothbrush. I meet my stare in the mirror and swallow, glancing at the door then reaching for the drawer below the sink. Sure enough there's a pack of new toothbrushes and a tube of toothpaste in there. Who stops potential morning sex to brush? Me, apparently. I get to work before my brain kicks in and convinces me that this isn't a good idea.

There's a knock at the door before I finish. "You decent?"

I pause, mid brush. Just freeze and stare stupidly at the door in the mirror. "Yep," I call, my toothbrush still in my mouth, my heart thundering against my chest.

And then he's there like some bed-headed sleep god. Shorts low on his hips, feet bare, scratching his chest as he moves to stand beside me and grabs the electric toothbrush from beside the sink. We watch each other in the mirror as we brush, butterflies fluttering, a grin stretching over my face in answer to the one he seems unable to stop from forming around his buzzing toothbrush. I lean forward to spit under the running water, wipe my mouth, then straighten. "How's your head?"

"Good." He smiles around his toothbrush again, brushes a little longer, then leans to spit and rinse too.

It's so *normal.* But so undeniably not normal. Not normal at all.

I press my lips together to stop myself from giggling at the absurdness of it all when he straightens, his big, tanned arm brushing mine, his own bottom lip disappearing between his teeth as he watches me. "All clean." The humor in his voice is still there, but so is something else. Doubt maybe? Wariness? Nerves?

I nod, not trusting my voice not to just pack up and leave if I try to talk, my tummy folding in on itself. The haziness of this morning disintegrating no matter how hard I try to keep it pulled up around me.

He holds my stare in the mirror, moves behind me and presses a kiss to where my shoulder meets my neck, his arms wrapping me from behind. "Nothing has to happen."

"I know." I turn in his hold and blink up at him, uber aware of his hands on me—of the fact that neither my body nor my mind are sliding into their usual panic mode over his closeness. "But I want it to."

His eyes crinkle again, his tongue sliding over his lip before he dips his head and kisses me with a slow easiness that flattens out the folding in my tummy. "Okay."

I nod, my fingers sinking into his hair, my lips barely leaving his. "Okay."

Hands on my hips, he lifts me, guiding my legs around his waist and holding me under my ass, he walks us back out of the bathroom.

The sun's almost up, the heavy floor-to-ceiling curtains backlit by a soft morning light, the white sheets of his bed still crumpled at the bottom of the mattress. He dumps me in the middle then climbs onto the bed, his fists planting on either side of my hips, his gaze roving my face as he moves up over my body.

I expect him to pounce, to sink into me and get right to it.

He doesn't.

He just hovers there above me, chest rising and falling with his breaths. "I need to know what you're thinking."

I wet my lips, reasons, worries, wants, needs, all suddenly rattling around my head with that one question. "I'm scared."

His mouth tugs down. So does mine. That wasn't even nearly what I planned on saying.

"We don't have to."

I shake my head and run my hands up his muscle-roped forearms. "I'm not scared of the sex." My lips press together while I try to find the words, the truth. "Okay, that's a lie, I'm a little bit scared of the sex. But I'm more scared of what comes after. I can't … I don't know if I'll … I don't want to hurt you."

His dimples flash beneath his stubble, his mouth turning up into a half-smile. "I'm tougher than I look." He drops down onto his elbows and presses his lips to mine. Once, twice, then again, finally settling his big body against me, nudging my legs apart with his knees.

My eyelids flutter and my knees hitch up, my heels digging into his ass at the oh so casual maneuvering of his pelvis right back to where it was before.

And when he deepens the kiss, *Jesus*, it's like somebody's turned up the heat—back-lit my skin from the inside out. My mouth falls open, a little pant escaping and then my arms are around his neck, and my back is arching, my shoulders lifting off the bed so I can get closer—kiss him harder, deeper, my body moving of its own accord, one hundred percent driven by how mind-numbingly good he feels pushing against me.

His breaths come sharp, minty, and addicting, both hands sliding beneath my head to angle me better, to hold me still while his mouth debases mine in the most dirty-beautiful kiss I think has ever existed. His hips rock harder, rubbing, and grinding, and pushing his body against mine over and over and over, and oh my … there's throbbing and pulsing and contracting of muscles I swear I forgot I had—internal, external, a building, aching, living undercurrent of pressure. "Holy fuck, don'tstopdoingthat." I pant against his parted lips.

With a rough moan his hands move to my ass, tilting my hips up so his shallow thrusting can go deeper, his shorts and mine the only thing between us. It's all-over stimulation, his face presses into my neck, every inch of his body dragging over mine, my clit, my pussy, my belly, my breasts. My breathing speeds and my body bows with every push and pull and slide of his skin. I dig my fingers into his hair and move with him, a keening, writhing, building climax blanketing out everything in a slow but so-intense-even-my-moan-is-too-enthralled-to-make-a-sound tidal wave that vibrates through every single muscle, every tendon, every *brain cell*, leaving me a trembling, panting puddle of something that used to be me.

He's watching me when I finally manage to pry my eyelids open, his tongue peeking out from between smirking lips.

"Jesus." My blush is instant, my nose wrinkling, face scrunching. "That was … you didn't even take your clothes off … you didn't even—"

"Don't worry about it." His laugh does delicious things to the shockingly hard parts of him still crushed to me as he brushes a curl from my face. "I'm fine."

"No, you're not." Planting my feet on the sides of his thighs, I attempt to push his shorts down his legs. "Take these off."

"Laia, you don't have to—"

"—I want to." I cut him off and slip my hand between the elastic of his jersey shorts and his *low,* lower abs, my pulse thumping in my throat and in my ears and pretty much everywhere when crinkly hairs tickle my knuckles just before my fingers reach his silky, hot hardness. It's not a lie. I really want to, more than I've ever wanted anything. I wrap my fingers around him and stroke from the base to the tip and back, then repeat, marveling at the lack of nerves I feel—the rightness of being here, now, with him like this.

His hips shift and that internal heat switch flips somewhere inside me again, pushing a drugging warmth up my neck.

His breath hitches and his mouth goes slack then clamps shut. "Fuck, Laia." He pulls from my grip and sits back, kneeling, sexy as sin and twice as handsome between my thighs, the soft morning light casting warm shadows over his face and over the dips and ridges of his body.

His loaded stare trails over my rumpled clothes then up to my face and I see it then, something that was never there with Damon, even in the beginning—acceptance—of me, of who I am, of *how* I am right now.

Maybe he's my prize from the universe for surviving the last few shitty years.

Something I actually get to keep. For the first time since I met him, I let myself go there, let myself admit that I want more than just a way to distract myself from my past. I want him.

I don't think, don't dissect or second guess, I just hook my fingers into the waistband of my pajamas shorts and push them down my hips.

Without a word his hands cover mine, guiding my shorts the rest of the way down my thighs, lifting my legs so he can slip them over my feet then setting them back down on either side of his knees. His gaze drops then lifts to my face. And then he's over me again. Kissing me again, that easiness still there in every lazy sweep of his tongue and graze of his lips, the warmth of his chest pressing into mine, the weight of him surrounding me in the best possible way.

I'm barely aware we're moving until he's already on his back, me on top of him, his hands smoothing up my spine beneath my tank then all the way back down over my hips and down my thighs in one long uninterrupted caress.

I pull back just enough to be able to focus on his face, his eyes, to read his expression.

He licks his lips and scans my face right back, a smile tugging at the corners of his mouth. "Your move."

"You want me to…"

"Whatever you want." His face sobers, those blue, blue eyes patient and willing and telling the utter truth. "I want you to do whatever you want."

"To you." I bite the corner of my lip to stop my face from splitting completely with my grin. "Whatever I want?" Nerves—the good kind—skirt down the back of my neck. Whatever I want. I kiss him deeply, finishing with a drawn-out suck of his bottom lip that makes him growl deep in the back of his throat and lift his head, trying to drag it out until I'm out of reach.

The brave, boldness only he seems to bring out in me, sparks to life. I sit up and pull my tank off, leaving me butt naked and straddling him. His stare darkens as he takes me in, his lips, still wet from my attention, parting, hands settling on my hips, not to guide or to control, just there, his thumbs rubbing my hip bones as he waits.

I rock onto him, just a tiny shift of my pelvis, then another, then another, setting off a slow spiral of heat up my spine, my hands pressed flat against the solid ridges of his abs. His mouth falls open, his fingers flex into my skin. So, I keep moving, keep teasing, keep dragging those graveled moans from him until it's not enough, until I need him as naked as I am and moving inside me.

"I want you," I breathe on a barely-there moan, lifting up to push at his shorts until he's in my hand, hot and thick and so, so ready. "Tell me you have protection." I glance up from where my fingers are wrapped around him, still lifted up onto my knees.

"I have protection." His laugh is deep and dirty, he sits in one easy movement, his arms wrapping my waist, mouth taking mine in a kiss so hard, so filled with want, my head spins. I love everything about it, love the lack of finesse and control, the way he kicks his shorts the rest of the way off and pulls me back down, trapping his veeeeery naked cock between us before he reaches blindly for the nightstand, a lamp toppling, the drawer rattling.

He breaks the kiss to rip the foil wrapper open with his teeth, his chest heaving, his eyes on my face as he slips it from its packet. "You sure?"

I nod and shift back in his lap, watch as he rolls the condom down his length, abs pulled tight, lips parted, a breath caught in his throat. And then he stills, and I'm caught in his stare again, our ragged breaths loud in the silent room. He's waiting for me to back down, to flinch back. I don't—I won't—not this time.

I lift up onto my knees again, my teeth sinking into my lip, my hands smoothing up over his sculpted shoulders, fingers digging into the hair at the nape of his neck as I position myself above him.

His head tips back, his eyes wide, one hand holding my hip, the other guiding himself into me.

I lower myself a fraction and the tip of him nudges me, slipping in, pushing past my body's resistance, thick and round and, *oh my god this is happening.* Our mouths hover in a not-quite-kiss, our noses bumping, our pants colliding as I take him slowly, inch by inch until there's no space left between us. I'm filled by him. Contracting around him. Trembling all over him. My thighs shake, everything pulsing a dizzying rhythm, my heart, my core, even the nerve endings behind my eyeballs.

"Fuck, Laia, you feel—"

I tilt my pelvis and whatever he's saying disintegrates into a groan. I brush my fingers over his brows, down his cheeks then press my mouth to his and move in a slow, grinding circle that drags my clit over the base of his cock in a way that has me moaning against his lips and doing it again, and again, and again. Kissing him was already addictive but kissing like this—with him moving inside me is—I angle my head and suck his tongue, my hands still stroking his face, my body moving in sure thrusts and deeper grinds. It's everything I'd forgotten I'd been missing.

His grip on my hips tightens, quickening my movements, driving in deeper, longer, harder, his lips on my jaw, his teeth on my neck, his mouth finding my nipples and sucking, lapping one then the other, guiding me back until my shoulders hit the bed and his big body moves over mine, thrusting into me with long deliberate strokes that arch my back and push me further down the bed.

There's teeth and tongues, the scrape of his stubble punctuated with guttural growls of approval, of encouragement. Touching and pulling and moaning. I can't get close enough, can't take enough of him. With every instroke he fills me more, pushing me higher, closer to the overwhelming edge. My head spins, my muscles shake, but he keeps on going, keeps thrusting, keeps driving into me until on a garbled moan of who-the-hell-cares-what I implode and explode, my body freezing, my back arched, my core contracting so tightly around his thickness, a hiss rips from lips pressed to my jaw and he follows me right over with one more full-body thrust.

I'm snapped back to reality far too quickly. One second, he's relaxed, the heaving of his chest slowing against mine, eyes heavy lidded, mouth curved into possibly his sexiest smirk to date, the next, he's on his back beside me, the muscles in his neck corded, his eyes squeezed shut. Pain. He's in pain.

"Your head." I sit up, the sunlight filtering through the curtains dimly lighting the tightness to his face when he turns it to me. "I didn't think." I brush his hair from his face. How could I not think? "The doctor said to take it easy." My throat tightens.

"I'm ok." He tries to sit up, but his eyes squeeze shut. "Ahh, Fuck."

"I'm taking you back to the hospital." I start to clamber off the bed.

My arm is grabbed before I get far. "Laia, relax. The pain meds have just worn off. I should have set an alarm to take them an hour ago."

I narrow my eyes, half off the bed, one foot on the floor the other tucked under my bum, my teeth raking over my kiss-swollen bottom lip.

His gaze strays down. Mine follow.

I'm still naked. *Very naked.*

My cheeks flush and I grab the top sheet to pull it around me then hurry into the bathroom to get a glass of water, glancing at my reflection in the mirror as I fill the glass. My hair is a riot. My cheeks are even pinker than before. And my lips are definitely swollen. What the hell did I think I was doing?

By the time I've made it back, the duvet is up around his waist.

"Here." I hand him the water then shake two pills from the bottle on the nightstand into my hand and hold them out to him. "If you're not any better in twenty minutes, we're going." I perch on the side of the bed and adjust the sheet around me, scanning his face for signs he's playing down the pain.

"Deal." He sighs heavily and lays back into the pillows, his eyelids drifting closed.

"Shouldn't we … talk about—" I clear my throat and shake my head. "Never mind, I should probably…" I glance over my shoulder, to the bedroom door.

"Laia."

I look back and he shifts over to make room for me, holding the covers up, opening one eye. "Come back to bed."

Nothing sounds better right now than curling up with him for another hour, but what if I've damaged him? What if I damage him more?

I glance down to where he's still holding the covers open for me. *Everything* is on show. Eve-ry-thing.

He's hard. *Again.* I force my attention up and focus on his face. His eyes have clouded. Busted.

"Fine. One more hour." Face flushed, I crawl into his arms, turning so my back is to his chest, almost purring when his big arms slide around my waist and he squeezes me to him, one hand settling on my ribs, just below my breast, the other on my hip, his body and everything attached to it pressed into my back.

There's no way I'm getting back to sleep like this.

"Felix?" I whisper, after laying still for what feels like an eternity.

"Laia." There's a gruffness to his voice that makes it clear he's about as far away from sleepy as I am. Lips press against the side of my neck, he tugs the sheet I'm still wrapped in away to smooth his hand from my ribs up to my breast, rolling my puckered nipple against his palm.

"How's your head?" My voice is no more than a breath.

He chuckles into my neck, the puff of warm air lifting tiny hairs all over my body. "All better." He presses his pelvis into me and his hardness slides between my thighs from behind, parting the lips of my sex until the head of his erection nudges my clit.

"You're wet." His growl is rough and graveled when he thrusts again.

"We shouldn't," I murmur on a pant, "what if your head explodes? What if you get brain damage?"

He laughs, the same ridiculously sexy laugh from before and thrusts again, his hands enveloping my breasts, molding and squeezing and teasing my nipples between his fingers and thumbs until I'm pushing into his hands.

"You don't play fair." I arch back onto him, all sensible thoughts fleeing my mind.

His cock slides easily over my clit. I am wet. So wet. It should mortify me. It does the opposite.

"Fuck." His growl is low and dirty in my ear, lifting goose pimples over every inch of me.

I slip my hand between my legs to push the tip of him tighter against me, then rock against him, every slow thrust of his hips coaxing a fresh spike of need through me.

"Fuck, Laia," he moans against the skin of my neck, his movements growing faster until the heat of a new climax starts to unfold inside me. The constant rub of him, right there but not inside, teasing out the best kind of frustration. My heartbeat picks up, loud in my ears. I pulse and contract, blood bubbling in my veins. Everything in me focused on the feeling, the slide of him until it's too much. I let go. My orgasm comes at me. Dazzles me. Sparkles me. Melts me. My moan is embarrassingly long and drawn out. My hips tilt back, and I push back onto him, the shift in angle letting him slide in completely. Stretching me, filling me, shifting everything into high definition. I clench and pant and grind back harder, taking him as deep as he'll go until his hands find my hips and he thrusts in hard, dragging me back to meet him again and again until his whole body tenses behind me and he lets go with a growled-out moan.

We tense at the same time.

That should not have happened.

TWENTY-SIX

Laia

"How is little Miss nurse today?" Kenzi grins up from behind the reception the moment I'm within hearing distance.

My teeth sink into my lip, heat rising up my cheeks like some sort of confession lava before I've even made it around to the business side of our workstation. "Fine. Good. Great." I think I manage to pull off some sort of smile. I've showered. I've washed my hair. I'm wearing my freshly laundered uniform, but still, Felix's smell lingers. I think it's stuck up my nose. All fresh air and ocean and peppermint and *sex*. If I've any hope of getting through this day without floating off into *lalala-I-got-laid-and-it-was-spectacular* land, I need to learn how to breathe through my mouth.

"How's Fee?" Kenzi's frown lowers her brows, but a knowing smirk is still hanging out there on her pretty face.

The heat creeps up into my hairline. I might as well have a sign reading, *I fucked Felix* on my forehead.

"He's fine." I rummage in my purse to avoid Kenzi's interest.

"I called this morning. Both of your cells were switched off…"

I glance at her and sink down into my chair. "How's Mylo this morning?"

"Grumpy." Her sigh is long and tired as she presses her fingers into her temples.

I spin my chair around to face her. "Grumpy?"

With another deep sigh she leans back, her chair creaking as it swings around. "Grumpy." Her smile is small, forced. "I'll tell you what. I won't push for details of your night if you don't push for details of mine."

"Understood." I nod, then press my lips into a line. I've never seen Kenzi anything other than cheery, or hungover … but even hungover she always keeps her cheeriness. "If you need to talk, you know I'm here, right?"

"Thanks, Laia." She throws her phone into her purse and stands, her shoulders drooping with the weight of whatever happened last night. "I'm cool. It's nothing I can't handle."

I tilt my head. "You want me to come to yours after work? We can have a girls' night. I'll pick up ice-cream. Or alcohol? Or both?" I pick up my pen and grab a sticky note. "What's your poison?"

"I love you for offering, but honestly, I'm fine. Besides, it's Saturday, I'm working in the bar." She yawns, covering her mouth. "And right now, I'm looking forward to a lazy afternoon in my pajamas after last night's drama."

"Okay, but if you need me, I'm here." I reach up to squeeze her fingers in a gesture that couldn't be further from *like me* if it tried.

We catch it at the same time. I curl my fingers back. It's too late. Kenzi's face has morphed from drained to down-right intrigued. "What have you done with my prickly little Laia?"

I roll my eyes but can't help but laugh. "If you need me, I'm just a phone call away." I press the button to power up my computer and swing my chair until my knees are beneath my desk.

"I know you are." Kenzi's nose wrinkles before she snorts and walks around to the front of our desks, shrugging the strap of her purse into place. "Oh. Yeah. It's my mom and dad's anniversary next week. They always do a big barbeque. You're coming."

"Sure, that would be great. What day? I'll see if I can make it my day off."

"Already sorted it with Pete." She grins wide.

"Sounds amazing." Something warm and, dare I say it, happy spreads through my chest and I am powerless to stop it from showing on my face.

"Whatever you guys got up to last night looks good on you, Laia." Her eyebrows wiggle. And just like that she's back to her normal self. "My parents still live in the house me and my brother grew up in. It's about time you saw a little more of the island. You'll love it."

"I didn't know you had a brother." I smile at the unexpected information. I don't know why I assumed she was an only child. Probably because this is the first I've heard of him.

"Yeah, Ollie. He's been the pain in my ass for twenty-one years." Her chuckle is pained but it's clear in the sparkle behind her eyes that there's a whole lot of love there. "He's studying in New York. He's a big city boy now." Her lips pinch as if she isn't entirely happy with the situation.

"Will he be home for the party?" I rest my elbows on the polished wood of my desk.

"Not this year, I'm afraid." She glances at her watch. "I'll tell you all about him another day. My pajamas are calling me."

I watch her go. That warmth spreading until I'm grinning like a fool.

Clua is beginning to feel a whole lot like home.

Felix

"Felix?" Mylo's voice shouts through from the bar.

"In the office." I recline in my high back, leather desk chair, my feet on the desk, a pack of crushed ice balanced on my head and my cell pressed against my ear.

"Yes, mom, I'm fine." I hold my finger up when Mylo sticks his head around the office door. "No. No, you don't have to come. I'll see you at the party next week." I pinch the bridge of my nose and listen to my mom's near-hysterical quick-fire questions. Someone that wasn't me filled her in on the accident. I should have called her last night, *before* the Clua gossip machine got to her. "Mom. Mom, it's okay, I told you, I'm fine. Unpack your bags. You live fifteen minutes away. I'll call if I need you." I hold the phone away from my ear. The woman can talk. "Okay. Mom, I have to go. I'll see you next week. I love you. Okay. Bye."

The down point of living on a tiny island. News travels … fast.

"How's the head, man?" Mylo nods towards the pack of ice when I throw my cell onto my paper-strewn desk.

"Will be fine as soon as the meds kick in again," I grumble, leaning further back into my chair, holding the pack in place. "How are you feeling?"

"Fan-fucking-tastic." He folds his arms across his massive chest, the bandages on his hands, stark white against the black and gray of the tattoos on his forearms.

I sit up and throw the ice pack into the bin under my desk at his uncharacteristically miserable tone.

"Wanna talk about it?" I frown up at him, the ache in my head pulsing with the movement. "You and Zi get home alright?"

"Nothing to talk about." He shakes his head, a strained smile tipping his lips. "Just having one of those days." He sits down on the chair in front of my desk, his huge frame dwarfing the matching low back version of mine. "So, you and Laia?"

"Me and Laia." I nod, unable to keep a grin from splitting my face as I link my fingers behind my head and lift my feet back onto my desk.

I haven't been able to think of anything else all day. The way she felt wrapped around me. Her face when she came apart beneath me. The feeling of being inside her bare. It was stupid—really fucking stupid, but, fuck, it felt incredible.

"The look on your face tells me everything I never wanted to know." He shakes his head.

I shrug, neither confirming nor denying. We haven't discussed what to tell people yet. But man, just thinking her name fills my mind with all kinds of vanilla scented visions. I'd thought she was going to hightail it home the second we got up. Exactly what I usually do the morning after.

She didn't though. She stayed for coffee and toast when I asked her to. Her shyness and awkwardness were there, but the flinching didn't make a single appearance. She even kissed me goodbye.

A kiss that almost had me dragging her right back to bed.

I force my mouth from the grin I can't seem to control and drag my hand over my jaw, meeting Mylo's amused stare and clearing my throat. "So, what can I do for you?"

"I'm going to see a man about a van this afternoon." He leans forward, resting his elbows on his knees. "And seeing as you too are now in need of transportation, I figured you might wanna come?"

TWENTY-SEVEN

Laia

Leaning forward to see over the dashboard of the truck, I pull the blinker down and turn onto my street—*my street.* I smile. I can't help it. I have a street, and a home, and a Kenzi and, after this morning, I think I might even have a Felix too. And the most shocking thing? I think I *want* to have him. For real. Not just to distract me or make me forget. I just—I like him. More than that—I think I *trust* him.

The smile I've barely managed to remove from my face all day falters as I round the bend to the bungalow. A red Mustang is idling by the curb. *My curb.* I pull into the drive, watching it in my wing mirror, my heart clunking against my ribcage, unease settling around me like a scratchy second skin. Of the few people I know here, none of them own a Mustang. My tummy drops. I shake my head. It doesn't have to mean … I blow out a slow breath, my fingers trembling as I turn the truck's lights off. The hopeful happiness from just seconds before now, so far gone I'm finding it hard to believe I had the audacity to feel it at all—to actually believe it was here to stay. The sun set an hour ago, and the security light above the garage door isn't doing a whole lot to banish the rising nerves winding their way up my spine.

It's nothing. It *has* to be nothing.

Still staring at the Mustang, I cut the engine, failing miserably at keeping my flailing heartbeat under control. It could be anybody. But why here, in front of my house? The question doesn't do anything to steady me. I grab my cell from my purse then sling the strap over my shoulder, glancing into my wing mirror again, swallowing past my bone-dry throat. Nine-one-one. I swipe my cell open and dial in the number. This is ridiculous. *I'm being ridiculous.*

But what if I'm not?

The door opens with barely any trouble for once, and I slide down from the truck, the heels of my gray pumps hitting the concrete drive with a dull click. I'm being paranoid. My cell still in my hand and my heart still stubbornly lodged in my throat, I slam the door closed.

The Mustang's door opens before I manage to take a step—before I even figure out where I was stepping to. My stomach doubles in on itself, every single time I was stupid enough to stand up to Damon flashing in my mind in a slide show of tears and pain and regret.

I hit call, my breath caught in my lungs, the second it takes for the low red door to open refusing to tick by. It's him. It's over. The police won't get here in time. Nobody will.

A Converse covered foot swings out of the car, followed by the rest of Felix.

It's Felix. Not Damon. Felix.

A laugh puffs out, releasing from my chest in a weird sort of hiccup as I watch him walk towards me. Relief and the dwindling adrenaline spinning my head by the time he makes it to me.

"Hey." His gaze moves over my face, his almost smile falling when it drops to the screen of the cell still clutched half-way to my ear. "What's wrong? What happened?"

"Nine-one-one, please state your emergency."

The faraway voice has me staring dumbly at my cell too. Wait. Shit. I lift it to my ear, my cheeks blazing with my over-reaction. "Yes. Sorry. False alarm. Sorry. I thought I saw something." I glance up into Felix's concerned face. "No, I'm fine. Sorry again."

I close down the screen. "I thought—" I press my lips together, the truth the only thing I can come up with to explain myself. "I thought you were someone else."

His jaw ticks, his neck contracting with his swallow. "Who?"

I hold his stare, pull the one side of my bottom lip through my teeth then glance away from the pity already beginning to form in his eyes. "You should probably come in."

He follows me to the front door, waits silently as I unlock it then slip off my shoes and drop my purse on the console in the entrance. He doesn't touch me. Doesn't smile or say a word, just watches me, jaw tight, forehead creased. I haven't even told him yet and things have already changed.

I pad through to the kitchen, the tiles cool on my tired feet, the spike of paranoia from minutes ago making me shiver despite the warm night. It wasn't him. But it could've been. It could've been and I'd have been just as useless and helpless as I ever was.

"Laia."

I start at Felix's voice behind me, my fingertips pressed against the kitchen counter, eyes fixed on the grain of the butcher block worktop. "Damon used to beat me." My cheeks burn, shame at myself for being so weak back then making my hands shake—making every part of me shake. "He beat me every day for years, and I just—let him."

I flinch before Felix's hands even make contact with my shoulders, not even his nearness or his fresh-air and mint scent enough to drive out the chill.

His hands fall to his sides when I turn, his brows knitted, his face tight at whatever he's reading on mine.

"He told me if I ever ran, I'd better not stop because if he found me…" I lift my chin, force myself to hold his stare. "I thought—I didn't recognize the car. I thought—"

Felix's steady gaze moves over my face, his chest lifting, his jaw ticking, a million unreadable emotions flashing behind his blue, blue eyes.

Seconds pass, the weight of his pity, his *judgment*, heavy on my shoulders. I shouldn't have said anything. My chin trembles along with the rest of me, but I lift my hand, my fingers curling slightly before they touch his cheek. "Say something."

This time it's him who flinches, his gaze refocusing on my face. "You're cold."

I pull my hand back to my chest. "I'm fine."

His throat contracts and he shakes his head. "Where's your bathroom?"

Ten minutes pass and he's still not back. I don't know what I was expecting, but it wasn't this.

The view when I walk through the bathroom door is almost enough to make me forget it all.

Felix—his beige cargo shorts pulled tight where he's leaning over the bathtub. Solid muscle and smooth, tan skin exposed where his white T-shirt has ridden up his back.

He straightens as the door clicks closed behind me, his hand lifting to the back of his neck when he turns.

My stomach sinks. I know that move.

It's his I'm uncomfortable move.

"Felix, if—" I take a step towards him and rub my forehead, steeling myself against his excuses, or reasons, or whatever he's about to throw my way. "If this has put you off, I get it." My teeth rake my bottom lip, but I hold his stare. Better him to decide I'm not worth it now than later.

His eyes darken and narrow, his jaw clenching and releasing as he closes the distance between us and tucks a curl behind my ear, curving his body back so he can meet my lowered gaze. "Laia, I don't think there's anything you could tell me that would put me off."

I shake my head and look away, looking anywhere but into his face when my chin starts to tremble again. Crying doesn't help anything.

"Don't." His warm, steady hands cup my jaw, forcing me to look at him. To meet this head on. "This changes nothing." His thumbs brush my cheeks, the truth of his words written in the serious tilt to his lips and the hard line of his brow.

I nod jerkily in his hold, swallowing past the ugly sob blocking my throat.

His hands slide lower, tracing down the side of my neck.

I inhale a shuddering breath.

He trails them further down, over my collar bones to the top button of my blouse, "You know what you need?" The corner of his lips lifts into a half smile when he slips the first button from its hole, then the next, and the next until the pale pink lace of my bra peeks between the white silk.

I lean into his touch. It does the same thing it always does. Smooths the jagged edges of my past until I can almost see past them. Almost *feel* past them. "What do I need?" My voice catches at the openness in his stare.

"You need to get into the bath." He undoes the rest of my buttons then slowly tugs my blouse from where it's still tucked into the high waist of my skirt. "And relax." His voice is soft, genuine, his eyes on mine even as he gently pushes my blouse over my shoulders and guides it down my arms, letting it float almost weightlessly to the floor. "No more crying. No more fear. He's not here. I am."

I lift my chin in a small nod.

His warm hands return to my shoulders and urge me to turn from him.

I bite back a smile at the mass of bubbles floating atop the over-full tub and breathe in the comforting vanilla scent of my own soap.

He runs a finger down the curve of my spine then slowly unzips my skirt, letting it fall in a puddle around my feet.

"I'm not going anywhere." His fingers slip under the clasp of my bra.

A groan escapes when he unclips it and pushes the lace from my body, my nipples tightening as his hands slide down my sides to push my panties down my thighs. "But know this, Laia." He straightens again and wraps his arms around me from behind, the cotton of his T-shirt soft against my naked back. Warm and comforting. "If that son-of-a-bitch ever shows his face around here, he'll have me to worry about."

And just like that, the weight I've carried since I left Damon lifts—just a bit—but it's enough to let me breathe a tiny bit easier.

If he ever does find me again. I won't be alone.

"Get in the bath," Felix whispers into my ear and walks me forward, his presence behind me begging me to reach back and touch him. Begging me to show him how much this means to me.

The slight bite of heat when I slip, first one, then the other foot into the water almost makes my eyes roll, goosebumps flaring over every inch of me. Exactly the way I like it. I sink down into the bubbles and my eyelids flutter closed. Perfect.

This is perfect.

He's perfect.

He's still watching me when I open my eyes again, leaning on the vanity, arms folded, the serious lines of his forehead and the slight pout to his lips impossible to read. "You can talk to me. You know that, right?"

I press my lips together and hold his stare.

He tugs on his ear, his chest expanding. "About anything."

I rest my arm along the edge of the bath and flex my fingers, the ache in my ring-finger knuckle throbbing. "You know what almost hurt more than the physical stuff?"

His jaw clenches and for a second, I hesitate. He'll think I'm ridiculous.

"What?"

I blink up at him. "The way he took away my … *me.*"

Something flickers over his face, and he crosses his legs, shifts against the vanity. "You can get you back."

"I know." I sink my finger into a little point of bubbles. "And I think I might be. I'm baking again. I've even made friends here. And then there's—this." My cheeks flush when I lift my gaze from the bubbles. "You … I mean … I don't mean we're … I know this isn't anything." I barely resist sinking completely under the water and staying there. Indefinitely. This is why I don't share.

His rough chuckle sets a desire-flavored buzzing off in my tummy, but that's nothing compared to the full-body vibrations when the crinkles around his eyes stay even after his smile fades.

Tension crackles thickly in the steam-filled air.

The flip from caring concern to undiluted sex when his gaze drops to where my breasts break the bubbly surface of the water is undeniable. He's not lying. My past hasn't put him off. At all.

"It's kinda lonely in here." I lift myself up the rolled edge of the bath, suds sliding down my body, my nipples tightening even more with the sudden change in temperature.

The corner of his mouth quirks. "You're supposed to be relaxing."

I arch an eyebrow and purposely allow my gaze to move down his body, all the way to the tell-tale bulge beneath his shorts. "I *am* relaxed. You?"

His groan is almost pained. "Laia, I don't want to—"

"You don't want to what? Break me? Scare me? I'm no more fragile now than I was this morning."

"I don't think you're breakable." A muscle in his jaw flickers like he's fighting some internal battle. I'm not sure if he wins or loses, but he stalks across the bathroom. "Your tub isn't big enough for two." The muscles in his forearms tense when he grips the edge of the bath and leans down to press a kiss to my forehead then dips his face so that his eyes are level with mine. "Just enjoy the bubbles."

The scent of him blended with my vanilla soap makes breathing like a mini party for my nostrils. Without so much as a slither of doubt, I slide my hand around the back of his neck and kiss him. My tongue teases his the second his lips part and I shift in the water, sending a little wave over the side.

He jerks back.

Something inside me freezes. A spark of fear shooting down my spine.

It fizzles as quickly as it sparks at the sight of his wicked grin as he grabs the back of his T-shirt and pulls it over his head in that sexy way men do.

His abs … that *V*…

He offers his hand out to me, a dimple flashing in his left cheek.

I tuck my fingers into his grip and let him pull me to my feet, water and bubbles cascading down my body.

I'm barely on my feet before I'm lifted into his arms.

My heart does a somersault in my chest, his touch already soothing everything back to bearable. "I'm soaking you." My giggle is breathy, my wet skin slipping against his chest as I wrap an arm around his neck. "Don't drop me."

"Never." His laugh is seriously the stuff of romance novels. A touch of gravel, with a hint of a rasp and a whole lot of delicious deepness.

I yelp when my ass hits the cold, polished concrete that tops the vanity, but the discomfort is instantly forgotten when my knees are nudged apart, and he leans his big body between my thighs.

"I've thought of nothing but this…" He flexes his hips and dips his head to press a kiss to my jaw, right beneath my ear. "All day."

"All day?" I slide my hands up his chest and over the round muscles of his shoulders, his skin hot against my palms. "Fun."

His smirk lights his eyes, and then his gaze flicks from my face to the mirror behind me. The smirk disintegrates, and whatever heat was there morphs into something cold. And shocked. And *pissed.*

My blood congeals.

"Tell me that wasn't him." His stare stays fixed over my shoulder.

I don't have to look to know what he's seen. I try to push him back so I can slip off the vanity, suddenly uber-aware of my complete nakedness and the marks my time with Damon left me with.

He grips my hips, holding me still. The muscles in his throat contracting are the only thing I can bring myself to look at. I forgot they were there because that's what he does—he makes me forget. He makes me feel like a normal scar-free person. But I'm not. I never will be.

"It's nothing." Before my chin can tremble. Before I can push him away, I'm wrapped in his arms, my face pressed into the crook of his neck, his hand covering the thin, jagged white scar on the back of my hip.

His body warms my rapidly cooling skin. "Tell me." He clears his throat. "Tell me what he did to you?"

I shake my head. "You don't need to do this."

TWENTY-EIGHT

Felix

I force myself to breathe in. Then out. Then in again. How the fuck could anyone hurt her?

Laia gently pulls back from where she'd hidden her face in my neck, her eyes glassy, her gaze wary and sad. So fucking sad, I want to find the prick and rip his fucking head off.

"Do the scars bother you?" Her voice is no more than a whisper as she glances to the side of the vanity then reaches for the hand towel by the sink and holds it awkwardly over herself.

My eyebrows twist up in the middle, my fingers flexing where they're still wrapped around her. The lack of color in her cheeks is all I can focus on. "There are more?" I swallow down the bile burning up my throat just thinking about what she's been through to get here.

Her mouth presses into a line and she fidgets with the edge of the towel held up almost to her throat. "There are more … but only if you know where to look. He wasn't stupid."

"Show me." My jaw aches with tension, my voice ragged even to my own ears. My chest is raw, like something's clawed its way in there and settled in for the long haul. Fury? Vengeance? Whatever the fuck it is, its roaring at me to protect her. To keep her safe. To find the pathetic bastard and see how brave he is against a real man.

Her tongue peeks out to wet her lips and her chest lifts with a long inhale before she covers my hand with hers and pulls it from her waist.

I steel myself against the very real possibility of that wall slamming down and never coming up again.

Still holding my gaze, she lifts my hand to her collarbone and presses my fingers to a slight ridge there.

The whole world spirals and zooms in on that one ridge, and it's like the air's been sucked from not just my lungs, but the whole damn room.

"He threw me down the stairs." Her lips form a slight O as she releases her breath.

I run the pad of my finger over the bump that's invisible beneath her skin. Simultaneously horrified and awed that she's trusting me with this … with her.

I nod. I think. The movement's so tiny I'm not even sure I make it.

She straightens a little. Like a tiny show of defiance against whatever memories are playing out in her mind as she swaps the hand holding the towel with the one covering my fingers. Then she guides my fingers to where her earlobe meets her head and the slightly raised scar hidden in the crease. "He dragged me back up those stairs."

There are no words.

She moves my hand to her ribs and this time her chin does begin to tremble. "There are more, Felix. But this is the one that saved me."

I press my palm against her ribs. Her skin's still damp from the bath, still a little pink and warm.

"He had to take me to the hospital." Her lips curve into a slight smile and she shrugs.

Shrugs like what she's just told me hasn't gutted me—hasn't just completely ruined me.

"The nurse treating me figured out what was going on, and the next day I was out of there."

Silence settles between us. Thick and full of questions. I bring my hands up to cup her jaw, stroking my thumbs over her cheeks, tipping her head back. How many black eyes were hidden beneath the lotions and potions on those shelves? How many split lips? Bloody noses?

How many times had she needed someone to protect her, and nobody came?

Her hand slides over my wrist and her eyebrows raise. Like she's waiting for me to speak. My gaze drops to a line of slightly darker skin across her forearm, and I take my hand from her face to lift her arm, flicking my gaze from the scar to her face.

Her laugh is shocked. Slightly wobbly, but it's nowhere near as bitter as I'd expect. "This one was all me. Ovens can be mean when you're not paying attention."

That she can laugh at all after living the life she has fills my chest with a rush of appreciation for the strength it must have taken her to move forward.

I brush my thumb over this scar as well.

"Say something," she whispers.

"You—" I clear my throat and the catch in my voice. "You inspire me." I clench my teeth. "You're brave, and so fucking strong."

She starts to shake her head, pink staining her cheeks.

My mouth is pressed against hers before she gets the chance to brush off my words. I don't think I've ever been happier to see a woman blush.

There's no hesitation in the instant parting of her lips or the stroke of her tongue.

I pull back and scan her face. She's flushed. Just the way I like her. I cup her head and tilt to the side to press a kiss to the scar on her earlobe. "And no." I tug the towel from where she's still got it held up over herself. "The scars don't put me off." I press another kiss to her collarbone, then bypass her seriously tempting breasts and lift her arm to trail my tongue up her ribs. "They don't put me off." I twist myself around her other side and kiss the back of her hip and the jagged white line there too. "At all."

Her yelped out giggle eases any residual tension from my shoulders when I straighten again. I slide my hands over the curve of her ass and pull her tighter to me. And when she wraps her legs around my hips and clasps her hands behind my neck, the rush of feeling that spreads through my chest has me pausing. Staring at her face. Trying to figure out how the hell we got here.

"Felix." The corner of her lips twitch and she clenches her thighs around me.

I lift my chin and my eyebrows. "Huh?"

Her fingers sink into the hair at the nape of my neck, and she frowns, humor shining in the green of her eyes. "You're staring."

My gaze drops to her mouth. "You're worth staring at." I lean in and press my lips to hers, lingering there until her eyelids flutter open again.

"In that case." She arches her whole body into mine and deepens the kiss. Long and slow, it has one of my hands flexing on her ass the other sliding up the side of her neck, my thumb brushing her jaw, my body pushing her back until her shoulders meet the mirror behind her.

The noises that leave her have me kissing her harder, angling my head to take it deeper.

She pants against my lips, her knees hitching up my sides, heels digging into my ass, hands dropping to the button of my shorts.

Breathing hard, I pull back and tug her hands from my waistband. "Wanna know what else I've been thinking about all day?" I meet her stare, my tongue touching my top lip before I plant my hands on the counter either side of her hips and kiss her jaw, breathe in her vanilla scent, and graze my teeth down the side of her neck before meeting her heavy-lidded stare again. "These legs." I slide my hands over her knees and push them further apart, my gaze moving over her flushed face. "Wrapped around my neck."

Laia

If my face has ever been this hot before I can't remember. My nose wrinkles, and his eyes narrow.

"What?"

"Nothing." I press my fingers to my lips, then my whole hands to my burning cheeks. "It's nothing."

"Laia." His voice is a low grumble, his hands still on my knees, still holding them shamelessly apart, but his stare never strays from my face. "Talk to me."

I shake my head. "Nothing. I can't—"

"—You can."

I grimace. It's not attractive, but let's face it neither are flaming red cheeks. "Fine, I've never … nobody's ever—"

"—Made you come with their tongue." His lips tick up at the sides like he's trying not to smile.

My mouth closes with an audible pop. "Yes, I mean no. Never. I mean, I've only ever been with … and he, well he wouldn't. He didn't like to reciprocate even when I—"

"—Stop talking. Please." Pressing the butts of his hands into his eyes, he leans back, head tipped to the ceiling on a long, drawn-out groan.

"I'm sorry. I shouldn't have—"

He instantly drops his hands and cups my face. "I'm not mad at you. Never you." He clamps his mouth shut then takes a long breath and the smile he was fighting wins out after all, spreading across his face. "Let me do this, Laia."

"No. Yes. What if you don't—" I press my lips together but hold his stare apparently no longer capable of finishing a sentence.

"Trust me." His eyes flash with a confidence that has me nodding despite the nerves and memories.

His gaze moves over my face, his smile straightening into something much, much more serious. Then, moving slowly like he's still waiting for me to back out, he leans in. "Trust me."

"I do."

The kiss starts soft, gentle even, his tongue barely tickling mine, his hands still cupping my face, big body curved over mine. He moves with care, slow and controlled, but for once, it's not enough to make me forget what's about to happen.

"Relax." He kisses my chin, the side of my jaw, his hands sliding down my sides and over my waist tugging me to him until I'm perched right on the edge of the counter and my shoulders touch the cool glass of the mirror again. "If you don't want this—"

"I do," I blurt out, earning myself one of his crinkly-eyed smiles.

"Okay." His fingers flex on my hips, his thumbs at my hip bones, his tanned skin vivid against my paleness.

"Okay." I nod.

His attention flicks down then he leans in and presses a kiss to the edge of my jaw, bristles scratching down my neck, over the rise of my breast. My chest lifts and falls in sharp little pants. And then his lips seal over my nipple, and my hips jerk up off the counter, my head coming away from the mirror, body curling over his. I twist my fingers into his hair, my mind finally, *finally* quieting, zoning into the drugging splice of heat shooting from my breast to my core.

He moves to the other breast with a rough groan, his teeth grazing over the tip.

"Holy shit," I breathe against the top of his head, his clean, fresh air scent filling my head, my heels digging into his lower back as his big body moves against mine.

And then he shifts lower, his hands back on my waist, holding me still, his tongue trailing down the center of my belly. My fingers tighten in his hair and my heartbeat kicks up until it pulses in the dip of my throat. This is happening.

His chin bumps my pubic bone, his wide shoulders pushing my thighs apart. This is really happening. My abs tense and I release his hair to grip the edge of the countertop.

His rough chuckle puffs warmth over my lower tummy. "Laia."

"I'm good." I'm not. I think I might faint.

"Laia, look at me." He rests his chin on my belly and squeezes my sides.

I bite down hard on my lip and force myself to look down my extremely naked body to his intense blue eyes. My legs are hanging over his shoulders. Hanging. Over. His. Shoulders.

"You can say no." His brows lift.

I shake my head, my attention caught on the slow pull of his bottom lip through his teeth, my whole body flushing.

He holds my stare, slowly pulls back then he kisses me. Long, slow and right, *right* there.

A pant catches in my throat and my toes curl, but he doesn't stop. He does it again. And again. *And again* until there is nothing—*nothing*—left in my head but him and his tongue and *I cannot believe I've spent twenty-seven years without this in my life.*

TWENTY-NINE

Laia

Smothering a yawn with the back of my hand, I turn the page of the book I've got propped up against my bent knees then turn it back again for about the hundredth time since I sat down out here. The sex on the page just keeps morphing into flashbacks of last night. Vivid, detailed, *toe-curlingly* high-definition flashbacks of last night. Felix is—I bite my lip, a squealy grin pulling at my mouth. He made me come on the bathroom sink. Then the floor. Then again against the wall and twice more in my bed. His mouth, his fingers, his … I shake my head and try to focus.

"Laia? Are you back here?"

At the sound of Mrs. Devon's voice, I push my sunglasses onto the top of my head. "In the backyard."

Unannounced visitors seem to be my new normal lately. I have to admit, it's kinda nice. I pull my tank on over my bikini top, unroll the legs of my cut-offs, and attempt to cool down my cheeks before she makes it around the side of the house and through the gate.

She appears holding a bouquet of lilies tied with a green ribbon. "I found these by the front door."

My stomach instantly tightens. Flowers. I swallow down the knee-jerk unease but can't seem to tear my gaze from the elegant white petals. Or force myself to stand from the wooden sun lounger I'm camped out on.

Mrs. Devon's smile fades as she lays the flowers onto the empty lounger beside mine. Today's yellow, paisley-print mumu poofs out at the sides as she sits down beside them. Her face, shaded by the canopy of palm leaves above us, turns sober. Worried. And a tiny bit scared. "Who do you think they're from?"

Pretty flowers for my pretty lady.

"Laia?" Mrs. Devon's soft fingers curl around my forearm.

"Excuse me?" I flinch. Shake my head. Slip my arm from her grip. "Sorry, I was just..." I paint on a smile. "They're beautiful." The words sound brittle even to my own ears. They're not from him.

"Who do you think they're from, Laia?"

"Felix." They have to be from Felix. It's the only thing that makes sense. "I should probably get them in some water." I stand to pick up the flowers, my fingers trembling. "Ice tea?"

"That would be lovely, thank you." Mrs. Devon tilts her head, scanning my face. "Are you sure everything's okay? You're very pale."

"Yeah. Yes, I'm fine. I just wasn't expecting them." I take a tiny breath of their sweet, heady, horribly familiar scent, barely resisting the urge to drop them.

Her eyes narrow, causing even more fine lines to spread out around them. "I'm actually here to let you know I'll be gone for a few weeks."

"Nice. Where are you off to?" I ask as I turn on auto-pilot from her concerned stare and head through the French doors to the kitchen to grab a jug of ice-tea from the fridge.

She's gazing out over the ocean by the time I've fixed our drinks.

The ice cubes clink against the side of the glasses when I place them onto the small wooden table between the two loungers.

"I'm going to see my son in Hawaii. But I can hold off if you need me to?" She holds my stare, head tipped to the side, hands lifting as if to take my own before they drop back into her lap. "Are you sure you're okay, Laia?"

"Flowers?" I wince and pull myself up in the bed, pain shooting through my tender ribs.

"I'm sorry about last night." Damon lays the pink carnations in my lap.

Dressed for work in his gray suit, his face is the epitome of regret. Almost.

My teeth sink into my cheek when I meet his chestnut eyes, and his mouth breaks into a rueful smile as he runs a finger over the bruise across my cheek bone. "You always know just what to do to make me lose my temper."

"Laia?"

I blink. Swallow. Shake the past from my mind and refocus on the now. It's not him. It can't be him. "No, honestly, you should definitely go. It's your son! You must be so excited. And Hawaii!"

"You sure? You seem—"

"I'm fine. I'm just … I'm not feeling so great today. Lots of late nights and early starts." I hold her far too perceptive gaze. "I'm really sorry, would you mind if I go lie down?"

It takes me ten minutes to reassure her that everything's okay and another ten to assure myself I'm not going mad after she leaves.

I lean down, my elbows on the breakfast bar, and stare at the flowers, cock my head and stare some more.

Here, have some roses, I'm sorry I gave you a black eye, but you know I hate it when you're late.

Here, have some daisies, forgive me for breaking your rib, but you know how I feel about your friends.

Here, have some lilies, I didn't mean to fracture your wrist. I thought you were leaving me.

You forgive me? Right?

Bile burns up my throat. I check the bouquet again for a card. Any sort of confirmation that they're from Felix.

There's nothing. I swallow thickly and flick my gaze around the empty kitchen, through the arch into the hallway and the locked front door beyond it.

THIRTY

Felix

Muscles burning, my fist connects with the punching bag in two sharp hooks, then two more from the other side.

Focus on the burn. Focus on the sweat dripping down my back. The release of breath with every strike. Focus on anything but the truth that's unfurling in my gut—in my chest—turning over in my mind.

I put way more force than necessary into my last right hook then grip the heavy bag with both hands and rest my forehead against it, its familiar leathery scent calming to my ragged breaths.

Even with my eyes open I can see her. Her pouty lips turned up into a smirk. Her cheeks and their constant flushing. Her eyes when they flash with whatever she's feeling.

Her scars.

Her strength.

Laia.

I grab the towel hanging from the weight bench and drag it over my face, walking over to the floor to ceiling windows of my home gym.

From up here there's nothing but trees. Huge, towering, Big Leaf Magnolias, the sun filtering through in speckled rays, coloring everything green. Not another person for miles.

Solitude. The only thing that's kept me sane these last few years. Now everything just makes me think of Laia.

The Beach Hut had been mine and Rosa's dream. After the Marines I put every ounce of myself into getting it up and running. For her. For me. For us. Her memory is in every corner of it. I'm proud of what it's become. Proud I was able to finish what we started. I still am.

This place though. I turn from the window to the decked-out gym. The first room I renovated. The first place after Rosa I felt any semblance of peace in.

I've never pictured sharing this place with anyone else. I grind my teeth against the conflicting emotions that tighten my chest. Against the thought that took up root last night and hasn't budged since.

Until now.

I'm ready to move on.

Fuck. I throw the towel onto the bench and leave the room. Move through the hallway, my bare feet soundless on the hardwood floors. Down the curved staircase and through the living room, straight to the drawer built into the fireplace.

The slice of pain that accompanies the contents of this drawer still dries my mouth. A box and a polaroid.

I lower myself onto the sofa and turn the small, delicately carved wooden box in my hands, brush my thumb over the initials carved into the top before I flip it open, my heart thudding painfully against my ribs.

The ring slides onto my finger, easy, like I never took it off. I drag my hand over my face and release a ragged breath before I pick up the smaller ring with my pinkie and the faded-with-age photo. We're not even looking at the camera. She's sitting on my knee, her head tucked beneath my chin. The smile on my face makes my eyes blur every time. I had no idea—no fucking idea.

I brush my finger over her cheek in the photo. She'd want this for me. I tighten my fist, both rings glinting against the sunlight from the living room windows. Rosa would want me to be happy. Laia makes me happy.

A knock at the front door pulls me from my thoughts.

"Come in."

The door opens and all I can do is stare.

Laia. As if I've summoned her. Standing there, her green eyes fixed on mine. Her eyebrows quirked up in the middle, fingers twisting in front of her. "Felix. Hey."

"Hey." I clear my throat and stand. "Come in."

Pink stains her cheeks as her eyelids flutter and her gaze moves over my bare chest. "I tried calling … I can come back if you're busy. I just wanted to…"

I rake my hands through my hair, the tiny diamond sparkling from my pinkie when I drop them again. "No. I need to talk to you about something."

Her bottom lip disappears between her teeth as she steps from the entrance. "Everything okay?" Her flip flops click against her feet with every step closer she takes.

Denim shorts and a white tank, her hair pulled back from her face, she finally looks up at me from beneath her eyelashes and the now familiar tug of protectiveness in my chest makes itself known. For better or worse I'm done fighting this. I'm ready.

The second she's close enough, I slide my hand around the nape of her neck and pull her to me. Brush my lips over hers. Breathe her in.

Her lips part, her tongue flicks against my top lip and she almost, *almost* leans into me. But then she stops. Slips her hands over my pecs and pushes me back. "You wanted to talk?" Her gaze flicks to the engraved gold band on my ring finger, then to the one on my pinkie and a frown creases her forehead. "Are those … are they your wedding rings?"

"Yes." I drop back down onto the sofa, twist them both off and tuck them back into the box.

"Is this her?" She lowers herself onto the coffee table in front of me, her knees between my thighs as she picks up the polaroid, her gaze flicking over the photo. "So young." Her voice is quiet, her attention still fixed on the photo. "This is one of Mama Den's." She blinks up at me, her lips parting, cogs turning. "Rosa was your one. Why did you break up?"

"We didn't." I cough to clear the roughness from my words. It never gets easier saying this out loud. "She … Rosa…"

"You still love her."

It's not a question. I grind my teeth but meet her stare and nod. There's no point in lying. "She was the love of my life."

"I get it." Her smile is shaky, but she blinks and looks down at her fingers. "You want her back."

"Laia, Rosa is dead…"

"I mean, me and you … you just got caught up in the … wait. What?"

I hold her wide-eyed stare, the dull ache, the bone-grinding finality of those words still hard to breathe past.

Her mouth opens. Then closes. The color in her cheeks fades. "I didn't mean … I mean … she's dead? Rosa died?" Her breath seems to leave her along with whatever she's trying to say. "Why didn't you tell me?"

I shake my head and flip the box shut, walls I hadn't even realized I'd built around myself reinforcing themselves against her pity.

Heavy silence thickens the air between us, all the things I wanted to say, needed to explain sitting like lead in my stomach. "Does this change things?" I run my tongue over my bottom lip, my eyes narrowing on the confused crease between her eyebrows.

"Should it?" She drops her gaze to my throat then meets my stare head on. "I still want to try this. With you. Unless you don't. Unless *you've* changed your mind." Her lips press together, and she holds her breath. "Is that what you wanted to talk to me about?"

My eyebrows lift and the pain of the rings and what they mean eases for the first time in a long time. "I haven't changed my mind about this." My gut clenches, but I lean forward and cup her face anyway. Tilt it up to mine and rub my thumbs over her cheeks. "I won't."

Though the confusion in her stare is still there, her pupils dilate and the warmth of her sharp exhale tickles over my skin. "Okay."

"Okay." Hiding nothing, I dip my head and press a kiss to her mouth.

Her lips part, her tongue sliding over mine as she smooths her hands up my forearms. Before I'm ready for it to stop, she presses her forehead to mine. "I got the flowers. They're lovely." Her grip tightens on my wrists holding my hands to her face. "Thank you."

My frown is instant. So is the rising panic paling her face when she sees it.

"I didn't send you flowers."

Laia

The world just stops, all pretense of brave, strong, happy Laia falling away like she never existed in the first place.

I jerk my hands from Felix's forearms and pull back from his hold, fear, like a lead weight around my neck, threatening to drag me down.

A shaky breath rushes from my lips. "Who then?" I press my fingers into my temples, then meet Felix's freaked-out blue stare. "If it wasn't you, then who?" I don't know why I'm asking. I know who. I knew the minute I laid eyes on the flowers who they were from.

I knew, I just didn't have the guts to believe it.

"What's wrong?" Felix's big hands lift to my shoulders, his face darkening with concern.

I flinch away. Shake my head. Get to my feet between his legs, my mind spinning, trying *not* to come up with the obvious truth. "They're from him. I know it."

Felix's whole posture changes, lines creasing his forehead, tension hardening the muscles in his big body. Normally, I'd drool. Right now, the only thing I can think of is all the different ways Damon could hurt him. Destroy me through destroying him. And Kenzi. And Mrs. Devon. He'll take all my happy and wring it out of my life like he did before.

"I can't do this. If he knows about you…" I shake my head and fix my stare on the crease between his pecs. "He'll hurt you. I can't … I won't let that happen. I need to go, I'm sorry. I need to leave." I try to scramble over his thigh.

"Laia. Calm down. You're not making any sense." He's on his feet and my face is cupped in his hands before I get anywhere.

"You don't understand." My gaze moves over his serious face. "I didn't want this. Didn't want to care this much about anyone." It just makes everything harder. A big fat tear escapes my eye and trickles down my cheek.

He wipes it away with his thumb and curves his body back so his face is level with mine, giving me no other option but to look at him.

"Please." I blink back another tear before it gets the chance to spill. "You don't know what he's capable of."

"And he doesn't know what I'm capable of." The crease between Felix's dark eyebrows deepens, but his gaze doesn't falter. I don't think he even blinks. "I won't let him hurt you, Laia. And if he tries" —his nostrils flare— "Let him try. Let him give me an excuse."

I blow out a puff of air, my heartbeat only slightly less erratic, but the thickness in my throat is impossible to swallow down. He's here. I can feel it.

"There's only one florist on this side of the island. We can phone them. We can figure this out. You don't have to do this alone anymore. Let me help you. Please."

I lick my dry lips at the strength in his gaze and the sureness of his voice and nod. A tiny jerky movement I'm not even sure he sees.

"Don't run."

My chin trembles, but I shake my head, the panic receding just enough for me to release my breath.

He presses his lips to my forehead and wraps me in his arms, my cheek against his chest, his heartbeat pulsing against my skin until mine slowly drops to match its steadying rhythm.

"I don't want him to take this from me," I whisper against his warm skin, my arms sliding around his waist. It's selfish of me to stay. To put him at risk.

But I'm not sure I can give this up.

Curled on the sofa, I chew my thumbnail and peer up at Felix. He's still shirtless, still wearing just his loose training shorts. Still watching me like I might bolt at any second. He's not wrong. In the past five minutes I've come up with at least fifty plans of escape.

Cell pressed to his ear, he smiles reassuringly down at me. "Great. Thank you. Bye."

He lowers himself down onto the chunky wooden coffee table and rubs his hand up my calf. "They just sacked a delivery guy for smoking weed on the job. Apparently, he's been messing up all of their deliveries for weeks."

I suck my bottom lip and lift my gaze to the wooden beams of the ceiling to stop any more tears. I want to believe him—want to get back how I felt this morning, when my head was filled with tongues and butterflies and a sureness that I was finally moving forward with my life—that I was finally breaking free of my past. "I don't know if I can do this, Felix."

When I drop my gaze back to him, he leans forward and presses his lips to mine once, twice. The third time I kiss him back, sink my fingers into the thick dark hair at the nape of his neck then pull back, my head already shaking. "Even if the flowers aren't from him, it's only a matter of time."

That crease reappears between his eyebrows. "I can handle him, Laia. Him and anything he throws our way."

My thumb lifts to my mouth.

He pulls it back down before my teeth find the jagged corner of my nail. “Trust me.”

A fresh wave of emotion trembles my chin, but I nod. “I do. It’s him I don’t trust.”

THIRTY-ONE

Felix

I cut the engine and dip my head to see out of the Mustang's windshield and up the stone path that cuts through the forest. There are fewer Big Leaf Magnolia and palms on this side of the island. More rubber trees and xate plants.

A reluctant smile pulls at my lips.

"Ex-a-te?" I shake my head and run my fingers through the fern-like leaves.

"No, silly. It's spelled X-A-T-E but it's pronounced shhhha-te." Rosa flicks her wide brown eyes up from her sketch pad and wrinkles her nose. It's smudged with charcoal. "If you're bored you can still make it to go fishing with the guys. I won't be offended." She shrugs and the wide neck of her faded turquoise and gray tie-dye T-shirt slips down her shoulder. "Watching me draw plants isn't exactly a fun first date. I figured I'd have this finished by now. It's due tomorrow."

"I don't mind. I like watching you draw." I reach over to where she's sitting cross-legged in the dirt and brush the black mark from the tip of her nose. "I think I'd like doing just about anything with you."

Her smile in response to my lame attempt at charm tightens my chest in a way I haven't felt before. I'm pretty sure I could see that smile every day for the rest of my life and never get bored of it.

My heart thuds heavily as I peel my fingers from their white-knuckle grip on the steering wheel and lean back in the seat blinking away the vivid images. Coming back here always brings them out. The memories. The starry-fucking-eyed sureness that we'd have forever. I swallow thickly and tug the key from the ignition before climbing out of the car with a grunt of discomfort.

I miss my pickup. This one is too low. Too small. Too *not me.*

Shoving my hands into my pockets, I wrap my fingers around the smooth gem-like glass I found on the beach this morning and kick at a pebble on the first flat stone of the path.

I suck in a lungful of humid air and lift my gaze to the crisscross of trees above and the tiny fractions of blue sky beyond them. It's crazy, but I always expect to see some sort of sign when I'm here. In her place. Some sort of hint from the universe that she's up there and not just … *Gone.*

I force my feet to move. Force the rest of me to follow down the winding path, up steps so old I wouldn't be surprised if they were from the beginning of time. I concentrate on how my Converse flatten the green moss that covers each step and steel myself against what waits for me at the top—the reason I'm here.

I never imagined I'd get to this moment. If I'm honest, I never thought I wanted to. But now that I am…

The image of Laia's awkward smile yesterday when she agreed to come to Zi's parent's party with me lifts a little of the weight. Makes it easier to breathe as I reach the last step. It's a big deal. My parents will be there. My friends too. It'll make things official. *Real.* Laia deserves real.

The clearing beyond the end of the path steals what little air I have left in my lungs and every single thought from my mind. My attention's not drawn by the mass of turquoise ocean beyond the small, flat grass-covered cliff-top, or the cloudless sky beyond it.

The only thing I see is the headstone in the middle of the clearing and the woman on her knees beside it. I knew she'd be here. She's been here every Thursday morning for ten years.

Visiting her daughter.

She turns when I near, and I'm sucker-punched in the gut like I am every time I see her. Rosa was her mother's double. Looking into Rosemarie's face is like looking into a future that was taken from me. Her waist length black hair may be streaked with gray and there may be more lines around her mouth and eyes, but the resemblance never fades.

Her face breaks into a wide smile and she lifts herself onto her feet when I stop before the carved stone plaque. "Felix. What a lovely surprise." She brushes her hands on her loose green dress and holds her arms out.

I lean down to hug her. Lavender and lime. The scent takes me back to the hundreds of meals we shared in her tiny cottage not far from here. I should visit her more.

If she wants me to after I say what I've come to say. The thought of her hearing about Laia from someone else doesn't sit well. And it's only a matter of time.

"Rosemarie." I kiss her cheek before I pull back. "How are you?"

She lets out a soft sigh when I release her. "I'm good, sweet boy. You know…" Her dark eyes flit to the headstone and her smile falters.

I know.

My hand lifts to the tight muscles in the back of my neck. "I came here to … I wanted to talk to you about something."

Her head tilts to the side and she watches as I try to find the right words. "You've met someone." Her lips tip up and she closes her fingers over my forearm. Artist's fingers. Short nails, strong grip. Muted colors forever stained into her now age-lined skin.

"How did you know?" I cover her fingers with my hand.

She lets out a soft laugh. "I guessed as much at the market last month. Mama always said that when the lemons grow big a change is coming. I saw you with her. Saw your face when you looked at her and I hoped…"

"You hoped?" I'm powerless to halt the frown from creasing my forehead. This is not how I expected this to go down.

"Felix, Rosa would have never wanted you to be alone forever. And neither do I." Her stare holds my own, nothing but truth and sad acceptance shining from her face.

I release the breath caught painfully in my lungs. "I came here to…" I shake my head and shove my hand in my pocket, my gaze dropping back to the name on the stone. To the swirls and dots identical to my tattoo engraved beneath. "I dunno…"

"To say goodbye?" Her wide eyes blink, shining with emotion, her smile small. Sad. But full of understanding. "It's okay. You can say it."

My jaw tightens. It's hard to breathe past the knot in my throat, but I nod.

"She'd be happy for you." She cups my cheek then turns to look out over the ocean. "It's time."

I nod again, the warm salty breeze tugging at my hair.

"Don't be a stranger, Felix." She squeezes my fingers one last time before she goes.

I watch her turn. Watch her walk away.

And then it's just us. I rest my hand on the top of the headstone and squat down before it. My insides twist so tightly they ache as my gaze moves over the engravement. The pebbles and ornaments. The tiny bottles of sand I've brought back from every new beach I've visited over the years.

I clear my throat and take the ocean-worn glass from my pocket. "I found this on the beach this morning." I place it beside the other trinkets. "It made me think of you." Scrubbing my hand down my face, I let out a long sigh. "This doesn't mean I'll forget us, Rosa. I just … she makes it better. She makes *me* better."

THIRTY-TWO

Laia

Be careful what you wish for, baby girl.

I push my fingers into the soft pie dough and glance at the time on the oven, puffing a curl from my face, picturing my dad's half amused, half smug lip quirk.

His words are definitely more than apt today.

Simon called. He wants twenty pies by tonight for tomorrow's breakfast shift at the hotel. They're already on the menu.

Felix is supposed to be picking me up in fifteen minutes to go to Kenzi's parents' party.

And I'm still in my pajamas.

I should have said no. Should have told Simon I need more time. I have other commitments. I *need* more time.

It's too late now though. I've committed.

I hunker down and peek into the oven. *No.* The lights on, but … I jerk open the door. "*No.*" No heat. The pies crusts are raw. These should be done by now. "No, no, no, no, no," I whisper, bashing the buttons semi-hysterically. They need to be done by now. I need the next four in and baking. "Why are you not working?" A knot ties up my stomach when I lift my gaze to the mango mixture and the new chocolate and chili filling, I finally perfected at two this morning with no Felix to keep my nightmares at bay. He asked me to stay at his place. I didn't. I couldn't. Some silly part of me figured staying there, with Felix, is like letting Damon win by default. Even if the flowers weren't from him.

I worry my bottom lip between my teeth and push those thoughts back. I need to find an oven. Kenzi's already at her parents' helping set up. I can't ask her to come back to let me into her place. My eyes sting and my pulse thuds in my ears.

I can't let Simon down. This is my chance.

A knock at the front door has me freezing, still crouched down, finger mid-jab of the oven's timer button.

Panic prickles down my spine. I don't want to let Felix down either. It's a big deal going to this party together. Like *together* together.

I hurry to the front door, peek through the looky hole then swing it open.

Felix's gaze takes a slow trip down my body, over my pajamas then back up to my face, a dimple appearing in one of his cheeks. "Though I really, *really* love those shorts, I think the party might be a tiny bit more formal."

A puff of a laugh escapes before my face crumples. "I can't come—Simon wants more pies, and my oven, and…" I shake my head and move back when he steps across the threshold. "I'm sorry. I can't get everything done *and* go to the party. I'm letting everyone down."

"Slow down." He grips my shoulders then smooths his hands up the sides of my neck. "What's wrong?"

His touch settles my nerves enough for me to pull in a deep breath. The buttons of his white shirt dig against my palms when I press them to his chest, my gaze lifting to meet his. "Simon's asked for twenty pies by tonight, but my oven is broken. It's not working, and I can't mess this up. I can't let him down. I need an oven and more time. And you … you look so … good. *so you*, but I can't go with you. I'm sorry. Please don't be mad."

"I'm not mad."

"You're not mad?" He's not mad. He's not even scowling. My head shakes, my eyes stupidly teary at the little half-smile still playing on his lips. Of course he's not mad. He's Felix. Not Damon. He's the anti-Damon. "You should still go, though. Mrs. Devon left me a key. Maybe I can use her kitchen." I wipe my hands down my shorts and glance through the arch into my mess of a kitchen, momentarily distracted by the flowers peeking out of the trash can.

"Use my oven."

My head snaps back to him. "Really?" His oven would work. His oven would more than work.

He shrugs a shoulder and rocks back on his heels. "Yeah."

My smile is huge and toothy. "Really, really?"

"I like watching you bake." He grips my hips and runs his teeth over his bottom lip before it curves up into a smirk. "Especially if you keep the shorts on."

"Wait. No. What about the party?" I pull out of his hold. "You can't miss it because of me." I push my fingers into my tied-back hair. "I'll figure this out. I'll call Mrs. Devon. I'll go to her place. You should definitely go to the party." I shake my head. "This is my problem. Go. Have fun." I might have admitted to myself that I like him. And even that I want more with him, but depending on him to fix my problems? That's not a hole I'm prepared to fall into. I don't ever want to owe anyone again for anything. Not even Felix.

His big arm is wrapped around my waist, and I'm pulled back to him the second I start for the kitchen. "I'm not going without you." He catches my lips in a soft kiss and I melt, literally puddle by his feet. "Pack up everything you need and let's go."

My teeth sink into the inside of my cheek. "I just … I don't want to get used to you fixing things for me."

His forehead creases and he scratches at the scruff over his jaw. "What if I like fixing things for you? What if fixing things for you is my new thing?"

I frown hard and shake my head. "I don't want to owe you anything."

His face sobers instantly, his eyebrows lowering as he scans my face.

"I didn't mean … I meant…" My thumb lifts to my mouth, my teeth finding the corner of my nail. "I shouldn't have said anything."

He gently tugs my hand back down. "Let's get one thing straight, Laia. When I offer my help, it's because I want to. No strings. I'm not that guy."

My chin trembles and my cheeks heat, but I nod, my fingers twisting in front of me. "You're right. I'm sorry. I—"

My words are cut off with another kiss. A kiss that feels a lot like distraction. I part my lips. He slides his hands down to my ass and lifts me easily, pressing me against the wall in front of the wide-open front door.

Switch officially flipped. I rake my fingers through his hair and arch into his hold, my lips hard against his until he pulls back, half panting, half laughing. "And no more apologizing." His eyes twinkle as he slides me down his body until my bare feet hit the cold tile, then he wanders off beneath the arch that leads to the kitchen.

If baking with Felix when we were *just friends* was fun, then baking with him now that we're more is something else entirely.

I bend to shut the door of his sleek, stainless-steel oven and peek through the glass at my pies. "Last batch in."

My ass is stroked, his presence behind me—comforting. And nice. And *hot.*

"I think baking might be my new thing too." His voice is rough but tinged with humor. He's been like this all afternoon. Touching, laughing, *helping.* Not at all bothered by the mess I've made of his kitchen or my occasional flinch when his touch catches me off guard.

I straighten in his hold, my back pressed against his bare chest. He lost the shirt the second we walked through the door.

I'm not complaining.

Still in my pajama shorty shorts and a white tank, I rest my head back on his shoulder, my gaze flicking to the huge clock hanging on the charcoal accent wall of the kitchen. It's already seven o'clock. The sun's low in the sky, casting the kitchen in a warm, orange glow through the floor to ceiling windows in the living room. "Thank you for helping me." My hands drop to cover his when they wrap around my waist. "You can still make it to the end of the party if you don't mind leaving me here to finish up. I told Kenzi we'd come if we can … I can't, but you can."

His lips trail up the side of my neck, his nose pressing into my hair. "*Or* I could just stay here, and we can make *naked* pies."

A laugh bursts from me as I turn in his hold. His hands slide over my bum, his chest expanding when I tickle my fingers over his pecs to his shoulders. "By the time this batch is done, and I've packed up and taken them to the hotel the party will be done. You should go." I glance back at the pies covering almost every surface of Felix's kitchen and the mess I've still to clean up. "There's no reason for you to miss the whole thing too."

"I'm looking at my reason." The dimple in his cheek flickers, his gaze dropping to my lips then lower still before lifting to meet my stare again. "Besides, you've got chocolate on your top. I should probably stay and help you with that."

I lean back and examine my tank. Sure enough there's a big blob of chocolate filling right down the front. I shake my head, my teeth sinking into my lower lip when I return my attention to Felix's raised brows. "What did you have in mind?"

"You. Me. Shower."

I watch him out of the corner of my eyes, barely managing to fight the grin trying to take over my face. He's driving my truck, one arm resting out of the open window, the other on the wheel, the warm night air ruffling his black curls.

We've just dropped the pies at the hotel. And all I can say is—*thank God for delivery entrances.*

If Simon was surprised at my newly appointed pie delivery guy, or the fact I was wearing a man's button-down shirt as a dress, he hid it well.

I tuck my foot under myself on the bench seat and twist to face Felix as far as my seatbelt will allow. "Thank you for today. You've no idea how much it means to me."

His dimple appears when he glances my way, the angles of his face dimly lit in orange by the passing streetlights as we head out of town towards my place. "If baking days always end up with you naked, then you, lady, have got yourself an assistant for life."

A flash of him carrying me through to his gray, stone-tiled shower and washing every inch of me fires my cheeks up to dangerous temperatures.

We nearly let the pies burn.

I press my palms to my face and let out some sort of breathy laugh. "It's been a good day."

"Best I've had in a long time."

His rough voice curling around his words in that sexy-ass Cluan lilt keeps my grin stretched across my face. "Me too."

We pull up my drive, and I puff out a sigh when he cuts the engine. I'm not ready for today to be over.

I've got it bad.

The nerves and unease I usually feel at the mere thought of growing attached to a man—*to anyone* don't appear. Not even a little bit.

"I think I like you, Felix Ashur." The words are out before I can stop them. My eyes pop and I moosh my lips together to stop anything else from escaping. "I … I mean…"

"Well, Laia…" A crease appears between his eyebrows and a bemused smile lifts one side of his mouth. "Laia…?"

"You don't know my last name?" This time I definitely snort. "You've seen me naked, and you don't know my last name?"

He unclips his seat belt and pins me with a smirk so filled with humor and sexy and all the things I'm really growing to like about him and holds out his hand. "I think it's time we were officially introduced, don't you?"

I wrinkle my nose. "I'm not sure we're *there* yet."

"I've been inside you, Laia. We're there."

"Cavana," I blurt out and slide my hand into his before my cheeks just give in and explode all over the cab. "My name is Laia Cavana."

His fingers tighten around mine and he pulls me to him, his other hand lifting to cup the side of my neck. "Nice to meet you, Laia Cavana."

"Yeah … you too."

"I need to get to the bar for a bit, but I can come back." He brushes my hair behind my ear and happy flips in my chest, spreading right to the tip of my nose. "Or you can come with?"

I shake my head. "Do you mind if I don't?"

"Nope." He kisses me lightly. "I'll be an hour, tops."

This feels good and right. *I feel good and right.*

"Okay." I lift my chin and press another kiss to his lips.

"Okay." He grins, and I swear it's almost as goofy as mine.

THIRTY-THREE

Laia

I'm still all floaty and Felix-drunk when I step through the front door and lock it behind me. He'll be back in an hour. That gives me time to put fresh sheets on the bed and hide my overflowing laundry basket. I kick my flip flops off and drop my bag on the console table by the door.

Only one thing better than climbing into a freshly laundered bed … climbing into a freshly laundered bed with Felix.

I'm not sure how I got to this place, but it doesn't suck at all.

I touch my fingers to my pendant. I hope mom and dad can see this, that I didn't let Damon win. *Feel* that I'm happy again wherever they are.

Not bothering with the hall light, I pad through to my bedroom, my feet silent on cool tiles.

Hand on the light switch, I glance out the window. A shadow in the back yard catches my eye and the air in my lungs evaporates. Just gets up and departs, all traces of my smug happiness disintegrated. *Someone's out there.*

The humidity of the night is suddenly thick and cloying. I cover my mouth and force myself not to blink, still staring out of the window into the darkness.

Stay calm. Maybe I'm just imagining things. I try to get my whirring mind to focus. My lungs to start working again.

Phone, I need my phone.

It's in my purse. My cell is in my purse by the door. Heart pounding, I force myself to focus on the darkness beyond the window.

This time I'm positive. It's not my imagination. Swallowing down the panic trying to climb up my throat, I make myself move silently back through the hall to the front door.

My hands are shaking so hard I almost drop my cell when I finally manage to find it in my purse. I pull up Felix's number, trying to listen over the roar of my pulse in my ears. Back pressed against the wall, I edge towards the kitchen in the dark, torn between being sure this is nothing more than paranoia and sheer terror that it's not.

Nothing, this *has* to be nothing. I pause under the arch that separates the kitchen from the hall and peer through the French doors. Something moves past them and it's definitely man-shaped.

My breath chokes me, my eyes stinging with the need to squeeze shut and pretend that this isn't happening.

Stay calm. I press call and hold my cell to my ear with both hands.

It rings and rings.

Panic builds with each unanswered second that passes, clawing from my chest, threatening to rip right out of me.

He's not going to answer.

"Laia?" Felix picks up just as I'm about to cut the call and phone the police.

"Felix," I whisper, dropping to my butt on the floor, my back against the wall, my fingers shaking so badly I can barely keep the speaker to my ear. "Felix—I think someone's outside the house."

"You what?" His voice, loud in the eerie quiet skitters across my already frayed nerves.

"Shh—please—someone's in the backyard." My breath leaves me, a sharp sob finding its way through my shaky grip on staying calm. "I don't know what to do."

"Don't do anything, Laia. I'm two minutes away."

I close my eyes and focus on his voice, focus on the image of his face in my mind.

It works—kind of. For a brief second, I almost tell him to turn back around.

Then the handles to the French doors are rattled.

What little grip I have on stopping myself from losing my shit evaporates. This is it. He's found me. He's really found me.

I give in to the panic, hot tears rolling down my cheeks. I press my lips together in an attempt to stay quiet.

"Laia?" Felix's tinny voice calls to me from my phone. "Baby, talk to me. Stay on the line."

"Someone's trying to get in the kitchen door." Fear snakes down my spine, I can barely breathe past the knot in my throat.

"Fuck. Okay, Laia. I need you to stay calm. Can they see you?"

My tongue scrapes like sandpaper across the roof of my mouth, terror prickling over my skin. I shake my head. "It's dark. I don't think so." This cannot be real. This isn't happening. Please don't let this be happening.

The front door handle rattles as if in answer to my delusional praying.

"Felix! He's at the front door. Please. Hurry."

"I'm right around the corner. Sit tight." His voice cracks on the last word. "I won't let him hurt you. Just stay put."

I move my head in a jerky nod, unable to get my mouth to form words.

"Laia? Laia! Talk to me." The panic in his deep voice only adds to the hysterics building in my throat.

"Laia, fuck. Say something."

The rumble of the truck's engine and the screech of its breaks loosens the twisting in my chest, and I give up trying to hold the phone to my ear and just hold it to my mouth instead. "I'm here. I'm okay."

"Laia, I'm outside."

I hear his car door, footsteps, the hard banging on my front door.

"Open the door. It's me."

Relief so acute it almost winds me, brings on a fresh wave of tears as I stumble through the darkness to open the door.

Felix

I've only been this scared once in my life. It burns up my spine and twists my insides in a grip so tight I can barely breathe past it.

I turn my back to Laia's front door and squint into the shadows, a fury I'm pretty sure I've never felt curling my fists so tight my fingers are numb.

If that worthless piece of shit is here looking for her, he'd better pray I don't get my hands on him.

After what seems like an eternity, Laia opens the door.

Her eyes are wide—glassy with fear, her bottom lip trembling like she's only just keeping it together.

I drag her to me before she gets a word out, crushing her to my chest. She shakes, almost violently, but doesn't pull back or resist my touch. She sinks into me, wrapping her arms around my waist, her fingers gripping the back of my T-shirt.

She's barefoot and still wearing my shirt. I rub my hand across her back. Partly to comfort her, partly to assure myself she's really there.

"It's gonna be okay." I tug her back to look into her face. Fuck, she's pale. I swallow hard, taking in the pinch to her lips, her wide eyes, the tears wetting her cheeks.

My fingers flex on her biceps. Breathe. Losing my shit won't help anything.

I pull in an exaggerated breath, my nostrils flaring, then release it slowly. "You okay?"

"He was here. He tried to get in." Her head shakes, the muscles in her throat contracting and releasing. "It's him. I know it's him. He's here."

"I'm going to look around out back." I try to pull away, twisting to look over my shoulder into the garden, the feeling of being watched prickling down the back of my neck.

"Don't … please don't leave me alone."

Her broken whisper locks into place something in my chest.

I cup her cheeks and walk her backwards through the door. "I'm not going anywhere."

I move in a weird sort of daze, calm, like I'm not ready to shred a man to bits, like a fury isn't bubbling just beneath my skin.

Laia's quiet. Nervous. Flinching every time I so much as look at her.

It's like going back in fucking time—like any progress we've made has been blown out of the goddamn water.

I place a hot cup of sweetened tea on the counter beside where she's perched. She's changed into leggings and a shapeless gray tank. "Jackson will be here any minute."

A muscle in my jaw ticks at the almost violent tremor of her hands when she picks up the mug, nodding and blinking and not meeting my stare.

I'll kill him. I will fucking kill the son-of-a-bitch.

"We need to check that whoever it was isn't still out there." I turn and lean against the worktop beside her, ignoring her flinch as I wrap my arm around her shoulders and tug her into my side.

She doesn't pull away, she just carefully puts her tea down and leans into me, reaching up to link her fingers through mine on her shoulder.

The tension buzzing at the base of my skull eases a little. Maybe not back to square one.

Her sigh is long and weary. "I'm going to have to tell them about Damon." She lifts her gaze to mine, fresh tears wetting her cheeks.

"Laia, what that" —I grind my teeth and force my anger down— "what he did to you wasn't your fault. You've nothing to be ashamed of."

Her eyes shine with a fear that tears at me, but she nods.

If anything had happened to her…

I hold her gaze and move so I'm standing in front of her. "I don't know what I would have done if something had happened to you. Us—this." I press my palm to her chest over her heart. "I want this for real. I want your long stories and your short stories. The good and the bad. All of it."

She blinks slowly, sucks her bottom lip into her mouth and for once I've not a clue what she's thinking even though she's staring me straight in the face.

I rub up the back of my neck and prepare for that wall to slam down—for her to shut herself down from me again.

It doesn't. She doesn't.

Color slowly creeps up her face for the first time since I walked through the door. "Me too. I mean yes, I mean, what you said." She rolls her eyes and presses her lips together, her nose wrinkling like it always does when she gets flustered.

I guide her knees apart to get closer. She doesn't flinch, she just leans into me and buries her face in my neck.

Banging on the door puts a halt, for better or worse, to any more admissions.

I kiss her forehead and smooth my hands down her arms. "That'll be him."

Laia

I stand behind Felix and grip the waist of his shorts as he opens the door. I know it's Jackson, but that does nothing to stop my heart from pounding in my eyeballs.

He nods at me over Felix's shoulder in his black Clua police uniform, his shield glinting in the hallway light where its hanging around his neck. Calm and controlled. This is the first time I've laid eyes on the man, but after our girl's night and Rae's stories I feel like I already sort of know him.

"I'm sorry for the trouble." I stare out into the blackness behind him, my heartbeat picking right back up again.

"No worries, Laia." He lifts his chin. "Jackson, by the way." His dark eyes are, steady, *kind.* "If you don't mind, I'll take a look around out here, see if we can't figure out what's going on.

He turns and the handgun holstered on his hip catches my attention.

Maybe I should get one too. I swallow thickly. Stupid idea, with my luck I'd probably end up shooting myself by accident.

Felix's big body practically vibrates with tension as he closes the door then turns to face me, linking his fingers through mine. "I think it's time you tell me exactly what this guy wants."

I nod and let him tug me through to the living room. Sit numbly on the sofa, my fingers twisting in my lap.

"Me, Felix. He wants me." Tears and fear and shame prick behind my eyes and I tighten my jaw to stop myself from crying. It doesn't help anything. "He warned me he'd come for me if I ever left…" I blow out a breath then swallow thickly, lick my lips and lift my stare to meet his. "He won't stop."

Felix's eyebrows are tipped up, his lips pressed into a severe line.

"I don't know what I'd do if he did something to you, or Kenzi or—"

"He won't get near enough to hurt us." Felix's hands cup the sides of my neck, and he rests his forehead against mine. "I will keep you safe, Laia. I promise you, I will keep you safe."

A long ten minutes passes before Jackson makes it back from checking out the backyard.

Knees pulled up to my chest, hand clasped tightly in Felix's, I watch him sit on the sofa opposite.

He looks between us, not a trace of a smile on his face, and the lingering hope that it was just kids messing around or a thief trying his luck vanishes.

"Someone's been watching the place," Jackson starts, a deep furrow between his eyebrows. "There are footprints in the sand outside your bedroom window, and smudges on the glass." He flicks his gaze to Felix, then back to me as he leans forward to rest his elbows on his knees. "Is there anybody that would have reason to be watching you? I'll send someone over to pull some prints from the door handles, but if you've got an idea of who it is…"

I press both hands to my mouth and nod, the need to run from this whole messed up situation strong. I could just pack my bags and be gone on the first ferry off the island.

Disappear again. Start over new.

"Her ex," Felix grinds out, winding his arm around my shoulders when seconds pass and I've still not said a word.

I square my shoulders.

Leaving isn't an option. This is my home now.

Both men are staring now, waiting for me to explain.

"My ex, Damon was … is…" I swallow again trying to dislodge the lump in my throat. "He's … he told me that if I ever left him, he would find me, and when he did, he'd…" I shake my head and look at the floor, my cheeks cold and clammy. "He found me in the place I moved to in Arizona and now he's found me here."

My voice sounds defeated, even to me.

Felix's grip on me tightens, but I can't seem to make myself react.

"I can't say whether it was him, Laia." Jackson steeples his fingers, his elbows resting on his knees, his voice still so calm I could believe that he's never lost his temper in his life. "But there's definitely been *someone* out there. I'm gonna need a photo and his details. If he's here, we'll find him."

"It's him. He's here. I can feel it."

THIRTY-FOUR

Felix

I unlock the front door of my house and push it open. She's been quiet the whole drive here, lost in memories of God knows what. I don't want to know, don't trust myself not to hunt the bastard down. If he's here—if he thinks he can take her from me in any way shape or form…

Her bags in my hands, I hold the door open with my back and let her walk past me into the house.

"Thanks." She wraps her arms around herself and stares at the floor as I close the door, her face devoid of color—of everything that makes her who she is, and it kills me.

Her bags thud to the ground when I drop them by the bottom stair. She looks so small, so fragile against the massive door it's almost hard to look at her knowing what she's had to survive, what must be going on inside her head.

I sigh sharply and take a step towards her. "You can stay here until we figure this out, Laia. For as long as you want. You're not in this alone anymore."

She'll never be alone again if I can help it.

The instant I'm within touching distance, she's on me. Arms wrapped around my neck, breasts crushed against my chest, lips on my chin, my jaw, anywhere she can reach.

Hands on her shoulders, I gently push her back. "Laia, this isn't—"

"He's in my head." Her bottom lip trembles. "I need him out of my head." Wide green eyes blink up at me, begging me to make it go away, breaking my fucking heart.

My jaw clenches so hard it aches at the fear and broken sadness shining in her gaze.

A tear slips down her pale cheek and, in that moment, I'm pretty sure I'd do anything she asked me to.

"I can make you forget." I dip my head and brush my lips over hers. Walk her back until her back hits the door, then kiss her again, harder, holding her face, tipping her head back so I can tilt my head and take it deeper.

She pulls in a breath and arches her body into mine, nipping my bottom lip with her teeth, sucking my tongue and moaning into my mouth, her hand snaking down between us, gripping me through my shorts.

I break the kiss on a pant. "Bedroom."

"No. Now." She shakes her head and reaches for my T-shirt, pushing up my body, until I have to help her pull it over my head.

Staring at my chest, she slips off her tank and her bra, her face still ashen, the skin around her eyes tight.

This isn't seduction. It isn't romance. She wants to forget, and she's using me to do it.

My tongue slides across my bottom lip when she glances up to my face as she pushes her leggings down. The warm night air thickens with the stress rolling off her when she meets my stare, pools of emerald green begging me to take over until the only thing in her head is me.

"Please." Brows tilted up in the middle, lips turned down, she takes a shuddering breath and something inside me shatters.

I wrap my hand around the back of her neck and kiss her long and hard, my tongue sliding over hers, my fingers knotting in her hair until her breath hitches in her throat and her eyelids flutter closed, the tightness around them easing. Her whole body arches into mine until her breasts brush my pecs, the tension in her muscles easing a little more with every touch of my tongue and graze of my lips.

I pull back. Press my forehead to hers, both of us panting, my hands engulfing her delicate neck on either side, thumbs brushing her jaw.

Not even a second passes before the tightness is back, that fucking haunted pain dulling the green before my very eyes.

"I'll make you forget." My voice is rough, barely more than a growl as I drop to my knees before her, my gaze fixed on her face. "I'll make you forget." I press a kiss to her belly.

Her fingers sink into my hair, and she takes another long breath that lifts her small up-turned breasts, but she nods.

Still holding her stare, I press my mouth to the smooth mound of her sex and guide her leg over my shoulder.

The scent of her fills my head. Vanilla. Sweet and clean. The knowledge that I'm the only man to have ever had her like this, to ever have touched her like this, stirs something primal inside me. I part her folds and run my tongue from her ready entrance to the hard knot of her clit then press it flat against the tiny bundle of nerves. Her hips rock, her fingers twisting in my hair. Lips closed, I suck gently and her back comes away from the wall with a hiss of my name.

My cock throbs, painfully hard in the confines of my shorts. I ignore it and keep going until she's pushing onto my face, her eyes closed, her mouth open in a wordless plea.

A low growl vibrates from my chest as I hold her open and thrust my tongue into her. She circles her hips, her movements jerky, her muscles pulsing around my tongue until I replace it with my fingers, thrusting them hard and fast, sucking her clit, letting her grind onto me until her body goes rigid, her grip on my hair grows almost painful and she comes, sagging against the door once the tremors stop.

Laia

My heart is beating so hard it can't be healthy, my breathing coming in fast pants, spinning my head, my whole body is buzzing with … I don't even know what, I can't think.

I stare down my body to where Felix is on his knees watching me carefully. Concerned. Worried. I shake my head, but can't find any words, still riding high on happy just-orgasmed endorphins.

The moment doesn't last nearly long enough. As soon as the fog clears the fear returns, fisting my windpipe until it's suffocating me—until Damon's in there again.

"More," I whisper, my voice not my own.

"Laia, we should talk about this." Felix links his fingers through mine, his intense blue stare pleading for something I just don't have to give right now.

Bravery. Strength. The ability to face this head on.

"I need you." I sink to my knees in front of him. With shaking hands, I reach for his shorts—for his belt buckle. The moment he's inside me, I'll forget—be taken to that place where nothing else exists or matters beside the two of us and how he makes me feel.

"Laia," he groans when I snap the belt from its buckle then undo the button beneath. "This is not the way to deal—"

"I don't want to deal with it, I want to forget it." I shake my head and lower his zip, free him from his shorts and wrap my fingers around his solid girth.

His hand covers mine and my gaze snaps up to meet his heavy-lidded stare. "Please. I can't—" my breath hiccups in my throat.

His eyebrows lower, but he doesn't pull back, he adds more pressure and guides my hand over the length of him, his attention staying on my face, concern written in every hard line of his forehead and tick of his jaw.

It's too much. Too open. *Too raw.*

I drop my gaze back to our hands, the crown of his cock, slick and dark, his abs pulled tighter with every slow stroke.

The need to have him inside me is almost overwhelming.

Without a word, I lift myself onto my knees and straddle his hips, at the first touch of him between my legs I meet his stare again, my mouth falling open as I lower myself onto him.

"Laia, I…"

I quiet whatever he's about to say with my mouth on his and push down again, my breath stuttering at the stretch to accommodate his thickness. Hands on my hips, his gaze flicks to where we're joined then back to my face and his pupils dilate. And then he's pulling me down, filling me with an almost pained groan.

Everything just *clears*, my mind focused solely on the feel of him parting the tight walls of my core, on how his hardness pushes past my body's resistance. Exactly what I need. I grind down into his lap, claiming every inch, every solid millimeter of him. His fingers dig into the soft flesh of my ass, but he doesn't guide me, just lets me ride him, lets me take my pleasure from him any way I want until I'm clenching around him, pulsing, and tightening and squeezing, my clit rubbing against the solid wall of muscle at the base of his cock until sparks shoot up my spine and everything else just falls away.

His stare stays locked on mine, eyes intense with worry and heat and lust.

I rock faster, take him deeper. "Harder."

His breath brushes my face, and his grip on me tightens, guiding me up and dragging me back down, thrusting into me, harder and faster until an oblivion-inducing climax starts to grow in the depths of me.

A ripple of heat unfurls to the pounding rhythm of my heart, enveloping me in a wave of sensation, of mind-bending, fear-numbing sensation. I link my feet behind his back and writhe against him, riding the crest of it, dragging him with me until with a hoarse whisper of my name, he crushes me to him and follows me over.

Still panting like I've run a marathon, I stroke his serious face, brush a damp curl from eyes that watch me carefully, intensely, *protectively*. I smooth my thumb over the twitching muscle of his jaw, and trace the full line of his bottom lip, completely sure of only one thing.

I love him. I'm not going anywhere.

I wake with the sunrise.

Wrapped in Felix's arms, I can almost kid myself that everything is fine—that everything is *going* to be fine. If it wasn't for the fact that I know it's not. Nothing's going to be fine, and nothing can stop the niggling voice in the back of my mind.

Run. Run. Run.

I lie there, listening to Felix's steady breathing, trying to keep my mind from straying back to last night and what would have happened if he hadn't picked up the phone.

Damon tried to get in.

Every time I close my eyes, I can see him. His face. The sneer that curled his lip a second before his fist connected. The cold smugness that lit his eyes if I cried out.

All of it on repeat.

I need to get up, I'm freaking myself out.

With huge effort I wiggle free from Felix's arms and tiptoe from the room, grabbing his T-shirt from the floor as I pass.

He doesn't even twitch. I'm not surprised, he barely slept last night. Neither of us did. *My fault.*

My eyes flick to the huge windows before I sneak out the door. Was it really just yesterday I was looking out of that window, happy and content and safe?

I stare at the ceiling to stop the tears, my breath releasing.

Coffee. I need it.

In the kitchen, I spoon coffee grains into the machine and fill the pot with hot water. I need to jumpstart my frazzled brain. Last night, the decision had been simple. I love him, I'm staying. He won't let anything happen to me.

But now, in the cold light of day, it doesn't seem fair. Felix has a business, friends, *family*. I can't expect him to put that all to one side for me. He shouldn't have to, and I don't want him to. I won't rely on anyone to keep me safe. I can't. Not anymore. Not when I know what's coming.

I know what Damon is capable of. He followed me here, he'll follow me away from here too.

I should leave before anyone gets hurt.

Leave them all behind.

Felix. Kenzi. Mrs. Devon. Mylo. Pete and Simon. Rae and the girls. *Clua.*

My stomach rolls and my eyes water just thinking about it.

I run to the sink and wretch, my insides doing their very own interpretation of a Mexican wave, cold sweat prickling over my forehead. I don't want to go.

Deep breaths. Deep, *deep* breaths.

I curl my fingers around the cold metal of the sink until my insides quiet and stop trying to take leave of my body. Apparently, my stomach and my heart are in cahoots against my head. They don't want to go either.

At the sound of footsteps upstairs, I straighten and wipe my cheeks.

"You're up early." Felix's voice is rough with sleep.

I turn with a quick smile, then return my attention to pouring a mug of freshly brewed coffee.

"Couldn't sleep." I shrug, hoping he won't notice how my hands shake as I add milk and sugar. "You want?" I try to keep my tone light like my whole world didn't just implode on itself last night—like I don't have to make the decisions between keeping him with me or keeping him safe.

He doesn't need to know anything until I've made up my mind. I move to lean against the island in the middle of the kitchen, glancing at him over the rim of my mug as I take a sip, the milky caffeine not even enough to warm my insides.

How can he be this beautiful? This good? *Meant for me?*

"Coffee can wait." He closes the distance between us, removes the mug from my hand, places it on the counter then plants his hands on either side of my thighs. "Are you okay?"

I bite my lip and nod—force myself to smile.

"Good." His gaze drops to his white Beach Hut T-shirt and where it stops high on my thighs. "I like your outfit."

My skin heats under his inspection. "My clothes were still down here after…" I trail off, tugging at the hem, gaze roaming the plains of his naked torso, drawn down to the green checked pajama pants hanging low on his hips. I was a woman on a mission last night. And each time I'd woken, he'd been ready and willing. "I'm sorry." I look away, embarrassed. "About last night."

"Don't ever be sorry for that." Hands on my waist, he lifts me to sit on the kitchen island, the marble cold against the backs of my thighs. His palms smooth over my knees, guiding them apart so he can lean between them. "As methods of distraction go…" He cups my face and presses his lips to mine in a soft kiss that instantly takes the edge off. "Yours are good."

I wrap my arms around his neck and kiss him back. "You taste like toothpaste." I breathe in, letting his heady scent fill my head and push all thoughts of leaving from my mind.

"And *you* taste like coffee." He kisses me again then sighs long and hard, his shoulders dropping, his dimples fading. "Are we gonna talk about last night?" A black curl has fallen over his forehead.

"Can we not?" A smile tugs at my lips and I run my fingers through the thick strands of his hair, pushing them back from his face. "Not yet."

When he lifts his gaze to mine, my heart stutters. I love him. The feeling is as strong now as it was last night.

"I like waking up with you here," he whispers, his hands flexing on my hips then moving to wrap me in a tight hug, his face pressed into my neck. "You smell like me." His nose runs along my collarbone before he pulls back and hits me with his dimples. "And sex. I like it."

His cell ringing cuts through my Felix-haze quick sharp, refilling my brain with the shitstorm that was last night. "Who would be phoning at this time?" I glance over to where his phone is charging on the other side of the kitchen.

With a resigned sigh he steps back, his hand lifting to rub the back of his neck. "Jackson said he'd call first thing."

I straighten and cross my ankles, gripping the edge of the black marble worktop.

"Jackson," Felix greets his friend and turns to lean back onto the worktop opposite the one I'm sitting on, his serious blue stare not moving from my face. "He did?" His eyebrows rise. "Okay, thanks, man." He nods slowly. "I'll let her know."

My mouth goes dry, my lungs shrivel, my heartbeat thuds, too heavy for my chest, barely audible over the ringing in my ears.

It's one thing to think he's here—to be *almost sure* he's here. It's another thing completely to have it confirmed.

I cover my mouth with both hands. I think I'm gonna throw up. Or faint. Or throw up *and* faint. "He's here."

Jaw ticking, Felix folds his arms over his naked chest, his gaze scanning my face. "Jackson went to the port to see if he'd arrived on the island."

I nod jerkily and press my lips together, blinking back the stupid, useless tears.

"He went through customs a week ago."

My heart sinks, my blood going cold in my veins. "He's here."

"Was." Felix moves back to stand between my thighs, rubbing his hands up and down my arms. "A Damon Black checked in and boarded the first Mexico-bound ferry this morning."

"I don't understand. He *was* here, but now he's just gone?"

"Jackson thinks something's off too. He's going to keep the detail on your place, but you're staying with me until we know more."

I nod silently.

"Talk to me." He curves his big body back so he can look into my down turned face.

I shake my head and plaster on a smile. "What's there to say, he found me."

THIRTY-FIVE

Laia

Kenzi folds her arms and leans back in her chair, a stubborn set to her jaw. "I'm not leaving, so stop telling me to, woman."

"Your shift finished over an hour ago." I focus on my computer screen and not on my over-protective friend.

I switched my cell on this morning to a dozen missed calls. And arrived to work to hugs and tears and a shed load of worry. She hasn't even told me about the party. She hasn't even pulled me up over the fact that Felix bailed on the party to help me with my pies. And that is not the Kenzi I know.

I don't want my shitty past to change things. I don't want to be just the girl that everybody is worried about. And I *really* don't want to talk about Damon and what I think he's up to. If he's here, or if he's really gone.

I want to talk about pies, or Mylo, or man bans. Hell, I'll even talk about Flappy Eyes right now. Anything to distract me from the constant replay of door handles rattling and the knowledge that Damon knows where I live, and I've not started running yet.

"So, we're sure he got on the ferry?" Kenzi pins with worried eyes, fiddling with the strap of her purse.

My heavy sigh starts at my toes and works its way right through my body until it blows past my lips and my fingers still on the keyboard. "So, the guys at the port say."

"You don't sound convinced."

I finally spin my chair to look at her. "I'm not. I don't get why he'd track me all the way here just to turn around and leave again. None of it makes sense, but I can't—I *won't* put my life on hold, not again."

"Does Pete know? I think Pete should definitely be told. He can hire an extra security guard or something. Or we can get Mylo to do it." Her eyes are wide. Worried. And about as scared as I feel. "Mylo would totally do it." She bites her lip, already pulling her cell from her purse. "I'll call him now." She pauses and her lips twist to the side. "Or maybe you should call him. Things are kind of weird between us right now. Oh. Maybe we can get Jackson to post someone here."

"Kenzi." I reach over and clasp her bouncing knee. "Calm. Please. He's just one guy." *One fucked-up sociopath of a guy.* I swallow down the unease that's been twisting my gut all day and force a smile. "Felix will be dropping me off and picking me up until we make sure he's not coming back. Okay?" I widen my eyes when she shakes her head and opens her mouth to say more. "Okay?"

She nods, but her bottom lip pouts out. "Okay."

"So, you can go home now. You're working in the bar tonight. You need to go home and chill out. I'm fine. I'm safe. I promise." I offer her what I can only hope is a reassuring smile.

She lets out a yawn, covering her mouth with both hands. "I did have a pretty late night." She blinks and the Kenzi I know and love is back. "We missed you at the party. And Fee. You guys were the talk of it until Rylie showed up and refused alcohol."

I stop spinning back to my desk and twist back to face her.

The mischief sparking in her eyes settles something inside me. Like a little bit of normality. "So, Rylie wasn't drinking? Why would that be talk of a party?"

Her face breaks into an excited grin. "Rylie is my partner in wine. She never misses an excuse to party."

I shrug, still completely lost.

"She's pregnant, Laia. She found out after our girls night when her hangover lasted a week."

"That's great news. Wait. *Is* that great news?"

"She and Kane have been together forever. It's great news."

The happy on her face is fleeting, her lips turning down and her eyebrows tipping up in the middle. "You left Arizona when he found you there. Does that mean you're going to leave here too?"

I can't meet her stare. Can't lie to her and tell her I'm one hundred percent staying either. "I want to stay, but I won't if it's going to put everybody else at risk."

"You're safe in Clua with us—safer than out there on your own. But if you leave, I'm coming with you. Don't even try to stop me."

Tears of a different kind sting behind my eyes and before I know what I'm doing I've got my friend in a bear hug.

If she's surprised, she doesn't show it, she just rubs my back and hugs me right back.

THIRTY-SIX

Felix

Laia sinks down into the warm water and lies back against my chest. Her hair in its usual knot on the top of her head, tickles my chin as she makes herself comfortable.

"Is this the kind of treatment I should expect every night? Bubble baths and back rubs?"

"Maybe." I take a sponge from a shelf built into the wall and squeeze water over her shoulders, watching the bubbles snake over her sun-kissed skin. "It's been a rough couple of days." Shifting beneath her, I lift my leg and rest my foot on the edge of the tub to give her more space. It's a big bath, but I'm not exactly small. Can't say I was thinking about sharing it when I fitted it.

A comfortable silence settles around us. I like having her here. In my home. I like picking her up from work, knowing she's safe. Having her with me.

Closing my eyes, I allow myself to drift and just enjoy her skin against mine and the feel of her fingers trailing over my leg. Being with her like this may not have been in either of our plans, but I'm having a hard time thinking of anywhere else I'd rather be.

"You never did tell me what this means." Laia's question breaks the quiet, her fingers following the lines of the tattoo on my calf.

"I think we should get this," Rosa says in her musical lilt, holding up the picture she's pulled from the printer in the library.

I shake my head and take the paper from her. "I thought you wanted to get something that means something. This is our wedding gift. I don't want some ancient crap." I turn the paper upside down. "Come on. No one even knows for sure what it means."

"No, you come on, Fee, this does mean something—look." Pulling her waist length black hair over her shoulder, she nudges my arm up so she can sit on my lap. "Look at this part here…" She lifts the paper so we can both see. "These two lines, see how they curve and bend with each other?" She runs a finger along the two thick black lines that run from one side of the image to the other. "To me, they are us."

I still, watching her face light up the way it always does when she talks about art.

"And these dots and swirls, the way they fit perfectly into each other on either side, they're our friends and family. It's us Felix. I think we should get this."

Nuzzling my face into her neck, I breathe in the citrus-fresh scent of her perfume. "How can I say no to that?" I press my lips over the gentle thrum of her pulse. "If you say they're us, then I guess they're us."

"It was Rosa's wedding gift to me." I cough to clear the roughness to my voice. "She had the same design on her ribs."

Laia stops tracing my skin and turns just enough to catch my stare. "Felix, you don't have to talk about this if you don't want to. I understand."

I know she does. And for the first time ever the memories are there, still sad, still painful, but the emptiness that usually accompanies them is less. Way less. Like this little woman with the big green eyes and dark blonde curls is filling that space. Replacing the emptiness with her grins and her fidgeting and her pies and her kisses. I skim my finger along her jaw and tilt her head so I can see her face. "She was an artist. Did you know that?"

She shakes her head before she lies back down against my chest, her hair tickling my nose again. "I didn't."

"She could look at any image and find meaning in it. It didn't matter if the meaning she found wasn't what the artist had in mind. To her the best thing about art was that it's meaning was objective, completely unique to each person."

Laia lifts my hands and links her fingers through mine. "She sounds cool."

Pressing a kiss to her shoulder, I rub my thumb over the pulse in her wrist. "She was. You would have liked her."

"How did she … what happened to her?" Laia's body instantly tenses against mine, her ears flushing pink, her head shaking against my chest. "I'm sorry, I shouldn't have asked that. Don't answer."

I suck in a lungful of steamy, vanilla-scented air then release it. These thoughts do hurt. I doubt they'll ever stop. "I'm surprised you've not been told already." Dropping her hand, I urge her forward so I can stand, the memories too painful to sit still with. "She was hit by a car on her way to work. Died instantly. In one second my whole world was turned upside down. It was like one minute I had everything I'd ever wanted, the next I had nothing. She was twenty-one. We'd just signed the papers on The Beach Hut."

Laia's shining green gaze watches me as I climb out of the tub and grab a towel. She pulls her knees up to her chest. "I'm sorry, I shouldn't have pried."

The towel wrapped around my waist, I bend forward, my hands on the edge of the tub. "The road you were driving the day we met."

Her mouth falls open then slams closed again. "I had no idea."

"Laia, meeting you has…" I squat down until my eyes are level with hers. "I didn't think I would ever find this again. Didn't think I wanted to. Meeting you has made me—fuck. I don't know—it's made me give a shit after a decade of feeling nothing. Meeting you has changed everything."

THIRTY-SEVEN

Laia

For the next few weeks, life goes on almost as normal, if you don't count Felix's hovering, or the fact that Mylo has taken to dropping by whenever Felix can't be there, or the horrible, twisty, sick feeling that took up root in my stomach that morning and hasn't budged since.

I get it. I do. And I appreciate the concern and the protection. But after over aa year of living by myself, the lack of alone-time is starting to get kinda suffocating.

"The pies have been a pretty big success in the hotel." I grin over to where Felix is sitting across the island counter from me.

"I hear you sacked Mylo." Felix watches me carefully as he takes a drink from his glass of water.

He's right, I sacked Mylo from his unofficial bodyguard duties. He was exhausted between working all day on the Surf school, helping out in The Beach Hut, and appearing on my doorstep whenever Felix had to stay late at the bar. I wasn't sure when he'd been finding time to sleep.

I was going to tell Felix. Eventually.

I stare at my plate, chasing a cherry tomato around with my fork. It's taken Mylo three days to rat me out, or for Felix to bring it up. Either way, I haven't been looking forward to this conversation.

My tummy knots. I ignore it. Felix doesn't lose his temper. In fact, I'm pretty sure I have a worse temper than he has. But, even knowing this, and trusting him completely, the threat of confrontation still has a knack of setting me on edge.

I flick my gaze up to his steady blue stare. "It's been over a month now. It's not fair to Mylo. Or you." I automatically check for his tells. No jaw ticking. Yet. We're good. "Mylo has better things to do with his weekends, and I love you, but I *need* some time to myself, just like you must need some time to yourself. Now let's talk about my pies some more. The manager of Clua Coffees would like some samples." I beam a cheesy million-watt grin at him. "If I can get all of the Clua Coffees on the island on my books, I think I can hand in my resignation at The Castle. Maybe I'll even open my own pie shop one day, how cool would that be? You wouldn't have to deal with my pies taking over your kitchen anymore."

My excited babbling trails off at the dumbfounded look on Felix's face. His eyes are twinkling and his lips tilt in a lopsided grin I don't think I've ever seen him wear before.

"What?" I place my fork down beside my plate. "Do I have spinach?" I run my tongue along my teeth. "Stop looking at me like that." I wrinkle my nose when his lopsided grin evens itself out into a bemused smirk and he leans forward in his chair, scrutinizing my face.

I shift awkwardly. "Felix, what?"

"You don't even realize you said it, do you?"

"That I need a little me time?" I roll my eyes and stand to lift his plate along with my own. "Don't you need a little time to do man stuff?"

"No, not that—just." His dimples flicker in his stubbled cheeks and he shakes his head. "Nothing—nothing at all."

I screw up my face but can't stop my own smile from tipping my lips as I take the plates to the sink. "It's a good job you're handsome."

"I don't feel good leaving you on your own yet." He leans his elbows on the island and scrubs his fingers through his hair, leaving it sticking up all over the place.

I sigh. I can't help it. So, so handsome.

"And *I* don't like being a burden." I hold his stare as I turn on the hot tap. "Please, Felix, I just want to forget about Damon. *If* he comes back, then Jackson will know. They have his details at the port. And Rae has been giving me boxing lessons. Seriously—I'm almost ninja level already." I turn my attention to running the soapy washcloth over the plates and setting them on the drying rack. "Maybe he took one look at you and your friends and decided I'm not worth the headache. Picking fights with people bigger than him was never his thing."

"First of all," Felix whispers into my ear from right behind me, making me jump about a foot in the air. "You're not a burden. And second of all." —he kisses the back of my neck— "I like waking up with you." He bites my earlobe, wraps his arms around my waist and props his chin on the top of my head.

I meet his gaze in our reflection in the window above the sink. "Felix—"

"I just don't want anything to happen to you." His forehead lines in his reflection and my heart thuds at the honesty of his words.

He's not trying to control me or take my freedom. He just cares enough to worry. I *do* get it.

I twist in his arms to face him. "Do you expect us to live like this forever?" I run my wet hands up his forearms and the muscles under his smooth, tan skin twitch beneath my touch. "And as great as it's been having Mylo over every weekend and being with you every night, I want my life back." I bite my lip and watch his face as I change direction and push my hands under the hem of his T-shirt, stroking the ridges of his abs with my fingertips.

It never gets old having a man this perfectly molded.

"You're trying to distract me." His voice is rough and deep, and tinged with the gravel he always gets when he's thinking about getting naked.

"Is it working?" I lift onto my toes to kiss the ticking muscle in his jaw.

"I'm not happy with this, Cavana." His brow lowers into a scowl, but he dips his head so I can reach his mouth. *Only a little pissed then.*

I tease the seam of his lips with my tongue. "Don't pout."

"Your first night home alone, huh?"

I twist the key in the lock and push my front door open, holding my cell to my ear with my other hand.

Kenzi called the second I pulled into the drive. I finished my shift at the hotel then came straight home. By myself. It's sad how much I'm looking forward to finally finishing my book in a bubble bath with a nice cold glass of white.

"It is, and I can't wait," I say, careful not to show even the slightest hint of fear in my voice. It's there, but so is the *need* for a night on my own. Right now, that need outweighs even my ever-present tummy spins. "Being with Felix every night has been…" I squint, trying to think of the right word as I close and relock the door behind me, pulling the four dead bolts across. Our first argument. Who buys not one, but two extra bolts? The argument lasted precisely five minutes and a brief make-out session in the lock department of the hardware store. He won. Obviously.

"Intense, it's been really, *really* amazing, but pretty intense."

Throwing my keys and purse down by the door, I kick off my shoes and wander through to the living room. "I'm already missing him, but I'm so ready for some alone-time. I wanna shave my legs without worrying about leaving a mess in the bathroom. I wanna be able to pig out on chocolate without feeling like a fat ass because he's just done two hours in the gym. And the sex, my God, Kenzi, I've never had so much fantastic sex in my life—but my lady-bits need a rest."

"So, you don't want me to come over then?" The smile in her voice is impossible to miss. It's not just been me and Felix this whole everybody-look-after-Laia month has been draining for. Kenzi has been around almost as much as Mylo even though things between them are still strained.

I'm pretty sure I'm not the only one ready to relax a little.

"I love you for offering, but I think I'm good." I flop down onto my hugging sofa, wiggling my butt down into the soft cushions.

"I'm just a phone call away if you need me." Even over the phone, I can hear that she's no longer smiling.

"I know you are. Thank you, but I'll be fine. I'll see you tomorrow."

I cut the call and toss my cell onto the cushion beside me, closing my eyes and relishing the feeling of being alone for the first time in over a month.

It's not long before night brings darkness. And noises. And all-out anxiousness.

Okay. So. Alone time—not all it's cracked up to be.

My cell vibrates under my pillow. I reach for it groggily, what feels like about ten seconds of sleep officially over.

I flop onto my back and hold my cell above my face.

I missed you. Come see me at the bar when you get up. F x

I missed him too. Jumped at every noise. Hated not having him to curl myself around on the sofa. Missed being wrapped in his warm arms as I slept. Missed waking up surrounded by his Felix smell.

I just—missed him.

I'm on my way. Missed you too. L x

It's only eight. I suck. Girl power just died, and I don't even care.

After the quickest shower known to mankind, I throw on my denim cut-offs and a loose-fit gray T-shirt and hurry out the door.

I'm still twisting my damp hair into a bun when my flip flop catches on a large brown envelope that must have been propped against the door. It won't be for me. It never is. Mrs. Devon's son still gets some of his mail delivered to the bungalow. I normally rush it straight over to her.

But she's still in Hawaii, so it can wait.

I pick it up and stuff it into the purse slung over my shoulder. I'll swing by and leave it at her place when I come back to get ready for work later.

Felix

I glance over the delivery man's head as Laia pulls into the car park in that clapped out old truck of hers and the knot I've had in my stomach since she left yesterday loosens. I've barely slept for worrying. I didn't like not waking up to her. Not a bit.

The short, bald driver clears his throat and wiggles his receipt in my face.

I sign it without looking and absentmindedly wave him off as he climbs back into his delivery van and reverses back onto the road.

Laia jumps from her truck and slams the door shut, looking way more refreshed than I feel.

I drag my hand over my mouth and watch her walk towards me, hips swaying, pink flushing up her cheeks before I've even laid a finger on her. I keep waiting for it to fade—this effect she has on me. The need to be near her, to be the one that makes her laugh, or blush, or even wrinkle her nose.

Over a month in and it's still going strong. Stronger even, because now she's comfortable around me. No flinching or shying away. Just Laia.

Her stare roams my face then flits down to my workout gear. "You're sweaty." She wrinkles her nose, but there's no disguising the spark in her stare or the way her tongue just slid across the seam of her lips.

She likes me sweaty.

"I jogged here." I scratch my chest over my sleeveless T-shirt. "Found myself with some excess energy this morning." I can't help the grin that takes over my face when the slight flush to her skin deepens and spreads down her chest.

Has it really been less than twenty-four hours since I've made her go pink?

"I missed you." Her soft voice pulls me a step closer to her.

"Let's not do it again then." I slide a finger through one of the belt loops of her shorts and tug her to me. "I like you in my bed."

The sigh that leaves her a second before she presses her lips to mine is enough to have my cock straining against the light material of my basketball shorts. She leans in tighter and lifts onto her tiptoes, slanting her head to tease her tongue against mine. "I like me in your bed too."

I run my hands down her spine to her ass and lift her with little effort, wrap her legs around my waist and growl against her lips when she wiggles onto my dick.

It takes a whole load of self-control to walk up the steps and through the swinging doors into the empty bar and not just strip her naked right there in the car park. My lips barely leave hers to catch breath. Fuck, I could kiss her all day every day and never get bored. She kisses like she means it. Every. Fucking. Time.

And fuck if that's not addictive.

"What time does Jo start?" She asks between kisses, arching her back and clenching her thighs around me.

"Why? What do you have in mind?" I nuzzle her neck, run my tongue over her pulse as I walk us behind the bar and through the door to the back.

"I'd rather just show you." She threads her fingers into my hair and tugs my head back, rolling her hips and kissing me hard.

I kick my office door shut behind us and lower her onto my desk.

She slides her purse from her shoulder, tosses it onto the desk beside her with a flourish, then pulls me by the waistband of my shorts to stand between her legs.

"Tell me." I smooth my palms up her bare thighs until the tips of my fingers slip under the frayed denim of her cut-offs. I know she won't. She never does. Doesn't mean I don't enjoy trying to get those dirty words from her pouty lips.

"Less talking, more doing." She leans back on her elbows, knocking her purse from the desk. An envelope slides from the soft brown leather and lands on my foot.

My chuckle makes her grin as I shake my head and crouch between her legs to pick up the mess.

"Though this position definitely has potential." She sits up and strokes her fingers through my hair, her legs swinging on either side of me.

I kiss the inside of her knee, but her name printed across the front of the A4 brown envelope catches my attention and I lift to my feet. "What's this?" I flip it over, looking for a clue.

"Ah—it must have fallen out of my purse. It was on the doorstep when I left the house. Probably something for Mrs. Devon's son." She shrugs, wraps her legs around my waist and slides her fingers beneath the waistband of my shorts.

I don't move. Or react. Or even breathe. My stare still fixed on her name as I hand her the envelope. This doesn't feel right. "It's for you."

"I didn't even check. I just assumed…" She takes it from me and her smile fades along with every drop of color from her face the second she lowers her gaze to her name. She runs her finger over the hand-written letters and swallows thickly.

Shit.

"I—how can he be here?" She blinks up at me, eyes wide. Confused. *Scared.* "The port has his details. I thought…" Her head shakes and she blows out a trembling stream of air.

"Open it." I cover her hands, forcing mine not to shake with the weight of unease that's just settled in my gut. "It might *not* be from him."

"I can't." She shoves it back to me and pushes herself further onto the desk—away from it—away from me. "You open it."

My heart's thumping in my chest, in my throat, in my fucking eyeballs, but I hold her gaze and run my thumb under the seal, moving from between her legs to empty the contents onto the desk beside her.

Photos. My teeth grind until my jaw aches.

Grainy photos of us slide across the dark wood desktop, each one more graphic than the next. Her on her knees, my cock in her mouth. Her spread out on her bed, my face between her thighs. Me on my knees staring down to where my cock disappears into her from behind. And more. And more. And fucking more.

Fury crackles down my spine and I lift a trembling hand to massage the twitching in the back of my neck, every muscle coiled tight enough to split, every fucking atom of me roaring for this not to be real.

I should have known.

Laia slips off the desk to stand beside me, still oblivious to the world of shit that's about to smash her to pieces. I briefly consider hiding them—shoving them back into the envelope—let her stay blissfully ignorant. I can't though. I wouldn't.

So, I take a deep fucking breath and wait. Wait for her sharp intake of air. Wait for the wretch that wracks her body when she fully registers what she's looking at. And I feel it all with her. Her tears. Her numb shock. Her fucking desperation like it's ripping my own fucking chest out.

I can't look at her though. Can't tear my stare from the photos spread over my desk. Every touch. Every kiss. Every fucking moment, that sick fuck was there, watching.

He never fucking left.

THIRTY-EIGHT

Laia

I stare at the photos, blinking uselessly, my stomach rolling, Felix practically vibrating with anger beside me.

My stare flits from image to image, seeing them, but not. Feeling the violation, but still looking for a way for it to be some sort of mistake. It doesn't come. It's not a mistake.

An eerie coldness settles over my mind—over my emotions—over every part of me it can reach. Shock, I guess. Whatever it is, it clears the way for one single thought. One single, horrifying truth.

This is my fault.

I'd been stupid to think that this would ever work, that Damon wouldn't involve Felix. That I could actually be happy.

Felix lifts a photo, drawing my numb gaze. Taken through his kitchen window, I'm laying naked on the marble-topped island, my legs spread, Felix thrusting into me. It's just as graphic and soul-shattering as the other pictures, only this one is different—worse.

Felix's face has been scored out. Viciously. Evilly.

With intent.

My blood freezes in my veins, chilling me from the inside out when I pick up the next photo. Kenzi and Mylo—faces scored out. There are photos of Mrs. Devon, Jo, Rae, Rylie, Pete and Simon.

Everyone I care about.

Felix slams the photo in his hand down onto the desk. I flinch back a full step at the crack of the wood under the force of his blow.

"Felix, I'm sorry. I didn't think—didn't know."

He turns to face me, his jaw clenched tight, his hands fisted by his sides, his eyes burning with thinly veiled rage. He doesn't say anything. Not a word. Just turns back to the photos.

This is all my fault.

His business is here, his family, *his life*. And I've just come along with my fucked-up past and messed everything up.

I need to fix this.

Felix drags his hand over his face. "Stop. Apologizing."

I start at the hard edge to his voice, my eyes stinging as I watch him blow out a slow breath before he meets my stare again.

"Don't you—*ever* apologize for that piece of shit again, Laia." He grabs my shoulders and pulls me to him, pressing his lips to my forehead. "None of this is on you, you hear?"

I stiffen against his body, my arms wooden by my sides. I can't help it. Can't seem to make myself react to his touch. Or his words. Or his anything.

Whether he wants to believe it or not, I brought this mess down on him. *I did.*

"This isn't your fault." He repeats again, leaning back to look into my face.

I lower my gaze.

"Laia this doesn't change anything." He cups my face, tipping it back up to his. His scowl, the hurt in the tight line of his lips is painful to witness, especially knowing that it's because of me. "Laia." He juts his jaw before it clenches tightly again. "This doesn't change anything for me."

Finally, the dam my emotions seem to have been trapped behind cracks, and a whole lot of pissed seeps through. I shake free of his hold. "Are you crazy, Felix?" I sink my fingers into my hair and tug at the strands, hot tears escaping down my cheeks. "This changes *everything.*" My bottom lip trembles. I scrub my hands down my face and spin back to the desk. "I have to go. I need to leave. If I go, he goes."

"You're not going anywhere." Felix's hands clasp my shoulders.

I shy away from his touch and wrap my arms around myself. "Don't tell me what to do—not you—not now." My gaze darts to his desk and the images laid there then returns to his. "I should have left as soon as I knew he'd found me." I look away, unable to hold the hurt behind his eyes. "It is my fault."

"The fuck it's your fault." His roar is like a slap in the face. I know he won't hurt me, but right now, what I know and, more importantly, what I *feel* are completely different things.

I'm shaking and backing up and verging on an actual fucking breakdown. "Felix, please. Just let me go."

"Damn it, Laia, do not pull that wall down." Both his hands lift to the nape of his neck and scrub up the back of his head. "I'm not him. I'm not trying to control you." He drops his hands to his sides, palms up. "If you run now, he'll find you again." His fingers find mine, link through them, squeeze them in all their numbness. "Stay here. With me. Let me help you."

It's no good. It won't work. Nothing will work. "I—I can't. I'm sorry." I stare at our linked fingers, still shaking my head, still barely stopping my stomach from lurching up my throat. "There's nothing you can do."

"I'm calling Jackson. I'll get Mylo. We'll hunt him down, Laia. I can fix this—*we* can fix this." Desperation saturates his rough voice, his eyes pleading, his thumb running over my knuckles.

I shake my head.

"Laia, I love you. Do *not* let him ruin this."

"No—" My chin trembles, a sob escaping. "Felix—you can't—I can't." My face crumples. He can't love me. It's not fair. More tears fall, more cracks splintering everything inside me. I let him drag me to him, wrap my arms around his waist, press my face into his chest and breathe him in.

His smell. His heat. His strength.

He shifts, but doesn't release me, even as he pulls his cell from his pocket. "We will sort this out, Laia. Trust me."

I listen to him tell Jackson everything, his body against mine tempting me to change my mind. He thinks he can protect me, and maybe he can, but at what cost? What if Damon decides to post the photos on the internet? Plaster them all over town? Show them to his family?

The thought of leaving Felix is literally turning my stomach. But what are my options? Stay here and wait for Damon to come out of whatever rock he's hiding under? Wait for him to make his move? To hurt someone around me to get to me? I wouldn't put it past him, and I couldn't live with myself if someone else gets hurt because I'm too selfish to do the right thing. I close my eyes and breathe in his Felix smell. Try to burn it into my mind. Fresh air and peppermint and him.

The second he cuts the call to Jackson he has the phone to his ear again. "Mylo, I need your help, man." He kisses my head then releases me to walk back to the desk to pick up the envelope.

"I didn't expect to see you here so early."

I jump violently at Jo's unexpected appearance in the office doorway.

"Not now, Jo," Felix snaps, gathering the photos back into the envelope, his cell caught between his chin and his shoulder.

The smile falls from Jo's face, her brow creasing as she looks between us. "I'm making coffee. Thought you might want one," she mutters, already halfway back out the door.

"I'd love one." I try to keep my voice light and glance over to where Felix is talking quietly into his cell. He covers the microphone with his hand, "Do not leave until we figure this out, Laia. Please."

I stare at his worried face—commit every detail to memory. "I won't," I lie, forcing my lips into a brittle smile.

Jo is busy setting up the coffee machine when I get through to the bar. Watching her back, I silently pull the door that leads from the bar to the storerooms and Felix's office closed, turn the key then slip it into my pocket.

If he can't get out, he can't stop me.

The further away from this island I am, the further away Damon will be from the people I love. I should have left the second I knew he'd found me.

"I left my purse in my truck." If Jo had gotten the chance to know me a little better, she'd have been able to hear the lie in my voice.

She doesn't. And now she never will.

"Okay." She nods over her shoulder then reaches up to pull some mugs from the shelf above the machine. "Milk and sugar, right?"

"Right." I walk out of the Beach Hut, praying I'll have enough of a head start to get away. I'm doing the right thing. I'm doing the *only* thing that makes sense.

Go home. Pack some clothes. Leave on the next ferry.

My plan is simple. I repeat it over and over as I climb into my truck. As I start the ignition and pull out of the car park. As I take the winding tree-lined road. My cell starts buzzing in my purse as I round the final bend to the bungalow I've grown to think of as home. Bile rises in my throat at the thought of leaving. I force myself to refocus.

Home. Bag. Leave … Home. Bag. Leave.

The image of Felix's face flashes in my mind. The first time he kissed me in the doorway. The night I told him everything. The million ways he looks after me every, single day.

He loves me. He told me he loved me, and I didn't even say it back.

Tears sting again, my chest aching, stomach rolling. What am I doing?

I blow out a breath and shove open the truck door with my shoulder, but it doesn't budge. My chin trembles with my blown-out breath. I don't want to go. A sharp sort of half-sob escapes before I can reel it in, wiping my eyes roughly with the palms of my hands. This time I shove hard enough that pain shoots through my shoulder and the door groans its way open. I've survived starting over before. I can do it again. I climb down from the truck.

But that was before when I had no one. This time I'm not alone. This time I have Felix—I have friends—this time I have a life worth fighting for.

I stop walking up the drive, the numbness of my determination cracking. *I have a life worth fighting for.* My cell starts vibrating again. I can't do this. I can't leave. I won't. I shove my hand into my purse to find my phone then swipe my thumb across the screen as I hurry to the front door.

"Felix. I'm not leaving. I'm—"

I should have paid more attention. Should have sensed something was wrong the moment I set foot into the house.

THIRTY-NINE

Laia

Even from behind, the lean lines of his body are unmistakable. He turns like he has every right to be here, his lips tipping into a casual smile.

Damon. In my house. In my kitchen. *Eating my pie.*

It's been over a year since I've been in a room with him, but it might as well have been just yesterday. Fear crackles down the back of my neck and I'm thrust back to being that weak, scared, trapped girl. My mouth goes dry, my hands tremble, my cell slips from my fingers and clatters to the floor.

In khaki shorts and a white polo shirt, he looks like he's stepped from the pages of a Ralph Lauren advert. Clean cut and wholesome.

Only I know better. I know the viciousness that hides beneath that golden tan and white-blond hair.

His chestnut eyes narrow, his gaze slithering down my body. "I always did like your pie."

I fold my arms and back up a step. "What do you want?" A ridiculous question. I know exactly what he wants—me. I swallow down the acidic taste in my mouth and force myself to stay calm. I'm done running. It's time to face this. "How did you find me?"

"Did you think I wouldn't?" His head cocks to the side, irritation tightening his features as he stabs his fork into the middle of the pie. "A sofa and a dress? I hope they were worth it."

My mind stutters, the blood seeping from my face. My inheritance account. He had access to it. "How?"

His flat, smug gaze pins me, his lips curling into a sneer. "*You*, Laia. *You* signed the paper that gave me access. So lost and stupid after mummy and daddy died, you bumbled around like a fool. You should thank me, I could have taken it all, I *should* have left you with nothing after what you did to me."

Mouth dry, memories from the days after my dad died so close after my mom clambering over themselves, foggy and grief-riddled—useless. I can't … I don't remember signing anything, but I must have. How though? How could I have been so stupid?

His loafer creaks on the floor as he takes a step. Towards me. Prowling. Predatory. Vicious.

I step back, my mind snapping back to the present. "Felix will be here any minute." I blurt out, backing up some more until I'm almost to the arch that leads to the front door. "He was right behind me…"

"You never could lie." Damon takes a step from the counter, his top lip twitching like it wants to curl again, his gaze locked on mine. Steady. Calculating.

I almost hate this bit more than the physical stuff. The faux-calm before the shit storm.

"You're coming home with me."

"You're insane if you think I'm going anywhere with you." My voice shakes, but I square my shoulders, pressing my lips together to stop my chin from giving away the tears on the verge of escaping.

He closes the distance between us in a couple of long strides.

My body reacts on instinct. I bolt.

I don't make it.

He has me against the wall before I even get under the arch. His hot breath skids over my cheeks, his fingers digging into my shoulders, forcing me back. "Did you show him the photos?"

"You're sick." I jerk against his hold, twisting my face from his, the cloying sweetness of his aftershave turning my stomach.

"I asked you if you showed him the photos, Laia?" A hand on either side of my face, he forces me to look at him. His stare is hard, cold, filled with a familiar detachment. "Because they're the closest he's gonna get to fucking you again."

I shrink back at his crude words, humiliated anew by the knowledge that he's been watching us. Watching *everything*. "You shouldn't have come here." I try to duck under his arm, the key in my pocket digging into my thigh. If I can just get to the door.

With an impatient sigh, I'm slammed back against the wall, his fingers wrapping my throat. "Always making things hard. It's like you enjoy making me do this shit."

I claw at his hands, sucking in panicked breaths against the pressure around my windpipe, my vision swirling, my legs flailing uselessly. The key in my pocket digs me again. I reach for it desperately.

"How did you think this would end, Laia?" He thrusts his thigh between my legs and presses his face against mine. "Did you really think I'd just let you leave me?"

"Damon, please," I croak out and kick out a foot, connecting with his shin. He doesn't even flinch. Panic thickens in my veins, threatening to immobilize me. If I give up now, that's it—my life in Clua is over. Determination sparks and keeps on sparking. I need to fight. I need to end this. Pushing the key between my fingers, I slip it from my pocket and stab it into his shoulder with everything I have.

He grunts, but his grip doesn't ease, he just leans back and cracks me across the cheekbone with the back of his other hand. It's a familiar move. It shocks me still, pain radiating from the point of impact across the side of my face, unlocking the trapdoor in my mind I've managed to, mostly, keep closed since I left him. The one that holds the memories of what I've been through, of what *he* put me through. All of it. Every break, every bruise, every split lip, and black eye.

I can't go back. I won't.

His fingers tighten and my vision blurs, my mind swimming, the terrifying oblivion of unconsciousness pulling me under. Stay awake. *Fight.*

They loosen a second before the blackness takes over.

"No you don't." He shakes me roughly, banging my head against the wall.

I wheeze and cough and gulp down air, my lungs burning, my head pounding. "I won't go back with—"

"You will." His mouth is on mine before I finish, his tongue forcing its way between my lips. I writhe back against the wall, tearing my mouth from his. He pushes harder, both hands on my face, holding me still, biting my lips, crushing his solid body against mine. It's not a kiss. It's painful and vicious and punishing. Meant to cow me. Meant to remind me who's in charge.

It doesn't work. Not anymore.

I bite back—hard, sink my teeth into his tongue when it thrusts into my mouth.

"Bitch." He jerks away, wiping his mouth with the back of his hand. "You want to play rough?" His mouth twists into a sneer and he grabs my chin and squeezes, crushing my cheeks between my teeth before licking his tongue past my lips.

My whole body heaves, rejecting the taste of him. The feel of him. Everything about him.

I should have stayed with Felix. Why didn't I just stay with Felix?

Damon's laugh is cold and hard and exactly the way I remember it, and, just like that I'm weighed down by the memories, dragged back into helplessness, into being nothing more than a victim, a sad statistic.

Until he gropes me through my bra.

Something inside me splinters, roars from the tips of my toes to the top of my head. I buck and kick and go for his face, nails raking down his cheek.

His hand, now fisted in my hair, yanks hard, dragging my neck into a painfully awkward angle.

I watch him press his fingers to the thick red welts, spanning from his eyes to the corner of his mouth. When he pulls them away, blood speckles them and his eyes bulge. I snort-laugh. It's a little insane and a lot hysterical, but it's not crying, and going by the furious glare he fires my way, it's hitting a nerve. So, I keep doing it.

It's short-lived, though. His fist slams into my stomach. The air, and my laugh, abandon me in a whoosh. I want to double over. Want to curl in a ball and wait for it to be over. His grip on my hair keeps me on my feet. Keeps me upright and far too present. I close my eyes and wait for the next blow.

"Get your hands off her." Felix's roared warning cuts through the ringing in my ears and I'm instantly released.

Relief, love, terror, panic—they all rush in as I slide down the wall.

He's here.

Surreal and almost in slow motion, Felix pins Damon to the worktop and lands one punch, then another, then another, all connecting with sickening cracks to the middle of his face. His body was limp after the first strike.

Pain shoots in every direction, but I drag myself to my feet, one hand splayed on the wall, the other wrapped around my middle. "Felix." My voice is hoarse, sore, barely loud enough to hear. "Felix, stop. You'll kill him." I lean my back to the wall and touch my lip gingerly, wincing when I find the split.

He freezes, one fist in the air the other wrapped in Damon's blood-spattered shirt, his shoulders heaving, his big body practically vibrating.

Cramping pain in my abdomen steals my breath and almost my balance. I hiss out, I'm not sure what.

Felix is on his knees in front of me before I open my eyes again, his hands on my cheeks, my neck, skimming my arms, hovering where I'm holding my tummy, like he's scared to touch me, scared to do more damage. "Laia," he whispers, desperate, worried, *scared.* 'What did he do to you?"

Even swallowing hurts. I grind my teeth and straighten, lean my weight back against the wall. "It's okay, I'm okay." I attempt a smile, then cover my stinging lip with my fingers. The cramping starts up again. "Ah. No. Not okay."

He shoots to his feet, cups my cheeks, scanning my face. "Did he—"

"No! No." I grip his forearms. "I just—I think I might need a doctor." I scrunch my sore face and drop my head into Felix's chest.

What happens next, happens so fast it leaves me breathless. One minute Felix is holding me, his big arms wrapped around my shoulders, his hands rubbing my back. The next, he's out cold by my feet.

I blink dumbly at Damon, his busted nose, the blood on his shirt, the broken fruit bowl in his hand. "The fucker broke my nose." He drops the bowl then presses both hands to his bloody nose. "I'm done fucking about, Laia. We're going home."

Running on nothing more than adrenaline and a whole lot of hate, I lunge for him, smack him in the face, screaming like a she-devil, the pain in my body numbed by the need to finish this. The need to see *him* bleeding on the floor.

He fists my hair again and drags me off him, my arms flail and scratch, and punch, my legs blindly kicking any part of his body I can reach. A flow of curse words I don't think I've ever used spit from my lips.

I'm slammed against the wall. But I keep fighting. Keep screaming. My scalp is on fire from his grip on my hair until he finally throws me to the floor and climbs on top of me, holding my flailing arms to my sides, straddling my waist, grunting with effort. "One way or another, you're coming with me."

"I'd rather die," I spit and struggle against him, knee him in the back and smash my head off his chin.

His face twists with rage and his fist connects with my cheek hard enough to rattle my brain and shoot stars behind my eyelids.

I blink. Try to focus. Try to get my brain to work again. Something moves behind him. I think. I blink again, my mind skirting consciousness.

"I warned you."

My eyes snap open. Felix.

The smirk falls from Damon's face, but before he can react, Felix's arm snakes around his neck and drags him backwards off me.

His face turns red, then purple, his arms and legs jerking in a desperate attempt to free himself from Felix's hold.

Still flat out on the floor, I lift my head and watch the fight leave him. Hold the stare of his bulging eyes.

I should stop this. I can't. *I don't want to.*

The crash of the front door being thrown open vaguely registers, then Jackson is on them, prying Felix's arms from Damon's neck.

"He's not worth it. Felix—let him go, man. He's not worth it."

Time slows, their shouts muffled. Felix finally releases him and stumbles back a step, head bleeding, fists clenched, chest heaving.

I drag myself to my feet. Ignoring where Damon is moaning on the floor. Jackson's already pulling out his handcuffs.

He can break his neck, garrote him, throw him off a bloody bridge for all I care. The only person I'm interested in is swaying and bloody, and staring at me, looking as shell-shocked by what just happened as I am.

FORTY

Laia

"I need to see Felix," I plead to the doctor examining me.

"Felix can wait. We need to make sure nothing's broken." His warm hand urges my arm up. "You've got a nasty bruise right here." Eyebrows pinched together, he presses his fingers against my tender ribs moving up them one by one.

I wince when his fingers press the side of my breast.

"That hurts?" The old doctor asks, his frown creating more lines in his already wrinkled brow.

I'm fine. "They're not broken." I've had broken ribs before. His features soften, and I focus on the patch of black by his temple in his otherwise completely gray hair, ignoring his pity.

"Please, can I go find him now?"

"How long have your breasts been tender?" His voice calm, he urges me to lie back on the trolley.

"I don't know." I shift up the paper-covered bed and try to breathe through a fresh wave of nausea. "I need to go."

"I'm just going to examine your abdomen, they mentioned cramping when you were brought in. Let me know if you feel any discomfort."

I close my eyes so he can't see me rolling them then sink my head back into the pillow and glare at the plasterboard ceiling. He's just doing his job. "The nurse already took a urine sample. No blood. No internal bleeding, right? The pain from before hasn't come back. I think I'm fine."

"Let's wait on the results."

I lift my head. That was a non-answer if I ever heard one.

The doctor just averts his gaze and presses his lips together, prodding my abdomen. "Any nausea?"

I scowl at the knowing look that crosses his face when I nod.

"I've been stressed. I get sick when I'm stressed."

"When was your last—"

"Enough. Please. I'm fine. *I feel fine.* I'm going to find Felix."

"I'll get a nurse to take you to him." Still frowning, he turns for the door. I pull my tank down and watch his white-coated back leave the sterile examination room.

This is the first time I've been alone since my house. It's all a bit of a blur. Dream-like. Surreal.

My brain tries to piece it all together—tries to patch the fuzziness into one coherent memory.

I know that Jackson was there. I know that Mylo showed up seconds after him. I know that I crumpled the second Felix came near me. I know that Damon was taken away in a patrol car. And I know that Felix held my hand all the way to the hospital, even when they were fussing over the deep gash in his head.

Then, we were separated to be checked out.

Five long minutes later, a tiny, bird-like nurse rolls a wheelchair into the room.

"Laia?" She doesn't even flinch at the mess I must be in. She just crosses the small room and goes to help me from the bed.

"I'm okay to walk." I get to my feet by myself. "No need for the chair."

"Hospital regulations I'm afraid." She shrugs a petite shoulder and turns the wheelchair, gesturing for me to sit.

"Have you seen Felix? Is he okay?" I lower myself into the chair.

"I haven't." She backs me away from the bed, then turns the chair with the practiced ease of a professional. "Let's get you to him."

I chew on my lip and stare at my hands. There's blood under my nails. Mine, or Felix's, or Damon's. I've no idea. I twist them into fists, blink away the stinging in my eyes and focus on the white tiled floor of the corridor passing beneath my feet and the rhythmic thud of the wheels over the ridges between them.

"This is you." The nurse's soft voice drags me from my brain-fogged daze.

I pull myself from the chair, but before I can push through the door, it's opened from the other side, and I'm face to face with a middle-aged nurse.

"You must be Laia." A wide smile lights her round face. "He's been desperate to see you." She tucks a loose black curl behind her ear and glances back over her shoulder. "We've had our hands full trying to keep him still long enough to patch him up."

I nod dumbly, my gaze fixed past her on where Felix has stopped what he's saying to Jackson, his attention on me.

I stand by the open door, whatever adrenaline I've been running on since getting here officially running out.

"Laia?" Felix's voice cracks, his gaze flitting over my face, his brows tipping up in the middle at the mess I know he sees there. My lip is split, and the side of my face has already come up in deep, purple bruising.

His look of helplessness and worry and guilt is apparently all it takes to officially break me. My face crumples and hot, fat tears roll down my cheeks.

He's off the bed and pulling me into the room, cupping my face, carefully wiping my tears with his thumbs, and sitting me down on his bed.

"It's okay, Laia." He lowers himself down beside me and kisses my wet cheeks. "We're okay. It's over."

I touch the freshly stitched gash on his forehead and suck in a breath. "I shouldn't have run. I was coming back. I'd changed my mind. I was coming back."

Felix swallows thickly, his jaw clenched tight, his gaze fixed on my face. "I know, baby. I know you were."

Jackson clears his throat from beside us. I pull back to look at him. "What's going to happen to Damon?"

"He's been charged. He'll be transported off the island by tonight. Don't worry, Laia, he's going away for this." Jackson nods once, his gaze shifting over my messed-up face too. He's too professional to wince, but I know he wants to.

"I should've killed the bastard when I had the chance." Felix wraps his arm around my shoulder and pulls me into his side.

"Then it'd be you going to jail, Felix." Jackson scowls at him, dragging his hand over his mouth. "You sure left your mark, though," he chuckles darkly, folding his arms over his chest. "I don't think I've ever seen a flatter nose." He winks at me, then nods to Felix. "I'll leave you guys to it."

"Excuse me. May I?" The doctor that checked me over earlier steps into the room just as Jackson leaves it.

"Of course, come in." I wet my lips, twisting my hands in front of me.

"Miss Cavana, I'd prefer if we could talk in private."

I look from Felix to the doctor. "Why? Is there something wrong?"

"Nothing's *wrong*." The doctor's stare shifts between me and Felix again. "If you'd just come with me…"

"Did the tests show internal bleeding?" My hands drop to my abdomen. "I'm not in any pain, though."

"Miss Cavana if you could—"

"I'm not going anywhere." I grab Felix's hand, my fingers twisting with his. "Whatever it is you can—"

"—You're pregnant."

"I'm what?" All of the blood left in my face leaves it in a rush.

Felix goes completely still beside me, but I can't seem to force my eyes to move from the doctor.

"You're pregnant." The doctor nods and hands me the paper with the results of the pregnancy test. "It's positive."

"Like, with a baby?" I stare stupidly at the paper. With a baby. I'm pregnant … *with a baby.*

"I should hope so." A smile twitches at the corners of his mouth. "I'll get you in for a scan now so we can see how far along you are and make sure everything's okay."

Felix's big hand covers my shaking one with his own and I finally manage to turn my stupefied gaze to him. I'm pregnant. With a baby. With *his* baby.

"Laia?" He scans the paper and then my face, his brows pinched up in the middle. "A baby."

I nod, shake my head, and press my fingers to my mouth, unable to form a single word. Shock. This must be shock.

"Say something."

I shake my head again.

Pregnant. With a baby. "I…" I puff air into my cheeks. "I should have known. How could I not have known?" I freeze and cover my tummy with my hands. "What if Damon … he hit me … what if it's hurt?"

"Look at me, Laia," Felix whispers softly, winding his fingers through mine.

His eyes are shining, bluer than I've ever seen them, his jaw clenched, his nod jerky, but sure. "It's gonna be okay. We can do this."

Can we? Can I? A million thoughts fight for space in my exhausted mind. The idea of having a family of my own has never even crossed my mind.

A baby. Felix's baby—*our baby.*

"We can do this, Laia," he repeats, not an ounce of doubt in his voice.

Fresh tears roll down my cheeks, but I nod too. "I think we can."

Felix

"I can't see anything," I mutter, squinting at the grainy black and white image on the screen by Laia's head. If I didn't have to stay in this fucking wheelchair, I'd be able to get closer.

"This, right here." The sonographer points at a peanut-shaped blob in the middle of the screen. "Is your baby." She looks between us, her eyebrows raised. "Can you see it?"

Emotions I've never felt before clamber up my throat. This morning I could have sworn I was on the edge of losing everything again. Now, I'm on the verge of having a life I never imagined possible.

Laia's fingers tighten around my hand, and she nods, her eyes glued to the little monitor. She's bruised and cut, but I'm not sure I've ever loved anything more. This is real. I blow out a long breath and squeeze back. This is really fucking real.

"Going by the measurements, you're seven weeks."

When Laia turns from the screen a smile is tickling the corners of her lips. *First night.* I got her pregnant on the first night. An answering grin splits my face, primal pride filling my chest. First fucking night. I'm not sure what caveman part of me is at work here, but I feel like I've just grown to ten fucking feet tall.

"Let's see if we can see the heartbeat, shall we?" Brow creased in concentration, the sonographer rolls the wand across Laia's abdomen. "Gotcha." She pulls a pen from the white bun on the top of her head and uses it to point to a thrumming dot in the middle of the peanut-blob-baby. "Can you see the fluttering?"

Awe. Pride. And a whole lot of love. I stare stupidly at the flickering dot. Laia's flickering dot. My flickering dot. *Our flickering dot.*

"Look what we made." Laia's voice breaks through my grinning, caveman stupor.

I'm going to be a dad.

SIX MONTHS LATER…

Laia

"Do you think my head is fat?" I ask over my huge bump to where Kenzi is sitting by my feet.

"Your head is not fat." She rolls her eyes. "It's pregnant." She spoons her ice cream into her mouth.

My carton is empty already. I pout my lip out. "My head *is* fat. No more ice cream for me."

"I'll believe that when I see it." She leans over to feed me a glob of her Rocky Road goodness.

I close my eyes and moan. Nothing has ever tasted better. Ever. My head is fat. So are my feet *and* my ankles. Even my ears are fat. But ice cream fixes everything.

Flopping back onto the huge gray sofa, I glance over to the door when it opens and blood rushes directly to my fat lady parts when Felix walks into the living room.

I moved in the day of Arma-Damon and never moved out again. Felix insisted. And I didn't put up even a little bit of fight.

It's taken time for the bruises, both physical and mental, to fade, but we're getting there. It helps that Damon pleaded guilty for a plea deal—that, even so, he'll be in jail for a long time. And it definitely helps that I have my little Clua family to get me through the freak-outs and late-night flashbacks when they inevitably show up.

But, back to the fat lady bits—nobody warns you about the horniness. It's twenty-four-seven. All. The. Goddamn. Time.

My gaze roams greedily from Felix's sweaty curls, down his hard, shirtless body and loose basketball shorts to the tips of his running shoes.

I take it back. There is one thing that tastes better than ice cream.

"How's my favorite pregnant lady this afternoon?" He shoots me a grin and leans over the back of the sofa to kiss my ever-growing bump, his hands smoothing my loose green dress over my tummy.

"Up here, handsome." I grab his ears and tug his head up to plant a kiss on his lips.

His mouth curves against mine and he sucks on my bottom lip until a breathy sigh escapes me. He *so* knows what he does to me.

"Gross, guys."

Felix pulls away when a cushion bounces off his head.

"Your knocked-up woman needs more ice cream." Kenzi stands and slides her feet into her flip flops. "I need to go. *I* have a hot date tonight."

"Tell?" I struggle, not unlike an upside-down turtle, to pull myself up to sitting. *I know nothing of any real-life men in Kenzi's life.* "How is it possible you've been here all afternoon and you haven't said anything about a hot date?" Truth be told, Kenzi has been zipped up tight these last few months as far as men are concerned. Mylo going back to Miami last month seems to have made life with her man ban significantly easier for her.

Or maybe not.

"I was joking." She blows us both a kiss. "My hot date is with my sofa, and Imogen Keeper's brand new and extremely hot, but *fictional* super-soldier. You can have the *book* when I'm done. I'll call you and your fat head tomorrow."

"Fat head?" Felix takes Kenzi's place on the sofa by my feet and pulls them into his lap.

"You can't tell me you haven't noticed my epic fat-headedness." I circle my hand in the vague direction of my face and stick out my bottom lip again.

"I love your head." His warm hands slide over my feet, his fingers pressing into the arches then beneath each swollen toe.

I groan and lay back onto the pile of pillows behind me.

I'm fat and round and filled with baby, but I've never been happier.

"Feel like getting out of the house?" He lifts my feet from his lap and stands, holding out his hands to help me up.

"Why? Where are we going?" I hold my hands up and let him pull me to my feet.

"I" —he presses a kiss to my nose— "have a surprise for you."

"You do? Is it more ice cream?"

"Better than ice cream."

"If you walk me into a wall, I'm taking you down with me." My eyes covered by Felix's hands, I reach behind me and tuck my fingers into the waistband of his shorts. "And I need to pee."

"Baby, when have I ever let you fall? And there's a toilet where we're going." The smile is clear in his voice.

"Just a few more steps." He pulls me to a stop. "Annnnnd, open your eyes." He drops his hands and I blink to focus.

"This is?" I stare up at the window of the building we're standing in front of then spin in his arms to face him, confused. "I don't get it."

"Laia's Palace of Pies."

"What?" I screw up my face, baby brain has clearly struck again. I have no idea what this is. Unless. I glance back at the shop then narrow my eyes at him.

"Okay, the name sucks, that was Kenzi's idea. This place belongs to a friend of mine. It'll be up for sale as of tomorrow."

My mouth falls open and I try to force my brain to catch up with what he's saying. I told him about the promise I made to myself about using my inheritance to set up on my own. I just never expected him to … I blink back the wetness hovering on my eyelashes. "It's perfect."

"I thought so." He nods slowly, the smile on his face heartbreakingly nervous. "He's waiting on your offer before he puts it on the market."

"I'm gonna buy a shop."

"You are. If you want to."

"Holy shit," I half laugh, half sob-choke. "I don't know what to say." I cover my mouth and shake my head.

"You don't have to say anything." He chuckles roughly, rocking back on his heels. "It's your dream, your decision. I just want you happy."

"I am." I bounce up on my tiptoes and plant a kiss on his mouth. "I love it. It's perfect. *You're* perfect. Thank you." I spin back to face the building, *my* building.

I'm gonna buy me a shop.

"It needs a lot of work, but we don't have to do anything until after the baby arrives. Mylo's offered to do the refurb when he gets back if you want him to. I just—you said you wanted to set up on your own—to keep that promise to yourself and your parents."

"You remembered." Tears well, and I grab his hand, tugging him around until he's standing beside me, facing the shop. My shop. "I can't believe you remembered."

"Of course, I remembered." He dips his head to kiss the top of my hair.

"I love you, you know that?" I tilt my head to rest it on his shoulder and rub my hand over my bump, hoping, more than ever, that my parents can see me—see that everything is okay, that everything is better than okay. That I'm happy.

"I do." Wrapping his arm around my shoulders, he pulls me tighter against his side. "The feeling's mutual."

I have no idea how I got here, surrounded by pies and people who love me, but it doesn't matter. In this moment, the only thing that matters is that I've made it.

I'm finally safe in Clua.

THE END

ACKNOWLEDGMENTS

First and foremost, I'd like to thank, you! The person reading this. Thank you for taking a chance on me and my story. I can only hope you fall in love with this lovely little Cluan world as much as I have.

Tricia, Heidi, Emily, Nat, Brenda and Rosie. My write or dies, my cheerleaders, my motivation, and my inspiration. Without you women I would never have finished this book or had the guts to send it out into the world. You've made it better and I have no doubt that you've made me better.

It's been a long road here, but we made it.

I can't not mention my insta-girls. We may be new friends, but your support makes me happy every single day.

Special shout out to my other egg, and ma wee Stace, I've lost count of how many drafts of this story you've read by now.

And not forgetting my girls, here, there, and everywhere. I'd love to name you all but I'm lucky enough to have the problem of having too many of you to list by name and keep to one page. From Jed to Ibiza and many places in between, you ladies have read, and re-read and jumped on board with my smutty words from day one, and for that I'm forever grateful.

And finally, my little family. You are my heart, and without you nothing would work.

I love you all.

ABOUT THE AUTHOR

Wife, mother, writer of smutty words with a whole lot of love … and kissing … and cocktails … and even a little sprinkle of suspense.

In other words, she writes the kind of books she loves to read.

Elle lives on an island with a husband, three almost teenaged little people, a big orange dog, and a passion for writing sexy contemporary romances that will have you sighing, crying, fanning your face, and big-smiling by the end of them.

SAFE IN THE CLUA is the first in the White Sand Series.

BOOK 2:

SURVIVING IN CLUA (Mylo and Kenzi's story) COMING END OF SUMMER 2022.

But if you can't wait that long … Keep your eyes peeled mid-summer for STAYING IN CLUA, a White Sand's novella that'll take you right back to the island and all the people there.

Keep up to date with release dates, give aways, and all the book stuff by following her on…

www.instagram.com/ellewyleewrites

www.goodreads.com/ellewylee

or signing up for her newsletter

www.elle-wylee-author.mailchimpsites.com

Printed in Great Britain
by Amazon